AL
EYES

AL EYES

MICHELLE A. MARIE

First paperback edition August 2022

Cover Design by MiblArt
Edited by Rebecca Grubb

ISBN: 978-1-7379382-0-0 hardcover
ISBN: 978-1-7379382-1-7 paperback
ISBN: 978-1-7379382-2-4 ebook

Published by Indoor Cat Publishing
michelleamarie.com

Dedicated to those who have been underestimated.

You're stronger than they think.

And to my younger self: Fly, girl. Fly.

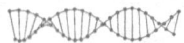

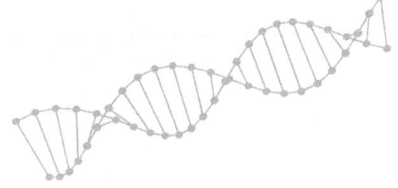

PART 1

WHAT IS
A BOY?

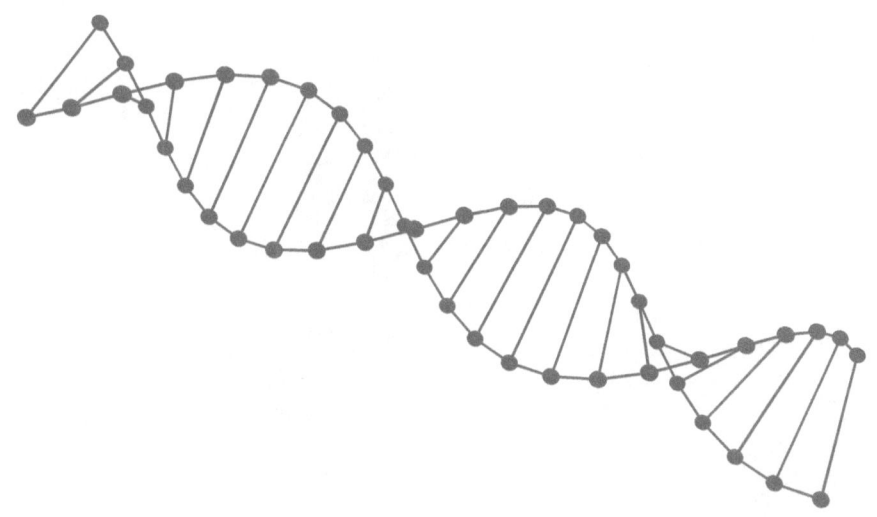

CHAPTER 1

The roof of an abandoned warehouse wasn't exactly a comfortable place to take a nap, but Al's aching muscles demanded she try. Too bad her hands weren't a good pillow. She shifted to her side and grimaced as the concrete's chill seeped through her uniform.

Before she was assigned these nightly Scanning missions, Al's fine chestnut hair had framed her oval face just under her chin on either side. Now a tangled and matted mop with bangs had taken its place.

Wrinkles and crusty smudges stained her dark-gray shirt and pants, and caked mud from many escapades had dried thick on her black lace-up boots. Her black cap, marked with an *S,* and a dark-green jacket with patches of black lay in a crumpled heap on top of her brown rucksack. The bright brass buttons on the coat's cuffs provided the only contrast to the uniform's otherwise gloomy color scheme. She would've used it to rest her head, but it smelled like sweat.

With a heavy sigh, she sat up, right into the path of the sun's retreating rays.

She squinted and recoiled. "Good. Leave, stupid sun."

Though she had given up on the idea of sleep, at least the cruel star wouldn't be around much longer to mistreat her. How nice that the fiery ball could sleep every night without fail.

A shadow steeped the roof in darkness as Hayashi Island skirted across the horizon, as weightless and unhindered as the pastel-stained clouds that sponged the sky. The glittering halo of light behind lent the landmass an ethereal glow.

Al scrunched her nose. "Must be horrible for the fancy people living up there."

She looked at her calloused hands and her short fingernails that housed layers of dirt. Frowning, she rubbed her palms on her pants, but then winced and clutched her side.

After checking her surroundings, she gingerly lifted her double-layered shirt, breathing through clenched teeth. A thick white binding covered her chest and half of her stomach. With labored breaths, she pulled the binding from the spot that dug into her pale skin and adjusted it lower.

The island's shadow left the roof, and she glared at the emerald sky jewel. "Yeah. Horrible."

The twilight's overpowering midnight blue crept up to swallow the pink and gold from the dying sunset. Then a quiet and beautiful darkness enveloped the world. Tiny dots of light emerged, struggling to flicker within the black, like muddied diamonds.

Al relaxed back onto the roof with a faint smile, but her face grew solemn when she gazed into the dark.

Most of the stars had finished burning out a long time ago and with only a few remaining speckled across the sky, the only significant light source the night had to offer was from the halfmoon. World leaders had blown up the other half hundreds of years ago during the days of space exploration in a last-ditch effort to combat coastal erosion, a decision they made after forcing the lunar colonies back to Earth. At least that's what Al remembered Mr. Fukuda explaining during one of his lectures in new-world history.

For a fleeting moment in time, space teemed with life, potential, and hope. Now, it was just as empty as it began, abandoned without a goodbye.

Al understood that feeling all too well.

"Are you an orphan star too?" She reached up toward the nearest faint glow. "I don't know who my birth parents are either..."

She scoffed at the thought, letting gravity pull her arm to her side. If her guardian, Maddox Finn, had his way, she probably never would. But she wasn't going to let him keep her in the dark anymore. She didn't have many clues yet, but if she could find enough, maybe her life would make more sense.

She sat back up, her scowl deepening as she stared out past the dusty, broken shacks below, toward the towering outlines of the capital in the distance.

Electricity was difficult to generate, not that Astova City showed much concern for that. The glittering buildings never slept, and the giant electric wall that protected the living inside from the dead outside always stayed on. Though Astova had avoided the worst of the radiation from the past war, the technology that remained was random, much like the individuals who understood how to use such knowledge.

People Maddox's age called that war The Consequence.

The only consequence Al cared about was the one that had trapped her in a bunker and kept her from interacting with the outside world for most of her life. At seventeen, Al was friends with more walls than people.

Footsteps snapped her out of her thoughts, and she glanced over the ledge. Yanking her shirt back down over her hips, she gave a brisk wave. "Hey, bud!"

The nineteen-year-old Filipino below saluted back with a beaming smile as he stepped onto the rusty rung of a nearby ladder.

Despite his boyish face, his body was toned and befitting of his age. He wore the same wrinkled uniform, although his was cleaner, and a gold hexagon engraved with an *L* was pinned to his left lapel—the emblem of a Lead Scanner.

His short brown-black hair was layered and floofy, smooshed down on the sides by a pair of coffee-colored flying goggles. A few strands poked out from under the straps, falling in front of his friendly, deep-brown eyes.

He reached the roof, bringing the scent of chamomile. After tossing his satchel next to Al's, he pulled a metallic packet from his pocket. "Wait...you weren't relaxing on the job, were you, trainee?" His confident voice held an air of playful resentment as he walked toward her.

"No, no..." Al leaned back onto the roof with a cheeky grin. "*Now* I'm relaxing."

"Al, you're supposed to be keeping watch."

"Oh yes. My apologies, Captain Zeek." She shot up with a sarcastic salute. "Incoming dust particles from the west. Evasive maneuvers recommended. Come on, this assignment is boring."

"You see, this is why *I'm* the leader." Zeek puffed up his chest. "*I* take my job seriously." He chucked the packet, and it smacked her right in the face. "See? Gotta be prepared for anything." Zeek laughed as he took another packet from his back pocket. He tugged down the wrapping, revealing a protein bar, and took a bite. "Next time, you go scouting and I'll stay behind and rest."

Al scrunched her nose as she ripped open her packet. "We wouldn't need to go scout for more snacks if *someone* hadn't eaten them all."

Zeek shrugged. "Okay fair, but I can't help that my metabolism is fast. Gotta refuel to rule, ya know?"

"Oh, is that what it is? And here I thought it was because my best friend was taking advantage of his seniority." Al took an aggressive bite and crossed her arms as she chewed.

They didn't speak for the next few minutes as they stared at opposite ends of the sky. Only the sounds of crinkling wrappers and the faint, hollow wail of the wind traveling through the holes of the metal fixtures below filled the void.

"Hey, you still mad at me? I wasn't gone that long..." Zeek sounded like he was trying not to laugh, so Al refused to respond. If he wanted to reconcile, he'd have to try harder than that.

"If you could fly a Keev-ship anywhere in the world, where would you go?"

Al turned to face him. "Well, that's random."

"Oh, thank God you're talking again!" Zeek feigned relief and clutched his chest. "The doctors told us it was impossible. But I believed!"

Al rolled her eyes and smiled in spite of herself. "Okay fine. I forgive you for ditching me. But do it again, and you're toast."

"Well, that doesn't sound so bad. Toast is tasty."

They looked at each other and let out hearty laughs that bounced off the roof. The silence returned, but it was peaceful now.

"To answer your question..." Al leaned back on her hands and stared at the sky. "I wanna go beyond the world. I wanna see the moon!"

"The moon?" Zeek almost choked on the water he sipped from his rubber jug.

"Yes, the moon! An old land of magic and mystery, untouched by human hands for centuries." Al scooted closer to Zeek as she mapped out her words with her hands. "Imagine the possibilities! The gold! Maybe we could even find moon fairies! I read an old legend once that said they ride giant rock rabbits and eat rice cakes!"

"Moon fairies, huh?" Zeek smirked. "I'd sure like to meet one of them."

Al clasped his hands. "Of course! I'd want you to go with me!"

Zeek stared at their touching fingers, the blood draining from his face. He jerked his hands from her grasp and looked away. "Yeah...sure."

Al tensed. *Wait! Is that not how men express friendship?* They high-fived all the time and some men even slapped each other's butts in the locker rooms, so why was this gesture any different?

An older, authoritative voice rang out from Zeek's satchel. "Unit Twenty-One, what is your current position?"

Zeek scrambled to his bag. He pulled out a circular radio and clicked the receiver. "Operator, this is Unit Twenty-One. We are currently in the Harmon Industrial District. Ready to receive orders, sir."

"We have a Code One, and your team is the closest to the target. Intercept immediately. Use of force is permitted. Tracking ID and location are being sent to your tracker now. Backup is on the way."

"A Code One?" Al's stomach constricted as the words registered in her brain. Out of all the situations they had trained for, why did it have to be this one? Why them? Why her?

"Roger that!" Zeek clipped the radio onto his belt and turned toward Al, his face lighting up like fireflowers.

"Time to shine! Let's go!" He pulled on his cap, hoisted his satchel over his shoulder, and shot down the ladder.

"Zeek, wait a minute!" Al rushed to the ledge and looked down, but he had already disappeared.

She caught up to him just as she shimmied into the other sleeve of her jacket, her satchel threatening to slide down her arm. The scent of oil and rust saturated the air.

Following the blinking dot on the tracker in Zeek's hand, they weaved and darted through dark alleyways crowded with jagged pieces of roofing and wooden beams. Al had to duck under awnings and corroded piping, while Zeek's head hardly moved at all, an advantage of him being several centimeters shorter.

Al was lucky she was tall for a girl though. Otherwise, her boy disguise wouldn't be as convincing.

She wrung her hat as she rummaged through random topics in her brain, anything to distract herself from what she was about to face. She was so lost on her train of thought she almost crashed into Zeek, who had stopped to hide behind the metal carcass of an assembly crane.

"Earth to space walker!" he hissed.

She stared at him and only one haunting thought echoed within her mind: Code One—a runaway woman.

He motioned with his head. "She's over there."

Al tensed. This was happening. This was real.

Zeek stowed the blinking device back on his belt and readied his gun. "We'll corner her so she can't run away, though by the looks of it, she might not be that hard to catch."

Al nodded without thinking as she poked her head out from behind the machine.

A barefoot woman limped away from them heading toward an embankment, blood dripping from a gash on her right leg.

Did she try to remove the tracking device herself? How desperate was she? When the government installed tracking devices, they attached them to the bone.

Al tried to stop her gasp. "Her hair it's—she's Altered!"

"Al, focus. We got this." Zeek put his hands on her shoulders. "I'll give the signal and then we'll take her down. Just like we practiced, okay?" His whisper was almost too loud.

Why was he so excited? This was a life-and-death situation.

Al shoved her cap onto her head and took the gun from her belt, freezing when she saw her reflection in the barrel. Which button was the stun function, and which one fired the killing bullet? Could she even take a life if she had to?

"Go!" Zeek jumped out from behind the machine as he rushed toward the woman, who bolted like a frightened deer.

He squeezed the trigger and a rippling pulse of low-frequency energy slammed her in the shoulder. She stumbled face-first into the dirt.

"Gotcha, bitch!" Zeek thrust his gun into the air with a cheer. "Look at that, Al! I got a perfect shot!"

Al, who had crumpled and clung to the metal side of their hiding place the moment Zeek started his attack, unfurled her body and approached the scene with timid steps. "Okay, yeah cool. You got her, Zeek. Now let's report in so they can take her away already." Al avoided the woman's gaze, trying to steady her wobbly gun hand with the other.

The woman burst into shrill hysterical laughter. "Are you serious? The government acts like Scanners are an elite team of soldiers, but you're nothing but children! Babies!"

Al flinched. She had heard despair could warp someone's mind, but Al had to agree with her. The school staff sure didn't seem to care about throwing inexperienced minors into danger. She scampered to Zeek's side and spoke under her breath. "This mission seems a bit too high ranked for us, doncha think? You're not concerned that—?"

Zeek smirked as he reached into his satchel. "I got this."

He sauntered toward the woman, twirling the end of a blue, neon rod on his index finger. Crouching next to her, he struck the rubber bar against her wrists and the material morphed into an enclosed figure eight restraint. "Look lady, no offense, but if you didn't want to be captured, you should've just stayed in your little house of lust."

"Screw you!" She looked like a fish realizing it couldn't breathe anymore.

"Not at all interested, lady." Zeek put his hands up as he turned away and pulled the radio from his belt. "HQ, this is Unit Twenty-One. Zeek Landers and Alec Finn, reportin' in." He lifted his finger from the receiver. "Did ya like that, Al? I made it rhyme." Her friend flashed that ever-confident smile of his as he set his bag down, but Al found no comfort in it this time. The binding squeezed her torso like a piece of fruit being juiced.

"Go ahead, Unit Twenty-One." The operator's voice again.

"Concerning the Code One—target located and captured. Requesting immediate retrieval at Harmon District section one-nine-seven."

"Request received. Please remain with the target. A recovery team will be with you shortly."

"Yes, sir!" Zeek tossed the device on top of his bag and began his victory dance. "And just like that, my promotion to Senior Scanner is practically guaranteed. Hell yeah!"

"Zeek, doncha think you're being a little extra right now, considering the situation?" Al shifted her gaze to the woman.

"Gotta learn to celebrate your victories, bud." He hopped on top of a rundown generator, putting his hands behind his neck and leaning back with a sigh. "Doing your civic duty never felt so good."

Al approached the woman, her nerves slowing her steps. Logic told her to keep her distance, but when would she get another chance to see a woman like her up close?

Though her clothes looked expensive, dirt, blood, and various other unpleasant substances stained the fabric. Half of her pastel-purple hair fell out of a ponytail tied with a piece of pink cloth with white flowers. She was beautiful, even though the grime tried its best to conceal that.

As Al passed behind their prisoner, she noticed the letters *P* and *G* tattooed on the woman's wrist. "So, what's a Personal Girl doing all the way out here?" Al didn't mean to verbalize her thoughts, but curiosity forced the question out of her.

You got this Al. Just show her you're a man. A strong intimidating man!

She stowed her gun and tried to deepen her voice. "If you tell us who your accomplices are, we could negotiate for a lighter consequence." *Oh yeah. Real convincing, Al.*

The woman glared at her with dark-brown eyes. "I'm not telling you shit."

"Don't bother, Al. The Altered aren't even worth talking to. Besides, the interrogators will make quick work of her later. She made her bed, so just let her lie in her dirty sheets." Zeek jumped to his feet. "Gotta take a leak. Keep an eye on her until I get back, kay?"

"What? Zeek don't just—" She turned toward him, but he had already vanished around the corner.

The woman's voice grew weak. "I don't want to die! P-please."

Al swallowed as something tried to claw its way up her throat. It felt like guilt.

She helped the woman sit upright. "I can talk to the Head Scanner. I can try to help you somehow..."

"Oh, how very kind of you." The woman's quivering lips morphed into a sneer, and she let out an agonizing scream that mixed with the sickening sound of cracking bone.

Al had no time to respond as the woman pulled her arms out from behind her back, the blue, neon restraint sliding down her left wrist. Her now-broken thumb dangled at an unnatural angle on her right hand.

The woman's crazed eyes were like Medusa's. Al couldn't move.

"How dare you live while we suffer!" The woman lunged at her, knocking them both to the ground.

Kicking and scrambling, they rolled over each other several times, tumbling down the embankment. When they landed at the bottom, the gun flew from Al's belt, skidding across the dirt. She tried to reach for it, but a horrible, searing pain ripped apart her nerves as the woman stabbed a pocketknife into Al's right hand. The tip sank all the way through, blood pooling in her palm and soaking the ground beneath.

Al's whole body spasmed. She wanted to scream, but she didn't know how to scream like a boy.

She bit down hard, causing blood and muffled, high-pitched sounds to trickle from her lips as she struggled to lift her throbbing hand. Every movement sent waves of sharp, unbearable pain through her arm. Before she could sit up, the woman shoved her back to the ground, pressing the barrel of the gun against her neck.

Al remembered where the safety lock was now.

The woman switched it off with ease, her chipped man-icured nails clicking against the hilt. Breathing through clenched teeth, the woman brought her mouth to Al's ear. The neon restraints hummed with an electric buzz.

"You...you're not really a man, are you?"

Al couldn't tell if panic or the unforgiving binding had forced the air from her lungs. Her thoughts coagulated like the blood in her hand.

"Surprised?" She pulled away, her shadow shrouding Al in darkness. "You must have thought it'd be easy to sell your lie. Since men and women have been segregated for so long, many have forgotten the nuances. But it's my job to know what men are. The moment you touched me, I saw your face, smelled you, I knew what you really are!"

The P.G. was right. Al was a liar.

"Al!" Zeek bounded down the hill toward them, his hand reaching for his gun. The woman whipped her head around and shot him in the leg without hesitation and he skidded the rest of the way down, gritting his teeth. "Damn it..."

"Don't worry, little boy. I haven't forgotten about you."

Al wheezed his name as the barrel of the gun, now hot from the freshly fired round, pushed into her throat.

Zeek's voice strained as blood from his wound seeped through his pants. "Not just anyone knows how to handle a gun like that...you really are one of those damn terror-ists, aren't you?"

"Typical Naturalist! Lumping all us Altered in with that group!" the woman seethed. "I suffered and waited years for my chance to escape! Someone like you wouldn't sur-vive one day as someone like me!" She whipped back to face Al, both hands gripping the hilt of the gun. "And you! Someone like you doesn't deserve to live!"

A gunshot echoed between the buildings.

Something warm and sticky made it hard for Al to see. Someone grasped at her arm and another set of hands wiped her eyes.

"Stay with me!" Zeek's voice.

A flicker of sight returned and the woman's crumpled body appeared beside her, a hole blasted through the side of her head. Gleaming scarlet and squishy pink particles covered the immediate ground.

Al rolled to her side and vomited. The knife still protruded from her hand, but she couldn't feel it anymore.

"Take them both to the trauma center immediately."

Al thought she recognized the other man's voice, but with her vision fading, she couldn't confirm his identity. His tone sounded so soothing. She felt like sleeping.

"Al! Hold on!" Zeek's voice again.

Then darkness consumed her.

Al opened her eyes, and the blinding light from a nearby window greeted her. She squinted and blinked, but her eyesight only adjusted to reveal something just as unpleasant.

"Oh, fish on a stick. Did they use what the patients threw up to paint the walls in here? What a horrible color." She clutched her head, the nausea returning.

As she struggled to sit up, she noticed her attire had been changed to a white jersey and pants. Panic shot through her and her hand jerked to her chest. She relaxed when the binding's familiar grip hugged back, but that comfort dissipated as every tiny nerve in her now-bandaged right hand throbbed with sharp, searing pain.

Gentle snoring and pressure on her legs forced her brain to change subjects. Zeek sat in a chair, his top half spilling over onto the bed with his head resting on his folded arms. He wore the same hospital garments and his brown goggles had slid sideways against his forehead.

"I'm surprised they let you keep those things on." Her smile faded as she noticed the cast peeking out from beneath his left pant leg and a pair of crutches lying on the floor. "Even more surprising that they let you in here with that leg."

As she watched his face, relaxed in sleep, she ran her hand over his thick hair. Soft. Warm. Harmless. A stark contrast to the bloody event they had just experienced.

Al wanted to cry, but she forced herself to hold her breath.

Only girls cried.

"Is there a reason you're petting me?"

Al froze. How long had Zeek been awake? His hair looked so soft she had touched it without thinking. *Recover! Recover!* "Well, good morning, princess." She dug her knuckles into the top of his head. "So ya made it back to the land of the living after all."

Zeek sat upright in his chair, laughing. "Looks like you made it too. Well, seeing that you're still alive and all, I'll go get one of the nurses to get us some lunch." Zeek's voice strained as he stood, leaning on his crutches. "Catch you later, bud!" He hobbled out the door like a newborn foal. The last of the rubber squeaks faded, and then she was alone, alone with her tormenting thoughts.

The woman discovered my secret so easily. Was it because she was also a woman? Al had been careless. Women were dangerous. As long as she stayed away from them, she could still survive.

What will Maddox do to me when he finds out I messed up? This was the first time her secret had been revealed, but he probably wouldn't be forgiving.

If someone hadn't shot the P.G., would Al have been the one with the hole in her head?

Wait! Who changed my clothes? Maybe her death was just delayed.

Her heart spun like a hyperactive spider and she clutched her chest, willing it to calm down. She pulled the blankets over her head, closed her eyes, and tried to steady her breathing. When she collected herself, she waited, unmoving in the silence. Then, a bitter smile crossed her face as she arranged her fingers into a gun and stretched out her hand. She pointed her finger gun at the window—toward the distant capital—and pulled the trigger. Her face hardened, and she brought her finger gun to the side of her head, pulling the trigger once more.

CHAPTER 2

Al's bare feet hovered in midair as she ran. She didn't know where or why, but the urge to move propelled her forward. Pastel blurs surrounded her like a watercolor painting. Panting, she collapsed, her knees hitting solid ground blanketed with orange and red leaves. A magnificent oak tree materialized overhead and bent a thick branch toward her as if to shake her hand, but the bark morphed into the body of a woman, snapping and cracking as she broke free.

She hovered above Al with a twisted, rooty smile. "Someone like you doesn't deserve to live."

Al couldn't move. The face staring back at her was her own.

A gunshot.

The other Al's face and body split in half and sprayed a geyser of blood and pink flowers. Clumps of hair and skin melted off like candle wax, sealing Al to the ground in a cocoon. Soon, nothing but a gleaming white skeleton remained frozen above her. Al screamed until her lungs ripped themselves from her chest.

Al jumped awake with a startled cry, the legs of her wood-en chair skidding across the concrete floor. The sound would've reverberated off the tall walls of the lecture hall had there not already been a throng of youthful voices clamoring around her.

"Yoo oh kahy der, bud?" Zeek stared at her, his mouth full of food and his hand motionless inside a green snack bag. A few chips had scattered across the table and onto the floor where his crutches rested. "You were thrashing around and making strange noises."

He returned to munching the goat-butter crisps, crumbs falling on his red blazer. The letters E.B.A., embroidered in gold on his breast pocket, shimmered in the light.

Right. She was still alive.

When she had returned home yesterday, a hastily writ-ten note from Maddox waited for her in her room.

The incident at the trauma center has been dealt with. One more slip-up and you won't be allowed outside anymore. His words echoed in her head and guilt sloshed in her stom-ach. Who had he killed to keep her secret safe? She had to be more careful. She didn't want to go back into the dark.

"I'm fine, Zeek." Al sat back down and as she rested her forehead against her hand, a twinge of pain radiated out from the center. The stitches on either side itched and burned, splitting her skin underneath the black fingerless glove she wore. Death had failed to take her, but his bite marks were still fresh.

"Zeek! Can you sign my racing goggles?" A young boy stood in front of the table where they sat, his arms outstretched, eyewear in one hand, a pen in the other. His braided black hair sat atop his head like a handsome crown, complementing his dark brown skin. He wore the same school uniform as Al and Zeek, but it was smaller, cuter.

Zeek pointed double finger guns at the boy. "Sure kid! It's Russell, right?"

The boy nodded over and over as Zeek took the object from his hands. "Yes! Yes! Russell! How did ya know my name?"

"I see you in the front row all the time! Gotta know the name of my number one fan, right?"

Russell looked like a moth seeing an electric light for the first time. "Number one fan?"

Al smiled. Lunch hour was the only time that students, regardless of age, could meet. This was also the time Zeek's adoring fans would stare at him from afar or, in Russell's case, gather their courage and speak to him.

Al's attention drifted away from the fan meet-and-greet and out across the bell-shaped hall. Dark mahogany framed four tall windows on her left that allowed the afternoon sun to flood the room, casting miniature shadows of boys sitting on tables, eating, and running about, on the adjacent wall. There were a wide variety of skin tones among her classmates, but they all had natural hair and eye colors, most of them black or brown. Just like all Naturalists did.

A red banner with *Elite Boy Academy* sewn in gold, hung above the teacher's desk in the center of the hall, and above that, two ornate picture frames held the faces of people Al couldn't care less about: the founder of the school on the left and the current director on the right, both young, both men.

Above them, an enormous frame that almost grazed the ceiling housed the smiling face of Astova's dictator, Vilroy Vax. Every time she looked at his portrait, something seemed off, almost as if the painter had pasted Vilroy's head onto the body of someone else. He wore a space suit, but his head and brown eyes were way too small inside the helmet.

Al laughed through her nose. If his likeness was to scale, where did his brain fit?

Zeek handed Russell the now-signed goggles and put his hands on the boy's shoulders. "You keep practicing and one day you'll be winning races too." He flashed his signature smile and Russell's head shook in earthquakes again as he cradled the goggles like a baby bird.

The boy ran back to his group of friends and they crowded around him, some turning toward Zeek with gaping mouths. Zeek shot even more finger guns in their direction.

Al shook her head with a smile. "So, Mr. Celebrity, ya think you'll be back to normal in time for the next Keevship race?"

Zeek sighed. "The doctor said it would be a few months before my cast could come off, so I'm not sure." He looked down at his leg. "Gotta do physical therapy too..."

"That bad, huh?"

"Well, at least I'm alive, right?"

"Yeah..." She gave him a weak smile. "So, the academy contacted Madd—my dad," Al tried to hide the stumble in her words, resting her cheek on her hand. She would never get used to pretending that man was her father. "But since he's off on another science convention trip, I still haven't talked to him yet. He'll probably yell at me when he gets back, whenever that is. What about you?"

"Oh, my family definitely knows what happened." Zeek crossed his arms. "You should've seen how mad my old man got when he read the tube letter. Accused the academy of trying to kill another one of his children."

Al grabbed her elbows and looked down. "Evie seemed like a sweet girl. She shouldn't have died like that."

"She shouldn't have died at all." Zeek tightened his fists against the table. "Those Altered bastards are always blowing up shit. Once I've graduated, I'm gonna blow *them* up and see how *they* like it." His shoulders sagged. "As her big brother, I should've protected her, and as your best friend, I should've protected you, too."

Al touched her neck where the barrel of the gun had been. "It's not your fault, Zeek. I shouldn't have gotten so close. And you gotta stop blaming yourself. Evie wasn't your fault either."

He met her gaze with a sad smile. "You're gonna be a big brother too someday, so make sure you watch out for them, okay?"

"I will." She clenched her fist at the lie.

"Such an *endearing* family moment."

Al stiffened. That voice. It belonged to *him*.

Perryn Keevie stood before them like an ominous tower, his near-black eyes protected behind a pair of thin, stylish glasses. His wavy black hair that split from the center of his forehead framed his face with perfect symmetry.

"Perryn." Zeek smiled through gritted teeth as he extended his hand. "How've ya been?"

"I'm afraid I'll have to decline your gesture of comradery due to the high risk of contamination." The way Perryn spoke reminded her of an old AI system, cold and precise. He avoided Zeek's hand in the same way, resituating the shiny black messenger bag draped over his shoulder.

His uniform was identical to theirs, but instead of a red blazer, a black trench coat hid his frame, the white button-up shirt underneath tucked in, ironed, and immaculate. A multicolored, striped tie and black-and-red-checkered pants showed the same level of care. He was perfect, and it was annoying.

Zeek raised his eyebrows as he retracted his hand. "If you keep saying stuff like that, you're going to keep scaring people away."

"I am above such things as friends." Perryn pushed up his glasses with a black-gloved hand and peered down at Al.

She glared back and refused to blink even when her eyes stung.

Keep your mouth shut, Al. He wants you to react.

Zeek shifted his gaze from Al to Perryn and sighed. "Right. Well, you certainly didn't do me any favors, *friend*. You used a blast bullet. That's overkill. You could've just waited for the public execution. It was my first mission as Lead Scanner, and I got my ass chewed out by Mr. Lann."

So that's what happened. Wait! Al frowned, her eyes turning inward, toward her nose. The voice she had heard just before passing out was Perryn's? That's why it had sounded so familiar. *Did I seriously think his voice was soothing?*

"No! I refuse to accept that!" She covered her mouth. Despite her determination not to speak in his presence, she hadn't lasted very long.

Perryn pinched the bridge of his nose. "You were reprimanded because of your lackluster performance, Mr. Landers, not due to any of *my* actions. I deemed the situation too dire to keep that rabid woman alive. In fact," He turned toward Al, a slight smirk curling the corner of his mouth. "You should thank me, *Alec*. I saved you."

His words burned her ears like hot oil. Did he have to use that name? Did he have to speak to her at all?

She scrunched her nose and kept her gaze on the table. "The day I thank you is the day you die and disappear from this Earth, you pompous ass..."

Perryn leaned toward her, his hands behind his back. "Oh? Should I inform the faculty of your *little* death threat?"

Al growled under her breath and started to stand, but Zeek stuck his arm between them. "No, no, of course not!" He laughed with an uneven rhythm. "Al is still recovering so—"

"Yeah, recovering from Perryn's existence!" She shot up from her chair.

Even though Perryn was four years older than her, she was five centimeters taller, a fact she relished. She straightened as far as her shoulders would allow and stuck up her chin, bobbing her head from side to side. Five centimeters taller was still taller.

Perryn's smirk disappeared, and he grabbed Al's collar in an almost graceful motion, pulling her toward him. His eyes were ice. Hers were fire.

The other boys stopped their murmuring, their heads turning to watch the skirmish. Zeek attempted to intervene, but Al shot him a glare from the corner of her eye. With so many peers watching, she had to hold her own.

"What now, huh?" She pushed out her lips into a pronounced pout. "How is the mighty Perryn Keevie gonna get even with me for irritating him?"

Perryn's grip on Al's collar tightened as his eyes narrowed. "For someone so insignificant and worthless, you sure make an awful lot of noise."

"Yeah?" Al cocked her head. "Well, you've got plenty of money to shut me up. I'll send you a bill."

Perryn scoffed and jutted his jaw out into a twisted smile. Maybe it was the crowd forming around them or because Perryn deemed it not worth his time anymore, but he relinquished his grasp on her, and she fell backward into her chair.

He reached into the pocket of his black trench coat and pulled out another pair of black vinyl gloves. "Mr. Landers, do keep your trainee in line." His voice returned to its normal temperature. He took off his gloves and replaced them with the fresh pair he had pulled from his pocket. "I would hate for our interactions here at school to affect your Scanner standing or..." He turned to face Zeek. "the business relationship you have with the prime minister."

Al continued to glare lasers at Perryn as Zeek wobbled to his feet, the muscles on his face constricting. He bent his arm and held his fist out in front of his heart—the Astovan military salute. "Of course. I am very grateful to Prime Minister Keevie for all he has done for me and my family."

"Good." Perryn turned his back to them. "Oh, and get well soon."

He ascended the stairs to the back of the lecture hall like a lone wolf and the other students returned to their boisterous conversations as if nothing had happened. More filled the room, finding their seats, while the younger ones packed up their belongings. Some began talking amongst themselves as they left, informing the new arrivals of Al and Perryn's altercation.

Al kicked the floor and crossed her arms. Perryn always ruined everything.

"I don't know why you provoke him so much, Al." Zeek sat back down with an ungraceful plop. "He honestly could just snap his fingers and then you and I could find ourselves with a one-way ticket to body bag island."

"I don't care! He's such an ass!" Zeek was right, but Perryn was an itchy sweater. She couldn't help but scratch. "Just because he's the only Elite Scanner and the prime minister's son, he thinks he's better than us!"

"I know, Al." Zeek put his hands against his temples. "But the Keevie family's relationship with our beloved leader Vilroy must be respected."

"Yeah, but—I mean, today aside, he doesn't even fight his own battles, Zeek. He's a cheater! Getting Goon One and Goon Two to enact his revenge for him. If he fought like a real man, maybe I would respect him more."

Considering her personal situation, Al noted the irony in her statement.

"If *someone* didn't irritate him all the time, then maybe he wouldn't have to retaliate?" Zeek poked his friend's shoulder.

Al swung up her arms. "I can't win, Zeek. I upset the man by breathing. Remember the day I transferred here?"

"Best. Food fight. Ever."

"Yeah, well, before you sat with me, all I did was say hi to the guy and you know what he said back?" Al straightened and made an exaggerated frown. "I don't talk to gaijin. Oh, ho ho ho ho ha." She pretended to push up a pair of glasses on her nose.

Zeek laughed. "A what?"

"I had to look it up. It means outsider. I don't get it. I was born here!" She draped herself over the table, letting her hands dangle over the other side.

Zeek nodded as he patted her on the back and then opened his notebook.

"Oh, notes!" Al bounced upright and began pulling paper scraps of different colors, sizes, and textures out of her bag, arranging them in front of her like a tattered tablecloth. Using her left hand, she jotted something down in clumsy letters.

Zeek turned toward her with a thin smile. "That again?"

"Of course! And I just added some new info." She pushed a piece of yellow paper against his nose. "Let's recap so we know where we stand in our investigation."

"Sorry officer. Wounded leg."

"Oh, come on, it's important!" Al pulled the paper back and began reading. "Perryn Keevie is most definitely a villain bent on destroying me as seen by the following evidence, with a total of one hundred fifty-seven out of two hundred forty-five interactions resulting in negative altercations with his goons. Most notably the Trash Can Incident of last year."

She shuddered and switched to a different scrap, continuing to read aloud.

"If that wasn't enough to find Perryn unbearable, his father sponsors Zeek for the Keev-ship races. Money's great and all, but for me, fancy gear and working seatbelts aren't enough payment to deal with the jerk-ass buttface who comes by the hangar every time we work on the ship to "check in" on us. New information has surfaced that may reveal that Perryn avoids conflict in big crowds? Also, germs may be a deciding factor in the battle to come against this crafty foe. Further research is necessary." Al finished reading and set down the last piece. "Well? What do ya think? Any new ideas on how to defeat him after hearing all that?"

"Jerk-ass buttface?" Zeek stared at her. "Really?"

"It's great, right?"

"It's something, alright."

The door of the classroom burst open, hitting the wall behind it, snapping their mouths closed. Mr. Fukuda entered, carrying a stack of books. He dropped them on the desk and began writing out the words *New-World History* on the chalkboard, leaning back so as to not sully the blue gingham collared shirt he wore.

As the murmuring died down, Al glanced over her shoulder.

Perryn sat alone in his usual spot, a seat at the top of the stairs, with his shiny black boots resting on the table and a book covered in a plastic film in his hands.

A few young men rushed down the steps, their bags half-open and their arms full of papers. When one boy dropped a flurry of pens, he abandoned them without looking back.

Al raised an eyebrow. *Every writing instrument for itself.*

The boys scurried into other vacant seats below, their shoulders hunched and shaking. Perryn, however, looked oblivious to his surroundings, as if nothing mattered to him except his book. Al figured nothing else did.

She squinted as she read the title in a hushed voice. *"Quantum Physics, A Study of The Spaces Between Us,* huh?" She looked back and forth between her table and Perryn's. "Well, if you ask me, there's still not *enough* space between us."

Zeek bit his lips together just before his laughter fell out, causing a strained raspberry to escape. "Next time," he whispered. "We'll definitely have a battle plan to take down the evil Oni, okay?" He extended his fist toward Al, who bumped it with her own.

"Yeah, let's sneeze in his face!" Her voice reverberated within the hall.

"Mr. Finn, Mr. Landers, are you planning to disrupt my class today as well?" Mr. Fukuda called up from the front of the room and pointed his chalk at them with a stern glare.

Al and Zeek apologized with halfhearted excuses, and the class erupted into cheers. The two troublemakers looked at each other and joined the raucousness as their teacher struggled to quiet the class with threats of extra homework.

Once the class had settled, Mr. Fukuda took something from his shirt pocket and plopped it into his mouth, his stare vacant as he reached the podium. "And now it's time for everyone's favorite time of the year, our annual Altered Awareness training. Hooray..."

The class let out various groans and sighs, and Zeek stiffened beside her.

Al looked at her gloved right hand and frowned.

Mr. Fukuda gestured to the door with stiff arms. "To help me with this riveting topic, a guest from the capital has chosen to visit us."

The door to the classroom opened and twenty soldiers dressed in red military jackets and white pants marched in unison across the floor to stand in an organized line on either side of the room. They gripped long rifles that matched the white of their gloves.

Following them, a troop of four soldiers surrounded a tall man as he ducked to pass under the doorframe. Surprised murmurs rippled through the air as the soldiers parted.

"Class, please give Prime Minister Keevie a warm welcome."

Al's head shot up. As everyone around her rose to their feet, erupting into applause, the binding tightened against her chest.

Mr. Keevie bowed, his stiff gray-brown hair remaining motionless atop his head. Stubble of the same gradient surrounded his chin and traveled up the sides of his face, forming a *W*. He wore a dark-blue suit over his broad build and pinned to his breast pocket was an ornate gold letter *K* with Keev-ship wings protruding from the back.

Al turned toward Zeek, but he was already on his feet, clapping hard, with his crutches tucked under his arms.

The prime minister lifted his hands to quell the crowd. "Thank you! Thank you!" His voice was low and commanding, not all that different from his son's, just much older.

She had seen Mr. Keevie before, as he often made public speeches, but with father and son now in the same room, Al realized just how different they looked. Mr. Keevie was as white as the Altered Awareness pamphlets being passed around, and his nose was much higher on his face. Al had never seen Perryn's mother before, so perhaps he took after her more.

As she turned back again, Perryn's intense glare shot past her toward the front of the room from behind the pages of his book. His eyes shifted and locked with hers, but he quickly moved his book to obscure his face.

Al scrunched her nose and scribbled on her notes again. Perryn had at least inherited his father's same smug attitude.

Mr. Keevie lost his smile and paced at the front of the room as he spoke. "As we all know, there was once a dark period in our history where a poisonous belief pervaded society, a belief that began even before I was born. Humans claiming the right to custom-make the DNA of their child. Characteristics such as eye color, hair color, and height. Simple. Harmless. Until it wasn't."

Zeek and the rest of the class let out boos and disdainful comments while Al gripped the underside of her chair.

"Those in power continued to fuel society's obsession with 'innovation,' authorizing even more extreme desires. Intelligence. Strength. All manner of inhuman attributes. These individuals dared to call themselves The Perfect Generation, as if they were better than us! But we all know their real name!"

"The Altered!" The class's yelled responses were out of sync.

"Despite our small numbers, we, the Naturalists, fought to keep our genes untouched just as nature intended, but what happened to us when we tried to defend our right to live? The Altered sought to destroy us with nuclear bombs!"

The entire class jumped to their feet again and Zeek pounded his fist on the table, his yells wild with adrenaline.

Al sank lower into her chair.

"In the wake of The Consequence, our beloved leader, Vilroy Vax, rose to power, unanimously supported."

The boys cheered and chanted Vilroy's name in unison. Al stood, joining with timid cries as her face broke into a forced smile.

"How can you tell an Altered from a Naturalist?" Mr. Keevie's voice boomed above the noise.

"If they don't have natural hair colors!" a boy yelled.

"And if they don't have natural eye colors!" another cried.

Al cringed.

"Ah!" Mr. Keevie raised his index finger. "But some may insist their hair and eye colors are simply rare instead of artificially constructed. Remember, less than one percent of our fellow Naturalists don't have dark hair and eyes. So how can you truly tell?"

"Their fingerprints!" Zeek's voice exploded with enthusiasm and Mr. Keevie grinned in such a way it sent another wave of nausea through Al's stomach.

"Yes, my boy! Their fingerprints will reveal their treachery!"

The crowd erupted into another loud frenzy, their voices resembling what Al imagined the eerie creatures living beyond the wall might sound like.

"Boys of the future, remain vigilant! Only you can prevent them from rising to power again! And remember! Never trust an Altered!"

Al slumped down into her chair, her head spinning as the clapping and cheering continued. She glanced back at Perryn once more. He was muttering something under his breath as his gaze shifted to the pair of discarded gloves on the table in front of him. Using his book, he brushed them onto the ground, stepped on them a few times, and kicked them away. They cascaded down the stairs to the next row, joining the fallen pens from earlier. Elevating his feet once more, he relaxed into the seat and returned to reading his book.

CHAPTER 3

Al's stomach continued to kick up into the back of her throat even after Mr. Keevie left the room, the soldiers marching out in the same grand fashion as they had arrived. The moment their squeaky boots disappeared down the hallway, she rushed to the bathroom, her lunch threatening to emerge.

If he had suspected me at all—! Al shook her head. She didn't want to imagine it.

When she returned to her seat, Zeek gave her a sympathetic look and teased her for not managing the side effects of the antibiotics they were both taking.

Teachers and subjects changed throughout the afternoon, but Al still couldn't shake her apprehension, staying lost in her thoughts until the end of the day.

As Mr. Dubois prattled on about the physics of trajectories, her gut twinged again. She clutched her stomach and grumbled. "If I had to live with Marcus Keevie-level intensity every day, maybe I'd be a jerk-ass too..."

A book slammed closed behind her and she tensed. *Crap! Did he hear me?*

The clock in the courtyard let out a loud, metallic chime and the students began shuffling about, their conversations roaring back to life.

Mr. Dubois tried his best to yell the weekly assignment over the noise, but as a man of average height and with the disposition of a flighty bird, the mass of boys ignored him, pushing and shoving each other as they tried to leave.

Perryn descended the stairs, pausing on the step closest to Al. She waited to see if he would speak, but he stowed his glasses and walked away.

As she returned her supplies to her bag, she stuck her tongue out at the spot where his cancerous presence had infected the room. A group of students rushed her table, begging Zeek for a retelling of the heroic Scanning mission that left his leg in such a state.

Al tapped his shoulder. "Catch ya later, supernova!" She grabbed her bag and saluted him before pushing through the wall of packed bodies. As soon as she emerged, a wave of flailing arms and writing tools swallowed Zeek whole.

She exited into the hallway, weaving through the other students that milled about. Sunlight shone through the giant stained-glass windows, beaming rainbow blocks onto the marble floor. Each pane had a different mosaic scene that seemed to narrate a story, but Al didn't understand what any of them meant. Mr. Fukuda had said that the building used to house followers of some sort of almighty being.

This deity, depicted as a regular man in the windows, performed magical feats like walking on water and splitting fish and bread into more fish and bread. The ancient religion had died out long ago, leaving all the details vague and confusing. Most people didn't believe in such things as gods taking up residence in the sky, rather, they worshiped the pure, untainted, genetic code of human beings.

The Naturalists ran the government with this belief, and the Altered tried to dismantle it by any means necessary, killing innocent people and scarring families like Zeek's without hesitation. They were the enemy. Then again, the Naturalists followed Prime Minister Keevie, a man whose veins popped out of his neck during his speeches about keeping women and the Altered in their places. Which side would make a better ally?

Al shook her head and focused on the windows. She thought they were rather pretty, but couldn't bring herself to believe in these so-called miracles. Whoever or whatever this omnipotent entity was, they had abandoned the world long ago. She was on her own.

Al rounded the corner and pushed through the double doors that opened up into a massive cobblestone courtyard. Shielding her eyes with her bag as the sun's rays pummeled her, she dashed behind a support pillar and waited for a group of soldiers in red to pass.

Tall shrubs and giant neon-colored flowers lined both sides, and in the middle, a glass fountain with clear bubbling water revealed all the odd things people decided to toss inside. Built as an homage to the current capitol building of the same design, a tall, thin structure made of purple glass shot into the sky from its center.

On one side of the fountain, nestled behind some gingersnap apple trees, was the fruit and vegetable garden, maintained by the school's nutritionist and gardener, a grandfatherly fellow who insisted on being called Mr. Shrub. That couldn't possibly be his real name, but Al didn't mind indulging him. Sometimes he'd try to share stories about his younger days, tales of the world before The Consequence, but the patrolling soldiers always stopped him. Such propaganda was forbidden, a mandate from Astova's "beloved" leader.

The soldiers disappeared, and she lifted her bag over her head, running past the other side of the fountain where a giant leafy arch outlined the entrance to a kilometer-long maze. Within its pruned walls, a variety of bright flowers grew lush and large, creating unique rainbow curtains. Al often ventured into the darkness to clear her head, or to find a moment of peace without the constant anxiety of feeling watched. The Elite Boy Academy didn't provide many of those, not for her.

If Al were normal, she would've attended Madame Quinn's School for Proper Ladies with the other girls. Al had seen the noodle-shaped island of Elbion on a map as a child and thought it looked like someone had taken a bite out of one of its sides.

Elbion was almost as fortified as the prison island of Marn, the upgrade to security sparked by an Altered attack three years ago, the same one that had killed Zeek's little sister.

The girls lived at the school from the time they could walk until they married, only interacting with men from their family at specific times throughout the year.

A third of the population had died during the war between the Altered and the Naturalists, leaving women only two options. Become a wife and repopulate the Earth or become a Personal Girl, a name that meant exactly what it sounded like. Either way, all women were caged birds. The only difference was the type of man who would break her wings.

"Okay, that's enough, brain. We good." Al patted her temple and continued running, the wind tugging at her messy, short hair.

Al used to care about her appearance, but when she learned from her women studies class, taught by Mr. Belford, that girls were clean, soft, and beautiful, she gave up. Al couldn't be any of those things, no matter how much she wanted to.

Leaving the courtyard, she made her way to the top of a grassy hill, and then, hopping aboard a piece of scrap metal, she slid down the slope, her hair receiving an extra layer of tangles by the time she arrived at the bottom.

A dull-blue gym stood before her, a worn dirt track spiraling out behind it. Plastered across the outside of the building like paper skin, several versions of the same poster displayed a well-dressed man waving from a podium or a buff scientist pointing a pencil. The same phrase sprawled across the top in fancy red lettering.

Vilroy Vax, The Vaccine for The World.

Al glared at the row of eyes that seemed to follow her. These posters were likely just an artist's interpretation, considering Vilroy never made public appearances, which is why his image varied so much across the city. Nevertheless, Al made a habit of memorizing every face on the off chance she met the real one someday.

As she pushed open the gym door, she passed a few upperclassmen who joked about the colors their skin would turn if a scorpiopine stabbed them. They smelled like sweat and ignored her as she hurried to the locker room. She entered the doorless concrete room and searched, pulling back shower curtains, and checking under bathroom stalls.

After someone almost caught her last year, she learned to leave the lecture hall early so she could change clothes without anyone seeing her. She managed to scramble into a stall and lock the door, but whoever they were, they apparently thought it would be funny to stuff her abandoned blazer at the bottom of the dirty towel bin. The thick sour smell clung to her for weeks, no matter how many times she washed her jacket.

After one more room sweep, Al approached her locker. Reaching into her bag, she pulled out a round, palm-sized device and removed her black glove, her stitches burning again. Pressing the device against her right index finger, a needle punctured her skin with a light click. A tiny droplet of blood bubbled up onto the tip.

Placing the device in her mouth for better leverage, she pulled a thin rectangular mesh from the side compartment and placed it on top of her pricked finger. The mesh formed a clear film that tingled against her skin as the blood spread out underneath and melded against the ridges of her fingerprint.

She tucked the device into her bag and kicked her locker. A compartment fell open with a metallic clink. After entering a six-digit code on the keypad, she placed her index finger on the adjacent scanning panel and with a monotone beep, the rusty green locker door swung open.

"Well, unlike you, Maddox, at least your sneaky gadgets are reliable." Al scrunched her nose and threw her red blazer into the open locker.

Before The Consequence eye scans were all the rage, but now, fingerprints taken and recorded at birth were the modern social security card.

Al was a thief when she used this device. Whose identity had she stolen? He was probably dead, or the system would've caught her by now. If the war hadn't taken out the holonet, surveillance programs would've found her too.

She glanced around the room again before unbuttoning her white shirt and tossing it alongside her blazer, revealing the white boa constrictor clinging to her chest.

Purple and yellow splotches in the shape of lines and odd indents swirled across her skin. Clenching her teeth, she shimmied the black glove back onto her right hand and then untied the side of her binding. The sharp pain punctured her sides.

Unwinding the lowest piece, her lungs expanded. She took a deep breath and then coughed several times, steadying herself on her locker. After taking a few more labored breaths, she pulled the binding tighter across her chest and dressed in her shooting outfit, wincing when her injured hand found an uncomfortable angle. Though it would be awhile before she could handle her gun properly, she still needed to appear strong.

She peeled off the thin film from her fingertip and shoved the crumpled leftovers into her bag. Retrieving an eye dropper bottle from her satchel, she headed to a row of bathroom sinks.

Holding the bottle above her eyes, Al let a few drops of clear liquid fall into each, blinking several times. Muddled brown stared back at her in the dingy mirror as her irises turned darker.

Al's arms and legs weren't like the attractive limbs the P.G. girls had in the erotic brochures. Hers were riddled with muscle, and pale like a ghost.

She gripped the sink.

No wonder you make a good boy. You're such an ugly girl.

She tossed the bottle back into her bag just as two tall, burly men dressed in shiny black uniforms entered the locker room—Perryn's bodyguards.

"Can I help you?" Al narrowed her eyes and clutched the open part of her shooting jacket, pulling it tighter to her chest.

The men moved to stand on either side of her. "Seems you were causing trouble, Mr. Finn." The taller of the two spoke. His rather high-pitched, slimy voice sounded funny coming out of a person with such intense black eyes and a thin spiky haircut.

"Heard you threatened Mr. Keevie." The other's voice was deep and filled with gravel. Shaggy black hair covered his eyes, but the mustache under his nose was well-trimmed.

"We would love to toss you into the compost bin again. Omoshirokatta na!" He turned to the taller man, and they snickered together.

She clenched her fists and jaw, forcing herself into submission.

"Well, I suppose you've been warned now, Mr. Finn. Have a nice practice." The two men laughed, continuing their conversation as they left the room like dissipating storm clouds.

Al kicked a row of lockers with an exasperated yell and slumped down on the wooden bench, dropping her head into her hands. Her palm throbbed against the glove and her lungs seized in her chest. Trapped. The outside world had more space than the home she was once forbidden to leave, but she still wasn't free. How was she different from any other girl?

"Al! Are you okay?" Zeek's voice echoed from the doorway. "I saw Perryn's goons. Did they do anything to you?"

"Oh, Zeek. Hi. No, I'm fine." Al stood and turned away from him as she finished buttoning her jacket.

He almost tripped over his crutches as he made his way to the bench. "Liar."

"What?" She closed her locker door. "I told you it's nothing." *Let it go, Zeek.*

Zeek sighed. "I still don't believe you, but sure." Al wanted to open up to him, but it was too dangerous. "I don't know why you talked me into this. What's the point of us coming to class if we can't even shoot right?"

"We can still learn from watching." Al tugged on his arm. "Here!"

She pulled him over to his locker, the one right next to hers. They had planned it that way. She hit the door with her fist and when the same keyboard and scanning panel popped open, she punched in a code.

Zeek held his index finger over the scanner and his locker clicked open. "Since when have you known my pin?" He scrunched his eyebrows.

"Since forever! You wrote it inside your notebook. Remember when you let me copy your aviation notes?"

"Oh God, what else did I unknowingly write in there?"

Al laughed. "Come on. Let's get ya suited up!"

"You serious?"

"Oh, I'm very serious!" She took Zeek's undershirt and jacket out of his locker with a playful smile. "You can still be part of the team this way!"

"You're really weird. You know that, right?"

"Yep! And that's what keeps things interesting!" She tossed his clothes into his face with a giddy laugh and sat on the bench across from him. The garments slipped off his head and into his lap.

Zeek sighed. "Fine." He hesitated as he gripped the edge of his shirt. Keeping his eyes on the ground, he pulled the garment over his head, revealing his tan, blemish-free skin.

Al's face fell, and she touched her side where the binding constricted her. His skin was beautiful. Hers looked like rotten fruit.

Zeek pulled down his undershirt and slipped one arm into his white shooting jacket, but when he tried to pull on the other half, his elbow got stuck halfway.

"I gotcha, bro!" Al jumped to the rescue.

"No! It's fine! Just stay over there!" Zeek waved his half-empty sleeve like a white flag as he struggled to push Al's hands away.

"Come on, Zeek! You clearly need help! Why are you being so stubborn?"

"I said stop, Al!" Zeek pushed hard against her. Losing his balance, he fell forward, landing above her on the bench, his arms outstretched on either side of her head. His eyes widened and his body grew rigid.

Al froze. *Red flag! Red flag! Get your butt outta of this!* Only a few layers of fabric separated him from the truth.

"Zeek..."

"...yes?"

"Look! Your hands are both free now!" She laughed and wiggled her fingers in front of her face. "You're welcome!"

Zeek scrambled off of her, turning to face the wall.

Al touched her chest, letting out a silent breath. *Fish on a stick that was close.*

Any semblance of silence that had existed evaporated into squeaking boots and slamming locker doors as a bunch of teenage boys rushed into the room like air released from a can. Then their pants started falling.

Why everyone wanted to compare that odd thing between their legs was beyond her. Al, of course, couldn't participate in the size Olympics, having no baton of her own. Hers was only a stuffed sock.

"Um, I'm gonna head to the shooting range and find us the best seat for watching practice." She retrieved Zeek's fallen crutches and set them against the bench. "See ya there?"

Zeek waved without turning around and Al headed out of the locker room, keeping her gaze to the floor.

CHAPTER 4

"What do ya mean Zeek isn't my Scanning partner anymore?" Al catapulted from her chair.

Her sleep schedule had returned to normal for the first time in weeks since her community service began, but as she stood in the Scanner's processing office, she realized her vacation was too good to last.

"He's gonna be my partner again once he's better, right?" She slumped back down in the chair and tried to regain her composure.

The gray-black eyes of the teacher in front of her were dull and tired, like his voice. "Look Mr....Finn, was it?" He lifted a sheet of paper to eye level. "I don't make the decisions, I only enforce them, so I wouldn't know." He leaned back in his green velvet chair, letting the page glide to a floor already littered with a sea of other papers.

The brass buttons on his striped vest reflected the light from the single lamp that dangled from the ceiling.

"If you have a problem with the new partner selection, then talk to the one who approved the transfer. Now get out." He gestured toward the door with a lazy arm as he covered his face with his bowler hat and placed his feet on the blue desk that separated them.

"And who would that be?" Al clenched her teeth, trying to quell her anger.

The teacher sighed and bent down to open a drawer, sloshing through the pile of disorganized papers it held, with slow and burdened movements, as if he was a sea-sloth in disguise.

Al tapped her foot against the dark tile as she looked around the office for anything that could distract herself from the names she wanted to call him.

Three walls were dark green, and the one behind her had an automatic sliding door with ceiling-to-floor frost-ed glass windows on either side. A large poster hung on the wall behind the teacher's chair with several il-lustrated faces of a man and woman, each drawn from a different angle, their hair pink and eyes a golden hue. The words *How to Spot an Altered* were printed in black at the top.

"Here." He held out the paper just far enough so he wouldn't have to leave his seat. "Now, please—woah man-ners!" His voice showed its first sign of emotion as Al ripped the sheet out of his hand.

Stamped in the left corner of the page was a bright golden *K* with Keev-ship wings sprouting from behind. The Keevie family crest.

Al crushed the paper in her fists. "I'm gonna kill him."

She stormed out of the office and down the wood-en hallway, passing rooms and almost bumping into other members of the all-male staff. Reaching the dou-ble-doored entrance, she pushed through them and con-tinued sprinting.

Perryn Keevie. Zeek's warning to leave him alone crossed her mind, but the reassignment form, now shoved in her pocket, was an obvious declaration of war. She wouldn't back down.

After searching all his usual spots, she retreated to the courtyard, seeking comfort from the blinding sun under a leafy apple tree. She steadied her back against its grainy trunk and tried to catch her breath. Mr. Shrub had already gone home for the day, but Al wished she could hear him talk about plants. At least then, something would be familiar. She could still pretend she was okay.

"Your breathing is distracting. Can you stop?"

Startled, Al turned to face the bark, but then chided herself for thinking, even for a split second, that trees could talk. It was him.

"Perryn!" She marched to the other side.

The concentrating reader didn't look up from his small book as he sat against the trunk, even as Al stood above him.

"Correct. *A*-plus for you." He turned a plastic page with a gloved hand.

"What the hell do you think you're doing?"

"Reading."

Al pulled the crumpled piece of paper from her pocket and chucked it at his face. "I'm talking about this! Why the hell would you put me on your team if we hate each other?"

Perryn let out a quiet breath and closed his book. A flicker of irritation crossed his eyebrows as he stood. "For your information, this is a friendly gesture. There were no other available Scanner leaders, and instead of having you restart your training next year—"

"Friendly gesture, my ass! You ass!"

"Shall I infer you have an interest in my ass since you keep calling me that?" Perryn pushed up his glasses with a smirk.

"Wha—!" Al tensed, her eyes growing wide as she tried to recall everything she learned about girls in class. "I'll have you know, I love girls with their curly locks, pink lips, big boobs, and curvy hips. Even if I didn't, there's no way I'd like *you* because you're so egotistical, you'd suck at being in a relationship!"

Perryn stifled a laugh and placed his book in one of the deep pockets of his trench coat. "If you have any complaints, I am certain Mr. Lann would be more than happy to overturn an official Keevie decision."

Al frowned, realizing he was toying with her again. They both knew that no one ever went against what the Keevie family decreed.

Perryn nudged the unwanted paper ball with the toe of his boot. "Shall I fine you for littering as well?"

Al scrunched her nose as she snatched up the paper and shoved it into her back pocket.

Perryn touched his chin. "Hmm. Trash picking up trash. Hilarious." He smiled as he walked away.

"Hey wait!" Al dashed after him. "I'm not done talking to you!" She continued to rant, explaining her disapproval of their pairing in great detail as she followed him through the courtyard and into a grassy clearing that flattened into a black helipad in the center. Al only stopped when she heard the distant humming of an engine.

As the sound grew louder, she noticed a sleek black craft flying toward them across the overcast sky. Rounded and long, like a bullet, with *Keevie Inc.* printed on the side in white, the ship had barely touched the ground when an oval door on its side slid open. Perryn stepped inside and turned around to face her, gripping metal rungs near the opening. His smug smirk grew wider the higher he ascended.

"I will contact you later with details of our first mission!" he called out over the engine. "Oh, and I expect you to be punctual or I will be deducting points!"

Al opened her mouth to shout something back, but the ship was too high.

Soon the black vessel became a tiny speck of pepper in the soupy white sky.

"A beautiful ship like that is wasted on someone like him." She let out a frustrated yell and flopped face-first onto the grass.

The distant call of the bugle birds reverberated across the field as if to answer her. Their hollow bellowing mixed with the soft clicks of the spring beetles and buzzing bumblebutts hidden between the blades of grass around her.

A sudden pain spread across the back of her bare neck. "Give me a break, sun!" She rubbed the burning spot and pushed herself up off the ground. "I can't stay here." She touched her back pocket where her potential death sentence resided. "I gotta find Zeek."

She found her friend in the noisy dining hall, laughing and eating with several upperclassmen.

Supported by marble pillars, the building's ornate innards curved with symmetrical windows and upon the high vaulted ceiling, a hand-painted mural depicted various sailing vessels, ocean creatures, and splotchy landmasses, the names of which meant nothing to anyone anymore. Long banquet tables arranged in groups of four, ran the length of the room, filled with boys of all ages.

She approached Zeek, who had two metal trays in front of him piled high with mounds of delectable food. He was stuffing the last remnants of a purple meat into his mouth before he noticed her.

"Hey, bud!" He flashed her a huge grin, dabs of dark sauce clinging to his cheeks. "Have you ever tried BBQ teasel-grouse before? Your mouth gets all tingly from the trace amounts of poison!" He swallowed a huge gulp of amber juice from his cup. "Oh! I talked to the cooks and guess what? They're bringing back goat burgers later this year. Finally!"

Al hit the table as she plopped down onto an open seat. "Zeek, focus! I need to talk to you." She glanced around at the confused and offended faces staring back at her. Some were mid-bite. "Alone."

Zeek wiped his face. "Yeah, sure. Um, guys, do you mind?"

The young men groaned, and some mumbled "fame moocher" under their breaths as they picked up their trays. Al glared at them and gestured to her groin with both hands as they shuffled away to another table. "Get some!"

"Sorry 'bout that." Zeek flexed his arm. "Want me to beat em up for ya?"

"I'm used to being called that by now. It's not a big deal, but this—this is." She pulled out the crumpled reassignment form, smoothed it against the table, and handed it to Zeek.

He took the wrinkled page and opened his mouth to speak, but Al stopped him. "Just read." She waited for realization to change his expression as his eyes traveled the length of the document, but it never did.

"Wow." He touched his chin and set the paper down.

"Wow? That's it? Just...wow?" She was hoping he would've shown a little more concern for her safety.

"Yeah, well, when I heard I was being put on leave, I figured you'd be assigned to someone else. Who'd have thought it'd be Keevie, huh?"

Al let her cheek hit the table, her words muffling. "I should just accept my demise now, I guess."

Zeek patted her on the back, then paused for a moment, appearing to be contemplating something, but then a hungry grin tugged at his lips and he grabbed his fork and dug into the bowl of noodles on the second tray.

"Hang in there. Perryn's the only Elite Scanner for a reason. Like me, he's serious about his job too. At the very least, his pride will keep you safe, even if he doesn't like you." He slurped up a big bite of the creamy noodles and the drops splattered across the table like blood.

Al gulped. "Yep. I'm definitely gonna die."

Another week passed and the dreaded assignment day arrived.

The grass was crisp as Al climbed up the hill toward the landing pad with her drawstring backpack. A purple gradient dyed the edge of the early morning sky, the sun not yet bleeding into the pattern. The fresh, cold air filled her lungs. There was still time before the summer heat emerged to drink away the dampness of night from the meadow.

Al shivered and gripped the straps of her pack.

Today's mission required a different Scanner uniform made of a lighter material and no hat. As she reached the top of the wet field, Perryn's figure came into view, his back turned toward her. He wore the same black outfit as she did, but today, his favorite trench coat was missing.

Al grumbled to herself. "I guess Zeek was right about him being serious about his job. He got rid of the only thing in the world that he allows to touch him."

Without his dark companion to hide him, Perryn's body looked thinner and less muscular than Zeek's, but his proportions were perfect. Al rolled her eyes. *Of course they are.*

As she got closer, she noticed Perryn was also missing his glasses. She couldn't help but stare. He looked so different. It had to be a trap, an attempt to distract her from the mission. She wouldn't fall for it.

"Good morning, Mr. Finn." Perryn's voice was so formal it made her laugh.

"Heya, *Mr. Keevie*," she quipped, swinging her arm. "Wow, today our outfits match the color of your soul. Am I right?"

Perryn cleared his throat.

Al opened her mouth to goad him further, but then straightened like a board when she realized two other men were with him. The museum curator, Mr. Vasiliev and the Head Scanner, Mr. Lann, eyed her with raised eyebrows. She'd insult Perryn later.

"From those of us at the Astovan Museum, we thank you!" Mr. Vasiliev was a short, round man with fair skin and spoke in an accent that matched his refined and rich outfit. "Our theme for the fall exhibit is 'Humanity,' so please bring back items you feel fit that description." He pressed his hands together the way a tree mouse did when eating corn.

"Everything you need for today's mission can be found in these." Mr. Lann's voice was warm but stern as he presented Perryn and Al with large duffel backpacks covered with zippers and pockets.

He was a bald, burly man with a black mustache and warm brown skin, and Al couldn't decide if he was more like a commanding general or a kind grandfather.

"You'll find your helmets and biosuits onboard our Keev-ship. You can change into them when we get closer to our destination."

A wide smile crossed Al's face. Keev-ships. What kind would they be using? What engine model would it have?

If I get to fly, maybe this Scanning mission won't be so bad! She was so engrossed in her flying fantasies she forgot to pay attention to Mr. Lann's briefing.

"…lose signal…depth…radiation present…"

"What?" Al caught the dangerous words in Mr. Lann's latest sentence.

Perryn closed his eyes and sighed through his nose.

Mr. Lann rubbed his chin. "Are you sure your trainee is qualified for this mission?"

"Alec Finn, age seventeen, height—180.34 centimeters, mental fortitude—eightieth percentile, physical fitness—eighty-fifth percentile, third-fastest climber in his grade based on last year's tests, sir." Perryn's voice was firm and confident.

Al saluted as she stumbled over her words. "Oh, uh, yes! I just get distracted sometimes, sir."

It was common for Scanner leaders to have access to their team member's health and fitness information, but to hear her stats coming from the mouth of the grim reaper's minion sent chills up her spine.

Mr. Lann shook his head and walked toward the landing pad, Mr. Vasiliev bouncing along behind him.

"Heh, didn't know you'd vouch for me like that." Al twisted a strand of hair between her fingers.

Perryn shot her an icy glare, and her breath caught in her throat. His laser eyes were much more intense without their glass shields, and they almost disarmed her. He lifted the pack onto his shoulders as if it weighed nothing and headed toward the platform. She scurried after him, dragging hers behind her.

When she saw the ship that waited for them, her apprehension faded away as quickly as the rippling air caused by its hydrogen-based exhaust.

The triangular body was a rusty orange but painted smooth with windows that looked like suns. This ship was almost the size of Perryn's, but the design and fine details made it an expensive and exclusive model. Only three had ever been made.

"Is that the Taiyou 17?" She pressed her thumb and index finger against her chin. "Judging by the sound of that engine, I'd say you have yourself a triple-core lithium-based battery which allows it to reach speeds of up to one hundred rotations per hour!"

Mr. Lann laughed. "I see what you pay attention to now."

Al touched the back of her neck. "Sorry, I've just never seen one in person before." A huge smile swept across her face. "It's my absolute favorite ship!"

Perryn flinched.

"Well, how about that?" Mr. Lann's smile deepened. "Did you know that Mr. Keevie here was the one who designed the prototype?"

Al froze, her voice deadpan. "Never mind I hate it."

"Please, Mr. Lann," Perryn pinched the bridge of his nose. "I prefer to keep my work and private life separate, if you don't mind."

"I am aware. Just wanted to brag about my favorite student for once."

The pilot emerged from the ship, beckoning Mr. Lann and Mr. Vasiliev inside. They left Al and Perryn alone on the ropeway.

"Why do you have to ruin *everything*?" She had stepped in a mud puddle and Perryn was the mud. "I can't even like a ship because you're connected to it."

"Is that your criteria for liking or disliking things?" A hint of boredom laced his words.

Al crossed her arms. "Yes, actually! I make it a point to hate all the things connected to you."

"Better add yourself to that list, then." Perryn ducked as he entered the ship, leaving Al with her mouth agape.

She let out an exasperated grunt and mumbled as she knelt, stuffing her smaller backpack into the bigger one. Hoisting it onto her shoulder, she took one last look at the tiny outline of the school sleeping in the distance and said a silent goodbye to those she cared about.

When Al had told Zeek about the mission, he promised he'd set an alarm to see her off. Judging by his bedhead and the strange combination of sweatpants and a pajama shirt that greeted her this morning, he almost didn't hear it.

Maddox still hadn't returned home, but he sent a tube letter filled with criticism and worry over her injured hand. Al's adoptive mother, Molly, who had been reading his words aloud during their breakfast, had stopped mid-sentence to call him a fussbadger. He really was.

Al ducked under the lip of the door and stepped into an orange metal world. Four attendants wearing black-and-white flying outfits appeared to have been waiting for her, and she apologized as they latched the door shut. They hustled past her down the metal hallway, their footsteps echoing within the belly of the ship. She followed them and entered the passenger area.

A bluish metal cargo box secured by thick straps sat dead center and a set of four plush black seats, bolted to the floor, hugged both its sides. The pilot, wearing the same flying uniform as the attendants, double-checked the gauges on the cockpit dashboard and conversed with the copilot about takeoff procedures.

Al looked for an open seat and noticed Perryn had already made himself comfortable with a plastic-encased book titled *The Origin of Species*. She didn't want to be near him if she could avoid it, but Mr. Vasiliev had taken a window seat and the only other one available was the space next to Perryn. She wasn't about to miss the incredible landscape because of him.

Gripping the straps of her bag, she let out a breath. "Excuuuuse me." She stepped over Perryn, the large pack knocking the book out of his hands and onto the floor.

He sighed, picked up his papered friend, and dusted it off. After stuffing her bag under her chair, Al sat and spun to face the window. "Take off! Take off!" She bounced in her seat.

From the corner of her eye, she saw Perryn's hand moving toward her and when she whipped her body around to confront him, their noses were almost touching. His eyes reminded her of black diamonds and he smelled like a deep, dense forest.

He smiled as he pulled the strap across her shoulder and buckled it at her side. "Safety first."

He sat upright in his seat and Al could only stare at him, her heart rattling in her chest and the roaring engine shooting vibrations through her feet.

"Oh, and by the way," Perryn opened his book, his smug smile growing. "Disrespecting your Scanning leader, minus twenty points."

Only strained, partial speech left her mouth in protest, the shock from him being so close still squeezing her lungs. She reached under the seat in front of her and grabbed the helmet of her biosuit. Slamming it over her head, she crossed her arms and turned to look out the window as the ship lifted off the ground.

CHAPTER 5

The steady engines caused a low-pitched humming to resound throughout the hull of the ship. Outside, a tiny dark shadow, projected on the green fields below, chased after them. The neighborhoods looked like they had shrunk to the size of a dollhouse, a toy she had to leave behind in the bunker the moment she became a boy.

Fruit trees and wheat wove together like a topiary quilt, a tall patch of green next to a flat patch of gold. The vegetation grew scarcer before the scenery morphed into brown and gray buildings swirling with smoke from tall, cylindrical stacks. Zeek had told her how he often traversed the factory district's piped veins searching for parts for his Keev-ship. The concrete and metal scenery lasted until they reached the capital.

Al lifted the visor of her helmet.

The alabaster buildings with their solar panels and glass siding shimmered in the midday sun. In the center of the city, a triangular prism-shaped tower extended far into the sky. Its fluorescent purple hue sent beams through the window and colored Al's skin.

She gripped the lip of the windowsill. Vilroy lived there.

Only his most trusted guests visited the top floor, which overlooked the entire city, while the members of his party worked in offices below him. Maybe Vilroy was there now, looking out at her. She ducked into her seat.

The ship continued to pass over the city's parallelogram buildings and past the racing arena until they reached the edge of the capital where a giant electric barrier rippled the air as bands of heat radiated between its T-shaped pillars.

"This is Team Delta requesting deactivation of the frying pan for mission seven one eight seven. Over."

The pilot's voice made Al turn her head. Perryn was no longer beside her. Only his book remained, resting in the center of his seat.

"Why do you call it the frying pan?" Al tossed her question toward the front of the ship with a giggle as she unfastened her seatbelt and stood.

"Well—" The pilot leaned back in his chair, stretching out the coiled wire attached to the receiver in his hand. "Have you ever seen what happens when something gets too close to it? Pfffftszz!" He shook his body, pulling his hands tight against his sides.

Al shifted her eyes with a pinched grin. "Sure wish I could pfffftszz somethin' in there."

"That thing's got a huge shock radius too, so the flying monsters don't get into the city."

"You're clear for passage, Team Delta." A robotic voice echoed inside the cockpit.

Al turned back to the window and watched the milky rippling air dissolve into long bands of electricity. The horizontal lines split down the middle and pulled apart like a door, revealing a dark tangle of trees and foliage beyond.

As the ship lurched forward through the now-open space, Al noticed a large group of soldiers gathered on the other side, all wearing breathing masks. They directed two separate lines of people through a tall archway at the bottom of one of the T-shaped pillars. The line entering the city had rag-dressed people carrying empty baskets or pulling carts, while the line exiting the city had similar individuals hauling dense bundles on their backs or tugging full carts.

A soldier near the archway shoved a man as he passed, and several other soldiers inspected a cart, removing items as a woman held back her protesting partner.

Al let out a small gasp. "Are they—"

"The Altered, yes." Perryn spoke behind her and she jumped, hitting the ceiling.

She crumpled back into her seat, holding the sides of the helmet. "Why do ya gotta keep sneakin' up on me?"

"Lack of awareness increases your probability of death." He picked up his book and sat. "We will arrive shortly."

"Yeah, you'd know all about being short, wouldn't you, Perryn?"

"I am only 4.5 centimeters shorter than you. Or if you prefer, 1.77165 inches. The difference is not that noticeable."

"One point seven—what? What are inches? Sounds stupid."

"Yes, and you would know all about being that." Perryn smirked and opened his book.

With a silent huff, Al crossed her arms again and sank back into her seat, her brain still sloshing around from the recent impact. He got her when her thinking was impaired.

Typical cheater.

As soon as the ship's tail cleared the opening, the electrical ribbons of the forcefield connected once more behind them.

The knotted trees below twisted in unnatural positions and everything was dark and dirty, like a thick layer of black dust had always rested on top of the world. Even the sun looked dingy.

"We're really goin' out in that, huh?" Al gulped. *So much for a fun adventure.*

The ship flew for another thirty minutes before landing at a docking bay that looked as distressed as its surroundings. As the landing gear locked with the stabilizers, the crew grabbed their breathing masks and bounded down the hall toward the door.

Al's breakfast somersaulted in her stomach. "It's been years since the fallout, so I didn't expect it to still look so...intimidating." Her helmet made a gentle clunk against the glass as she watched the crew outside refuel the ship.

"This is where the Polonium clouds originate." Perryn flipped another page in his plastic book. "Everything in this sector looks like this."

"Great! Fun for the whole family."

A shout came from the back of the ship, signaling an all-clear.

Perryn stood, tucked his book into his bag, and headed toward the exit with it. Al let out a nervous whimper as she grabbed her own bag and followed.

Once at the back of the ship, the crew helped Perryn and Al into their biosuits, their helmets attaching with a distinct whoosh and click. As the men perused the checklist on their clipboards, nodding their heads, Al thought of astronauts. Were they also scared to leave the safety of their ship and go out into the unknown?

Al stepped outside and felt a tap on her shoulder. It was Mr. Lann.

"Best of luck out there, son!" The triangular regulator covering his mouth and nose muffled his yell.

She nodded, but didn't feel the least bit reassured. Mr. Lann trudged down the ramp toward Perryn, leaving her alone at the now-closed door. Mr. Vasiliev pressed his face against the window. Wide-eyed and mouth agape, he was a scared mouse now, even though he had been so energetic before they took off.

"Well, guess I'm really gonna die now." Her voice echoed inside the airtight suit. She labored down the incline of the landing and off onto the dusty ground. Every step on the soot-like film left behind a white boot-shaped indent, like stepping in snow but with the colors reversed. "Yep. Yep. This is definitely the end."

Mr. Lann saluted as he re-entered the ship and the crew rushed in after him. The door latched shut and the ship's engines roared, kicking up black clouds like tiny tornados. Al dropped her bag and threw her hands up to block the swirling particles, but then put them down with a sheepish grin when she realized her biosuit provided enough protection.

The ship lifted off the ground and floated into the grimy sky until only an eerie silence remained. Then she was alone. Alone with her worst enemy in a land of literal death.

"We need to begin our descent down the ridge before nightfall." Perryn's voice echoed within her helmet with metallic static from the internal com system.

Al looked at the sky, wishing the ship would return. "How long is that gonna take?"

Perryn didn't answer and he had gone a significant distance before Al realized she was being left behind. She pulled on her duffel backpack and rushed after him.

When she caught up, she slowed to match his gait, a frown spreading across her face. "If I died because you left me behind, wouldn't it make you feel even a little bit bad?"

"I told you where I was going." Inside the hollow helmet, Perryn's voice seemed extra cold. His bag obscured the top of his head. "If you choose not to follow, that is your mistake."

Al scrunched her nose. In normal circumstances, she would've kept up the fight, but decided she better wait until she reached the campsite to irritate the only human for kilometers who knew how to survive in Death Desert.

Why is he such a stuck-up cactus? Maybe in his twenty-one years of life, she was the only person who had dared to stand up to him. Al smirked as she crossed her arms. If he wanted to be a cactus, she'd be a chainsaw.

For the rest of the walk, neither of them spoke. At first, it was awkward and unnatural, but then Al realized she rather liked the silence, even though the scenery made it hard to relax.

The flaky, splitting trees towered above them, their black leaves creating a dark velvet canopy. Several maroon plants dripped a black ooze and within the bubbling pools beneath their fleshy petals, the bodies of small animals were still decomposing.

"I half expect a zombie to jump out and eat us at this point." Al cringed as a bubble burst and sprayed tiny droplets of acid upon a tree mouse's half-submerged body.

How did the Altered live out here? They could enter the city to work and buy supplies, but they couldn't stay. Something about cross-contamination always came up when anyone mentioned them.

Other than their steady footsteps and the occasional distant animal screech, silence prevailed. Each time an otherworldly cry disrupted the air, Al jumped, but Perryn continued his pace, unfazed.

The sky hadn't changed at all since they began their journey, so Al couldn't tell how much time had passed.

Hours? It could have been days for all she knew. The sameness that surrounded them repeated like a conveyor belt, even when Perryn stopped at the edge of a ridge.

"We have arrived." He set his bag down and removed ropes and pulleys from inside.

Al inched closer to the cliff and looked down. The deep, gaping mouth of a giant cavern smiled up at her with jagged, rocky teeth.

"We're not really going down this way are we?" The thought of falling forever through the dark crushed any remaining excitement she had tried to hold on to.

"What did you expect? An elevator?" Perryn sighed. "Make yourself useful and help me."

Al backed away from the ledge, laughing. "Come on! I'm sure there's another way..."

Perryn threw down his ropes and stormed over, roughly grabbing Al's wrists, holding her in place as he spoke.

"If we fail to reach our destination before dark, we will be easy targets for scorpiopines or any of the hundreds of other predators roaming this area that would happily paralyze us with neurotoxins and then tear our limp bodies to pieces while we are still conscious. Wakatta ka?" He frowned through the glass.

Al tensed and pulled her wrist out of his grasp. His bare eyes really needed to come with a warning label. "Okay, okay. I got the download."

Together, they tied the ropes to a sturdy tree and routed them through a set of metal pulleys on their belts. Al glanced across the ravine to the opposite side where crumbling structures, leftover pieces of someone's life, dangled and fell into the depths below.

"To think people actually lived here..." She tied a knot and pulled it tight. "It's just so sad."

"Time to go." Perryn finished looping the ropes through the pulleys on his belt and then heaved his bag onto his shoulders.

With nimble fingers, Al hooked herself into the ropes and resituated her bag on her back. She looked over the ledge again and closed her eyes, trying to steady her shaking body.

"Lean into me." His voice tickled her ears.

"What!" Al's eyes shot open.

"If you fear heights, we can descend together."

"I'm not afraid of heights and I can do things on my own. Thank you very much!"

"Fine." He clicked on his headlight and rappelled down the cliff.

"Ahh! Leaving me behind again, I see! I'm gonna race you to the bottom!" Al launched herself off the cliff without hesitation.

"Must you be so loud? Our goal is the mid-section outcropping, not the bottom."

"Whatever! Wherever we're going, I'm gonna beat you there!" Al's nerves were still on high alert, but her brain distracted her with the thought of winning against him.

"May the best man win."

As Al descended, adrenaline flooded her veins. She felt alive and free, a sensation not that different from flying. She released another pulley on her belt, and the rope skidded down faster. As she zoomed past Perryn, she let out an excited yell.

The sound of his irritated grunt filled her helmet. "The ledge should not be much farther down. We will camp there for the night."

"Oh, you mean the ledge I'm totally gonna get to first?" Her laughter morphed into a sporadic cackle.

A faint light seeped into the pitch black below and Al slowed her descent as it grew closer until her feet touched a solid surface. The outcropping was wide with a tall rocky ceiling, and strings of dangling orbs draped on either side of the cave provided dim light.

Various containers stacked in piles lined the site and a cylindrical shower tucked in the far-left corner pressed against the craggy walls. Perryn swung into the opening next to her with an effortless dismount.

Al rolled her eyes. "Showoff." She caught herself smiling and turned it into an exaggerated frown when she noticed Perryn staring at her. He unhooked his belt from the line and headed into the back of the cave. "Hey, I got here before you!" She clenched her fists at her side. "You have to admit defeat! I'm the victor! I—" Her face smeared against the glass of her helmet as she fell forward, tripping on the rope still connected to her belt.

Perryn leaned over her with a smug smile. "Perhaps if you closed your mouth more often, your hand-eye coordination would improve."

Al slid out from under her oversized bag and lifted herself into a sitting position, feeling dizzy. "You're a jerk."

Perryn's eyes widened, and he threw off his bag.

She snorted. "Did your brain finally short circuit?"

Perryn reached toward her and she shut her eyes, clinging to the connection clasps that held her helmet to the biosuit. "I knew it! You really are gonna kill me!"

A soft pressure pressed against her shoulders and she opened her eyes to Perryn sticking a large piece of gray tape against her dome.

"You cracked the glass, probably when you fell just now." His tone seemed agitated. Was he scolding her?

She stared at him, her breathing uneven. "You caring about me is mega weird, bro."

Perryn narrowed his eyes. "It seems the radiation has already seeped through the crack and infected your blood."

"No wait! Really?" She flung her hands against the glass.

Perryn cleared his throat and turned away. "No, I was just...joking. Down here, the air is safe. When we return to the surface we might experience some issues, thus tape."

Al stared at him in disbelief before she scrunched her nose and crossed her arms. "If that's your kind of joke, can the punchline be me actually punching you? That wasn't funny."

He ignored her and placed both of their bags inside a metallic box with a clear lid. After a high-pitched beep, the box began humming and vibrating as a red arrow on the gauge outside ticked closer to one hundred percent.

Perryn walked to the shower and hit a button with his palm, gesturing toward the unit with an extended arm as the door slid open. Al continued to glare at him as she stepped inside.

The glass door slid shut behind her and water sprayed with deafening thunder, the sound amplified by the suit's material. Outside the shower, Perryn motioned for Al to spin several times and raise her arms, allowing the water and soapy mixture to cover the entirety of her suit. When the last of the water had disappeared down the drain, a thin blanket of mist filled the tube. With a ding like an oven, the door opened and out popped a fresh Al.

Perryn stood far from her as she emerged and directed her to wait by the black boxes while he decontaminated himself as well. Once clean, he took off his helmet, pulled his arms free from the suit, and fluffed his hair with his black-gloved hands. He took off the rest of his suit and hung it on a hook near the shower. Al watched him with her arms crossed, her biosuit still on. Perryn returned her gaze for a moment, but when the humming box dinged, he sighed and opened it, lifting their duffel bags from inside.

He removed a fresh pair of black gloves from his pocket and pulled them on. "I will collect extra supplies from Site B and should be back in about an hour. You are free to explore, just do not get lost. I will not look for you if you do."

He took a smaller bag from the larger pack and headed to the back of the cave, where it split into three rocky hallways. His footsteps reverberated against the walls as if mocking her until it was silent once again.

"Well, maybe I don't want you to find me." The metallic fabric encasing her was uncomfortable and cold, just like Perryn. She looked out into the vastness beyond the cave—pitch black, like the end of the world. Her stomach rumbled. She frowned at the tape on the glass, and then took off her helmet, digging a squished protein bar out of her pant pocket with an ungloved hand.

As she munched, Al imagined that within the orb lights dangling along the wall, captured lightning bugs bounced about, and the wires that held their prisons together were the ancient roots of an electronic tree. She laid back onto the cold ground, the last of the protein bar protruding from her lips. Boredom had arrived.

"Alrighty! Let's go explorin'!" She jumped up and shimmied off her biosuit, leaving it in a heap in the middle of the cave. Checking both ways for Perryn crossing, she dashed off in the opposite direction she had heard his footsteps leave. Her own now thundered down the tunnel like a hollow drum.

The same glowing bug lights lined the top of this corridor and continuous metal tubes of various sizes ran along the bottom. Al figured they transported water or gas somewhere. Deep scars from wheels crisscrossed the ground, and the walls were a mixture of rocks and earth, with occasional jagged metal pieces and stringy roots poking out from the crevices.

As she meandered through the tunnels, she disturbed a family of rock rabbits enjoying a cozy snooze in the wall. The cute defenders of naptime chased her away, and she laughed as she ran.

Resting against the hard wall at a fork in the hallway, she dumped debris from her boots. Gurgles traveled within the pipes and the scratchy gait of a scurrying animal came through the wall. After tugging on her boots, she stood.

The path before her split, one side another well-lit tunnel, the other ending in a misshapen hole in the wall. She headed toward the hole, ducked through the opening, and stepped into the darkness beyond.

The gigantic open space before her seemed to go on forever. In the middle of the roundness, a glowing purple wisteria tree radiated out giant roots like a wooden octopus. Al approached one and tried to wrap her arms around it. "Woah! This root's gotta be a meter thick, at least!" She felt tiny in comparison.

Above the bright tree, hundreds of tiny bioluminescent crystals covered the ceiling, creating intricate chandelier-like shapes. Their light reflected across the cave floor, sprinkling the blue-green foliage below with a kaleidoscope of dancing colors.

"And where there are cave stars..." Al ventured farther with hushed anticipation. "There are bound to be cave moons."

Nestled between two boulders, a cluster of beautiful pale blue flowers bloomed, each egg-round and surrounded by a delicate and layered white petal skirt. Al cradled one in her hand as she twisted the bud from the thick white stem. A clear liquid poured from the dislodged portion and she brought the bud to her lips and drank. Sweet nectar warmed her throat.

Rustling grass made her turn around.

A huge glowing stag moved toward her, bobbing his head with every step. His antlers branched upward like tree roots, curving and bending multiple times into a compact maze, and his incandescent fur swayed as if blown by wind. He looked straight at her with black pupils that took up a good portion of his face, only breaking eye contact when he stopped to nibble at bits of foliage.

Al slowed her breathing. She could almost touch him. With measured speed, she pulled one of the cave moons free and offered him the bud, reaching out her other hand toward his soft-looking nose.

"Al?" Perryn's distant voice echoed behind her, spooking the buck. His gleaming form disappeared beyond the giant tree like a sped-up sunset. Al chucked the flower into the void and wiped her hands on her pants before stepping back through the opening she came from. Marching down the hall and rounding the corner, she found Perryn wandering the corridor.

"You bellowed, your majesty?" Al swept her arm forward in an exaggerated bow.

"Oh, so you *are* alive. Good. You can follow me and help carry the rest of the supplies back to camp."

"Pfft, after a response like that?" Al raised an eyebrow, pushing past him. "You're on your own, buddy."

"Minus ten points."

Al dismissed him with her hand as she trotted down the hall. "Yeah, yeah. Whatever, Abacus!"

Al sat gazing into the dark void beyond the cave, a piece of moose jerky hanging from her mouth as she chewed. A fire crackled and popped in the center of their camp and its warmth hugged her through her sleeping bag. Other than staring at nothing, what else was there to do down here? Sleep tugged at her eyelids, but she kept fighting, waiting for Perryn to retire first.

Tucked inside his sleeping bag with his back against the cave wall, he read from the same plastic book he had started earlier that morning, his glasses once again resting on his nose. The thought of him watching her while she slept filled her with unease and she sank deeper into her fabric nest, gobbling up the rest of her jerky.

At some point, the bug lights went to sleep and only the faint orange glow from the embers shone through the pitch black.

She dreamt of following the luminescent buck, his four-toed hoofprints leading her deeper into the cave, past the wisteria tree, and to a clear blue lake. Rippling across the surface, her reflection smiled back. As she touched it, her face transformed into Perryn's. With a twisted smile, his vine-like fingers sprouted from the water and tangled with the strands of her hair, which had somehow grown longer. He yanked her down into the depths as she screamed, water filling her lungs.

Al jumped awake with a cry that echoed off the cave walls and a soft brown blanket that had not been there before she went to sleep slipped off her shoulders.

"Bad dream?" Perryn's voice didn't seem to hold much concern, but he glanced at her as he spoke. Sitting on his knees, he stirred a bubbling mixture in a black pot over another campfire. The smell of cinnamon wafted toward her. His glasses were gone again.

"It's nothing." Pulling the brown blanket over her head, she patted her chest and let out a breath. Her binding was still intact.

Perryn continued stirring. "We will explore Site C and D today and they are much deeper. Make sure your rope is secure. I will not save you if you fall."

"Sounds good..." The dream had startled her too much for her to counter his jest.

The spoon stopped scraping against the pot. "You sure you are alright?"

That did it. "Woah, woah, woah! I told you your kindness was creepy, didn't I? Cut it out." She scrunched her nose and hunkered deeper into her sleeping bag, like a caterpillar in a cloth cocoon. Her stomach growled, and she emerged like a disheveled butterfly.

Perryn sighed as he portioned out two servings of porridge. After slurping it down, Al gathered her gear and prepared for the long descent.

They spent several hours at Site C, where the ancient ruins of a shopping mall finally satisfied her craving for adventure. Ignoring Perryn's warnings of unstable infrastructure, she sprinted up and down the mysterious once-moving staircases and hopped over gaping holes in the crumbling checkered floor.

They explored a fashion boutique near the entrance where Al tried on frayed scarfs, dusty gloves, and strange hats, forcing some of them onto Perryn's head. He recoiled each time and deducted several points when she refused to stop. She ran out into the hall laughing, but when she rounded the corner, she almost shrieked.

Frozen stiff with an extended open hand, a lifelike woman dressed like a jungle explorer stared out with an unnaturally wide smile. The skin on her forehead had peeled back to reveal rusted inner mechanisms. Hundreds of other bodies in a similar state lay strewn about behind her. Though broken, they looked newer than the building.

Al chuckled through her nerves. "A robot..."

They sat near an old elevator shaft, munching on sandwiches for lunch, the ends of the Earth stretching out on all sides of the glass box into deep pockets of darkness. The small light positioned behind them warmed her back.

She took a sip from her water jug and looked up and down the control panel. The buttons were numbered one through twelve.

She smirked. "You were wrong about there not being an elevator, you know."

"Oh, my mistake. Welcome aboard. May I suggest floor thirteen?" Perryn deadpanned, his sandwich holding hand freezing in midair.

Al burst into laughter and hit him on the back. "Okay, I'll give you that one. It was good."

Perryn stiffened and turned away to take another bite. After spending a couple of days with him one on one, he seemed more like a moody bookworm than a demon. Maybe she could give him a chance.

Al pulled on her rope a few times, the scab on her hand twinging underneath her glove, before stepping backward over the ledge. Site D was just below. She looked down into the pitch black and the beam from her forehead light flashed across the reflective tape on Perryn's ropes.

"Did you die up there?" His voice was faint and echoey.

"If I did you would know because I would totally become a ghost and haunt you!" she called over her shoulder as she continued her descent.

"That would be incredibly horrible for me. No thank you!" Perryn's warm laughter bounced around the cavern, and it surprised her into smiling. He was becoming more human as time passed, and while unfamiliar, this new feeling wasn't so bad.

Their feet touched the next landing at the same time.

Al sent Perryn a beaming smile. "A tie, huh? Well, guess that makes us both winners—or both losers?"

Perryn cleared his throat, unhooking his rope from the line. "For this site, I suggest we split up to cover more ground, considering the size."

Al wasn't sure, but she could've sworn he sounded nervous. She shook the thought from her mind as he switched on a generator and the lights above them flickered to life. With a salute, she bounded off toward a broken staircase. "Right! See ya soon, Mr. Keevie."

Several hours later, the two spelunkers rendezvoused back at the ledge. After hooking themselves onto their lines, they hit a button on their belts and automatically rose into the air. They continued switching their lines at every subsequent level until they reached the top.

When they returned to their campsite, Perryn spread out his scavenged treasures atop a rubber mat. He alternated between brushes of different sizes and bristle strengths as he examined a thin rectangular object that had a silver pear and J logo branded on the outside.

Al stacked her loot to his right, among which were jeweled necklaces, a rusty hovercar license plate, and a pair of men's boxers in a dingy plastic packaging. A faded logo of fruit spilling from a cornucopia was printed in the corner. Searching alone through the crumbling buildings for artifacts had been unnerving, but other than a run-in with an extra-large spider or two, she had no problems collecting them.

She arranged her last item and sat next to him, rocking side to side with her legs crossed. "The things you found just look like primitive kitchenware to me."

Perryn scoffed. "This, Alec, is a genuine quantum computer."

"You say that like I'm suppose'ta know what that is." She giggled, continuing to sway.

"A supercomputer with the entire CPU fitting on a chip the size of a fingertip. This is the consumer lite version, judging by its size." Perryn rotated the item, checking for things only he understood.

Al stopped rocking and looked at her finger, her eyes crossing with sarcastic wonder. "Woah! Imagine a snack that small!"

Perryn shook his head, mumbling about homophones, and placed the computer back on the mat to continue his appraisal.

"Hey! Guess what? I've got something special to share!" Al produced a weathered book from behind her back. "Tada! I have no idea if it's valuable or not, but you're the book guy, so..."

Perryn froze, transfixed.

"Perryn?" She inched the book forward the same way she had offered the flower to the glowing deer, her eyes darting back and forth between her hands and his face. Then, as if struck by lightning, he jolted back to life and snatched up the book.

Al stifled a laugh.

Scuttling over to his bag, Perryn removed a waxy sheet of plastic and wrapped the book several times. The material shrank to its shape, creating a form-fitting seal. Al was hoping for at least a thank you, but wasn't surprised that he said nothing at all.

When Perryn returned to sit by the mat, he pulled a round, metal object from his pocket and clicked a button on its side. He set it on the ground and a blue hologram shot out from the top, projecting onto the cave wall.

Al's eyes grew wide like an amazed child as she scooted closer to him. "That's a P.M.D, right? And it's intact! Where'd you find it?"

"Inside someone's hovercar."

Their eyes met in a brief, reflective silence as Al's smile faded. They were collecting artifacts like adventurers, but Al suddenly felt like a grave robber.

The Personal Memory Device beeped once, and a rippling screen asked "continue" in chunky, white letters. Perryn clicked the button again, selecting the "yes" option, and the blue screen morphed into what appeared to be someone's living room.

Outside their tall windows, angular vehicles zoomed by without exhaust, and glassy buildings covered the entire skyline. An offscreen hand clicked a remote and a paper-thin holographic television screen materialized, revealing two women standing side by side in what looked like some sort of lab. The camera's angle obscured their faces, but the shorter one held a microphone and the other wore a lab coat, her white hair extending past her back into two long braids.

A charismatic woman's voice, robotic from the degradation of the device, emanated from its built-in speakers. "We never know when human imagination will lead us to something groundbreaking, but today might just be one of those historic moments! I'm Jeni Moss and this is the inside scoop!"

A catchy jingle played, and a smiling rainbow ice cream cone appeared and faded out from the center of the screen.

"I'm here with esteemed scientist Kera Lacey, who has recently discovered a way for us to live forever. I understand you call it the Death Clock Gene. Is that right, Miss Lacey?"

Al leaned closer to the cave wall. "What! Live forever?"

Perryn shushed her.

"Oh, yes, I suppose that is the colloquial term for it." Kera's dignified voice sounded much more youthful than Al expected for having made such a life-changing discovery. The same robotic quality clung to her words. "But here at the lab, we prefer to call it the Aevum Gene and the potential for immortality has not yet—"

"How fascinating!" Jeni over-articulated her words as she pulled the microphone away from Kera.

The scene shook as the person whose eyes were capturing this viewpoint looked down. Their hands scratched the scaly chin of a small animal with a red collar around its neck. When the viewer looked up, Jeni's wide smile and blonde hair took up the entire television screen. Even as the cameraperson tried to move away, Jeni attempted to remain the focal point.

"So, Kera, what's next for you?" She tripped and fell forward as the camera made a purposeful, almost irritated shift, panning to Kera at last.

Kera smiled a little as she pondered the question. "I'll have lunch with my boyfriend, I guess. Not much left to do after you cure cancer and beat death."

As Kera's face filled the projection, Al's whole body went cold.

Tightness.

She knew who she was.

Stabbing.

Clutching her chest, her head twisted against the ground.

Burning.

"Al! What is it?" Perryn's voice sounded muffled, like Al was drowning in a deep, cruel sea. Water filled her ears, her eyes, her lungs. She gasped for air and scratched at her sides like a crazed animal where the binding constricted her under her clothes.

"Al! Try to calm down." Perryn moved to her side, gripping her shoulders.

She continued to heave forward, oxygen refusing to enter her body. Perryn kept calling her name, but his voice disappeared with her air supply.

Al opened her eyes, and the pressure behind them made her head spin. Her entire body ached, but it was much easier to breathe. She tried to sit up, but something yanked her back. Still groggy, she looked up. Her hands were tied to a water pipe.

"What...?"

"Amendment fourteen—under penalty of death, no woman for any reason shall impersonate a man." Perryn's voice hit her like a guillotine.

She looked down. Her stuffed sock was still there, but her shirt was unbuttoned, and the binding was missing.

He saw. He knew.

Her mind swirled with thousands of screaming thoughts, each one crashing against her skull like a tsunami, urging her to run, to do something.

He sat with his back to her, the light from the roaring fire casting a flickering outline onto the metallic walls like an evil spirit had possessed his shadow.

"Rather ironic that the thing helping you blend in was the thing that ended up giving you away." Perryn's words held a sarcastic bite as he turned toward her. A halo of orange surrounded him like a fallen angel.

With each footstep, another sickening pang of fear thumped in her chest. He lowered his face so close to hers, his hot breath caressed her cheeks. His diamond-black irises stabbed her, and her heartbeat bled into her ears, drowning out her thoughts.

"You know how society is, Al. The only good woman is a dead one, or one you can fuck." He grabbed her chin with a gloved hand, forcing her to look at him. "Care to guess which one you are?"

A chill ran down her spine like a fuse, igniting her resolve. "Option C. The one that'll kick your ass."

Perryn dropped her chin with a scoff and with a swift flick of his wrist, he pulled a gun from his belt and pointed it at her. She flinched, but refused to look away.

"Why waste effort on a public execution when I can kill you right now? No one would even care. I am well within my rights in the eyes of the law and not just because my name is Keevie." His stare was harsh and unforgiving. "This is what men do, Al. They take what they want and destroy the things they no longer need."

"I'm not afraid to die." She glared at him. "I've been wondering how long of a run I'd have, actually. Two years is a bit short though. Thanks for ruining it!"

Perryn looked at her for a moment longer before lowering his gun. "Lucky for you, I have other plans." He returned the weapon to his belt and leaned against one of the black boxes near her, once again changing his gloves for a fresh pair.

"If you're suggesting I become your plaything, then I'd definitely rather die!" Al jerked forward, the rope digging into her wrists.

Perryn let out a long, hearty laugh as he turned away from her, a laugh that lacked any of the warmth she had heard from him earlier. This one was cruel. "Plaything? Do not flatter yourself. You are a child. I doubt you have the necessary skills to satisfy a man."

Al frowned, not knowing whether to feel relieved or offended. A child? He wasn't that much older. "Then what do you want?"

"For you to follow my every command."

Al blinked several times. "What?"

"Imagine the proud Alec Finn, bowing to her sworn enemy, or perhaps even calling him Master. Having power over you seems entertaining."

She scowled. *So that's his angle, to torment me.* "How do you know I won't just kill you once I'm free, huh?" The rope burned her skin.

Perryn turned around and smirked, running his gloved hands through his hair. "The futility of such a thought is laughable. I outmatch you in every way."

Al clenched her fists. He was right. She wasn't strong enough to physically overpower him and surprise attacks would be impossible now. He'd be expecting them.

"Even still, I have known you were a girl for quite a while. Why else would I put you on my team? And why would my bodyguards not accompany us to a location rife with potential 'accidents'? If I fail to return to the surface, I have instructed them to release your true identity and implicate anyone close to you—your family and dear Mr. Landers as well."

Her eyes widened as horrible scenarios flooded her brain. *No! I don't want anyone else to die because of me.* How could she have believed for even a second that he had any redeeming qualities? All that fuss about her helmet, the blanket on her shoulders, asking if she was okay. It was all an act. "How long have you known?"

Perryn turned away again. "Will you submit to me or not?"

She gritted her teeth. The wolf had trapped her. The answer leaving her mouth had a horrible taste. "Deal."

CHAPTER 6

Perryn set her free after she agreed to his proposition. No sense in keeping her tied up like that. He needed an extra pair of hands to continue the mission, even if they were stubborn.

They spent the next two days continuing to gather items but barely spoke, a welcomed reprieve from her constant need to instigate conflict. Glares were a side dish at every meal, however. She also moved her sleeping bag to the farthest part of the cave and created a barrier with the black bins. If he wanted to kill her, why did she think that would stop him?

Sitting on the cave ledge with her bare back exposed to him, she wrapped the binding around her chest, like a snake reapplying its shed skin. When she had passed out, there had been no time to focus on trivial things such as modesty. She had been unconscious. Thankfully, she had not required CPR. After he cut her free, her normal breathing rhythm had returned.

Perryn gritted his teeth. She had forced his hand due to improperly tied fabric, nothing more. Looking at her now though, the discolored splotches, new and old bruises, and faded scars running up and down her body stood out against her pale skin. Did her internal organs reflect the same injuries?

He frowned and returned to packing and organizing the items they had found. She was too open, too trusting of him. Had his aggressive display taught her nothing about men?

They would return to the surface tomorrow morning, but there was no way to come back from the consequences of this accident.

He picked up the P.M.D. and paused for a moment before placing the device in his pocket instead of with the other items. Anything showing women in positions of power, and Altered women at that, would be considered propaganda and destroyed. Something the prime minister would be more than happy to carry out.

The weight of the gun pressed against his side, and he closed his eyes. She had not wavered. Even as he glowered down the barrel of the gun, she had refused to avert her gaze. Her eyes housed a bright flame, an unyielding spark that sought to defy her circumstances.

Perryn scoffed and situated the last of his books inside his pack. *How naïve.* What did she know of the world? He turned to look at her again and all the air rushed from his lungs.

With one foot hovering over the chasm, she tipped forward.

"Ai!" Perryn sprinted toward her, yanking on her wrist just before her other foot gave way.

She toppled backward onto the ground, her body sprawling out like a paper shikigami.

Perryn stood over her. "What the hell are you doing?"

"What? What happened? Did I space out?" Bewilderment slowed her words as she held her head. A moment of clarity registered on her face, and then her innocent brown eyes bored a hole straight through him as she sat up. "Wait a minute. I thought you said you weren't gonna save me."

Shit! He looked at the offending hand that had touched her and placed it behind his back. "Hurry up and put some clothes on. Taku..." He retreated to his corner of the cave, mumbling under his breath, and began organizing the books in his bag, though they were already in order.

Keep it together.

Hurricane Al stormed toward him, picking up her jacket along the way. "Why would that matter? You've already seen me half-naked." She slipped her arms through the sleeves and stood in front of him. "Why did you save me?"

Play it off. "Are you seriously asking that? You must have forgotten our arrangement."

She scrunched her nose. "Yeah, about that. You never answered my question. How long have you known I was a girl?"

Divert her attention. "Why did you have such an adverse reaction to the P.M.D.?"

She stiffened and grabbed her elbows as her eyes darted around. "That girl...she's a traitor to the Naturalists."

A lie. "Who is she to you?"

Al pointed at him. "No way! You got one question, Mr. Keevie, and you just used it. That's it. The end!"

Mr. Keevie? "You are unbearably exasperating."

"Now tell me! How long have you known I was a girl?"

She had determination. He would give her that. Should he tell her the truth? He reached up to straighten the glasses that were not on his nose before he turned from her. "From the moment I met you."

His words continued to rattle inside Al's head the next morning as they broke camp and climbed out of the ravine back into the fresh contaminated air. If he had known that long, what kept him from blackmailing her earlier? He could've turned her in or killed her at any time, but he didn't. Was it safe to assume he wanted her alive? *He did save me from jumping off that cliff. But why?* Was it really because he wouldn't get to antagonize her? Or was it for another reason? No matter what she came up with, nothing about what he did made sense.

The orange Keev-ship had already docked by the time they reached the platform. Entering from the back, Al and Perryn walked into a plastic decontamination shower. The deafening sound of water spraying against nylon shook Al's sleepy nerves awake. Once clean, they removed their biosuits, secured the bags of treasures inside the cargo box, and took their seats.

Al stared at its blue lid as she buckled her lap restraint. Which bag held the P.M.D? The white-haired girl floated through her memory and she whacked her forehead against the window with a rather loud clunk, hoping the pain would prevent her body from jumping into another fit of panic.

The purple-black sky hid the beautiful scenery she had seen before. Only a few specks of light from the buildings below cut through the darkness. She allowed the humming of the engines and the soft outline of the rolling clouds to lull her to sleep.

When she awoke, the sky was more lavender and the lights within the ship were on. Her mind had decided not to torture her in her dreams this time. Rubbing her eyes, she pressed her soft black pillow to smooth out a crease, and it responded by making a strange breathing noise.

Her eyes shot open. She was resting on Perryn's arm. Stiff as a corpse, she inched upright, screaming inside of her head. She turned to look at him, expecting a terrifying expression to stare back, but he was asleep, his breathing even and quiet.

His hair had cascaded over his face like black lace as his head rested against the palm of his gloved left hand.

A new book, *The Selfish Gene,* lay spine up on the floor near his feet.

Al stared at him, and when she felt a small smile creeping onto her face, she realized she had been staring for far too long. She seized and turned away to stare out the window. After a few clouds zoomed past outside, she scrunched her nose and rescued his book, placing it back in his seat pocket.

"You should be nicer to your friends," she mumbled with a pout. As she turned to face the window again, she thought she saw him smile.

Once they landed at the academy's airfield, Mr. Lann gave a quick debriefing, then he and Mr. Vasiliev bid Al and Perryn farewell, leaving them behind in the foggy morning mist. The air was quiet and eerie, as if they had entered Death Desert again.

Al picked at the ends of the tape on her helmet, her small backpack feeling heavier on her shoulders than the gear-stuffed one she had left on the ship ever did. She wanted nothing more than to sprint away, back home, back to Zeek, back to normal.

Perryn took a step toward her, and she flinched.

"In total—" He pushed buttons on his wristwatch. "You earned seventy points out of a possible one hundred and fifty for your first A-ranked mission."

Al shot him an unamused glare but didn't dare speak.

He paced around her like a vulture as he continued. "I had to deduct many points for misconduct, you see."

She shivered, but she couldn't tell if it was from the early morning temperature or from Perryn's icy interrogation.

"Worry not, for I am a kind leader. I will give you a chance to raise your score if…"

Al continued to glare, tapping her foot against the crunchy ground as he stalled.

A smirk split his face as he stopped in front of her. "Bow to me again."

"Excuse me?"

"You referred to me as 'your majesty' in the cave and refused to help gather the supplies, therefore—"

"Really?" Al took a step toward him. "You're still upset about that? What're you, five?"

They locked eyes, the phoenix and the ice dragon waging another staring war.

A familiar voice called out to them through the mist, disrupting their stalemate. The two warring states turned as Zeek made his way up the hill toward them, leaning against one crutch to stabilize his steps, though his leg no longer had a cast.

Al's stomach lurched into her throat. *Not now, Zeek!*

"Welcome back, bud!" He embraced her in a giant hug, knocking her helmet from her hands.

"Yeah, good to see you too!" She struggled to speak between breaths and patted him on the back.

Perryn cleared his throat, and Zeek pulled away. "Heh...welcome back to you too, Perryn. How was the trip? Didn't get radiation poisoning did you?" He sent Perryn his finger guns with an awkward smile.

Al cringed. *Zeek, please!*

"Actually, now that you mention it," Perryn placed a hand on his chest. "I might have, as my breakfast appears to be making a comeback."

Al shot an irritated sideways glance at him. They hadn't even eaten yet.

"Oh, shit, man. I hope you get that looked at. That could be real dangerous!"

Al snickered. *Take that, you jerk.*

"What about you?" Zeek shot his finger guns at her. "You good?"

Al looked down at her busted helmet. Mr. Lann had encouraged her to keep it as a memento from the mission, proof she had survived in Death Desert long enough to come back, but the helmet was irreparable, much like her old life, which she had worked so hard to keep together.

"For the most part." She picked up the helmet and raised it with a weak laugh. "The only casualty."

Zeek touched her shoulder, his eyes narrowing with concern.

Al forced another laugh. "Really, Zeek. I'm fine. No worries."

"Yes. No need to concern yourself with Al's well-being." Perryn's smile knew things Zeek didn't.

"No need?" Zeek spun around to face him. "Al is my best friend, so if he gets hurt, of course it concerns me. Did something happen?"

Perryn raised his eyebrows. "While I appreciate your enthusiasm, Mr. Landers, Scanner confidentiality prevents me from discussing specifics."

Zeek dropped his crutch and moved toward Perryn, rolling his shoulders back and prepping his fists for launch. "Bullshit. I'm a Lead Scanner."

"First Al and now you? The disrespect for higher management just keeps spreading. Will it never cease?" Perryn glanced at Al and scenarios of bad endings befalling her best friend pummeled her imagination.

She jumped between them, pushing against Zeek's chest to hold him back. "Seriously, Zeek, I'm fine! I just lost my balance and got scraped up. That's all."

Zeek stared at her, his eyes flaring and his mouth twisting open. Backing down from a fight with Perryn was suspicious, but she had to protect him.

Please let it go, Zeek. Please.

Zeek threw a glare at Perryn, and Al wasn't sure the crunching she heard came from the crisp ground or Death cracking his knuckles.

Zeek let out an unsatisfied sigh and turned away from them. "If you say so..."

Al relaxed her arms, but her relief was short-lived.

"And minus another fifteen points."

Perryn's watch emitted several beeps.

"What?" Al stared at him, squinting. "He's not even on our team. How does that even make any sense?"

Perryn shrugged, resituating the bag on his shoulder. "I do not make the rules, Al—wait." He paused and his face broke into a smirk as he held his chin with his fingers. "My apologies. I do."

Al clenched her lips to prevent the gurgling magma of the angry volcano within her from spewing out. *So, he's gonna play really dirty then.*

"My bad..." Zeek rubbed the back of his neck.

With a heavy sigh, Al picked up his crutch and handed it back to him. "Don't worry about it. How's your leg?"

Zeek took the crutch with a soft smile. "Almost back to normal, I think." He glared at Perryn again. "Can't wait until we're back on the same team."

"Yeah..." She looked at the ground. "Me too..."

"Oh, by the way, Al, your dad is waiting for you out by the front gate."

"What? He's actually here?" *If Maddox didn't even bother to show up when I almost died, why make an effort now?* What ulterior motive did he have?

"Yeah! I saw him on my way over and he asked me to tell you."

"Great. Just great." Al hit her forehead, clenching her eyes shut. *Literally out of the frying pan and into the fire.*

When the three arrived, Maddox's tall frame leaned against the metal gate of the school's entrance. Tired dark-brown eyes stared out at nothing as he inhaled from the cigarette between his fingers. Strands of his short caramel-colored hair fell from a loose ponytail tied low behind his head as the wind carried the fumes away from his mouth. His trimmed boxed beard did nothing to hide his age, but his tweed suit and red scarf made him appear rather trendy.

"Hey, kiddo." His gruff voice still held warmth as he ruffled her hair.

He was going all out with the parent act today. Al looked up at him with an uncomfortable smile. "Hey ya…Dad."

If only he knew what had transpired down in the dark. This mistake was a million times worse than the trauma center incident. If she told him, Maddox would force her back into the bunker forever. *Goodbye freedom and any chance of finding my birth parents.* Then Perryn and Maddox would start a war as they tried to kill each other. *Goodbye Zeek and Molly.* No, she had to find a way out of this mess on her own.

"Hey there again, Mr. Finn!" Zeek gave the man a hearty salute.

"Mr. Landers." Maddox nodded at the sunburst of a man and then addressed the brooding dark cloud behind him. "Mr. Keevie." He let out a puff of smoke.

"You know smoking is bad for your health, sir." Perryn waved the dirty cloud away from his face. "It can end up killing you."

"Heh, life's a fatal illness, anyway." He sucked in another breath of tobacco. "What is it you kids say these days? Gotta live my best life?" He took one final drag before

dropping the cigarette onto the wet concrete and extin-
guishing it with the toe of his black boot.

"Yes, well..." Perryn paused. "I shall inform headquarters that Alec Finn has been safely collected by his father."

"Much obliged, Mr. Keevie. Enjoy the rest of your
weekend, boys." Maddox rose from the gate and headed
down the dirt road leading away from the academy. "Al?"

She turned to leave. "Catch ya later, Zeek."

"We still meeting up tomorrow?"

She skidded to a stop and breathed through clenched
teeth. Why did he have to ask that right now? Perryn was
still here. *If he realizes I'm gonna have fun, he's gonna squash it!*

"Uh whaaat? I dunno what you're talkin' about!"

"Yeah, remember we—"

"Are you sure that is the best course of action after coming back from such a grueling mission?" Perryn's voice
stabbed her in the back. "You should stay home and rest.
I *insist*."

And there it was, The Squashining.

Al cursed under her breath before turning around to
flash a smile. "Zeek, I might need to rest, actually. Perryn
has a point..."

Zeek stared at her in disbelief.

"We'll hang out soon. Promise!" She waved and dashed
after Maddox before anything else could happen.

CHAPTER 7

"So, how did your mission go?" Maddox's voice fell flat within the insulated cockpit of his gray Keev-ship.

Does he expect me to be grateful that he's paying attention to me now? Al stared out her window without answering him.

The sun had risen high enough to encourage the shop owners on Main Street to open their doors. A few men carrying trays of fruit pastries and steaming loaves of bread helped other men arrange them in an attractive pattern within a display case, their open mouths speaking words Al couldn't hear.

Next to the bakery, a neon-green building of equal size sported a large sign with the words *Exotic Pets* hand-painted in sloppy black letters. It featured crude drawings of animals with jagged teeth and spikes, but in the window, only rock rabbits, garden lizards, and horned beetles slept in their padded cages.

"Al? Did you fall asleep?" Maddox didn't take his eyes from the sky path, but reached out to tap her back.

"No. I'm awake." She brushed his hand away without turning from the window.

The ship hovered several meters above the cobblestone street, casting a warped shadow upon the shops below as they passed other crafts going the opposite direction.

A shiny cog hanging in the Gear and Gadgets Repair Shop window showed an eleven a.m. opening time and The Best Barber Shop next door already had a long line of men in various stages of hair growth waiting outside. Some stood with women who entertained their infants with homemade toys.

They passed the Fancy Florist, the only shop in the city owned by a woman. The sign that hung on the awning made sure to let the world know this information.

Outside the red doors of The Catch and Claw Café, which served the best roasted potato sticks in all of Astova, a few workers stood at wooden barrels, pulling out orange spuds and peeling them.

Couples of all ages decorated the empty stalls of the farmer's market with colorful produce, soaps, candles, and other handmade items while groups of soldiers dressed in red and white marched with high knees across the square, stun guns hanging at their hips.

"Look Al, I'm just trying to communicate. You know I worry about you, right?" Maddox's words sounded awkward, like cotton had filled his mouth.

"You say that, but you've always disappeared for weeks, sometimes even months on end, leaving me behind." She traced the roofs of the buildings on the glass with her finger. "Now that I'm older, the only difference is I get to go outside."

"Well—" his words caught in his throat. "I'm here now, making an effort, aren't I?"

Now I get it. "You mean, you're overcompensating."

Maddox stiffened and sighed. "Can't hide anything from you, can I?"

He turned the ship left, away from Main Street, and the concrete road below dissolved into a dirt one.

On either side, a dense collection of coniferous trees sprouted tall with fuzzy periwinkle or dark green needles. Other than the tree mice with their translucent wings and the bugle birds with thin, sharp beaks for extracting bark grubs, the road to the Finn family home had no neighbors.

"You know what I still don't get? Why would a Naturalist agree to take in someone like me?" Al stared at her reflection in the glass above the dash. "Don't you worry about getting caught?"

Maddox's expression hardened. "I promised your mother I would keep you safe—"

Al let out a sarcastic laugh. "Oh, yes, I'm very safe. On top of being a freak, let's have Al pretend to be a boy for an extra dose of treason!"

"You really want to try your luck at Elbion or be forced to live outside the wall with the other Altered? At least this way you can learn practical skills and actually have a chance to survive if something ever happens to me."

Al rammed her back against the seat. "Yeah, yeah, I know! I have your lectures pretty much memorized at this point. Remember Al, be aware of your surroundings at all times. Hide your fingerprints, Al! Don't cry in front of others! Act tough, but don't draw *too* much attention to yourself! If you mess up and someone finds out, it's either back to the bunker or death. Good luck, Al."

Maddox took in a quiet breath and furrowed his eyebrows. "Good to know you've been paying attention. As it stands, you have one chance left. The trauma center was hard to clean up."

How can he be so nonchalant about murder?

"I know that already." She glared out the window, recalling Perryn's warning and Kera's face. "I dunno why my mother wanted *you* to protect me, or why anything to do with her is always treated like some deep dark secret, but aren't I old enough to at least know her name yet?"

Maddox gripped the steering wheel, his fingers curling over the metal. "That's a story for another time."

"Yeah, exactly. Textbook Maddox."

They flew in silence until they reached home, where Maddox lowered the ship onto the metal stabilizer in the driveway and switched off the hydrogen-powered engine.

Their house was a round dome made of interlocking glass and metal hexagons with different gradients of white, gray, and clear. Solar panels ran along the top, blending with the pattern. The door was the only natural element of the structure, made of wood and painted a dark green, resembling the surrounding thick forest. A sea of white and black pebbles covered the front yard on either side of the cobblestone walkway, while groomed ferns and poppyroses framed the bottom of the dome like a floral skirt.

Al kicked the ship's door open and hoisted her bag over her shoulder. She grabbed her helmet and chucked it into one of the rose bushes before slamming the door.

Maddox cringed. "Please be gentle with her, Al. She isn't cheap."

Al rolled her eyes and grumbled to the front door, her feet crunching against the pebbles. If anything broke, she'd just fix it. It wasn't a big deal.

She waited on the steps, tapping her foot against the concrete as she crossed her arms.

Maddox eyed her rejected helmet as he reached her side and placed his finger on the circular scanning panel.

"Identity confirmed. Welcome home, Maddox Finn," Martin the AI's computerized voice greeted them as the door swung open.

Al rushed inside and was about to kick it shut, but Maddox snuck his shoulder into the opening. He let out a pained grunt before stepping through the door. "Trying to off your old man, huh, kiddo?"

Al looked down. "Sorry..."

He ruffled her hair and smiled. "Don't worry, I'm a tough cookie. It takes more than a door to take me down."

"Did someone say cookies?" A warm and airy voice called out to them.

From the kitchen, a curvy woman in her forties with peachy skin and dark, shoulder-length hair appeared in the entryway. She wore a frilly, long-sleeved white apron that hugged the pregnant bulge of her stomach as she stirred the contents of a mixing bowl with a spatula.

"Yes, we're back, Molly, and it's just us." Maddox shrugged off his jacket and hung it on the nearby coat rack.

"Good! I was tired of pretending that I knew how to bake these infuriating things." Her voice changed to a lower, more textured tone as she set the bowl on the counter, the mixture inside not resembling anything edible at all.

Molly pulled off her apron, tossing it and a pillow, onto a green armchair, revealing black pants, a red sleeveless turtleneck, and a much flatter stomach.

"Tough day? You look like a junk-dozer swallowed you up and spit you back out." She licked her thumb and wiped a smudge of dirt off Al's face.

Al rubbed her damp cheek. "You could definitely say that."

"Well then, let me whip you up something I'm actually good at making." With a knowing smile, she winked and headed into the wide silver kitchen and opened the triangular orange refrigerator. Two faded orange hand-prints, one adult-sized, the other a child's, overlapped in the middle of the glass doors.

Al smiled. She and Molly had built the cooler together, sitting in the middle of the living room, staining their clothes and the now dearly departed carpet with grease and orange paint. That moment was the only happy memory Al had of her childhood, having spent most of her life locked in the dark, cold bunker under the house. She didn't even have a proper bedroom until a few years ago. She frowned. *Thanks a lot, Maddox.*

"Sit! Sit!" Molly motioned to the glass dining room table with exaggerated hand swipes, as she stood on her toes to pull dishes from the middle shelf of the cabinet.

Even though Maddox and Molly had matching finger band signatures engraved under their skin, Al wasn't sure they were actually married. There were too many secrets to keep track of in this house.

Something sizzled in the pan on top of the convection cube and a sweet aroma filled the room. Al slumped into one of the dining room chairs, and after Maddox took his boots off in the entryway, he sat next to her at the table.

With the clinking of dishes and a sprinkling of garnish, Molly arrived, plates in hand. "Chef's special. Molly's maple moose sandwiches!" She set them on the table with a proud smile as syrup oozed from the edges of the pancakes.

Al forced a smile back. "Thanks, Molly. You're the best."

Molly put her hands on her hips and beamed. "Naturally." She bustled back into the kitchen and returned with a cup and saucer. "And for my Dox, perfectly crafted—straight from the packet—barley tea." She placed it in front of Maddox as if performing a sacred ceremony.

He nodded with a soft chuckle. "Thank you, Molly. You know how to pour the hot water just how I like it."

She gave him a thumbs-up. "I got you, darling."

Molly joined them at the table with a pancake sandwich of her own, and while the adults talked about politics and town gossip, Al's stomach twisted relentlessly. What horrible things would Perryn make her do? The best option would be to disappear, live a new life beyond the wall, but then she wouldn't be able to find clues about her parents or see Zeek anymore.

"So, Al, I heard you got to fly on a brand-new Keev-ship this time. How exciting!" Molly's bright voice snapped Al out of her thoughts. "I've always wondered, why do you like them so much?"

Al's stomach relaxed and she smiled. "I like knowing what their insides are made of, what kind of magic makes them work."

Maddox dropped his fork, startling the other two at the table. "Don't mind me, just getting old..." He stared into his cup of tea.

"Thanks for breakfast." Al stood, put her dishes in the sink, and sprinted up the stairs. She bounded down the hall toward her bedroom and opened and closed her door with a loud thud before tiptoeing back down the hallway. *Espionage time.*

Keeping her back against the wall until she reached the top of the stairs, she sank onto her stomach and peeked out over them. Listening. Scheming.

Maddox stared out the window as he stood in front of the kitchen sink, the water running.

"Everything okay, Dox?" Molly came up behind him and squeezed his shoulders.

"She is too much like her sometimes..."

Molly turned off the water and cupped his hands. "I really think you should be honest with her before she finds out on her own. Al's a smart kid, remember?"

Al smirked. If the adults wanted to continue keeping secrets in her house, they needed to try a lot harder.

"More like a sneaky one." Maddox turned toward the stairs. "Al, I know you're listening."

The flattened girl scrunched her nose and hit the ground with a disappointed grunt. So much for being smart.

Maddox pulled his hands from Molly's. "We'll talk later." He made eye contact with Al as he crossed the living room and disappeared into his study in the back of the house, leaving her to sulk on the stairs.

Molly let out a defeated sigh and began scraping the squishy mixture out of the bowl and into the garbage. "You two are something else."

Still pouting, Al flipped onto her back, her hair falling to either side as she stared at the puffy white clouds through the glass ceiling. "He started it."

The sound of crashing waves and seabird calls filled her room as Al glared at the sky, lying in her round bed with her bare feet dangling over the edge. "I have to figure out how to stop Perryn from controlling me."

Her binding and stuffed sock lay in a messy heap on the floor near her dresser. Free from its grasp, she wore a loose-fitting white shirt and blue shorts.

A miniature model of a long red Keev-ship hung from the skylight in the middle of the room and a few painted posters of men standing in heroic poses in front of their ships were taped to the opaque glass walls. One of them was Zeek, his charismatic smile captured with perfect accuracy.

A seabird screeched by her ear as it circled the familiar digital beach scene flickering on her walls. Al groaned. "Martin, simulation off, please."

"Terminating simulation. Stress levels are still detected," the AI answered her as the digital ocean faded back to grayed glass.

"Yeah, the stupid seabirds were adding to that." Al sneered at the wall, but then gasped and touched it. "Sorry, Kelpy. Sorry, Potato." Taking out her anger on her friends wasn't right.

She sat up and traced the red scar on her right hand and then clenched her fists. "I'll figure out how to defeat you. Just you wait, Perryn!" She hugged her pillow to her face and let out a frustrated scream into its fibers, but a tiny and polite knock stopped her outburst. Tossing her pillow aside, she opened her bedroom door and craned her neck into the hall. "Hello?"

A metallic creature zoomed past her and landed on her wooden desk. As he jolted his shiny head from side to side, the smooth ovate leaf-shaped antenna that sprouted from his forehead bounced in a choppy rhythm. Behind his meshy cowlick, a tiny collection of solar panels ran down the back of his head. The same tech covered the tops of his knees and wings, when outstretched, revealed his inner mechanisms grinding and moving about.

"Cogs!" Al scooped up the crow and touched him to her cheek.

Even though the worldwide holo network had gone offline before she was born, this tiny flyer stored droves of knowledge within his byte-sized brain.

"Al. Al. Back. Back." The bird squawked with a cute, childlike timbre and fidgeted in her hand. He then hopped onto her lamp, but lost his balance, soon settling for the flat surface of the desk instead.

Al chuckled as she sat cross-legged on her bed. "Yes, I am! How've you been, Cogs?"

The crow tilted his head, his green jeweled eyes sparkling. "Maintenance. Good. Friendship. Low." He bounced across the desk toward Al. "Al. Here. Cogs. Happy."

"I'm happy you're here too! It sucks that Maddox never lets me take you out of the house. You could ride on my shoulder like my personal mascot." Al rolled her eyes as she mocked her guardian's words. "But it's too dangerous, he said. You might talk, he said."

Cogs tilted his head again and paused, the indicator light under his chin flashing blue. He opened his mouth and out poured Maddox's recorded voice.

"You have to leave Cogs here. We don't know who could be listening. We can't risk it. I'm sorry." Cogs closed his mouth with another squawk and bobbed his head.

"Oh." Al gulped. "When you put it like that, I guess he kind of has a point."

"Point. Point. Win game. Al?" His tiny coiled feet clicked against the desk as his leaf antenna waved from side to side like a tail.

"Yes, you win!" Al clapped her hands together and giggled.

Cogs opened his mouth and a short trumpet fanfare poured out, followed by a man's animated voice saying, "You did it!"

"We just need confetti and it could be a party! Wait— Cogs!" She turned to him, her eyes widening. "You know about things before the war, right?"

Cogs bounced on the desk. "Correct. I am Cogs."

"What do you know about someone named Kera Lacey?"

Cogs paused, the light under his chin blinking blue. He let out a sudden squawk as the light turned red. "Access denied."

"What do ya mean, access denied?" Al squinted. "Cogs, tell me about Kera Lacey."

The answer came much quicker this time but remained the same.

"Access denied."

Al scrunched her nose. "I shouldn't be surprised. More secrets." She stood and paced around the room while Cogs mimicked her actions on top of her desk. "What was it? That thing Kera was talking about? Avenue? No. Avery? Oh, fish on a stick, what was it?" She slammed her fist into her hand. "Aevum!" She faced Cogs, who was still pacing back and forth. "Cogs, tell me about the Aevum Gene, please!"

Cogs stopped pacing and tilted his head as he computed the information. His blue indicator light flashed a lot longer than usual, and Al held her breath. *Please work!*

The indicator light turned green. "Information. Found."

"Thank you, my smart, wonderful brain!" Al patted her head.

Cogs opened his mouth, and a woman's pre-recorded voice came out of his beak.

"The Aevum Gene, more colloquially known as the Death Clock Gene, has been a hot topic since its discovery, but today, the world finally saw its first glimpse at a new type of human, the kind that could live forever. Mia London has more information."

"Thank you, Gabriella. Supporters of the experiment have celebrated across the world with what're being called 'holy grail parties.' Sales of large goblets have more than tripled over the last week. While the discovery is being hailed a miracle by the scientific community, a strong voice speaking out in opposition is former fellow researcher, Vilroy Vax."

Al gripped her sheets. "Him?"

"I initially joined the project out of respect for my colleague and to satisfy my curiosity, but once I understood the full scope of her plan, I couldn't align myself with it anymore. We need to focus on more natural goals at this time."

Al shuddered. Hearing someone who would one day turn into the most powerful man in Astova speak with common citizens like a regular person made her skin crawl.

"We will continue to bring you more information as the story unfolds, but for now, from all of us at Inside Scoop, we wish you luck! So exciting huh, Mia? Now for your daily ozone levels, quadrant three is currently at a healthy eighty percent—" Cogs closed his mouth and the news report ended.

Al's eyes darted sporadically as she tried to process her thoughts. She was only hoping to find information on Kera, but instead, she discovered that Vilroy not only knew her, he also knew of her plan to create humans who could never die. "Woah..."

"Woah. Woah. A discovery." Cogs hopped onto her shoulder, his antenna standing up straight like an exclamation point.

Al stiffened as she looked at him. "Cogs, are you sure you're not connected to the holonet anymore? Like, really sure you're not transmitting a signal right now? This seems like the kind of secret info that would get someone's head chopped off."

Cogs paused, and his indicator light turned red. "Connection. Error." He ducked his head in and out of Al's hair as he played peekaboo with his reflection in the mirror on the opposite side of the room.

Al relaxed her shoulders. "Okay, so what happened to her? You would think someone who discovered something like immortality would be more famous. Maybe I could find her old address and retrace her steps that way?"

Cogs stopped moving as his little brain computed the question. A flash of green. "Hall of Records. Death. Life. Numbers."

"Of course!" Al had a name to put to the face now.

She shot up, causing Cogs to cling to her shoulder with a strange wailing not befitting a robot crow. Opening her closet, she shoved several boxes out into the center of her room, her head bumping into the few shirts hanging within. With more disapproving cries, Cogs gave up his perch and flew back to the desk, bouncing and squawking every time Al tossed something out.

She removed the last box, completely clearing the bottom of the closet, and then stuck her finger into a hole in the floorboard, pulling open a secret compartment. From within, she retrieved a photograph with burnt edges. The bottom left corner had a handwritten note.

Alisa-My Sweet Angel-Age 2 Months

It was cruel enough that Maddox had intended to destroy the photo without her ever seeing it, but he even wanted to keep her real name a secret by calling her Alec instead. That part at least made sense. The name Alisa belonged to a girl, something Al wasn't sure she'd ever be.

She turned the photo over and stared at the moving digital image of a smiling woman. Her two long white braids swayed in the wind and her icy blue eyes opened and closed as she patted a baby on her shoulder. Bundled in a red blanket, only the child's kicking feet were visible.

Al hugged the photo to her chest, her whole body encouraging her to cry, but she refused to give in. Cogs' antenna drooped to one side as he perched himself on top of her head, nuzzling his beak between the strands of her hair.

Despite Maddox's best efforts to literally keep her in the dark her whole life, Al had finally found a solid clue about her past.

"Kera Lacey. I know your name now, Mom."

Maddox looked up from his tiny screwdrivers and magnifying glass to check the schematics of his latest invention.

Deep gray on three sides and pure glass on one, the walls of his study room were covered with several shelves of books, a black chalkboard scribbled with equations, and a glass case that held an ornate purple kimono with a gold butterfly pattern.

Among the items on his well-organized desk were vials of cleaning chemicals, a few bottles of eye-dye he had made for Al, and his cup of barley tea. He took a sip from the white porcelain cup and tightened his lips. Cold. Rubbing his temples, he leaned back in his maroon armchair.

The clock on the shelf started to chime. "Already noon? I guess I can allow myself a break."

He stood and walked over to the glass wall, leaning his forearm against its cool surface. The sun shone through the needles of the trees outside, casting prickly shadows all over the room.

She saw through me, as clearly as I can see through this glass. Seventeen years and he still didn't know how to be a father to her, let alone a good one.

Turning away, he pulled out a book from one of the many shelves and opened the front cover to reveal a hollow inside. Nestled within a stained brown cloth was a heart-shaped gold locket. He flicked it open with his thumb and smiled as he watched the digital screens flicker, his eyes welling up with tears. Brushing them away with the back of his hand, he placed the book back on the shelf and retrieved a red handker-chief from his pocket to blow his nose.

He then retired onto the plush couch and rested his feet on the coffee table. "You would kill me if you saw where my feet were." He chuckled as he stared at the pendant.

The ticking clock invaded the silence surrounding him, and his face turned dark as he closed the locket in his fist. "Well, I'm done vacationing to memory lane. Don't know why I visit. The weather's always shit." He sat up and tucked the jewelry back into its secret nook. Sitting back at his desk, he returned to his project, the afternoon sun continuing to paint funny shadows around the room like a nursery mobile.

CHAPTER 8

Al dug her running shoes into the dirt, sweat trick-ling down her neck as her bangs stuck to her fore-head. With shoulders hunched forward and her dirty cloth-wrapped hands at the ready, she assessed the series of obstacles before her.

Tall trees bordered the backyard like a living fence, and strung between their branches, a blue meshy canopy fluttered in the wind. If not for that, the scorching sun would've reached Al's bare arms and legs.

She let out a long breath, the sweat-dampened bind-ings sticking to her back and chest under her white shirt. The stuffed sock rested in her room.

Another breath.

The black shorts she wore clung to her already-tired muscles.

Another breath.

Maddox stood beside her with his clipboard tucked under his arm, his eyes glued to his wristwatch, and his whistle held near his lips.

Cogs shuffled across his shoulder, watching Al with tilt-ing head movements. He wore a tiny paper hat behind his antenna with the words *Team Al* on the front, and with each cranial jolt, it slid farther down his head.

"Run four, start!" Maddox blew the whistle and Al sprinted forward, zigzagging across the dark lines drawn on the ground and hopping in and out of colored circles.

Reaching the end, she continued speeding forward until she reached an alternating line of thin, hollow hexagons that glowed blue. She leaped through each one, her feet landing in the middle of the raised blue podiums on the other side with perfect precision.

After crawling out from underneath a canopy made of sharp metal pieces, Al jumped back to her feet and raced toward a vertical wooden wall where a worn-looking rope dangled from the top. Al let out another breath before grabbing the rope and placing both feet against the wall.

Sweat soaked her entire shirt, and the muscles in her arms shook. She gritted her teeth and tried to climb, but after three steps, her arms gave way and she collapsed back-first onto the hard dirt, the wind knocked from her lungs. She could feel this one. It was going to leave a nasty bruise. She struggled to bend her knees as she gasped for air.

More injuries. More pain. More destruction to her already beat-up body. What else was new?

"Help. Help. Trouble." Cogs landed on her knee with cute squawks, the paper hat having completely fallen to dangle under his chin. Al's hand shook as she reached up to stroke his beak, and then both of her arms collapsed at her sides.

"Al!" Maddox was above her, holding his clipboard. "You almost had it, kiddo!"

Al covered her eyes with her arm and continued to pant. "No, no...I'm fine...thanks for...asking..."

"I'm sorry. I got a little overzealous. Are you okay?"

"Well, I'm not dead yet," she quipped, rolling onto her stomach. She felt like a bowl of noodles as she stood and the sting of fresh scratches bit into the back of her legs.

Perfect. Add it to the list of defects.

Cogs perched himself on top of Al's head and burrowed into her hair like it was a nest.

Maddox looked away. "I wish you wouldn't joke about death so much..."

"Why not? Would you actually be sad if I died?"

"Of course I would. Why would you ask that, kiddo?" He reached out to embrace her, but she shrugged him away.

"I'm not a kid! And I'm sick of getting hurt all the time! It's like all I've ever been to you was just some freaky science experiment for you to study." Al swallowed, but her throat felt dry and scratchy. She wouldn't cry, no matter how much she wanted to. She wasn't weak.

"I'm sorry." Maddox's hand fell to his side. "I pushed you too hard today. I just want to make extra sure you maintain your physique be—"

"Because you don't trust me to take care of myself, right?"

"That's not..." Maddox clenched his clipboard and looked down with a heavy sigh.

"Whatever." She headed toward the back of the house as Cogs squawked several times.

"Mean. Maddox. Mean." His antenna curled inward as he jolted his head from side to side inside Al's hair.

When the automatic back door slid open, Molly was sitting cross-legged on the living room floor, fixing a clock. "Did you beat your time today, dear?" She held up the timepiece with an exaggerated smile, but her expression turned into alarm as Al let out a frustrated yell.

"Kiddo? Dear? I have a name, ya know! Because I'm a human being? I'm tired of not being treated like one!"

Al thundered up the stairs with Cogs belting, "Mean. Mol-ly. Mean." until she slammed her bedroom door.

With her clean hair wrapped in a micro towel, damp from her recent shower, Al laid on her bed again, staring at Kera's moving picture.

"All these years waiting to know your name and I find it in the center of the Earth, after dragging myself through a radiated death park with the most egotistical guy in the world. Ridiculous." She scrunched her nose and rolled onto her back, the towel unfurling like flower petals. "I'm starting to think the only way he'll leave me alone is if I die."

Except for a few disk-shaped lights stuck into the ceil-ing, the night sky covered the room in darkness, the halfmoon now only a sliver of its normal size.

Al held the picture above her face. "Kera Lacey. Hall of Records. How to enter. Now I sound like Cogs."

Her crow friend was curled up on her desk in a little round bed, his eyes closed and his wings and antenna folded against him. He made a faint humming sound as his metal chest moved up and down.

Al set the picture aside and continued to stare into the sky through the clear ceiling, the soft fibers of a fresh shirt and shorts hugging her skin.

"If I can convince Zeek to go with me, I can use his military clearance. Then if hydrogen hits the fan, I'll just convince the authorities it was an independent Scanning mission?" She scratched her head with both hands and groaned. If she involved Zeek, she risked revealing her secrets, but only military families could access the Hall of Records. She would have to come up with a sneaky excuse to hide her true intentions. But even if she did that, how in the world would she go without Perryn interfering?

A light knock interrupted her planning.

"Al? Are you hungry?" Molly's muffled voice came through the wall.

Al clawed at the bed for the picture and shoved it under her pillow just as Molly opened the door.

"I thought you might enjoy a snack since you didn't join us for dinner." She held a tray with a plate of sliced oblong-shaped fruit stuck with toothpick swords. Al inched to sit closer to the pillow that hid her mother's photo as Molly set the tray on the desk.

"I brought the good stuff." Molly winked with her hands on her hips.

Al frowned but didn't budge. "Trying to win me over with sunset fruit, I see."

"Yes, and you better appreciate it, because this is the last of it," Molly teased, plopping onto the bed next to her. She took a piece and stuck it in her mouth before picking up another and swinging it like a pendulum in front of Al's face. "Hmm? You sure you don't want one?"

Al's stomach gurgled. With a sigh, she pinched the sword and stuck the piece of fruit in her mouth. She licked the magenta leftovers from her fingers, as a tangy flavor overwhelmed her senses.

"Look Al, I know we seem like stuffy old adults who just tell you what to do, but we really are trying to keep you safe. We love you!" Al could tell Molly was trying her best to reconcile, but no amount of explaining would change the fact that Al was trapped, forced to either live a lie in the light or the truth in the dark.

"All my life, I've been hiding. When can I finally stop doing that?"

Molly took in a deep breath and let it out. "I'm sorry, Al, my lovely, smart human being."

Al smiled. Molly had taken what she had yelled at her earlier to heart.

"I too wish you didn't have to live this way. Before The Consequence, women could do anything! They built spaceships, served as prominent defense leaders and they even cured cancer! Oh my gears, I doubt they taught you *that* at the academy."

Al shook her head.

"Back in my day, equal opportunities were the standard. Now, us women are reduced to being baby machines until we die! I don't care how low our population is! It's wrong!" Molly stuffed two more pieces of sunset fruit into her mouth.

Al touched the photo beneath her pillow. Maddox might be the tightest lid in all of Astova, but maybe Molly would open up. "Did you...know my mother?"

Molly stared out into the room and remained silent for a long while.

Al frowned. *Of course, she won't say anything.* Maddox's secrecy decree extended to her as well. Molly was easier to talk to, more understanding, but she was still loyal to her husband.

"We used to work in the same building." Molly smiled wistfully. "She was always so self-assured."

Wait what? Molly actually revealed something for once? What building? Is it still standing? I wanna ask, but I can't risk her knowing I'm looking for Kera. She'd tell Maddox for sure. But if the Hall of Records didn't pan out, maybe Molly could be a backup plan.

Al held up the sword toothpick. "Excuse me. Did you just give away secret information to the enemy?"

Molly crossed her wooden blade against Al's, her spunk returning. "Alas, my captor was too convincing, and I was compelled to switch sides."

"Okay fine, Molly." Al laughed, lowering her sword. "You're actually the best!"

Molly placed her hands on her hips with a smile. "Naturally."

When Al returned to school the next day, Perryn wasted no time in exercising his power. His commands were simple at first, like lending him a pencil, or holding the door open for him, but then his requests grew more annoying.

On the day the limited-edition goat sandwich arrived at the academy's cafeteria, the overlord demanded she wait in line to buy him one, using her own money. The line was so long that it ate away the entire lunch period and she never even got one before they sold out. He made her return every subsequent day to try again.

When she managed to get her hands on the fabled food, she presented it to him with triumphant pride, hopeful that he'd be appeased and stop tormenting her for a while. That was expecting a lot. He took the sandwich and, after hesitating, dropped it in a nearby trash can, making sure she could see him. Al wanted to dump the entire receptacle on his pristinely combed head.

A week later, Perryn told her to visit the library after school, and when she arrived, a table full of stacked books greeted her. A plastic film covered each page, and he instructed her to sanitize every single one. Al wanted to punch him in the face. His smug, stupid face.

She wasn't sure when she had fallen asleep, but when her eyes snapped open, the sky was dark and her body had slumped forward against the table now filled with sanitized books. As she sat up and rubbed a sore spot on her cheek, a blanket slipped from her shoulders. She bent down to pick it up, and her groggy mind presented her with a conundrum.

This was the second time a mysterious blanket had materialized out of thin air during her sleep. An uncomfortable weight, like an anchor, fell to the bottom of her stomach when she realized the only explanation.

She whirled her head back and forth, looking for Perryn, but she was alone.

"No." Al scrunched her nose as she balled up the blanket in her hands. This kind gesture didn't erase his misdeeds. Plus, all these extra side quests prevented her from hanging out with Zeek unless she saw him during class. When he confronted her about it, she had to lie to keep him safe.

She stared at the blanket again, more puzzling questions poking her brain. If Perryn could make her do anything he wanted, why was everything he requested so juvenile? It had been months since the cave, but Perryn still hadn't sold her out or tried to kill her. If he hated her so much, then why stall? Al rested her chin on her open hands. "Maybe he's not as evil as I thought."

That idea stayed with her even until a month later when they received another Scanning mission: helping the town of An Mi with a pest problem.

Because of An Mi's remote location, Perryn suggested they use his personal Keev-ship. He probably just wanted to show off. As she sat in his bullet-ship's soundproof lounge, she frowned at the expensive-looking, deep-brown material that lined the interior and rounded over the gilded windows. Plush black chairs bordered either side of the aisle, two in each row. Each one had a floating tray table, upon which a warmed hand towel and a container of pastel mints awaited use.

An attendant dressed in a black suit offered her a tall glass of sparkling liquid with an emotionless stare, but she shooed him away. With a bow, he turned and walked down the carpeted aisle and entered a rounded door near the front of the aircraft. Al craned her neck to catch a glimpse inside the cockpit before the stoic attendant latched the door shut, but it was a brief and unexciting view.

She scrunched her nose and sank so low in her chair she almost sat on the floor. "Why would anyone sit here? It's so boring. You can't see the engine, switches, lights, or anything." She leaned her head back on the seat, following the lines and rings in the dark wooden panels of the ceiling until her gaze fell upon Perryn, who was reclining in the seat facing her on the opposite side of the aisle.

His glasses had returned to his nose and his head rested on one hand as he perused a red book propped up in his lap. Al couldn't read the symbols on the front, but she recognized the cover as one of the last books he had forced her to clean before he allowed her to leave the library.

She returned to her chair, sitting on her knees, and peered over the top at his bodyguards, who sat several rows behind her. Only the tops of their heads and their eyes peeked out, like lions waiting behind leather boulders.

"Do you really have to travel with those guys?" Al ducked down in her chair and shuddered as flashbacks of fruit peels and the stench of garbage reached her nose.

Perryn kept his eyes on his book. "They are trained in flight safety for this specific Keev-ship model. An extra precaution should any accidents occur with the plane."

"Right." Al rolled her eyes. "Wouldn't want someone important to go down with the ship now, would we?"

Perryn smirked. "If their presence bothers you that much, you are more than welcome to jump."

"Sure!" Al clapped her hands together and pointed them at Perryn as she spoke. "If I can use your arrogance as a parachute, I should be fine."

He stifled a laugh behind his hand and turned a plastic page.

They reached the outskirts of An Mi about an hour later, landing on a grassy hill that overlooked a cluster of flat buildings. The remnants of a Keev-ship hangar loomed a few yards below them, its metal walls ripped open and, in some places, twisted into cone-like spirals. Something big and angry had done that.

She pretended not to notice the bodyguards as she followed Perryn to the back of the ship. They remained in their seats like statues with their backs turned.

By the time she reached the exit door, Perryn had already buckled himself into a protective vest and stowed his glasses. A pair of black earmuffs hung around his neck. Without a word, he nodded at the open compartments where the extra equipment was stored.

Al knew he wanted her to suit up, but mimicked his head motion with a questioning glance. Perryn made another, but much more pronounced head tilt toward the gear, and Al snickered.

"Stop messing around." Perryn unhooked a vest from the compartment and shoved it into her arms, which she almost dropped when he let go. He hoisted his bag onto his shoulder as the same emotionless attendant pulled open the oval exit door and bowed.

Perryn disappeared outside and Al scrunched her entire face, mocking his words as she donned her gear. Why was he so serious all the time? Life could end at any moment, so why not have fun once in a while? She stepped outside, grateful the late afternoon sun was sinking behind her.

Perryn had waited for her this time.

As they walked down the hill covered in tiny white and yellow flowers, she noticed the buildings didn't seem as sturdy as they had first appeared. Some had crumbled, spilling bricks, boards, and belongings from their sides. The roofs showed the same cone spirals protruding downward into the interior like stalactites.

They reached the bottom of the hill where a white archway welcomed them with a black sign hanging from the center by one chain link, threatening to fall. Bearing the symbols 安美 in white, a painted version of the same delicate meadow flowers decorated the sign on both sides. Passing underneath, the two traveled down a brick street, and an eerie silence soaked the air, only interrupted by an occasional gasp or a window slamming shut. Al gripped the straps of her bag. This town really did need their help. The houses grew more sporadic as the distant sound of men's laughter grew louder.

A group of fourteen men in their twenties, wearing the standard black-and-green Scanner uniforms, sat on top of crates, drinking beer, eating, or playing cards off to the side in the dirt, their vests and earmuffs strewn about. A few green tents dotted the campsite and bouts of congested snoring thundered from inside. The moment the men realized they had company, they stiffened, some dropping their silverware.

"Elite Scanner Keevie!" a man stuttered as he launched to his feet with a salute. Even his black mustache seemed to quake. "We, uh, we're just saving our strength for the fight!"

Perryn closed his eyes for a moment and sighed before walking straight through the middle of their circle. "If you die from being ill-prepared, I *will* include that in my field report." The men exchanged tense stares once he had passed.

Al followed her partner, cringing as she went. "Excuse us..."

They moved away from the group toward a towering beige wall that seemed to reach the clouds, stretching farther than Al could see on either side. In the center, a gaping hole spilled broken concrete and a giant letter *A* gleamed red with paint—the Altered's calling card. They had breached the wall and disturbed the creatures that lived within the dark forest on the other side, purposely throwing the town into disarray.

Al touched the scar on her hand. Why were the Altered so good at causing pain? Was it because they were hurting too?

A pair of young men, one standing against the wall, the other sitting on a crate, stopped their conversation when they saw Perryn approaching and retreated to the safety of their buddies in the circle. Al was about to sit on the crate, but Perryn reached it first. She sighed and hit her back against the wall. *Fine.* She was sick of sitting anyway.

The men snuck glances over their shoulders, and Al couldn't help glare back. "Why are people so afraid of you, Perryn?"

He raised an eyebrow. "That is a rather strange question, since you are the one asking."

"I'm not scared of you. You're just annoying."

"Kochira-koso."

"What's that mean?"

"Likewise. Same here. Touché."

"Ohhh, I'll have to remember that one." She turned to face the wall, placing her hands shoulder-width apart, and began stretching her calves.

"Why...?"

Al smirked. "So I can use it against you later."

Perryn pinched the bridge of his nose and sighed.

Al had to admit he was less annoying today, but that didn't mean she wanted to hang out with him. She still needed to convince him to leave her alone long enough so she could search the Hall of Records. Operation Find Kera was taking too long.

"Hey! Let's make a deal!" Al pushed away from the wall, a brilliant idea buzzing in her mind. "If I take down more of these pests than you, you have to agree to give me one day off from having to look at your jerky face."

"That would be a no."

"Oh! I see." Al leaned toward him, cupping her hand around her mouth as she whispered. "Afraid a girl might beat you, hmm?"

Perryn stiffened.

"Well, I guess that's that then. The mighty Perryn's downfall was swift and—"

Perryn covered her mouth with his gloved hand, and Al squirmed with muffled protests.

"Listen!"

She glared at him, but stopped moving. Beyond the wall, a low humming was growing louder, moving closer. *Wings?* The monsters were coming.

Perryn yanked on his earmuffs. "Men! Get off your asses and move!"

Just as Perryn's words left his mouth, hundreds of black-and-yellow insects the size of small children flooded through the wall, the sound of their wings oversaturating the air with painful frequencies.

The men yelled and dashed about as they scrambled to pull on their protective vests and grab their guns or beating sticks. Some sitting on the crates toppled over backward, spilling beer over their chests and the ones inside the tents burst out with half of their clothing trailing behind them.

Al struggled to pull on her earmuffs and flattened herself against the wall. For a moment, she thought her eardrums would burst.

"Stay here so you can avoid being killed!" Perryn's voice sounded far away as he ripped the gun from his belt.

"What's that?" Al yelled back. "Sounds like you're afraid you're gonna lose!"

Without waiting for his response, she charged into the circle of men, gun drawn, and ducked as one of the giant hornets swooped low, its bony legs just missing her. She swung her leg out in the dirt, turning to fire as it boomeranged back toward her, but just as her finger touched the trigger, the insect exploded, almost drenching her in green goo.

Standing beyond the carcass was Perryn, his gun outstretched in one hand, his whole body rigid. "This is not a game, Al!"

"Oh, it's so on, Keevie!" She leaped from the ground but then flinched as the leg of the hornet's fallen body twitched beside her.

A man's scream cut through the mess of falling goopy bugs and gun blasts.

Al whipped around and watched as a hornet skewered a man with its long silver stinger, piercing straight through his back and out his stomach. The man convulsed and his eyes rolled back into his head as the venom dripped down his legs and onto the ground, melting his clothes and skin. Without warning, the formidable flyer launched the man off its stinger and into the town. He slammed into a roof and crumpled to the ground like a rag doll, his body continuing to dissolve.

Al cringed just as another hornet charged toward her. *Not good!*

She ran close to the wall, leading it to a place where she thought she could find better leverage. Vibrations from its wings closed in behind her and she sensed another one join the chase. The binding dug its claws into her side. She hoped running this way wasn't a mistake.

In the distance, a dilapidated bell tower emerged; a long rope attached to the top swayed in the wind. *Perfect!* Gathering her strength, she willed her body toward it, pushing the balls of her feet into the cobblestone through her boots. She turned down a street between two houses and sent a few power shots at an already crumbling roof. It toppled, sending brick chunks and boards cascading down in front of the hornets, interrupting their flight. Their wings reversed as their long legs flailed in surprise.

Al dashed out from behind the buildings and climbed the rope, pulling her body up as fast as she could. When she was almost to the top, the hornets pushed through the settling dust cloud and barreled toward her.

"Come at me, bugs!" She wrapped the rope around her wrist and using it like a pulley, she pushed off the wall. Letting the rope slide through her palm, she pulled out her gun and fired multiple shots at the hornets, the low-toned, off-key bell ringing above her. One hit the leader, and it split open, floating to the ground as its wings registered the misfiring connections from its now-missing brain.

The other two shots missed, and Al's confidence evaporated. Her palm burned, and the binding dug deeper into her skin.

Just as she was about to slam back into the tower, the hornet rounded its body and pierced her vest with its stinger, pinning her hard against the concrete, and knocking the gun from her hand. The warmth of the melting vest spread over her stomach. Any second now, the stinger would pierce her skin. As she stared into the hornet's huge net-patterned black eyes, her labored breaths left her, but the air refused to come back.

A blast ripped through the side of the hornet's head. It staggered, and its wings slowed, dragging Al down the wall as it fell. They both hit the ground, and she kicked at the hornet's body, trying to push it away.

Perryn appeared at her side, pulling her shoulders. With arms almost too shaky for even finger strength, Al undid her vest and threw it off to the side before it disintegrated into a puddle of melted plastic and fabric. Heaving, as adrenaline surged through her veins, she leaned back against the wall.

Perryn crouched beside her. "I told you to stay put." The emotion in his voice was hard to place. Was it her earmuffs or something else?

"And let...let you show me up?" Al continued to pant as she clutched her side. She had tied the binding too tight again.

Perryn put his gun back on his belt. With delicate gloved fingers, he lifted the side of her shirt and untied the knots that held the binding. The cloth loosened and she gasped, grabbing onto his arms. Her head fell forward against his shoulder. As her breathing became deeper, easier, she released him.

"Th...thank you..." Her breathless words tousled loose strands of hair that dangled in front of her face.

Perryn frowned as he stared at her. Why did he look so confused?

He reached toward her, but then his hand jerked back to hover over his gun.

A high-pitched screeching resounded behind the houses as another crazed hornet ripped through the metal structures and wrapped its slender legs around him, pinning his arms to his sides. Gripping him tight, the hornet rose into the air.

Perryn!

Al dove toward her discarded gun and with sudden reserves of strength, she aimed at the hornet and fired. A power blast tore through a layer of skin on its back. Screeching, the wounded insect tossed its prey as it launched into the sky to join the other retreating bugs.

With a pained groan, Perryn hit the ground and went sliding through the dirt like an oversized sootball. He stood, his shoulders hunched and rigid as if breakable items surrounded him. The thick band of his earmuffs had slid in front of his eyes like one of those ancient VR headsets, and boisterous laughter exploded from Al's mouth as she clutched her sore sides.

"Kuso." He shuddered as he resituated his earmuffs. "I. Hate. Dirt." He relentlessly dusted himself off as he made his way back to Al, who rolled onto her back, continuing to laugh.

"Did I just save you? I think I did, Mr. Keevie!" She pointed up at him, her tired arm swaying like a limp noodle.

Perryn sighed as he turned from her. "What day do you want?"

CHAPTER 9

T hree days later, Al and Maddox flew to the charming renovated district of La Reina. Only twenty minutes from the academy, La Reina's elegant Victorian homes stood in perfect rows on either side of a sparkling street paved with solar panels. The gray ship's reflection rippled and hopped within them.

Wooden benches, berry shrubs, and tall lamps that twisted into swirls at the top lined the length of the block in equal increments. Instead of an electric barrier, the wall surrounding this neighborhood was eggshell white and covered in ivy and blushing-pink flowers.

The homes looked identical save for their exterior paint, which alternated between pastel pink, blue, and yellow. In the front yard of each, a dock disguised as a tree supported stylish Keev-ships on thick brown metal arms. Maddox had only just secured his craft onto the tree-dock in front of a multi-storied blue house when the door of the home burst open.

A woman with black hair tied in a sleek side ponytail and wearing a bright floral dress waltzed out onto the wide porch. As she waved, the green crystal jewelry on her wrist slid down her arm.

Al jumped down from the ship, her day clothes comfy and loose and her rucksack hanging over one shoulder. Maddox turned off the engine and scooted from his seat, his face twitching when she slammed the door.

"So good to see you both!" The woman's brown eyes smiled as the pair approached the white porch steps.

Tall grass dotted with purple and pink flowers covered the crisscrossed base of the home and metal baskets filled with a collage of beautiful, bright blossoms hung from the white porch banisters. A cloud of humming-fairies barraged them, burying their long purple beaks inside the petals.

"Good afternoon, Mrs. Landers." Maddox nodded at her.

"Please, come in. Make yourself at home. I got the iced tea ready." Her fluttery voice beckoned them as she turned, the stained-glass window on the door catching glints of green light from her bracelet.

"Apologies, ma'am. Today is a drop and go." He ruffled Al's hair, and she swatted his hand away with a low, irritated growl.

"Well, in that case…" Mrs. Landers disappeared behind the door and returned with a glass container wrapped in a thin glossy film. "Take some pancit." She handed the noodle and vegetable dish to Maddox, who accepted it with a gracious nod. "I used royal carp this time. Ay nakanu!" Mrs. Landers laughed and swatted the air as if hitting someone's back, and Maddox and Al smiled with amusement. "Zeek should be awake by now if you want to head up."

Al nodded, and with a flippant wave to Maddox, she stepped into the entryway, leaving the two adults to discuss the woes of parenting.

The Landers' three-story home had high vaulted ceilings and a wood floor blanketed with a handwoven red-

and-gold rug. Though the foyer was clean, the walls were not, covered with stuffed bookcases, shelves stocked with old-world knickknacks, chairs piled high with folded clothes, colorful bins filled with children's toys, and one antique grandfather clock.

To the right, a spacious living room sported blue wallpaper dotted with white flowers. Behind the manilla sofa set, an old red, blue, and white flag with a yellow sun stitched on the left side hung on the wall. Encased in glass, ribbons, medals, and awards in contrasting colors adorned the fabric, and in the very center, the name *Landers* gleamed with embossed gold.

Upon the mantle of an unlit fireplace, several moving pictures of men in military uniforms, some with white beards, others with younger features, stood in a row within metal frames. A digital shimmer cascaded over the images every so often, causing the occupants to repeat their movements on a continuous loop, just like the picture of Kera.

Mounted on the wall behind them was a wooden sculpture of a man nailed to a cross by his hands and feet, another remnant of the ancient religion Zeek and his family practiced. Al still wasn't sure what the man had done to warrant such a punishment or why Zeek's family wanted to display such a violent image in their home.

She slipped off her shoes and headed for the wooden staircase on the left, but a wooly black-and-white beast almost knocked her over. Riding on his back, Zeek's three-year-old brother, dressed only in baggy pants, giggled and shouted as he held a metal ladle above his head.

Mrs. Landers' voice sounded through the house with parental warning. "Axel, how many times have I told you? Jeffrey is an *outdoor* panda!" She herded Axel and his trusty steed to the front yard as Al ascended the stairs, chuckling and dodging the wooden Keev-ship and soldier figures that a certain spoon-wielding child had left behind.

When Al reached the landing, a hollow, rubbery sound echoed into the hallway from an open door. Sitting on his bed, Zeek's preteen brother punched a balloon attached to a rubber band, his black bangs shrouding his eyes.

"Hey, Axis!" Al saluted him, and he stopped.

Without saying a word, he hopped off his bed and closed his door. After a moment, the same rubbery sound started up again on the other side.

Al shook her head and continued to the end of the hallway, where a plaque with chipped pastel-pink paint stood out from the olive-green walls. Yellow and pink flowers adorned the edges, and in the middle, the name *Evangeline* was written in a child's hand. Al gripped her bag strap, her chest tightening. *Evie.* She had never met Zeek's little sister before her unfortunate death, but the way he changed whenever he spoke about her meant she must have been special.

Pivoting to the right, she reached Zeek's room. His door was ajar. After knocking a few times and receiving no response, she let herself in.

The sheets on his bed had twisted off their respective corners into a clump and a single pillow rested against the bedframe on the floor. Bunched-up, khaki-brown curtains draped over his clouded window, tied with a knotted cord that looked impossible to undo. A side table stained with ghostly water rings of glasses past held his racing goggles and a sepia picture of a young boy with a toothy grin sitting atop the shoulders of a smiling man in uniform.

Al smiled. "You were such a cute kid, Zeek."

She picked up the pillow and sat with it on the bed, facing a giant map of Astova that covered the entire opposite wall. Scattered across the country, several places were circled in red, and off to the side, the words *traitors* and *next target?* were scribbled in the same color. Below the map, a desk overflowed with newspaper clippings, their headlines relating to the Altered, their attacks, and the death toll they left behind. One article title referenced the victory at An Mi, and she shuddered, remembering the hornet's oozy insides. Another sepia picture peeked out from underneath the mountain of paper, showing a smiling girl with black curls, a flower crown, and a frilly white dress. She stood in a garden in front of a white tower with a sign that read *Madame Quinn's School for Proper Ladies.*

Al sighed through her words. "Oh Zeek, I think you're getting worse." She stood and touched the circled town of An Mi on the map. "There's at least three new circles since I last came over."

An engine revving outside brought her to the window.

Two men dressed in dark-red military jackets, white pants, and black boots disembarked their ship—Mr. Landers and Zeek's older brother, Jack. Mr. Landers was no longer the young man from the picture, his face wrinkled with laugh lines, and a peppery beard sprouting from his face like regal pine needles. He greeted Maddox with a hearty handshake and a pat on the back as Jack stood next to them, motionless, his expression as stoic and blunt as his buzz cut.

The door creaked open behind her, and she turned to greet her friend. "Hey, bud! How a—" Her whole body tensed.

With a towel draped over his head, Zeek's wet hair clung to his face, and water droplets speckled across his bare shoulders and chest.

Al tried not to look down, but her eyes betrayed her.

She spun around to face the window with a strange, choked gasp as Zeek ripped the towel from his head and covered himself. Al closed her eyes and clung to the window-sill while Zeek scrambled through his dresser drawers. Then his room door slammed shut.

Al sank to the floor, her face still flushed.

Zeek leaned against the wall, his arms crossed, and his mouth turned up into a scrunched pout. "I don't know why you always freak out when stuff like that happens. You've got one too, so what's the big deal..." His words trailed off as he stared at the ground.

Al pretended to sip her iced tea through the straw, even though her cup was empty. *Please let it go, Zeek. Switch to a different topic.*

Plates with remnants of pancit sat on the floor next to cloth napkins and a handwritten note from Mrs. Landers.

"When I got your tube message yesterday, I was happy we could finally hang out again like we used to, but...I still can't shake the feeling that something's different between you and Perryn."

Al bit her straw. *No Zeek. Not that topic.* "We've clearly been arch enemies in our past lives and the war is just continuing in this one. Nothing's changed."

Zeek rose from the wall and touched the back of his neck. "You know you can always tell me if—"

"I'm fine, Zeek," she snapped.

"Woah. Excuse me for caring."

"Sorry, I'm just...tired." She wrapped her hands over her elbows. The sting of the rope still ripped through her palm even though only a faint pink line remained.

Zeek pulled at the loose threads hanging off his curtains, his face solemn. "Whatever you say."

Al forced a smile. "Hey, what's with the sulking? Didn't you read the whole message I sent? I might have found a clue about the Altered." A lie. Secret keeping was hereditary in her family. Her face fell. Al wanted to believe her mother was a good person, but if Kera was building humans that could live forever, did that change things? "Do you ever wonder why they're so extreme? They must have a reason, right?"

Zeek scoffed. "Who cares."

"But they can't possibly all be bad, right? So maybe—"

"What the hell, Al? There's no such thing as a good Alt!" Zeek hit the wall with his fist. "That's the kind of thinking that almost got you killed. And if you had died too, I—" He stopped and looked away.

Al hugged her knees closer to her chest. She shouldn't have said anything. "You won't lose me, Zeek. I promise."

"I'll hold you to it then." He marched to his side table and picked up his goggles. Strapping them across his forehead, he flashed her his famous smile. "So? This place must be pretty dangerous for you not to mention it in your letter."

Al released the tension in her shoulders. "Oh yes, a most dangerous place indeed. The Hall of Records."

"Books? Okay, way less exciting than what I was expecting, but sure, why not."

Al stood and hoisted her bag over her shoulder with a soft smile. "Come on! Let's try to get there before Perryn takes all the credit, okay? He knows too." Another lie.

"Oh, you bet we'll beat him!" Zeek bolted to his open dresser drawer and began pulling on a pair of socks. "Remember when he shot down one of the Altered's Scraper Sharks?" He lost his balance as he hopped on one foot. "The ship didn't even have anyone in it, but that's all it took for the Scanning board to create an all-new category just for him, promoting the guy to an Elite Scanner!"

Having conquered his pair of socks, Zeek grabbed his bag. "Maybe today we'll find something that'll prove to them *I* deserve a fancy new title too!" His gleeful shouts and stomps thundered down the hallway.

Al stood alone in his room, her smile crumbling. Zeek reacted exactly how she knew he would. This was manipulation. How was she any different from Perryn?

Once outside, they rounded the house to the backyard where well-trimmed grass couldn't hide all the forgotten toys scattered about. Near the ivy-covered wall, a green tarp concealed a long, bulky object. Zeek peeled off the protective skin and smiled a big, toothy grin.

"And there's my baby!" He hit the side of his bright-red Keev-ship.

The roofless model was much smaller than the commercial ones and fit two people, one in front of the other. While the T-shaped design was sleek and modern, the knobs and dials inside were a mishmash of different sizes and colors, elements left over from poorer days.

Al shook her head. "Never gonna understand why you named it The Prostitute, though."

Zeek embraced his ship. "No. Al. Don't mess with the name. It's what makes her, her. Plus, it gives the commentators something interesting to say."

Al raised her eyebrows. "Oh yeah, and they love you for it." They threw their bags into the seats and pushed the ship into the middle of the yard, the wheels of the landing gear ripping up bits of grass along the way. "I'm driving today!" Al scooped up her bag and plopped into the front seat, soft with black cushioning that had ripped in several places.

Zeek flashed a cocky smile as he leaned against his ship. "Are you sure you can handle her? She's *my* girl after all."

"Oh, get outta here." Al shoved her bag into his chest with a smile.

While Zeek stowed their belongings in the trunk, Al flicked a combination of switches and levers on the dashboard. "Wow! Do you really drive this thing with your stop gauges that high? I'm surprised you haven't exploded yet."

A row of lights changed from red to green as the hardware returned to its proper position. She pushed the triangular ignition button, and the engine roared to life.

"Hey! She's preset for speed, not safety!" Zeek yelled over the noise, hopping into the seat behind her. "Missing something?" He dangled her goggles in front of her face.

After strapping them across her eyes and placing a weathered brown headset over her ears, Al clicked the double belts of her restraint into the red buckles. Zeek had acquired them at an old-world auction late last year, where they were being marketed as "the last remains of a transportation vessel called a hovercar". Thanks to Perryn, Zeek had the funds to buy them.

Al shook her head. *No. Don't think about him right now.* She pulled the fuzzy mic toward her face. "Remember when you were still using rope?"

Zeek's laughter erupted in her ears. "Yep, I can still feel those barrel rolls in my thighs sometimes."

The arrow inside the temperature dial rose until it reached a red bar. Al twisted the hover release on her left and the ship lifted off the ground. As the landing gear retracted, she glanced back at Zeek, who pulled down his goggles and let out an excited shout with a fist bump to the air. "Fly or die!"

Al countered his yell with her own as she pushed down the throttle and they sped forward, the wind rushing past them.

Flying much faster than average ships, they made up their own sky path as they went, weaving around low-rise buildings, over wind turbines, and between trees, all the while letting out long, excited calls.

A flock of bugle birds bellowed in the distance as they began their ascent into the clouds. Al steered the ship to fly alongside them and together bird and human spiraled up, creating a red-and-white double helix formation in the sky. The feathered gliders broke away soon after and disappeared into the white sea above.

Only the open sky could offer Al the freedom she yearned for, allowing her to fly wherever she wanted, no Maddox to tell her she couldn't, no prying eyes to endanger her. The binding forced her to conform, but even that couldn't tie her to the ground.

She closed her eyes and stretched out her arms, the wind's chilly fingers wrapping around hers. "I wish I could stay like this forever..."

"I'm not sure forever would be long enough..." Zeek's voice was almost inaudible in her headphones.

She pulled her arms back into the cockpit with a grin. "Wow! You like flying with me that much?"

Zeek coughed uncontrollably.

"You okay?"

"Yeah—" he struggled between breaths. "Sky bugs."

As the adventurers walked down the crowded city street, the looming buildings above dappled the concrete in a collage of shadows. All manners of delicious smells from the colorful wooden stalls swirled around them.

Most of the milling bodies were men, but a few well-dressed women also shuffled by. One struggled to hold the hands of her toddler boys while juggling bags filled with glittering boxes. As they passed, Al hunched her shoulders and moved closer to Zeek. Women were dangerous. The gap between the two friends widened however, when he began visiting stall after stall, filling his mouth with tasty samples. Al sighed through her laugh. Zeek could never turn down free food.

Just as she was about to catch up to him, she careened into someone and they both fell to the ground with surprised yelps. As she rubbed her side, she noticed a fallen basket spilling with wooden figures of extinct animals. She looked up into the purple eyes of an older man.

"Al! Are you okay?" Zeek's voice rang out like an alarm bell as the bearded man stumbled, failing to stand. Zeek gasped before his lips curled into a dark sneer. "Do I need to teach you a lesson, you filthy Alt?" He loomed over the cowering man who shielded his face.

"Dada!" A little girl with indigo hair, dark skin, and the same purple eyes sprinted toward her grandfather, but stopped when she saw Zeek. She twisted the hem of her dress, her eyes wide and her mouth clenched tight.

The people around them averted their gaze and continued their business.

"Zeek!" Al jumped to her feet. "It's fine! I ran into him." Zeek tried to push her out of the way, but she stood her ground. "Let it go."

He let out a frustrated sigh, still glaring at the old man. "Watch yourself, Alt. You're lucky you're allowed to enter our city at all. Get your supplies and leave!" He tore away from Al and marched in the direction he had come from.

Al composed herself and bent down to help the man stand, but he spat in her face. "I don't need your charity, Naturalist!" He pulled away from her as his granddaughter rushed to his side and clung to his arm. She glared at Al with eyes too old for her age.

Al stood, wiping off the saliva with her sleeve, guilt stabbing her in the throat again. She was Altered like them, but they weren't the same. They were honest. Keeping her gaze to the ground, she turned and trudged after Zeek.

The Hall of Records was a tall, cylindrical building made almost entirely of glass, with floors slightly offset from one another as they spiraled to the top. As Al and Zeek ascended the marble steps, a few men in dark-blue uniforms were scrubbing a giant red *A* from its side. The two friends shared a tense, knowing glance before the automatic doors welcomed them inside.

Before they approached the security checkpoint, Al ducked into the restroom to apply her fake fingerprint. She returned to Zeek's side, trying to keep her breathing steady. If the soldiers caught her now, all of this would be for nothing, and Zeek would be implicated too.

He presented his family crest, a gold, layered circle with a fancy *L* curving inward, and the guards in red cross-checked the design in a thick binder. After scanning Al and Zeek's fingerprints, the men allowed the pair to pass.

Al let out a breath and put her hand in her pocket to pick away the fake skin. She had concocted a whole story to explain the fingerprint device, but because of Zeek's family name, a bag search wasn't necessary.

In the center of the hall, a thriving wisteria tree sprouted from a mossy circle, its purple blossoms fluttering across the reflective lacquered floor. From five stories above, a domed glass roof bathed the tree in afternoon sun. Other than a few men that sat contemplating large manuscripts at glass tables on the floors above, the building was empty and sterile.

Another pair of stern-faced soldiers stood off to the side in front of a dimly lit hallway blocked by a long metal chain. A sign reading *No Entry* hung from its rust-orange rungs.

Al shook her head. She needed to stay focused. Pushing herself forward, she approached a tall, unrailed staircase. A room directory was mounted on the wall near its base. She scanned the list in silence, realizing several of the numbers and names had been scratched out.

That's weird. I wonder what they used to say. Who—? She shook her head again. Kera was the only mystery she needed to solve right now. Al found the room she wanted to search and then made her way up to the first door on the second floor with Zeek trailing behind her.

Inside, the concrete walls were hard to see behind all the metal shelves stuffed to capacity with thick, dusty books, organized by the year printed on their faded spines.

Zeek sat down in a clear, egg-shaped chair suspended from the ceiling by a thick bar and crossed his arms. "So, what, or rather, who, are we looking for exactly?" He swiveled back and forth, his feet pushing against the legs of a wide glass table.

Al's stomach somersaulted. "Someone named, um, Martin Pliny." She wasn't about to blow her cover after making it this far, but the name she chose still felt obvious in her mouth.

Zeek tilted his head. "Never heard of 'em."

Al picked up a book and started searching, guilt scratching at her throat again.

The bookworms spent the next few hours scouring through census records until the table looked fuller than the wall.

Al slumped into a companion egg chair with a heavy sigh. "Now I understand why the holonet was so convenient. AI systems would've found something by now."

Zeek let out a sudden snort and continued snoring. An open book rested on the table in front of him.

Al shook her head with a small smile. "Or, at least, I would've known this was a dead end much quicker." She ran her hands down her face and looked at the bubbled ceiling. "More secrets…" She stood with a sigh and shook Zeek's shoulders.

He jumped awake, his goggles slipping down over his nose. "You can never have enough sauce!"

Al snickered. "Sorry Zeek, but this was probably a waste of time." She began placing books back on the shelves. "At least you got a good nap in."

"Well then, it wasn't a waste of time." Zeek returned his goggles to his forehead and stretched, his smile morphing into a loud yawn. "It makes sense, though. Detailed information about the Altered is only given to those with the highest clearance."

Al scrunched her nose. "Yep. Realizing that now."

"I could always ask my old man to look into it."

"No!" Al bumped the shelf, and a book fainted to the floor.

Zeek raised his eyebrows.

"Sorry." Her voice softened. "I just…I'm like you. I really want a cool fancy title. So we gotta do this without his help." The lies flowed off her tongue like water. Since when had it become this easy? She bent down and picked up the grimy green tome. "We'll just have to look somewhere else."

"Don't lose hope, bud! I've got an idea!" Zeek leaped to his feet. "Did you see the soldiers guarding that hallway? What do you suppose is in there?" He smirked and rubbed his hands together.

"Probably just a crumbling part of the building blocked off for safety reasons. That's really common with these older ones."

Zeek grabbed Al's shoulders and turned her to face him. "Secret information." He wiggled his eyebrows up and down.

"I think you inhaled too much mold."

"Oh, come on, Al. I know military procedures like I know the inside of my Keev-ship engine."

"As your mechanic, that's really concerning."

"Trust me!" He flashed his famous smile.

Al sighed. "Fine. But if we get caught, I'm telling them the truth."

"And what's that?"

"That it was all your idea."

"Are you sure this is gonna work?" Al looked up from the newspaper she was pretending to read as she sat across from Zeek in the café on the first floor. The men sitting around them provided just enough chatter for the pair to speak in hushed voices without being heard.

"Yeah. They only had one star on their shoulders, so they're newbies. They always get the green beans to do the boring jobs nobody wants. They'll be happy to leave."

Al gripped the table, her knuckles growing numb.

"Don't worry." Zeek moved in front of her gaze and puffed up his chest. "You're talking to the champ here." He guzzled the rest of his chilled oolong tea and stood. "Besides..." He pointed to the ceiling.

"Attention. The Hall will close in thirty minutes." A robotic voice echoed through the building.

"Showtime!" Zeek left a few coins on the table and then shuffled through the streams of men that trickled toward the front door as he headed for the guarded hallway.

Al squished the pastry she hadn't eaten with her fork and then, taking a deep breath, pretended to make her way to the restroom. As she darted behind a support pillar, she waited for Zeek to put phase one of their plan into motion.

"Hey there!" He saluted the two young soldiers with a smile.

They looked at each other before the one with brown hair spoke. "We're not supposed to talk to anyone."

His partner hit him on the shoulder with the back of his hand. "Bro!"

"Oh yes, my man, I know, but it's almost closing time, and I'd wager you both have gone the entire shift without any food. Am I right?" Zeek leaned closer squinting as he read their nametags. "Private Khine and Private Agbayani." The one with brown hair took a step forward, but his partner stopped him again and shook his head. "How about I buy you two a nice meal from the café? My treat!" Zeek shot finger guns at them.

"Hey wait...I know you! You're Zeek Landers, right?"

"That's me!"

"Wait! You mean *the* Animus? Your wins are legendary!" The brown-haired soldier pushed past his companion. "Will you sign my racing goggles?"

Zeek stood between them and wrapped his arms around their shoulders as he ushered them toward the café. "Of course! Of course! Oh hey, Agbayani! Are you Filipino, my man? So am I!"

Al poked her head out from behind the pillar. "I can't believe that worked." When the three new comrades had entered the café, she darted toward the hall and stepped over the chain.

The hall was darker than it had appeared from the lobby. Most of the lights had shattered and the ones that still worked flickered on and off. Unable to see in the dim light, she stuck close to the wall with uncertain steps. She was halfway down the hall before her eyesight finally adjusted.

Metal half-circle doors ran along the right wall, the swirling grooves of letters and numbers in the doorplates obscured by thick dust. She blew hard, dissipating the particles to reveal a name and a lab identification number, both of which meant nothing to her. She traced the letters of "lab" with her finger. Was it possible these were the rooms that had been crossed off the directory?

"Wait! A lab? Didn't Kera—"

The odds of finding it here were slim, but what did she have to lose? She rushed down the hall, blowing her tiny hurricanes on each adjacent door until only two remained. Lightheaded and with the unforgiving binding trying to cut her in half, she closed her eyes and steadied herself on the cold metal wall.

"Why does everything...I do...have to involve...breathing?" She glared at the nameplate and gouged out the dust from the first letter instead—a K.

She froze. *It couldn't be! Could it?*

Taking another deep breath, she sent multiple blasts over the rest of the letters, coughing as she inhaled some of the residue. Rubbing her eyes, she stared at the door as the dust settled, and almost stopped breathing.

Her mother's name appeared, engraved on the wall.

With her heart still pounding behind her eyes, she pulled and pushed at every corner and crevice, trying to figure out how to get inside. She slammed her fists against the door. "Why won't you open?"

A whirling noise squirmed from inside the metal and after a small slot at the top slid open, a long coil shot out.

Al jumped back. On its end, a flat, round screen reflected her perplexed expression.

"Identification, please." A female's voice poured out from an unseen speaker.

"Hello?" Al continued to search for a handle, running her hands over the smooth, cold surface.

"Identification, please." A thin blue line slid down the screen and a low-toned beeping came next. "Error. Please position your right eye in the center of the scanner for a proper reading."

"Okay?" Al blinked several times as she moved her eye closer to the screen.

"Identification accepted."

"I get it. *Eye*-dentification." She chuckled, trying to calm her nerves. "But wow. The security system is super busted. Guess they let anyone into secret labs these days."

With a rush of air, as if opening an ancient tomb, the door slid aside. Not knowing how long it would stay open, Al dashed inside.

The room was too dark to see anything beyond the faint light that shone from the door. Without warning, it slammed shut, and pitch black surrounded her. Al sank to the floor to lower her center of gravity. *I'm not tumbling down any stairs I can't see.* Would she be stuck in here forever?

Like a wave, rows of overhead lights snapped on with sweeping clicks.

"Would you make up your mind?" Al hid her face in her arms until her pupils readjusted, then she lifted her head and stood with wide eyes. "Fish on a stick..."

A short staircase made of perforated steel led to a cavernous room that spilled out beneath her feet. Wide desks covered in dingy cloth lined the walls with giant monitors mounted above them. They looked like larger versions of the computer Perryn had found. In the center of the room, hundreds of exposed red and yellow wires ran from the floor to the ceiling, snaking behind a circle of vertical containers that looked like enclosed metal beds. They surrounded a tall structure that fused with the metal ceiling and the grated floorboards.

Still dizzy from light pollution, she steadied herself on the yellow railing as she descended the steps. When she reached the bottom, dust had caked on her fingers.

She sneezed and wiped her hands on her pants. "I have no idea what I'm doing or what I'm looking for, but if there was ever a place for secrets to hide, it'd definitely be here."

She approached the monitors, pulling back the cloth and breathing in another cloud of dust. "Okay!" she coughed. "I take back what I said before, Zeek. Dust particles *are* dangerous."

Al inspected the drawers, but they were empty or locked with a key that probably didn't exist anymore.

Moving to the back of the room, she found a sign with the words *Wet Lab 1* hanging over a locked door. Without windows, she couldn't tell what was inside. She turned and ascended a set of steps to an elevated platform, where she found yet another covered desk. Only more dust awaited her. But when she yanked open the top drawer, buried treasure skidded across the bottom.

A metal picture frame held a well-preserved moving photo with three teenagers in lab coats sitting on the steps of a building that looked like the Hall of Records. The icy blue eyes and long braided pigtails of the young girl in the center were unmistakable.

"I found you." Al's throat tightened.

Two boys sat on either side of Kera. One was smiling and making peace signs with his fingers behind her head like bunny ears. He had short, stylish black hair and his dark-brown eyes kept opening and closing as the picture looped. The other boy had his arms crossed. His black hair fell to his ears, almost meeting the edges of the smirk that split his face. Unlike the other boy, he had green eyes.

Al flipped the frame over to remove the stand and when she took the photo out, she noticed something written on the back.

Kera Lacey

Calvin Hayashi

Vilroy Vax

~The Eternal Child Project~

"Hayashi? Like the floating island? Was the entire world involved in this coverup or something? None of this makes any sense!" She flipped the photo several times, trying to match the names to their faces. "Wait, hold up!" She squinted and brought the photo closer to read their nametags. "Okay so that's Calvin, which means Vilroy is the one with green eyes? But does that mean he's Altered or just a rare Naturalist?"

She slumped into one of the dusty chairs, her arms collapsing into her lap. "Is that why he always hides from the public? Because he's Altered?" Astova would nosedive into another war if the Naturalists knew an Altered ruled over them. "But why would an Altered mandate such hatred against his own kind? Then again, with all the bombings and chaos they cause, that could also be a reason he stays in his tower." Al covered her eyes with a frustrated groan. "I'm so confused."

Something about the picture made her stomach squirm, like disturbing the past had cursed her somehow. "The Eternal Child Project..." She read the bottom of the picture, noticing the smudged, illegible date. "The reporter mentioned a human who could never die. Could this be them?"

Was it possible that the child was still alive somewhere? Perhaps only Kera, Vilroy, and Calvin knew the answer.

"Too bad I'm not the Eternal Child." Being immortal would've been the perfect cheat code. "But I'm not special enough to be important like that."

Even though she had more questions now than when she had arrived, she had to get going. Zeek couldn't stall the guards forever. She wanted to take the picture with her, but it was too big to fit in her pocket and there was no way to fold it without damaging the thin screen. If Zeek noticed it under her arm, he'd ask too many questions, all of them dangerous. Taking one last look, she placed the relic back in the drawer.

After running down the steps, she turned toward the door, but the vertical beds in the middle of the room whispered her name on a persuasive frequency, and her curiosity overpowered her time-management skills.

Intertwining metal pieces supported the boxy frames and frosted-glass lids encased the tops. Each one had a three-digit number and the word *Life-Pod* printed in worn black letters along the side. Halfway between the top and bottom of the pod, a red handle protruded out. Al couldn't help herself. She twisted it with a gleeful smile and the lid sprang open.

Breaking free from disintegrated straps, a human skeleton, dusted with cobwebs and soot, fell forward on top of her, its black hole eyes staring into her soul.

She screamed and screamed, flinging humeri and femurs away from her, almost tripping over a rolling chair. Bolting up the stairs, she scratched and pounded on the door, searching for a handle that didn't exist. "I wanna get out now, please! Hello? Random voice lady?"

The door folded away, and Al tumbled out headfirst. She regained her bearings and jettisoned down the hallway that her strained eyes struggled to see.

Ducking under the chain, she almost tripped again as she pushed herself toward any escape route she could find. She smacked right into another skeleton, though this one had skin, clothes, and arms that shook her shoulders.

"Woah! Al, what's wrong?" Zeek's voice. "Did you see a ghost or something?"

"Yes!" She gripped his shirt. "Yes, Zeek, I'm sure I did!"

"Hey! You boys can't be here right now! What family do you belong to?" An older man wearing all blue and carrying way too many keys on his belt flashed a lightstick down on them from one of the upper levels.

"Let's go!" Zeek yanked her hand, and they bolted out the door and onto the crowded street—Zeek laughing, and Al still unsure if the world held too much light or too much darkness.

Zeek stared at the night sky dotted with stars and a half-halfmoon as Al lay next to him on a grassy hill. The bright city twinkled far below in the distance. He had flown them here, Al having been too shaken up to continue piloting.

Zeek grinned. *I got to be the hero and save him. Awesome!*

His ship was parked behind them and a dim hand lamp clung to its metal side. Aimed in their direction, it cast a faint halo around the pair like a circular barrier, though it seemed to have no effect on the winged and buzzing creatures of the night.

"Hah! That one was a real speeder!" Zeek pointed at the sky. "Don't think we saw this many last year."

Al rolled to his side to face him. "What I remember is someone eating all the food beforehand and then complaining about the lack of snacks, which forced us to lose our precious viewing spot. Maybe that had something to do with it?"

Zeek patted his stomach. "Well, you don't have to worry about that tonight."

"Yeah, lucky me." The wind seemed to waltz with Al's brown hair, stirring up the scent of sunset fruit.

"So, aside from your ghost friend, find anything interesting in the hallway?" Zeek propped himself up on his elbows, trying to ignore the sputtering engine in his chest.

"Nope! Just a lot of dust." Al's response was too quick, like he had rehearsed it somehow. Was he lying?

Al rubbed his nose as he sat up. "Ya know, I've always thought the vernal space showers must be like space rain. But I bet that jerk-face would tell me I'm wrong, though, using all his fancy scientific evidence and *oh so smart vocabulary.*"

Zeek frowned and touched his left leg where the bullet had left a scar. *The Altered destroyed everything.* If the P.G. hadn't shot him, Perryn would've never entered the picture.

Al had changed since coming back from Death Desert. There wasn't much to go on, but still, Zeek knew. Something in his gut jabbed him every time Al rushed after Perryn without protest whenever he called, or when he saw them after school, working on tasks that seemed more like hazing instead of training. Al didn't tell him about any of it. Al was silent, something Al was never good at. Zeek needed to know, and now they were finally alone.

Al might report me, but I don't know when I'll get another chance to know the truth.

"Hey Al?" Zeek steadied his breathing. "Do you like guys or girls?"

Al snorted. "What? I dunno. What about you?"

"I've been questioning that myself lately." Zeek stared at Al. "Because there's someone I might like."

"Oh really? Congrats, bud!" Al hit him on the shoulder. "Who?"

I must be really good at hiding it then. "Say I liked a guy. What would you think of me?"

Al shrugged. "That you're my best friend, Zeek."

Zeek's mouth fell open. "It's not weird or gross?"

"Nope! I know the government gets upset about it, but what do they expect keeping all the girls on a separate island?"

He didn't reject me!

Al scrunched his eyebrows. "But I don't really know what love is or how you get it. You meet your birth-partner on selection day, so maybe it happens then?"

He seemed like he was telling the truth, but maybe a different topic would give Zeek the answer he wanted to find. "What if the government actually allowed men to be in relationships? I mean, so long as they helped produce their quota of kids with their wife first."

"That depends. Could women be with other women too?"

Zeek scratched his head with a nervous laugh. Al's curious smile was cute. "I don't think so, since a woman's job is to have kids."

"Oh...right." Al scooted away from him.

What's with that reaction?

A family of lightning bugs dove in and out of the light border as if hopping in and out of dimensions while flying drunk. Zeek watched them dance, following the leader until his eyes landed on Al, who was glaring at him.

He flinched. "What? What's that look for?"

"I know you love the government, Zeek, but it's not *that* great."

"I do not!"

Al smirked and rolled toward him like a human roll cake. "Why so defensive if it isn't true, hmm?" Al attacked his side with several finger jabs. Every poke felt like a shot injecting his system with a cocktail of endorphins and anxiety.

"Cut it out!"

"Oh, come on, no need to be shy!" Al sprang up, clasping his hands over his heart. "The way the executive branch forcefully carries out laws is just so romantic. I can see why you're hooked."

With an irritated grunt, Zeek grabbed his friend's shoulders. "For your information, Al, the person I might like is an actual person!"

"Fine. Geez. I was only joking." Al pouted and looked down. "You're the one being cryptic here."

"And what if I liked a girl?" Zeek leaned closer to Al, feeling the warmth from his shoulders invading the nerves in his hands. Al's lips looked unsettlingly soft and his eyelashes were long and delicate. It wasn't normal for a guy to look so alluring. "What would you think, then?"

Al looked up at him with a beaming smile. "Why not both?"

Zeek sighed and brushed the top of Al's head before he stood and turned. "Got it."

"Got what?"

The fact you don't get it, that's what. "The bug. It was totally gonna eat you."

Al let out an exasperated groan. "You're really not gonna tell me who you like, huh?"

"Nope." Zeek faced her, forcing a smile. "Come on. Better head back before we get surrounded by bloodsuckers."

"Fine." Al stood and pointed at him. "But you gotta spill the oil eventually! I'm your best friend." Al marched toward the ship.

"Yeah..." Zeek clenched his fists and looked at the ground. "I know you are."

CHAPTER 10

A l sat in the lecture hall, staring out the window as Mr. Amari lead a demonstration on resetting broken bones. The students assisting him kept play-fighting with the splints.

Over the last few weeks, Perryn had continued to assign her more meaningless tasks, including sprucing up an old Keev-ship engine, and though she hated to admit it, that one had been kind of fun. July would arrive soon, bringing an end to their Scanning missions, but that just meant Perryn's tormenting would happen off school grounds where there were fewer witnesses.

"Maybe I should've just let the bee thing eat him."

"Al?"

"Huh?" She turned and a frowning Zeek stared back as he poked her arm with the eraser side of his pencil. Instead of notes, doodles of giant meterworms swallowing people whole covered the pages of his workbook. He tensed and smacked it closed, but she could've sworn one of the stick figures had glasses and Perryn's name written above it.

"I said, you're still coming over for your birthday, right?"

Between new clues about her mother, Perryn's strange requests, and trying to keep everything a secret from Zeek, something as unimportant as the day she was born hadn't even crossed her mind.

"Um, yeah! Can't wait." She smiled, but then realized her tyrannical boss would probably refuse to give her another day off.

"Maybe next year we can have a party at your place, huh?" Zeek returned to his notes and flipped to a blank page.

"But your house is the perfect size for everyone. Plus, my house is boring." Her house was full of secrets. "Hey!" She cupped her mouth and leaned closer to Zeek. "Why not invite the guy you like?"

He tensed. "Al, shut it! What makes you so sure it's a guy?"

Al bumped her shoulder against his. "You were trying so hard to be sneaky the other night, but unless you've been scaling the walls of Elbion without telling me, I'm sure."

He shrugged away and began copying what Mr. Amari had written on the blackboard. "I asked them already. They're busy."

Aha! I knew it! Al smiled as she opened her notebook. She'd identify Zeek's mystery man soon enough, but until then, she needed to focus on her own secret. How would she get another Perryn-free day?

She came up with many convoluted plans, but then, the day before her birthday, when they were tasked with collecting scrap metal from the industrial district, Perryn told her he'd be out of town for important business reasons. It was strange and convenient, but Al didn't want to look a gift moose in the mouth. The sight of his ship disappearing into the sky after they had delivered their haul might have been the best present he could've given her.

After she returned home, she stayed up late into the night, dancing and singing off-key as Cogs played old songs from his beak until a weary-eyed, messy-haired Maddox crashed her party. She fell asleep with her bird friend curled up in a ball near her head.

Dressed in a collared red shirt and black pants with a party hat strapped to her head, Al leaned against the wall of the Landers' kitchen, slurping pancit from her fork. The kitchen and living room dripped with colorful streamers, balloons, and red and white flags strung together on twine, and a giant hand-painted banner reading *Happy 18th Birthday Al!* hung across the second-floor banister.

All the men wore fancy shirts and slacks, while Mrs. Landers and Molly (pillow included) looked elegant in their modest dresses and jewels. Everyone had differently-colored party hats except for Zeek's older brother Jack, who sat at the base of the stairs feeding bamboo stalks to Jeffery the panda. Jeffery used to have a hat too, but it had mysteriously gone missing.

Arranged on the island in the kitchen, a homemade sunset fruit cake sported four candles. The white frosting sparkling with sugar crystals was smooth, except for a few child-sized finger holes that revealed the cake's purple insides.

Axel kept running past the kitchen window, soaring his wooden Keev-ship as he spun around in circles in the backyard. Axis lay in the grass, staring at the midafternoon sky, his arms and legs outstretched.

Mr. Landers and Maddox stood near the refrigerator and alternated between sharing opinions on the military's efforts to quell the Altered threat and exchanging jokes about the old world. None of the punchlines made sense to Al, but both men guffawed every time, as if any less of a response would've been considered an insult.

She set her plate on the counter, about to search for Zeek, but he appeared behind her.

"Bud!" He lowered his voice as he wrapped his arm around her shoulder. "You can't just leave behind an un-finished plate of pancit." He looked both ways. "My mom will make me stop being friends with you."

Al laughed, pushing him away. "Oh please, Zeek."

"I'm not joking. Do you remember Neel?"

"Who?"

"Exactly." Zeek wiggled his fingers in front of her face and made ghost-like moans.

Al rolled her eyes with a smile and though he tried to block her hand, her finger missiles still found his side. He let out an "oof" and then piled several hearty scoops of pancit onto his empty plate. Leaning against the island, he stuffed his face while Mrs. Landers and Molly sat on the couch in the living room. Her belly protruded out from her blue A-line dress. How she made a pillow look so realistic was impressive.

"How far along are you now, dear?" Mrs. Landers sipped iced tea from her poppy-rose-patterned teacup.

"About five months now." Molly beamed, patting her stomach.

"I'm so happy for you dear!" She touched Molly's hand. "After all those miscarriages, my heart was broken for you. You have a loving husband to wait so long for your second child."

Al scrunched her nose. *Yeah. I'll be the best big brother baby cotton could ever hope for.*

"I'm very lucky he didn't throw me away for a new wife. My Dox really loves me." She smiled and lifted her empty teacup above her head. "Oh Dox? Your pregnant wife needs more tea!"

Maddox shuffled into the living room. Taking the cup, he smiled in a way only Molly and Al would know was forced. "Dear, please don't overdo it."

"Oh, come now, darling. Pampering your wife is a privilege."

Mrs. Landers covered her mouth with her hand and giggled. "She's right, you know."

The two mothers burst into a round of warm laughter as Maddox entered the kitchen like a reluctant knight on a quest for his beloved. He trudged past Al and Zeek, heading to the counter where a punch bowl held pink tea, lemon slices, and ice cubes.

"Hey, Mr. Finn?" Zeek finished slurping the last noodle from his plate and set it on the island. "Jack and I want to take Al for a ride to celebrate. That okay?"

"He says yes!" Al jumped up, almost knocking over her leftovers.

Maddox sighed as he finished ladling a fresh serving of tea into Molly's cup. "Don't stay out too late. Tomorrow's a school day."

Al and Zeek gave each other a high-five with an enthusiastic yell before rushing toward the door. Jack was waiting for them, his coat and shoes already on. A hint of a smile traced his lips.

"Do you think what I'm wearing will be warm enough?" Al asked, pulling on her boots.

Jack and Zeek tried to hold in their laughter.

"Where we're going, bud, I don't think that's gonna matter at all."

With a thick piece of fabric wrapped around her eyes, Al stood somewhere where the ground vibrated. Based on the echoey reverberations of Zeek and Jack's voices, Al determined she was inside of an elevator going up, though there was no way for her to tell how high.

Zeek's potent scent of chamomile filled the enclosed space.

"Seriously, where are we, Zeek?" Al resisted the urge to pull off the blindfold. She wasn't sure she liked not being able to see, but she didn't want to ruin something that Zeek had put effort into preparing for her. "I know you usually take me to a new place I've never seen before, but this is ridiculous."

"I told ya." His voice floated into her right ear. "It's a surprise!"

As if to answer him, the doors opened with a bright ding and a change in air current flooded the space with the sound of men's lively voices and low jazz music.

Zeek gripped her shoulders and pushed her forward.

The hard metal flooring changed to a soft carpet and as she stumbled forward, unfamiliar smells pummeled her nose—a cloud of tobacco and charcoal, a sweet sugary perfume, or was it actual sweets? People passed in front of her, their forms appearing as shadowy figures through the layer of tan fabric.

When Al had just about enough of being pushed around, Zeek stopped. She searched with her hands and touched a flat surface in front of her. As she continued brushing over it, her fingers found a round object, which she tapped with her palm. The sharp ring of a bell caused someone in front of her to clear his throat.

"Sorry about that, sir!" Zeek's voice. He pulled her away to stand in a place without any landmarks for her hands.

"Name?" The man's voice bit with irritation and age.

"Landers, party of three."

"A member of our staff will be with you shortly." His presence disappeared.

"What a grump." Al crossed her arms.

"He looked like one too." Jack's unamused voice.

After some time, someone approached them and confirmed their reservation, then Al was once again pushed down a stretch of carpet, though the harsh party noises didn't follow her.

"I remember my first time." Their guide chuckled. Al couldn't tell his age, but his plummy voice gave him an air of dignified cheekiness. His shoes squeaked and clopped, like they were too big for his feet. "The blindfold is a nice touch. You kids are so creative these days."

"What are you talking about?" Al was certain she didn't like being blindfolded now.

"Don't worry, birthday boy. After tonight, you and Zeek will both understand what it means to be a man!" Jack's voice sounded like he had a wide smile. "Ow! What was that for, Zeek?"

He didn't respond.

"Here we are. Your room is down the hall and Mr. Finn's is right here. Enjoy!" The fancy man began whistling, and as his song and uneven footsteps faded behind her, Zeek cleared his throat.

"So, since this is your eighteenth birthday, Jack and I both chipped in to get you something special. I've never seen her before, but she was the most expensive girl, so she's gotta be the best. Even got a few of my other friends to pitch in too, though I didn't exactly tell them it was for you, since they sort of don't like you."

Al scrunched her nose. "Wow. Thanks." *Hold up. A girl? No no no no no!* "Are you guys gonna be with me?"

"Nah, we got a date with some twins." Jack's playful voice strained, as if squeezing something tight. "Zeek's still pure, so I gotta help dirty him up a bit!"

"Get off me!"

The loud creak of a door came from behind her, and someone pushed her forward.

"Wait, Zeek!" Al turned to face where she thought she had heard his voice last, with arms fumbling to pull off the well-tied blindfold. "I changed my mind! I don't wanna board this ship!"

Jack laughed. "Sorry Al, you're locked in there until time's up! Company policy. Tough it out or pray for a fire."

"This will be good for both of us." Zeek's voice was so quiet she wasn't sure she heard him right.

The air whooshed past her as the doors clicked closed, surrounding her in a stuffy silence smelling sweet and thick with spices. Al yanked the cloth blindfold up over her head. She needed to get out. The last time she met a girl, she almost died.

She rushed forward, pushing and pulling at the ornate curled handles, but the doors didn't budge. Jack was telling the truth. *Fire.* Maybe she could find a match. She turned and ventured into the room.

Three crystal chandeliers dripped down at different lengths, illuminated with flickering white candles, the only source of light in the room. Thick billowing fabric, dyed in maroon, dark purple, and red draped across the rest of the ceiling, outlining the top of the black walls.

She dashed past a glass table supported by the outstretched hands and purple tail of a topless wooden mermaid, where an assortment of fancy sweets and pastries, a bottle of wine, and two gold goblets waited for consumption. A velvet loveseat and a matching lounge chair framed either side.

Toward the back, she found an elevated four-poster bed with a white mesh canopy and red satin sheets that held secrets Al never wanted to uncover. Metal handcuffs dangled from the backboard. She took a step back. "Zeek, why the hell did you take me here?"

Across from the bed, an ornate vanity with three oval mirrors rested against the wall. *Drawers!* She crossed the floor and yanked them open, rummaging through lacy garments, whips and other strange objects. No matches, not even a lighter. "Okay, guess I have to knock down a chandelier." She turned and halted.

Fluttering like something out of a fairytale, several delicate and glittering dresses hung on a shiny rack. Like a fixated crow, Al ran her hands over the blue silk, the pebbly gold, the crocheted white. She bit her lip and looked around before taking the white dress from the rack, her face sparkling with the light of the tiny jewels embedded in the fabric.

The garment was heavier than it looked, poofing out like an upside-down flower at the bottom with a somewhat scratchy material. She stood in front of the mirrors and held the strapless dress to her chest, turning side to side. How long were dresses supposed to be? This one almost reached her calves. She flattened her bird-nest locks and then ran her hands along the soft stitching of the flower pattern. Clothes could be this beautiful?

"Would you prefer I wore that one instead?" A light and sultry voice tickled her ears as a pair of slender, glittering arms wrapped over her shoulders. The letters *P* and *G* were tattooed on her right wrist. A Personal Girl.

Al yelped, the dress falling to a crumpled heap on the floor.

Reflected in the mirrors, the most beautiful girl Al had ever seen in her life smiled back. Her blonde hair twisted up into a complicated pattern with a few tresses that framed her oval face, and her light blue eyes swirled with gray undertones like the ocean had been captured inside of them. Was she Altered or just a rare Naturalist?

A row of crystals dotted her cheekbones like a smile and sheer lavender gloves clung to her light brown skin. Her arms cascaded down Al's chest with soft movements she didn't know the human body could make. "Or you can wear it. I don't judge."

Al tensed and backed up against the vanity, almost slipping on the fallen dress. "I—I think there's been some kind of mistake, ma'am!"

"Ma'am?" Her laugh sounded like wind chimes.

The girl wore a thin-strapped top made of layered white feathers that hugged the outline of her ample chest. Below her toned stomach, she wore a matching pair of tiny shorts with the same delicate feathers sprouting out from her hips. Woven in-between the feathers, strings of jewels sparkled like gentle solar flares.

"My name is Angel." She tilted her head with a mischievous smile.

"How did...where did you come from?" Al couldn't look away.

"Heaven, of course." She moved closer.

Angel smelled like fresh violets, a scent that Al wished the locker rooms back in the academy would invest in.

"Miss Angel, um, couldn't we just talk instead? Talking is great!"

Angel giggled. "Don't worry, sweet boys like you are my specialty." Without warning, she lunged forward. Al tried to stop her hands, but it was too late.

Angel blinked several times. "Is this a sock?"

Her cheeks now flushed, Al shoved her away, and the Personal Girl flopped onto the floor with a forced, dramatic cry.

Al ran to the mermaid table and grabbed a knife. "Don't come any closer!" She held it out with both hands. "I told you to stop and now I—I have to kill you!"

Angel giggled. "Well, this is definitely one of the most eventful sessions I've had in a long time."

Al closed her eyes. She had to kill her. *You can do this, Al.* Unlike Perryn, this girl had no power over her.

The moment Al opened her eyes, she sped forward and pushed Angel against the floor, holding the knife just above her neck. Angel stared up with hard, unflinching eyes. This situation was familiar. The last time she met a P.G. their roles had been reversed.

Al's hand quivered. *Do it. Slit her throat. Don't you dare cry.*

"If I need to die in order for a fellow woman to live, I can think of worse ways to go." Angel grabbed Al's wrist and forced the knife down. Al gasped as blood trickled from the girl's neck. As the stream disappeared into the lavender robe bunched up underneath her, Angel laid her hands at her side in surrender.

Al held her breath and pushed the knife deeper into Angel's neck. *If you don't do this, Zeek, Cogs, and Molly, will die because of you! Hurry, before it's too late!*

Angel's eyes looked like stormy waves.

You'll die too. Al's shoulders trembled.

With a defeated yell, she threw the knife across the room and stumbled off the defenseless girl. "I can't do it..." She fell to her knees.

Angel hopped up as if she had been shot out of a spring-loaded chair. "Well, thank your conscience for that." Pressing the wound on her neck as she stood, she rushed to open a black door near the vanity. Inside was an ornate bathroom. Angel rummaged through several drawers and when she emerged, a white bandage wrapped around her neck.

"I don't understand." Al stared at her distorted reflection on the floor. "Aren't you afraid to die?"

"Men have treated me much worse." Angel pulled clothes from the drawers in the vanity. "Plus, if I die, I want to be stoic and cool! Not going to give my killer the satisfaction of seeing me crumble."

Al opened her mouth to respond, but Angel stuck out her index finger and then disappeared back into the bathroom, closing the door.

Should I continue trying to escape? How much longer would she be alive? Maybe Angel had a secret tube letter dispenser in the bathroom where she could inform the staff of Al's treason and that's why she was taking so long.

Al stared at the hand that had only moments ago tried to take someone's life, the same one that had a leftover scar from when someone had tried to take hers.

The door to the bathroom swung open and Angel had changed into a sparkling pink robe and a matching nightshirt and shorts, her jeweled makeup removed. Her hair was no longer blonde, but a dark brown instead. Silky and brushed to perfection, her straight locks rested at the small of her back.

Al looked away, her face hot. This hair color suited her better.

Angel stepped over the blonde wig and winged costume and shut the bathroom door, sauntering to the lounge chair with pink fluffy slippers covering her feet. When Al remained motionless on the floor, Angel rolled her eyes and pointed to the loveseat across from her. "Come sit."

Al stood on shaky legs and tried to string together an apology, but the words got caught in her throat.

Angel held up her hand and shook her head. "I probably would've done the same thing if I were in your position. Though, no offense, coming here was a reckless move. *I* wouldn't have done that." She picked up a cookie covered in cream from the table and took a bite, the whipped topping smudging on the tip of her nose. She giggled. "Why did you?"

Al walked toward her. "My friend sent me here as a birthday present...he doesn't know."

"You sure about that?"

"If he knew the real me, he'd definitely turn me in without hesitation." Al sank into the velvety chair, trying not to look Angel in the eyes. Without her wig and make-up, the girl was stunning, and her ethnicity ambiguous.

"Ooo girl, you have to tell me your story!" Angel clapped her hands together, her smile as radiant as her pajamas. "My normal policy isn't to pry into the lives of my clients, but it's been forever since I've spoken to a real girl. I can't help myself!"

The looseness of the nightshirt hid the size of Angel's chest, but Al couldn't help but remember how accentuated it was a moment ago. She touched her own and frowned. "Sorry to disappoint you, but I've never been a real girl in my whole life."

Angel wagged her finger. "What are you talking about? You're free! Freedom is what makes a girl real."

"I'm not free."

Angel snorted. "Well, you're freer than me." She shifted positions and shoved the rest of the dessert into her mouth. "Here. Questions are easier, right? Ask me one. Then I'll ask you one." She gestured toward Al, the glittery sleeves of her robe reflecting in the dim light.

Al watched the condensation drip down the wine bottle and fidgeted in her seat. Angel's demeanor was still so unsettling. She wracked her brain trying to think of something to ask. What did girls talk about, anyway?

"So…how did you become a P.G.?" She picked up a fruity scone and held it in her lap, unable to take a bite.

Angel let out a dramatic sigh and let her body drape over the lounge chair like a fancy sheet, her fingers twirling with the orange corded tassels along the bottom. "They found me sleeping inside a Snow White Casket when I was four, with a pair of white costume wings strapped to my back."

"A snow what?"

Angel giggled. "Wow, am I really that much older than you?"

"You don't look it. How old are you?"

"Okay, miss cheater. One question at a time." Angel put a finger to her lips. "The casket thing protects people from the sun and radiation by freezing them, I guess. I don't really know how it works. Either way, it's a relic from the past and since no one knows how long I was asleep, no one knows how old I am either."

"Oh…" *Maybe it's like one of those life pods in Kera's lab.*

"Anyway, when I opened my eyes, there were only flashes of images that didn't make sense, only remnants of feelings. I was told later that because of a malfunction of the whatever system, it had affected my memory and that I was lucky to be alive. Oh yes, what a wonderful paradise I woke up to!" She laughed and sat up, crossing her shimmering legs as she turned to face Al. "Then they found out I couldn't have kids." She paused, the waves in her eyes growing distant.

Al wanted to take a bite of her scone, but the silence was too loud.

"And now I'm a Personal Girl!" Angel's voice became sweet and fluttery again, the bubbling tide returning to the shore.

"Is that why your name's Angel, because of the wings?"

Angel raised her eyebrows as an inquisitive smile crossed her face. "Among other reasons. That's a ton of free questions, you sneaky cheat. My turn now. What's your name?"

Al brushed a few crumbs from her lap. "Al...ice."

Angel narrowed her eyes, still smiling. "Right. So, what about you, *Alice*? Why are you pretending to be a boy?" Angel popped the cork on the wine bottle and poured them both a glass.

Should I really open up to a stranger? Al glanced at Angel, who was resting her hands under her chin and leaning forward. She looked so excited. *I guess if I'm going to die soon, someone should know my story.*

Al took a huge bite of her scone. After swallowing, she explained in very limited detail a summary of her life story, redacting everyone's names, and anything that would put any of them in danger.

Angel hid her wide smile behind her hands as she sat on the edge of the lounge chair. "Well, you know how to control that 'jerk-face' who's blackmailing you, right?"

Al shook her head and picked up a goblet, taking a sip. "I don't think it's possible. He's really powerful." She grimaced, looking into the liquid. Why did wine taste like barbecued grapes?

Angel snorted. "All men are the same, girl. Hit that thing between their legs and down they go. Touch it juuust right and they do whatever you want."

"Huh! Why would I ever wanna touch it?"

Angel burst into a fit of laughter, almost knocking over her glass. It was easier to look at her now.

A three-note metallic melody sounded through the room and Angel sighed. "That means our time is up." She pouted and fell back onto the lounge chair. "And I was having so much fun too."

Panic turned the scone in Al's stomach sour as she stood. "How do I know you won't tell anyone my secret?"

"You don't." Angel shrugged, looking unsympathetic. "But us girls gotta stick together." A loud knock came from the door and Angel popped up from her chair. "Plus, I'm not too keen on getting involved with your drama. Ya girl's gotta stay alive too." She ushered her guest to the door, filling Al's pockets with extra scones.

Once the doors opened, a male attendant dressed in a brown suit stepped away and bowed. Al could now see why his footsteps had seemed so unique. Peeking out from just beneath his brown pants, two mechanical prosthetics rested inside a pair of black dress shoes.

The hall stretched down with a red carpet and the same chandeliers from Angel's room hung from the vaulted ceiling. At the very end, Al could just make out the lobby, still crowded with people.

The two boys who had dragged her into this mess sat on a cushioned blue bench, oblivious to the trouble they had caused. Jack leaned against the plain black wall smirking, his button-up shirt half undone on one side and smeared lipstick on his cheek.

Next to him, Zeek sat hunched over, his forehead resting on his clasped hands. When he looked up at Al, he gave her a strange smile that seemed broken and forced.

Angel tapped Al's shoulder and just as she turned, Angel kissed her on the cheek. "Happy birthday!" She disappeared behind the door with a flirty wave, leaving Al to touch her face with a blank stare as she turned back to face the hall.

Zeek gripped the edge of the bench, his teeth clenching.

"Come on." Jack stood and stretched his arms. "I better get you two *men* home."

They started down the hallway, passing other tall doors and men dressed in gold and silver with unabashed women draped on their shoulders like glittering scarfs. A man hiccupped from his crumpled position on the floor, a goblet tipped on its side between his limp fingers.

"So..." Zeek's voice trailed off as he stared straight in front of him. "How was it?"

Al tugged at the ends of her hair. "Well...I thought I was gonna kill her."

"Geez, Al! Going all out on the first go?" Jack laughed. "I'm sorry I doubted you." He wrapped his arms around her shoulders and ruffled her hair. She swatted him away and punched his arm.

They soon stood in front of the elevator, waiting to go down. Just like Angel's room, the building didn't have windows, so Al still couldn't tell how high up they were.

"What about you, Zeek?" She fixed her messy hair. "Do you feel more like a man now?"

Zeek clenched his fists. Jack opened his mouth to speak, but his brother cut him off. "I was a natural! You should've seen the faces she made! That they both made! I bet I was better than you, Al!"

"Okay, okay!" Al put up her hands in defense. "Good for you, Zeek."

Jack sighed just as the doors slid open and more men reeking of tobacco and beer stumbled out onto the floor with rowdy laughter. When the doors closed once more, Zeek and Al stood on opposite sides of the elevator, their backs turned toward each other.

CHAPTER 11

Zeek seemed distant, off somehow, ever since the night they both paid a visit to the glittering girls, but Al dismissed her worries. Maybe what men and women did behind closed doors changed a person. However, when Zeek started sitting next to his other friends in class and gave her curt replies or ignored her when she tried to speak to him, she knew he had changed too much. He stopped responding to any of her tube letters, and at some point, she received a notice that they were no longer being accepted at the Landers' residence. When she did find him alone, he'd pack up his belongings and rush down the hallway to join in a conversation or just disappear altogether behind a corner.

Angel was also an issue. There was no reason to trust her, but considering Al was still alive, the wind hadn't caught word of her secret yet. Keyword: yet.

Al groaned and put her head on the silver desk in front of her as she sat in Perryn's office. For such small things, secrets were incredibly heavy.

The room was tidy and sparse, with only a file cabinet against the wall and a triangular desk where Perryn sat across from her. How would he react if he knew about Angel? Would that fix anything or just make it worse? Everything was a mess.

"Is something wrong?" Perryn's glasses reflected her pouting face as he looked up from the stack of papers in front of him.

"Being a girl is horrible! Sometimes I really wish I wasn't one!" She slapped her mouth closed and shot upright. Since when had she become so comfortable around him?

"Perhaps, but then you would not be you." He looked down and continued calculating percentages on the top page.

What the hydrogen? Did he just say something nice? Al looked away as she played with a piece of her hair. "Um, yeah...thank you..." She stiffened. She was thanking him now, too?

"No need to thank me. I was merely curious why you were not as loud today."

"Wha—!" She sank deeper in her chair, her face falling. He was a jerk again. "What's next? You gonna tell me I failed my Scanning evaluation?" She'd have to repeat her training with him, and Zeek wouldn't be her partner next year. How many more years would this game of his go on?

"You passed."

Al unfurled her body. "What?"

He gathered the papers and straightened them against the table. "Though we have our differences, that did not affect my evaluation of your skills. You earned your score, Al."

She stared at her feet. What in Astova was happening? Was Perryn the bad guy or the good guy? She wasn't sure anymore. She realized she hadn't been sure for a while.

Several weeks later, on the last day of school, a small crowd of families filled the benches inside the gym. Mothers sat fanning themselves with the event leaflets or lace fans, while fathers clinked their mugs of beer against their neighbors'. Young boys ran through the gym, pulling red and blue paper Keev-ships with long, flagged tails behind them. Other than infants or married women, the bleachers only held men. Soldiers dressed in red and white stood at the entrances, their eyes hidden beneath tall, wide-brimmed hats.

Al sat in a chair on the makeshift stage with the nine other Scanner trainees, their leaders standing behind them at attention with their hands behind their backs. All wore their uniforms, stun guns at their belts.

Beads of sweat soaked the collar of her uniform—the long sleeves and pants felt like they were melting into her skin. Because winter lasted a lot longer than summer and the Scanning missions only happened during the school year, the academy had never invested in a summer version. She squinted and scanned the crowd.

When Molly, who seemed to have stuffed two pillows under her white dress for this public event, saw Al, she waved and called out her name. Al sank lower in her chair. Maddox looked up from helping Molly get situated and offered a weak smile, but Al frowned and ignored him, turning her head.

Behind her, Perryn had dressed like the other Scanner leaders but forwent his jacket. Without glasses to hide his defined features, he seemed almost regal. The shiny material of his uniform hugged his chest, showing every even breath he took. Had he always looked like that? Al wiped her forehead with the back of her hand, blinking hard. The gym was too hot.

"Relax." His sudden whisper had the opposite effect, and she snapped up straight, just as Mr. Lann approached the podium to speak.

"Esteemed Astovans, welcome to the annual Scanning awards ceremony. This unique partnership with the military began as a way for young men to assist in quelling the Altered threat, but it has grown into much more, providing opportunities for our students to go beyond their studies, learning not only real-life skills, such as leadership, endurance, and teamwork, but also offering a way for them to give back to our community. This year we saw over eighty-five requests fulfilled!"

As the crowd clapped, Al noticed the Landers family sneaking onto the benches. Mrs. Landers pulled Axis' hand as he tried to wiggle free, while Mr. Landers juggled food trays and several beer glasses. Jack hoisted Axel off his shoulders, and Zeek shuffled along at the tail end, his head down and his racing goggles strapped to his forehead. Al locked her eyes onto him like the targeting system of a warship, hoping he'd look up.

"On behalf of the academy, it is my greatest honor to present to you the following candidates for promotion to Senior Scanner, our highest rank." As Mr. Lann read each name, the leaders walked up to the podium and received a gold hexagon pin with a capital *S* engraved in the center. They then pinned the badge on the right side of their partner's green jacket. Al shifted her gaze behind her.

The gold *E* on the right side of Perryn's shirt reflected an identical, though tiny, version of herself within its polished surface. That's right. Perryn was in a rank all his own.

"And the candidates for promotion to Lead Scanner, who will be assigned their own teams next year." More badges, more names, more applause.

Al returned her focus to Zeek, remembering how they had sat in opposite places last year when he became a Lead Scanner. He still refused to look at the stage.

"And finally, the candidates for the completion of their first year of training. Alec Finn." Mr. Lann probably didn't mean to sound so surprised, but he looked up from the paper with a perplexed expression.

"Woo! Go Al!" Molly's voice stuck out above the clapping and Al stood, looking at the ground.

With perfect precision, Perryn walked to Mr. Lann and received a gold pin with a number one engraved in the middle. As Mr. Lann read off more names, Perryn returned, moving close to her.

The smell of pine.

His fingers grazed her shirt as he pinned the badge in place, but it felt like he was touching her bare skin directly. Al tried to swallow, but her throat was too dry, unlike her hands, which felt like waterfalls.

Their eyes met.

"Congratulations." When he spoke, all other sounds seemed to disappear.

Her cheeks burned. The frequency of his voice reached a part of herself she couldn't name.

As he returned to stand behind her, she forced herself to look at the crowd. Zeek stared back, but the moment their eyes met, he looked away. Al continued her solo staring contest for the remainder of the ceremony. Looking anywhere else was dangerous.

Once the ceremony ended, the families rushed to the stage with balloons, flowers, and cards. Some parents argued over the few artists hired to draw pictures for the event, the poor men being pulled or pushed in all directions by a swarm of proud mothers.

Just as Maddox, Molly, and the Landers Family approached the stage, Zeek slunk toward the exit doors. Al jumped off the back and ran after him. He wasn't getting away this time.

The moment she was outside, she called his name. He bolted.

She continued calling as she chased him up the grassy hill, through the courtyard, and into the maze. "Zeek! Stop running and talk to me, please!" Her breath was ragged as the binding dug into her skin. He disappeared around a bushy corner before she could see which way he went.

With a loud sigh, she stuck her hands into the leafy hedge and climbed. Hoisting her body up onto the wall, she balanced herself and started running. When she finally caught a glimpse of his hair, he had stopped, resting with his hands against his knees. She let out an exasperated yell and jumped down from the hedge.

Startled, Zeek sprang to his feet and turned to run in the other direction, but Al pulled out her stun gun and shot him in the shoulder. He fell face-first into the dirt. Panting, she trotted up beside him and propped him up against the hedge.

"What the hell was that for, Al? I don't want to talk to you!" Dirt had smudged across his cheek and his goggles had slid off onto the ground.

She pointed the stun gun at his nose. "If you don't shut up, I'll use it on your mouth too."

He glared at her but stayed silent.

She returned the stun gun to her belt and sat next to him. Taking off her Scanner jacket, she tossed it to the side, which provided some relief, but Al wished she could take off her shirt like a real boy. Their panting and the buzzing of the summer bugs that lived inside the hedges saturated the air around them.

"So, why are you avoiding me?" Al wiped her forehead with her sleeve.

"Who says I am?"

"You just did!" Al straddled his lap. Doing so caused his limp body to slide down the hedge and lie flat in the dirt. "Talk!" She put her hands on her hips and scrunched her nose.

Zeek swallowed as he darted his eyes down near his legs and back up at Al. "I thought you didn't want to hang out with me anymore."

"What? Why?" Al would've laughed if she wasn't so mad.

"I couldn't do it...I couldn't go through with it, Al...and when I heard you had, with that girl, I—"

"Wait. Hold up. You didn't do anything?"

Zeek looked away, his cheeks turning red. "Yeah, and since you did, I thought you would think I was weak, that I wasn't a man."

Al laughed. "Did your goggles cut off the circulation to your brain?"

"No, why would—hey!"

"For your information, I didn't do anything either."

"You...you didn't? But you said—"

"Yeah, I know what I said, but I was just trying to act cool." Al fiddled with the ends of her hair.

"Me too."

"Yeah, so who cares if you can't do it with a girl? That's not why you're my friend. You're one of the most important people in my life." She hit his chest. "So stop ignoring me and my letters!"

Zeek covered his eyes with his arm and smiled, his paralysis gone. "I told you if you didn't finish the pancit my mom wouldn't let you be my friend, right?"

"Too bad!" She rolled off of him laughing. "So, we good?"

"Yeah, we're good."

"That's a relief. I dunno how we'd get through the race next week if we weren't." She slapped his goggles against his stomach and sat up.

Zeek rose beside her and strapped them back across his forehead. "I had to get her ready on my own without my mechanic, though."

"Oh gee. Wonder why. Maybe don't ignore your mechanic so he can work on your ship?" She snapped her head in his direction.

"That's not fair! The last time *you* weren't busy was like five months ago."

"Yeah, blame Perryn for that."

Zeek narrowed his eyes. "Since when is he 'Perryn'?"

"Huh? Whaddya mean?"

"You usually refer to him as a butthead or jerk-ass or something."

"Oh, um, yeah he is." Al picked a leaf from the hedge and tore it into pieces.

Zeek let out a strained sigh as he stood. "We're gonna win this year too, right?"

"Oh yeah!" Al jumped up, the leaf particles falling to the ground like confetti. "Coming in for a landing is Zeek Landers!" She swooped her right hand low and then stuck her arm straight up with her elbow bent.

Zeek dipped his left hand the same way. "We're gonna win and be *Al* right!"

They high-fived, speaking in unison. "Fly or die!"

Al hummed while packing her rucksack as Cogs stood on her desk basking in a shaft of light, his solar-paneled wings outstretched, aimed toward the sun.

"This is perfect, Cogs!" Al set her bag against the wall. "School's over, the race is tomorrow, and no more Perryn!"

"Bye. Bye. Human." Cogs landed on top of her head, releasing a comical whistle that ended with a crash.

The smell of tobacco wafted into her room, a sign that Maddox was smoking in the kitchen. She grumbled and was about to close her door when the doorbell let out its grating chime.

"Molly!" Maddox yelled and dishes clinking together and shoes squeaking resounded below.

"Danger. Danger." Cogs zoomed into her closet and she pushed it closed just as Maddox reached the front door.

"Mr. Keevie. What brings you here?" Maddox sounded like he needed to cough.

"Sorry to disturb you, sir, but I have business with Alec."

Even though she was on the second floor, Perryn's voice still clutched her heart. She slammed her door and slid her back down it until she sat on the ground. "What now?" She had escaped, but he was back. Back to confuse her. Back to make her feel things she couldn't understand. A few moments later, she felt the vibrations from a light tap against the door.

"Al?" Maddox's voice. "Mr. Keevie has informed me that there is a follow-up Scanning mission that you need to participate in."

Of course there is.

Opening the door a nose-length, she spoke in a low voice, unsure if her tormentor loomed close enough to hear. "I think this is a trick, Maddox."

"A trick?" His voice sounded bland and unamused.

She opened the door all the way and pulled him inside before slamming it once more. "The Scanning missions have already ended. Why would he show up and say there was more if not to be sneaky?"

Maddox raised his eyebrows. "Is there something you're not telling me?"

She looked at her feet, Perryn's warning echoing in her head again. "No, I just wanna be able to fly with Zeek tomorrow."

Maddox embraced her and she pouted, letting her arms dangle at her sides. Why was he hugging her right now?

"Know that everything I have done, I did to protect you. I hope you will understand." His voice strained, as if holding back tears, but when he pulled away, his face showed no visible signs of distress. He must have been feeling guilty again. Maddox always picked the weirdest times to apologize to her, and he always had a knack for making it awkward. But a hug was still nice.

"You better get going. The sooner you complete the mission, the sooner you'll be able to focus on the race." He smiled with his hands on her shoulders.

She nodded. Maybe he really was trying to make amends this time.

The rucksack that she had filled with joy and anticipation now felt heavy with dread and regret as she slung it over her shoulder. "Cogs is in the closet, by the way. Please let him out when it's safe." She opened the door and stepped out into the hall.

"I will."

Al descended the steps, avoiding Perryn's bare gaze. His dangerous eyes wouldn't work on her if she didn't look at him. She said nothing as she rushed past him and out onto the gravel walkway where a yellow ship waited, hovering just above the ground.

Their flight was a silent one, as they sat next to each other inside of the fish-shaped ship. Their shoulders almost touched, despite Al's efforts to squish herself as close to the window as possible. She watched the trees outside fade into buildings and then back to trees.

Their silent driver wore a black-and-yellow-checkered uniform that matched his ship. On the dashboard in front of him, a Personal Girl figurine wearing a sparkling blue dress frantically bobbed her oversized head side to side with the turbulence.

When they turned and climbed a hill, Al swallowed her excitement. Wherever they were going, it was close to the Keev-ship racetrack. The blue and red flags waved at her from below. A few tents already lined the grass, and several ships were being parked near the track. She tried to get a good look through the gaps between the trees as they continued winding up the hill, but she didn't see Zeek's ship anywhere. Would he misunderstand her absence and start his silent treatment again?

The taxi-ship stopped with a slight jolt at the top of the hill. As Perryn paid the man with a few coins, Al stepped out.

Erected in the middle of the hill dotted with shrubs and wildflowers, a wooden shack slanted so far to the left that Al wasn't sure how gravity allowed it to stand. She tilted her head, trying to line her body up with the angle and almost fell over. The spiderwebs and decaying wood made it look like no one had accessed the front door in years. A rusty sign hung from its handle: *Reception*.

Surrounding the building in a circle, several glass domes stuck out from the ground like the eyes of a giant ground spider. She approached another rusty sign that had been bent close to the ground and read the faded letters.

"*It's A Bomb Motel?*" Al pulled her arms tight against her body, cringing at the rust.

Perryn sighed. "This is not how it looked in the brochure."

Al glared at him. "I hope it's filled with dirt and dust and germs and—" She began coughing on purpose. "Oh no. I think I'm sick."

"Come on." He approached one of the round domes near the back as the yellow taxi swam back down the dirt road.

When Al reached his side, the clear dome sat open on its hinges. She looked down into the pitch-black hole. "You know, liking the dark this much won't help people see you in a very positive light." Al snickered. If he was going to ruin her day, she'd do it right back.

Perryn flicked a switch that stuck out from below the lip of the metal molding, and a series of cone-shaped lights attached along the length of the dark tunnel lit up, revealing a ladder stretching several meters down.

"Get in."

"How do I know you won't just trap me in there forever?" Al shrank back from the edge with the sudden realization sinking like the hole in front of her.

"I had not thought of that, but since you mentioned it, I might reconsider. Go."

Al took a reluctant step onto the first rung of the ladder. She had traveled down a while before she looked up, expecting to see Perryn's evil smile pressed up against a closed dome, but he was climbing down as well.

"If you stop, I am not responsible for any broken fingers. Hurry up."

"Fine!" He sure was forceful and moody today.

When she reached the bottom, the space opened up into a trendy living area filled with silver appliances and a soft-looking white couch. Black trim accented the beige-paneled walls, and a mural of a blue night sky graced the ceiling, with tiny bright lights acting as stars.

"Wow! It's actually nice down here!" With a curious smile, Al began exploring the underground home.

Along the wall, fake windows cycled through moving pictures of a sandy beach, a pink tree with fluttering blossoms, a field covered in snow, and an orange-and-red forest, complete with an occasional fuzzy creature scurrying past. Toward the back were two bedrooms and between them was a modest bathroom. Scampering back into the kitchen, Al opened the fridge. Lining the shelves, trays wrapped in strange metallic packaging had pictures of appetizing food pasted on their lids.

Al laughed to herself. "I should bring back some of these for Zeek!"

"Al." Perryn's voice was behind her.

She jumped, causing the fridge door to slam shut. "Stop doing that!"

"I need to talk to you."

Al raised her eyebrows. "Um, you mean, you haven't been this whole time?"

Perryn walked away and sat at the silver dining table. "Sit."

"Okay, geez. I get it. Calm down, edgelord." Al scrunched her nose as she sat in the chair across from him.

Perryn rested his elbows on the table. His folded hands blocked his eyes from her view. "You will not be going to the race tomorrow."

The air in the room stabbed her with thousands of tiny, cold knives. "What?"

Perryn didn't move. "This is because you failed to do exactly as I instructed."

"What the hell do you mean by that?" Al catapulted from her chair, her hands slamming on the table. "I've done every single infuriating thing you've asked me to do! You—"

Perryn was the bad guy again, but it didn't make sense. He had saved her from the hornet, allowed her a day off, let her pass her Scanning training, and even congratulated her for it. Would a nemesis really do all that? Maybe she just didn't want it to make sense. "So, that kindness you showed me was all an act?"

Perryn flinched but kept his hands in their folded position. "Do not accuse me of things you assumed all on your own."

What was she doing? *Stop talking, Al. Just run already. So what if he's confusing. He's trying to keep you from the race.* "I'm done listening to you!" She turned and dashed toward the ladder.

Just as she started to climb, an interlocking disk slid over the top of the shaft, blocking out the light from above. She reached the top and pushed against the metal with her shoulders and pounded it with her fists, but the lid didn't budge. "No…" She slid down the ladder, her heart sinking with her. As she whipped around to face the table, Perryn lowered the remote in his outstretched hand.

"Did you forget who I am?" His eyes were so cold they almost scared her.

Why was he doing this? Regardless of the reason, she was trapped. She was always trapped. "I hate you!" Turning away from him, she ran into one of the bedrooms and slammed the door.

Al opened her eyes, her head wedged between a set of soft white pillows. She glanced at the side table and a clock told her the time: almost twenty-one hundred hours. Her binding crowded around it, spilling down the sides like fabric water, her stuffed sock a misshapen boulder.

She gripped the sheets and stared at the old constellations that didn't exist anymore dotting her ceiling. "I have to get that remote."

All men are the same, girl. Angel's voice entered her head.

"But I don't know how to be a girl like her. I don't even have the right clothes." She rubbed her hands over her face and then hit her cheeks twice. "I gotta try. He can't take flying away from me. No one can."

The stone floor was cold against her bare feet as she stood, wearing a black bandeau and boy shorts. There was no mirror in the room, but Al already knew she wasn't as beautiful as Angel. Her sides twinged with dull pain as she moved. She could feel the ugliness seeping into her skin. It always did.

She pulled a white button-up shirt from her bag and shoved her arms through the sleeves. The loose material at her sides covered her splotched skin. Even if she wasn't pretty, all she had to do was act like Angel.

Opening her door, she poked her head into the living room, but he wasn't there. The bathroom door was ajar, but he wasn't there either.

She gripped the handle of his door. No turning back now. A draft of hot air gushed past her as she pulled.

Perryn was asleep on top of his covers, one arm above his head, his black gloves still on. Under his sleeveless shirt, his chest rose and fell with each even breath.

Al steeled her nerves. *Now if he could just stay asleep until I'm ready.*

She approached the side of the bed, where his glasses rested on top of a closed book on the nightstand. Would the remote be in the drawer? She shook her head. He was smarter than that and she might wake him if she checked.

Smooth strands of hair formed a thin black veil over his closed eyes, and his lips were parted. Her heart began pounding behind her eyes and even though she wasn't wearing the binding, she found it hard to breathe. Maybe this was a bad idea. But how else would she get out of here? He wasn't going to hand over the remote if she just asked nicely.

Taking a quiet breath in and out, she straddled Perryn's body, hovering above him. Her bare knees sank into the bed as she sat on her heels, her shirt tickling her sides.

He let out a low groan and her cheeks grew hot, her confidence waning.

She covered her eyes. *You got this, Al.* He'd wake up, caught off guard by her charms, and have no choice but to set her free. She'd show him she wasn't a kid.

With shaking fingers, she reached toward his belt clasp, her heartbeat so loud she could no longer hear if her breaths were still quiet.

She froze. How exactly was she supposed to touch him? Angel never explained that part.

Gloved fingers squeezed her wrists, and she fell forward.

The smell of pine again.

She looked up into his harsh glare. "Perryn!" He was too close. "G—g—give me the remote..."

"I see."

In one graceful motion, he flipped Al onto her back, her shirt and hands flopping to her sides.

She stared up in wide-eyed bewilderment, his weight sinking into the bed next to her shoulders as he loomed above her. Their legs touched, the fabric of his silky pants gliding across her skin. His cold eyes seemed hungry somehow, as if he intended to devour her, but she couldn't look away, couldn't think. Was she even breathing anymore? He had paralyzed her with only his gaze.

He moved closer, his hair brushing against her now bare shoulder. Heat radiated out of him. "Do you know what happens next?" His soft voice caressed her ear, and she shut her eyes, letting out a small squeak as she clenched the bedding in her fists. This was a mistake.

"See? Do not act like you understand." He lifted himself from the bed, and the door slammed.

Al lay motionless, catching her breath, the smell of pine still lingering around her. What just happened? Too much, or maybe nothing at all. She wasn't sure. Her mind was a mess of loud, bouncing, incoherent thoughts.

When she sat up, his trench coat was missing. With her face still flushed, she stepped down from the bed. Steadying herself against the wall, it took everything in her not to crumple to the floor as she opened the door.

Fresh air rushed past her.

Stumbling to the bottom of the ladder, she looked up into the clear night sky. The hatch was open. Perryn was gone. *Freedom!*

She bolted back to her room and stuffed the binding and stray belongings into her bag. After pulling on her pants and resituating her sock, she jammed her feet into her boots, tucking the laces into the top. Throwing her bag over her shoulder, she ascended the ladder.

Without checking to see if Perryn was around, Al sprinted down the road. Did he mess up? Or did he intentionally set her free? She'd figure that out later. She needed to focus on running.

Perryn's eyes.

His lips.

His hair.

His voice.

Brain, shut up!

She let out a grunt as she ran, the night air taming the burn on her cheeks.

When she finally stopped to duck behind a bush, sweat dripped down her forehead. The Keev-ship track was just ahead. Perryn wanted to keep her from the race, but he sure didn't try that hard. He seemed distracted, not like himself. Maybe he'd try something tomorrow. With a frown, she pulled the binding from her bag and wrapped her chest.

Her breathing still labored, she ran toward the tents resting on one side of the track. Each one had a distinct logo or the name of the racer that slept inside printed on the fabric.

She found Zeek's, a brown one with *Landers* written in red. As she unzipped the tent and stepped inside, a knife swung past her in the low lamplight. She dodged, but ended up falling butt-first to the ground.

"Al? Is that you?" Zeek stood above her, weapon in hand. He wore a pair of dark blue sweatpants but no shirt and behind him, the layers of his black sleeping bag lay dislodged and thrown apart.

"Wow. I guess you're ready for anything." She grimaced as she stood.

"Where were you today? I had to get the ship ready all by—"

"Yeah, I know. I'll tell you later. Right now, I just wanna take a shower and sleep." She set her bag down and began rummaging through it. "Hey, can I borrow a micro towel? I forgot mine."

Zeek stowed his knife. "Um, sure. I think the community stalls are still open for another twenty minutes or so." He froze. "Wait. You're not...staying the night, are you?"

"Yeah?"

"But you always say you can't." He frowned, pulling his arms across his chest. "Al, what—"

"Like I said, I'll explain later. C'mon, please? I only got twenty minutes until I'm doomed. Towel?" She held out her hand, and he sighed.

Walking to his sleeping bag, he bent down and pulled the microcloth from his brown duffel bag. He held it up with his face turned away.

"Thanks, bud!" She yanked it from his hands and dashed out of the tent toward the showers.

Sleeping with the binding would be painful, but to be in the same tent as Zeek, she would have to endure its suffocating embrace tonight. Perryn's was way too dangerous.

CHAPTER 12

Someone tugged at her binding.

Her eyes shot open and Perryn hovered above her in the tent. Zeek was missing. She tried to call his name, but Perryn's lips silenced hers as he grabbed her wrists, pinning them above her head. He pushed his body against hers. She couldn't breathe. He released one of her hands and began caressing the bare skin under her shirt. Her whole body blazed like an engine fire as her vision turned blurry and dark.

She fell into herself.

Al shot up from the sleeping bag and buried her head in her hands. *What the hydrogen was that?*

"Bad dream?" Perryn stared back at her, but after blinking the sleep from her eyes, his hazy form morphed into a squinting Zeek. He was leaning against the tent, a blanket draped over his now-clothed shoulders. The beginnings of dark circles plagued the skin under his eyes and his hair stuck up in random clumps like an unkempt lawn.

Al touched her chest where her heart felt like it was trying to burst from her ribcage and let out a breath. It was just a dream, a stupid, meaningless dream. "Did you sleep at all?"

Zeek yawned. "Not sure. Too tired."

"Zeek! You're the one piloting today. You should've kept your sleeping bag and given me the blanket."

"It's fine." He rubbed his eyes. "Last night, you looked like you needed it more than I did."

"You better not crash or anything."

"Guess our survival depends on you then." Zeek stood and threw his blanket over her head with a laugh. "I'll go get us some breakfast. Their moose sausage is the best!"

Al remained under the blanket even after he left. The pocket of air surrounding her smelled like chamomile, like Zeek, a safe and warm scent. If only this barrier was strong enough to mask her presence from the world. Then she could disappear. Everyone would leave her alone. People complicated everything.

She wrapped her arms around herself, but stopped when she felt the binding slide down her side. Lifting her shirt, she noticed the tie had indeed loosened. She had been so exhausted last night, she must have undone it in her sleep.

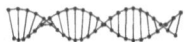

The wind was a healthy strength as Al and Zeek pushed his ship out onto the wide dusty track. They both wore black shorts and white shirts with long red sleeves, their respective last names running down their left arms in white bubble letters.

Several other two-seater ships already waited at their pre-assigned positions, refueling with large coils or with their pilots inspecting their instruments. As they continued past them, Al scanned her surroundings, looking for even the tiniest hint of Perryn's presence. Nothing.

Off to one side, behind a low-lying metal fence, was an elevated seating box painted in red with white diamonds running along the side. Snacks and megaphones in hand, several men filled the rows, wearing homemade shirts with the names of their favorite racers.

Zeek's number one fan, Russell, sat in the front row, kicking back and forth as his legs dangled off the bench. Based on his rapid hand movements, he seemed to be re-counting some sort of exciting story to his father, who sat next to him. They both wore shirts with the slogan *Landers Land Best* written in black.

Zeek cupped his hands over his mouth. "Russell! Thanks for coming!"

The young boy jumped on top of the bench and waved with both arms before turning back to his father, his hands twirling and weaving as he sat. Russell's father looked toward them and Zeek smiled, signing *thank you*. The bearded man nodded back with a warm wave.

Al noticed the *No Women Allowed* sign hanging from the entrance of the stands and glared. Nothing would stop her from flying, not a pathetic sign, not even the mighty Perryn Keevie. He was still missing.

Maybe he gave up? She couldn't be that lucky. He had to be lurking somewhere, waiting for the right time to enact his revenge. He must have let her go on purpose last night. No way Perryn was that sloppy. But why go through all the effort of trapping her underground just to set her free so soon after? Al scrunched her nose at the thought as she and Zeek reached their starting position at the back of the lineup.

Against the backdrop of the tree-lined hill on the op-posite side of the track, red curtains rippled on a wooden stage, where two men dressed in brown suits and bowler hats stood behind a podium that had a megaphone sticking out from its center. Jim was a short bald man and Mick, the taller of the two, had a bushy black mustache that looked like oversized toothbrush bristles. Shouting men, waving pens and papers above their heads, swarmed below them. The moment the crowd saw Zeek they about-faced and pressed up against the guardrail that separated the stage from the track, the position of their arms not changing.

Zeek let out a breath. "Oh boy."

"What's wrong, Animus? Not nervous, are you?" Al elbowed him in the side as they attached the hydrogen refueler coil to the ship.

"Pfft. Please. I'm the champion! Being scared is for losers." He struck a heroic pose before his face loosened. "Just, those guys don't understand the term 'personal space'. It's seriously a foreign term to them."

Al eyed the men dressed in fancy suits as they squished together like the colorful wires in a clock. The speed at which they jotted down notes every time Zeek glanced at them made it seem like they were proud parents fawning over their newborn child. Several teenage boys stood next to them wearing green cloth bands around their forearms, written with the name of the company they worked for. They juggled papers and equipment as their faces held various stages of dread.

Al snickered and motioned to the crowd with her head. "It looks like the new part-timers are just now realizing what they signed up for."

"But it isn't all bad." Zeek grabbed his goggles from the cockpit and after strapping them to his head, he pointed at himself with his thumb. "My face gets to be plastered on every poster around the city during race week. Imagine how many people are falling in love with me right now!" He clutched his heart and sighed.

"Oh, just get goin' already, will ya?" She pushed him toward the reporters and their voices raised in volume as he stepped over the railing and up onto the stage.

Jim and Mick quelled the crowd, but then a reporter from Keev-ship Daily began his barrage of questions. Al couldn't hear what he asked, but a huge grin crossed Zeek's face.

"Strong!" He paused and flexed his biceps. "Smart!" He pointed to his temples with both hands. "Sleek!" He brushed imaginary dirt from each shoulder. "Zeek!" He pulled out his finger guns.

The men below let out impressed gasps, and once again attacked their notepads with their pens.

Al cupped her hands over her mouth. "Make sure they get your good side!" She turned toward the ship, shaking her head, and pushed up her sleeves. "Alright, beautiful. Let's see how you're feeling this morning."

She hopped into the cockpit and flipped the fuel valve switch and the tank began to fill with hydrogen, the arrows on the dash quivering until they rose.

"Engine—stable. Fuel tank—seventy percent and climbing, internal temp—standby, landing gear stability..." She reached below the dash and twisted a nob that looked like the legs of a metal octopus. With a creaking noise, small tremors shook the cockpit.

Al sucked air through her clenched teeth. "Passable. Barely."

A slight crackling and then a burst of vintage brass echoed over the loudspeakers. Jim's voice boomed, his words elongated. "Gentlemen and Scoundrels! Welcome to Astova's annual Keev-ship raaaace!"

The crowd, now packed shoulder to shoulder with excited males of all ages, clapped and whistled. Other than Russell and his father, Al didn't recognize any of the faces.

Molly would have watched if she were allowed and Maddox had never shown any interest. Last year Mr. Landers and Jack cheered from the front row, but military business kept them busy this time.

"We've sure got a great turnout this year, right, Mick?"

"That's right, Jim, and speaking of a good turnout, just a friendly reminder that this year's race is, as always, sponsored by Keevie Inc., the main and best supplier of all your Keev-ship needs. Now please welcome Prime Minister Keevie for his opening remarks!"

The crowd responded with gracious applause, and Al's shoulders tensed as she swiveled her head toward the stage.

Zeek clapped and backed away from the podium, just as Marcus Keevie approached it, wearing a dark-navy suit. His smile was chiseled and hard like a statue's, like he had practiced the warmth right out of it. A few soldiers dressed in red surrounded him on either side and then Perryn emerged behind them, wearing the same clothes from yesterday. His bodyguards moved to stand beside him.

Al catapulted herself from the cockpit and crumpled to her knees behind the ship. He had finally appeared.

Mr. Keevie's low and zealous voice resounded out. "Keev-ship racing began as a way for Astovans to collectively heal from the Altered's cruelty."

Loud disapproving "boos" erupted from the stands, drowning out his next few sentences.

"Now a full-fledged sport of ingenuity and grit, we are immensely pleased to welcome new and old competitors alike to symbolize our right to take back the sky!"

The crowd responded with more enthusiastic cries as Al held her head. Perryn wouldn't cause a scene in front of everyone, right?

"Everything good?"

Al jumped as Zeek appeared, staring down at her with raised eyebrows.

"Um, yeah!" She hit the ship as she stood but kept her body below it. "Just uh, mentally resonating with the engine."

"Nice! Then let's get ready to kick some cloud ass!" Zeek held up his arm for their signature handshake.

Al laughed as she lifted her arm as well. "Don't ever say that again."

They high-fived and jumped into their seats, securing their goggles over their eyes. Al glanced at the stage again.

Mr. Keevie sat in a padded chair, a wall of soldiers blocking him from the dark prince who sat next to him with his arms crossed and his eyes closed. Was Perryn taking a nap?

Al scrunched her nose. *How nice for him to be unbothered by anything.* Sinking into her seat as far as she could, she crossed her arms too. She wasn't sure she could handle another encounter with his eyes. His irises were like black holes, sucking her soul from her body.

"Now to introduce this year's racers!" Jim spun away from the megaphone as Mick stepped up.

"New to the field wishing to dish out some judgment with his ship The Hand of God, Ramon De Los Reyes!"

A man wearing a long-sleeved white robe with a golden cross on his back stood inside a pure white ship closest to the front of the starting line. The crowd didn't seem impressed and booed. Frowning, Ramon returned to his cockpit with a huffy sigh. His mechanic, dressed in similar clothing, cowered in the seat beside him, hiding his face with a Bible like a shield.

Mick cleared his throat. "Okay Gents, put your gears together for the twin prodigies of the field, flying their ship, Static Resonance—The Ajith Brothers!" The identical twelve-year-olds stood up together, smiling and waving in unison, their adorable curls mirror images of each other. The crowd cheered.

Jim continued, his voice increasing with intensity. "Next up is a man who needs little introduction! Flying his ship The Croaker—The Croaker!"

A small section of the men screamed his name, repeating it over and over as a heavy-set man wearing a shirt a few sizes too small lifted himself from his cockpit and waved a greasy hand at his adoring fans. The double tail fin of his black and red ship featured a black frog with a mischievous smile and yellow eyes. Behind him, his much thinner mechanic with a scar on his cheek directed the crowd to continue with their feverish chanting.

"And who could forget this next racer who became a surprise favorite last year! The Incredible Mr. Wu and his ship—The Super Gentleman!" Mick bowed low as a tall, slender man wearing a black tux rose from his chrome polished ship.

Mr. Wu bowed, sweeping his black cape behind him, and then returned to his seat in a perfect, almost rehearsed way. The crowd cheered again, while some of the younger boys wearing capes of their own pressed their faces against the fence.

"Now! Your favorite daredevil, flying a ship also named after himself—Wicked Kris!" The crowd began chanting in unison as a flurry of fireflowers exploded from the side of the track.

A young man with dark brown skin howled as he shot down a zip line from the top of a light post using a metal bar. His black hair, spiked with green-and-purple tips, remained stiff as he somersaulted in the air and landed inside his cockpit where his partner waited. He thrust his hands above his head and let out another victory yell, and the crowd responded with more whistles and shouts.

"And now the racer you've all been waiting for!" Mick flung his free arm into the air as Jim jumped in front of him to steal the megaphone.

"That's right, folks! Your Animus flying in his ship the—The Prostitute!" Jim almost choked on the last few words. "Zeek Landers!"

Zeek rose from the cockpit as he laughed and flashed finger guns at the crowd. They responded with more loud cheers, and Russell beamed from the sidelines, waving his goggles. Al would've jumped up too but pretending not to exist inside a space that provided little cover required arms and legs inside the vehicle at all times.

As the pit crews pushed away platforms and detached fuel coils from the ships, she glanced at Perryn. Her chest tightened. He was staring straight at her, his eyes tired and murky, not at all the same ones that held her hostage the night before. As he disappeared behind the curtain with his bodyguards, she couldn't shake the feeling that he almost seemed sad. If Perryn Keevie could ever feel that sort of emotion. Al shook her head. He was the enemy. Plain and simple.

"Hello? Al? Let's go, spacewalker!" Zeek had turned around in his seat.

"Right!" Al saluted him. "Preflight check complete!" As she and Zeek pulled on their headsets, the ship rose to join the others hovering in the air.

The roar of all the engines at once drowned out the crowd, even though they continued to cheer through their megaphones. Only the lower tones of the announcer's voices stood out amid the noise as they continued to address the audience. Al switched on the internal radio within her seat and much clearer voices poured out from her cans.

"And as always, we wish you all a favorable wind!" Jim's words still held their exuberant flair despite the clear strain in his voice.

"And now, presenting the starting flag for today's race will be..." Mick began, his voice just as ragged.

"The lovely!" Jim continued.

"The beautiful!"

"The smoking hot!"

"Angel!" they both yelled together.

Al cringed. Following through with the celestial being's sensual suggestion had almost certainly stolen several years of her life. Maybe that's why Angel looked so beautiful. She handed out advice to her clients in exchange for their youth.

The sparkling girl sauntered down the starting line, the long blonde wig and silky white dress that barely covered her body fluttering in the wind. On her back, a pair of glittering wings bounced with each step and in her hands, she held a tall red-and-white flag with a black ship printed in the middle of the flimsy fabric.

"Hey, Al? Isn't that the girl you almost—"

"Yeah Zeek, and I don't wanna talk about it!" She threw her head into her hands. *If that memory could just be deleted from my brain, that would be great, thanks.*

Zeek tapped her shoulder and she looked up. With a smile, he held out a tag-shaped object made of yellow fabric with the outline of a black Keev-ship sewn in its center. She took the gift and waited for him to get resituated in his seat and pull on his headset before she spoke.

"What's this?"

"Good luck charm! Supposed to ward off crashes or something."

She chuckled. "Are you sure you don't need this then, Mr. Sleepyhead?"

"I got one too, so we match! See?" He held up an identical charm.

"Well, guess we've got double the luck then." She unzipped her pocket, placing the charm inside, and then buckled her chest restraint.

Angel had made it to the center of the track and flashed a series of huge seductive smiles and waves to the crowd, which left the men whistling and shouting things Al only half-understood. She lifted the flag above her head with both hands, her bobbing wings expelling small clouds of sparkles.

"Showtime!" Zeek's voice was thick with anticipation.

Angel waved the flag in a circular motion and slammed it into the dirt.

Go!

The ships shot off in loud bursts, creating a whining metallic symphony. As they zoomed forward, a tremendous gust of wind blew through the arena, causing an avalanche of candy, popcorn, and beer to cover the cheering spectators. The strong draft also blew up Angel's dress, and she feigned embarrassment with a halfhearted attempt to pull the fabric back down to Earth.

Jim and Mick's fevered voices faded from Al's headphones as the cold wind pushed up against her skin. The ground grew distant beneath them, but they leveled out at a height where their ship cast a tiny shadow upon the dusty track. The dirt soon faded into a mess of grass, rocks, and trees. Then, only red flags flying from tall light poles or high branches marked the route.

Al closed her eyes and stretched out her arms. Peace. Pure bliss. Nothing mattered in the air. There was only freedom.

The markers led them around a bend and into a forest where the sky path continued between a clear-cut in the treetops. Campfires, tents, and cheering men dappled the ground and the distant sound of clinking beer glasses reverberated through the air.

They exited the forest, wiping away the bugs splattered across their goggles, and an open field stretched out beneath them. Several families enjoying picnic lunches waved and cheered as the pair soared above.

Zeek pointed out two rival crafts in the distance, one belonging to Mr. Wu and the other to Ramon. "Okay! You ready, bud? Time to give these people a good show!"

"Roger that!" Al turned a knob near her feet and two cylindrical rockets retracted down from the back of the ship. She lifted a see-through cover on her dash, her hand prepped to push the red button it had concealed. As the other ships grew closer, Al and Zeek rose higher until they hovered a few ship lengths above their original altitude.

Al gripped her mic. "Boosters primed and ready!"

"On my signal—" Zeek flicked a few switches in the cockpit, causing their gliding assists to retract back into the ship. Vibrations rattled the shell as the rockets in the back revved up. He gripped the steering wheel, ready to dive. "Now!"

Al slammed the button with her palm and their ship slid through the air like a sharp knife, leaving the other two ships in their hydrogen dust. The intense force shoved their backs against their seats and any trace of summer heat froze around them. If the people under them had applauded the two friends couldn't hear them, as only the muffled sound of violent wind reached their covered ears.

Monitoring the meter on her dash, Al struggled to hold her hand above the button as Zeek aimed the ship down, the muscles in her arm activating against the g-force.

"Cut it!"

She slammed the button again and let out an adrenaline-fueled yell. "Woo! That was amazing! Nice piloting!"

"Yeah! Nice teamwork!" Zeek reached his hand above his head and Al leaned forward to high-five him. "Now let's catch up with the leaders, shall we?"

"Right behind ya!" Al laughed, throwing her fist into the air.

"Al! Can you turn around and see what's going on?" Zeek's sharp change in tone stripped away her excitement as he adjusted his side mirror. "What the hell is that?"

A huge black cloud billowed up from the distant arena behind them and several medical ships zoomed past below them, heading toward the smoke. There wasn't time to contemplate much more before a loud, grating beeping echoed in their headphones. *Not good.* Without hesitation, Al flipped the switches near her side.

"Al, that doesn't sound good!"

"Yeah, I'm aware! Just give me a sec!" She unhooked her seatbelt. With her headphones still attached, she ducked upside down and checked the pressure meter mounted in the cavern-like space between their seats.

"In the future, you should really move this to a place that's easier to access." Her voice strained as the blood rushed to her head.

"Okay, got it, but can you fix it?"

"There's a problem with the boosters. When we used it, something zapped the power supply. I told you not to misuse your stop gauges, didn't I?"

"Still didn't answer my question, bud!"

"I can try to fix it, but there's no telling how much time we have." She hoisted herself upright in her seat.

"Until what?" Zeek's voice cracked.

"We fall from the sky."

He swallowed. "I'll try to lower the ship so we don't have so far to fall."

Al opened a compartment next to her seat and pulled out a tool belt and a long metal cable. Wrapping both around her waist and snapping them together with metal hooks, she touched Zeek's shoulder. "See you soon."

He gave her a thumbs-up as she threw her headset in her seat.

Ignoring the blurring scenery below, she took a deep breath and closed her eyes. She wanted to let herself panic, to let all her fear bubble out, but she couldn't afford that right now.

Stepping over the side of the ship, she descended toward its underbelly using the assist handles that protruded out. The wind gnawed at her face and ripped at her hair as she reached the bottom of the ship, the pulley system activating with skipping jolts.

The ship sank lower.

Swinging under, she hooked both her ankles and left wrist into more handles. With her free hand, she pulled the seam ripper from her belt and attached the magnetic end to the ship's red skin. After twisting and yanking the tool, a section of the shell unlocked and slid open.

She let go of the seam ripper and it remained attached as she poked her head up into the ship's insides. It smelled like rotten eggs, meaning hydrogen was leaking somewhere into the hull. Al had added the scent for situations just like this.

"Oh, great. That's just great!" She began testing pipes with another tool from her belt and sorted through wires. This was her fault for not double-checking the stability of the engine before takeoff. Perryn had consumed her thoughts.

The ship let out a long whirling sigh as an overhead light flashed red. Then, as if suspended in a tractor beam, the ship froze in midair.

A sharp jab sank deep into her bones.

She was out of time.

The ship plummeted into a freefall, and Al screamed, the uncomfortable lurching sensation attacking her stomach. She struggled out of the hull and tried to climb back up, but her left ankle trapped her between an assist handle and the ship. Grasping for the seam ripper with both hands, she tried to yank her foot free. The tool broke away from the ship and Al fell backward with a terrified scream.

She dangled upside down by her ankle, the metal cable squeezing her waist.

As the green of the valley grew closer, she willed herself to reach up and untie her boot with one hand, as the other gripped another handle. Her abs burned and her fingers felt slow and sloppy as they fiddled with the laces. Somehow, Al loosened her foot from her shoe. She pulled it free and the boot plummeted out of sight.

With the last of her strength, she climbed back up and hauled herself over the lip of the ship and into her seat. She saw the back of Zeek's head just before she wrapped herself into a ball and sank to the floor.

The ship smashed into the ground.

When Al opened her eyes, everything blurred together and parts of her body felt numb. Soft grass surrounded her and someone above her called her name.

Where was she? What happened? What day was it?

"Zeek?" Her voice was breathy and slow as she sat up, holding her head. Her fingers grazed against a bandage on her forehead. "Zeek?" She attempted to stand, but firm hands pushed her shoulders down.

"Al, please remain still. You have a mild concussion."

"Perryn? What're you...? Zeek! Is he okay?"

"The medical team is escorting him to the trauma center now. They are confident he will wake up soon."

"Wake up? What? That's—" She grabbed her head again as sharp pain radiated out behind her eyes, but her vision returned. Perryn was kneeling in front of her. Dirt and dusty gray ash saturated his clothes. "How did you know where we were?"

"Zeek. He sent a distress call over the radio before you crashed." As Perryn looked toward the racetrack, she noticed a shallow gash across his left cheek. The blood was still wet.

So Perryn can get hurt, too. "Are you okay?"

His hands twitched against her shoulders before he released her. "The Altered detonated a bomb. It is not safe to linger here."

Her breathing malfunctioned in her chest. "What?"

"Al..." He stood and smudged the gash with the back of his gloved hand. "It is time I stopped lying to you."

CHAPTER 13

Giant chunks of the scorched black track had been ripped from the earth like uneven jigsaw pieces, and jagged metal, warped into unnatural positions, dangled from the remnants of the stands that still stood. Smoke billowed up from shattered solar panels, and pockets of fire outlining the blast zone raged, even as man-made rain poured from the emergency ships above.

Soldiers and medical personnel wearing biosuits collected and tended to bodies as they found them, piling them onto covered stretchers that floated into the bowels of a much larger ship, the living to the right, the dead to the left.

Al slammed the sun visor down and turned from the window of Perryn's ship, wrapping her arms around herself. He sat across the aisle, his arms crossed and his unwavering gaze on the back of the seat in front of him. His bodyguards weren't with him this time. Were they lost somewhere in the rubble?

A sickening tingle radiated down her throat and she stumbled as she stood, rushing to the bathroom in the back of the ship. After she had emptied the contents of her stomach, she wiped her mouth and slumped to the cold metal floor.

Her brain throbbed against her skull, her nerves, and muscles screamed at her, and her bootless left foot looked pathetic in just a sock. Was Zeek going to be okay?

She shivered and hugged her bare knees to her chest, closing her eyes. "I won't cry. I won't break."

It only felt like seconds before she awoke to Perryn calling her name and shaking her shoulders.

"Stop! What's wrong with you?" She ducked her head back into her lap as an intense light greeted her.

"Al, please. I know this hurts, but I have to make sure your concussion is not worsening."

"I'm fine! Just let me sleep!" She heard a click and the fake sun went out.

Her consciousness faded back into darkness, but like before, Perryn's penlight interrupted her short dreamless sleep.

She shoved his hands away. "Perryn! Seriously, I'm gonna—"

"Could you at least relocate? This is the only lavatory on board."

Frowning as she stood, she dragged herself into the aisle, the door to the bathroom slamming shut behind her. She moved back to the now-dimmed cabin, where the softness of the seats felt like clouds against her skin.

Beyond the windows, a black night swallowed up all external light except for the faint glow of the halfmoon that seemed to shimmer and glide over the moving ground. Or was that the ocean? Sleep claimed her before she could decide. Anglerfish Perryn continued to disturb her, but she lost count as her mind stopped processing the passage of time.

The heavy jolts of the ship's docking mechanism knocked her awake and a thin brown blanket slipped from her shoulders. Perryn again? He wasn't in his seat.

A fresh purple sunset kissed the skyline and tall jagged rocks descended like steps until they disappeared beneath a navy-blue ocean. How long had she been out?

She touched the bandage on her head and frowned, a new trophy to add to her broken-body collection. While the area was less painful now, her heart made up for the difference when the memories flooded back all at once.

"Al, time to go." Perryn's sudden voice was cold but lacked its usual bite as he walked down the aisle, a pair of boots in his hands.

She shook her head, wrapping the blanket around her shoulders. "I'm staying right here." Why did she even agree to go with him?

Perryn knelt beside her, setting the boots on the ground. "I promise. Everything you need to know is out there, not in here."

She fidgeted, turning away to stare at her feet and hide her mouth behind the blanket. His expression was foreign, but not because she didn't know what it was. Sincerity was a language she never expected him to speak. Since when had his presence become something comforting?

Al scrunched her nose. That was probably just the brain damage talking. She'd only accept his gift because proper shoes would be nice.

Dropping the blanket as she scooted back, she yanked off her brotherless shoe and pulled on the new pair, tying the laces. Soft cozy warmth flooded over her cold foot as it raced to catch up with the temperature of the other. She stood and tapped the boot toes against the metal floor to situate them and then followed Perryn in silence to the back of the ship, where he handed her a black hooded cloak to wear. Once he had donned his own, they stepped out onto the beach.

Sea salt and the sound of crashing waves tickled her senses as she plodded down a winding sandy path made of colorful stone hexagons. Several were missing from the intricate pattern. They approached a pair of towering sawtooth formations that jutted into the sky like pointy, fractured horns and the seabirds nesting above let out warning calls.

Al craned her neck as she entered the passage between them, the tall shadows staining her whole body in dark gray. "Where are we?"

"Petram." Perryn kept his back to her. "Watch your step."

Al touched the bandage on her forehead. "A little late to be worrying about falling." Why was gravity so obsessed with using her body for target practice?

Thick vines that covered the rocks spiraled up into a draping canopy and a few orange lemurdogs dangled by their fuzzy striped tails, howling deep, throaty calls from their tiny faces, a boisterous song echoing across the limestone.

Pockets of mosquitoes and tiny night bugs emerged as they continued through the dark ravine. The long sleeves of her racing shirt protected her arms, but fearing for her bare knees and below, she wrapped the thin cloak closer around her body and quickened her pace.

The smell of burning wood reached her nose, and the buzzing vanished.

As they rounded the corner, a flickering torch cast dancing shapes upon a stone door built directly into the rock. A man wearing a similar black cloak stood guard in front, holding a staff adorned with wings and two snakes coiling around the top. The black ibis mask that obscured his face muffled his words as he spoke.

"Thoth welcomes you to the house of wisdom and asks what gifts you bear." The man's other hand gripped the hilt of a knife that glinted in the torchlight.

Perryn stepped forward, pulling his hood farther down over his eyes. "Thoth himself stands before you and bears the seal of Ma'at." He produced a gold ring from his pocket with a pair of scales engraved onto its face.

The ibis man eyed the ring and then bowed, re-sheathing his weapon. He stepped aside and the round door behind him rolled open. As Al stepped through, several cloaked figures let out grunts as they pushed the door that sat within a shallow groove. When she and Perryn had cleared the opening, the figures released the round slab, and it rolled back into place.

Carved from the same rock she saw outside, the darkened cave-room had no windows. Orange and brown pipes, stringy lights, and multicolored wires intersected and twisted in the cavernous ceiling like a giant mechanical spider web. Several hooded figures shuffled about, whispering in languages Al recognized but didn't understand.

"So you're a god now? That's rich." Al kept her voice down as she moved to Perryn's side. "What is this creepy place anyway?"

"Headquarters."

"For what?"

He didn't answer and turned down a narrow corridor lined with more dim lights and metal railings. The hallway opened up into a footbridge and below, sweaty mechanics wearing clothes stained with dark colors were constructing Keev-ships amid steam and sparks. Al relaxed. At least something normal had appeared. She kept walking across the bridge, but just as she was about to reach the other side, she caught a glimpse of a red *A* on one of the wings.

Her stomach lurched. Those weren't Keev-ships.

She dashed to the railing and peered down. *Scraper Sharks!* What were *those* things doing here? She froze. Was this the Altered's base? Was Perryn working with them? She turned to question him, but he had already disappeared down another narrow corridor.

Rushing after him, she entered the hallway and a loud flurry of indistinguishable voices reverberated off the walls, pouring from the arched opening at the other end. She stepped through and the sudden brightness blinded her. She steadied herself against the wall until her eyes readjusted.

The lecture-style room had stone slabs for seating packed with people wearing black cloaks with hoods that obscured their faces. At the bottom of the steps, several people sat in a row on a stage wearing animal masks. A wrinkly banner with the image of an angry man with a giant red X painted over his face hung behind them. *Is that supposed to be Vilroy?*

Scanning the crowd, she found Perryn sitting in the corner, and he motioned for her to sit next to him. She took her seat and was about to start her barrage of questions when a booming man's voice called out.

"Settle! Settle! Friends, settle!"

As the view to the stage cleared, the jackal-headed man who had spoken returned to his stool and a woman wearing a cat mask stood next.

"We welcome you, brothers and sisters, to the gathering. Now our Ra, he will speak."

Her voice sounded familiar. Why? Who was she? Who were any of these people?

Loud cheers from the crowd and the man entering the stage distracted Al from her panicked thoughts.

The man wore a white cloak and a mask of a strange bird with accentuated eyes and a blue headpiece that left his mouth exposed. He lifted his hands, and the crowd hushed. "Yes, we welcome you, brothers and sisters. I, Ra, have heard the pain of our people."

Al leaned toward Perryn, her harsh whisper increasing in volume. "This is some weird, next-level cult crap, Perryn. Why did you bring me here? Is this the Altered's—"

"Just listen," he snapped.

She turned back to face the stage, gripping the stone slab. How was she supposed to do that when her mind was yelling so loud?

Ra, as he called himself, moved closer to the audience, his hands spread out like wings. He seemed familiar too.

"For many years, we have tried to free ourselves from the Naturalists and their egotistical obsession with pureness. For many years, we have suffered at their hands, losing sisters and brothers, daughters and sons, children and parents. We lost hope more times than we'd like to admit. I know I have. But today, those losses are no longer in vain! Today, we have finally eliminated the snake that sat at the right hand of that demon Vilroy Vax! Marcus Keevie is dead!"

"What?" Her stomach twisted as she stared at Perryn, but his face remained cold and unchanged, even as the crowd cheered. The binding dug into her chest and her lungs tightened. This was the Altered's base. This was their leader. Perryn had brought her to a den of killers.

"Yes, yes, it is truly a day of celebration, my brothers and sisters. But just as this victory ushers our efforts into a new era, so too must *we* enter a new era. Too long have we banded together in the shadows. It is time now for truth and light. Let me be the first to lead the way into this new revolution." The man removed his mask, and the crowd let out gasps and shocked murmurs.

Al shot to her feet, the hood slipping off her head. She covered her mouth, trying not to scream. The man under the mask was Maddox Finn.

His eyes widened when he noticed her, and when his gaze shifted to Perryn, they narrowed. For a moment, the sides of his mouth curled into a snarl, but his professional demeanor returned as he addressed the crowd. "Come, my brothers and sisters. Join us!"

The other animals on stage transformed into humans, and while Al didn't recognize any of the men, the woman under the cat mask was Molly.

Al shook her head as her breathing shallowed. How could the woman who gave such gentle hugs be here right now? How could she believe in anything that this group stood for?

"Join us!" the other members on stage pleaded in unison.

Al collapsed onto the stone slab, her arms falling slack. The reason Maddox was never around was because he was spending all his time here. The bomb. That was him. Him and Molly. All the bombs were them. "This isn't real...this can't be real..."

Perryn reached toward her, but then stopped and turned away, clenching his fist.

The cloaked members below removed their hoods and all colors of hair and eyes began to brighten the room like a rainbow garden. Many of them were women.

Maddox smiled and opened his arms once more. "Welcome to the future!"

"The future belongs to the Altered!" the crowd cried out in unison.

Maddox disappeared offstage the way he entered, and Molly and the other revealed members followed.

"Al." Perryn's voice was the only familiar thing left in the world. Where was she? This nightmare was the worst she had ever dreamed.

"Al!" Perryn shook her shoulders, and she looked at him, her soul numb. He held out his gloved hand, his eyes still shrouded by his hood. "Can you stand?"

She wasn't sure. Why did he seem so calm about his father's death? How long had he known about this place? She took his hand, and he helped her to her feet.

"This way." He let go as he turned toward the stairs and her hand felt colder than it had before.

She followed him down the steps, past the stage, and behind a dark curtain where two muscular men waited with crossed arms and stern glares. But when Perryn showed his ring, they bowed and let the pair pass. Perryn knocked upon the rusty-orange door behind them and it opened to reveal an office and Molly, who ushered them inside.

"I think she is still experiencing shock." Perryn helped Al to a chair.

"Brilliant observation, detective obvious! I knew this would happen. I told Maddox he should've told her the truth. I don't approve of the way you two have handled things." Molly turned toward Al, reaching for her. "Oh my gears! Your forehead!"

Al jumped out of her chair and shoved Molly away. "Don't touch me! Don't touch me, you liar!" Her throat tightened when Molly's face fell. "Just—don't touch me."

Molly stared at the ground and nodded as she moved to lean against the opposite wall. Al ripped off her cloak and tossed it to the ground.

"Once Dox gets here, we'll answer all of your questions."

"You better." Al slammed down into her chair.

Moments later, Maddox stepped through the door, his face solemn. Al glared at him as he brought a chair from out behind the desk in the corner of the room and sat, avoiding her gaze.

"Al—"

"How long have you been the leader of the Altered?" she cut him off.

Maddox leaned forward and rested his head in his hands. "Since before you were born."

Al gave him a bitter smile. "Figures. I'd ask you why, but I don't think I care."

"Al, please let—"

"Why did you kill Marcus Keevie?"

Maddox gestured toward Perryn, offering him a chance to speak, but when he remained silent, Maddox sighed. "Marcus Keevie was Vilroy's closest ally. Take him out and Perryn replaces him as the next prime minister. Since Perryn is sympathetic to our cause, he won't be helping the government wipe us out."

"Us?"

The eye-dye, the fingerprint re-creator, the hiding, the secrets, the meticulous planning. Maddox just happened to have a custom-made plan all laid out for her? She thought he had done everything out of love, but no. He was too good at lying, perfect even. "Maddox, are you Altered?"

"…yes…"

She shot Molly a glare. "And what're you? A robot?"

Molly pushed herself off the wall. "No! I'm a Naturalist. Dox is a…friend…a long-time friend and I'm helping because it's the right thing to do."

"Right thing to do? You've killed so many people!" Al leaped from her chair. "The attack on Elbion…that was you guys too, wasn't it?" She stumbled forward, her chest squeezing. "How could you look Mrs. Landers in the eye, knowing you killed her daughter? How could you look at Zeek?"

Maddox shifted his gaze, and Molly spoke. "That was a mistake. A terrible mistake." She held her elbows as she looked down. "That bomb was meant to destroy the building, not the people. But Al, sweetheart, the Naturalists keep killing people too, unarmed, innocent people, even children—"

"Oh, I guess that makes it all okay then, right?" Al snapped. Molly retreated to the wall. "The reason the Altered suffer is because of you! The Naturalists hate us because of you! They're terrified of us because they think anyone different than them is going to kill them! Wow! I guess it's true!"

Maddox hit the arm of his chair with his fist. "Al, you don't understand the complexities of what's happening."

"And whose fault is it that I'm so sheltered, huh?"

Maddox gritted his teeth and crumpled back into his chair. "I wanted to give you a normal life."

"Normal? Great job, *Dad*!" Al clasped her hands together in mock appreciation. "Did your guilty conscience dictate that one, too? Because it's been a grand old time. Oh! Also, Perryn's been helping by blackmailing me into doing weird stuff for him. Did you know that?"

"He what?" Maddox jumped from his chair and clenched his fists.

Perryn flinched and uncrossed his arms. "That is not exactly—"

"I'll deal with *you* later." Maddox turned back to face Al, his voice softening. "What he was supposed to be doing was keeping you safe in exchange for us taking out Marcus. Those were the terms." He rubbed his temples. "How did things get so complicated?"

Al stiffened as she turned toward Perryn. "But you…you acted like you didn't know anything! This whole time you…" She grimaced as pain radiated from beneath her bandage and down her neck.

"I made him swear to keep it a secret from you because then you would've found out about all of this shit before you were ready." Maddox scoffed. "But who am I fucking kidding? You'd never be ready for any of this. Thanks, by the way for bringing her here, Perryn, even though I specifically told you to keep her hidden until I came for you."

Al's eyes widened. Was that why Perryn took her to the motel? *That's why his excuse didn't make sense!* But if he knew a bomb had been planted at the race, why did he let her go?

Perryn took a step forward, his hood not quite concealing his glare. "If you honestly thought any of you could return to your normal lives after killing the prime minister, then you are the one who was not ready, Maddox. This is the safest place for her."

"So, what, you care now? Is that it?" Maddox pointed at Perryn. "Don't you dare lecture me about keeping her safe. I'm the only one who can."

Perryn took another step forward, his hood slipping off his head. "And yet, who did you call upon to protect her for the last two, almost three years? Right, me."

"Stop talking about me like I'm not here!" Al yelled. "I don't need either of you to watch over me! I'm not a baby! I can take care of myself!"

"Really, Al?" Maddox raised his arms as he walked toward her. "You never once stopped to think about how much I've done for you, have you? Never questioned why one day I suddenly allowed you to go to school after keeping you in the bunker your whole life? Did you think the trauma center was your only mistake? We all put our lives on the line. Just for you! You're welcome!"

Al took a step back. "I—"

"You're oblivious to everything, aren't you?" Maddox glared down at her, his eyes returning to the harsh and bitter ones from her childhood. "You're lucky there were always people there to clean up the messes you made or you would've been dead already."

Tears welled up in her eyes, but Al swallowed and pushed them down. She refused to cry in front of this man. He was a stranger now.

Perryn sent Maddox another glare. "I think that is an unfair—"

"Dox, you don't need to be so harsh with her!" Molly rushed to stand in front of Al. "We're in this situation because you two didn't want to explain things to her, so don't take your anger out on her. Oh my gears!"

Al almost let her expression soften out of habit, but Molly was a stranger now, too. "There's one thing you're still not explaining to me, then. I could've just lived outside the wall this whole time. Why go to such lengths to protect me if I'm such a burden? Why am I so damn special?"

Maddox sighed, and his shoulders sagged. "Al, kiddo, I'm tired."

The nickname cut into her heart like a searing hot knife. She wasn't going to let him play that card and run away. None of the clues she had unearthed from the cave and the lab gave her concrete answers about her past, but Maddox's reaction might.

"We'll have more time to discuss everything you want later, but right now, I need to return—"

"It's because Kera Lacey is my mom, right?" Al blurted out with an angry smile. "I'm a part of the Eternal Child Project, aren't I?"

Molly gasped, her hands flying to her mouth. "How did she...?"

"I said later," Maddox seethed, heading for the door.

"No!" Al ran in front of him, blocking his path. "No more lies! You're gonna tell me right now! Who am I?"

"SOMEONE WHO SHOULDN'T HAVE EVEN BEEN BORN!"

Maddox's words knocked the breath from her lungs, and she stood there, eyes wide and frozen. The realization of what he had said registered on his face, but before he could speak, she burst out the door.

She ran—past the colorful comrades, down the halls, and beyond the Scraper Sharks. When she reached the stone door, she dashed between the clamoring bodies already leaving and sprinted until she reached the ocean. She crumpled to the sandy shore, the coarse granules scratching against her knees.

The words didn't hurt. Somewhere deep down she already knew them, lived them, but now, someone else had confirmed it, had invaded her mind and stolen her biggest kept secret—that everything would be better if she was dead.

The world never wanted her.

Even though she wanted to cry, her body just wouldn't let her. So she screamed, long and hard, ripping at her sides to undo the binding, and tearing the sock from her legs and the bandage from her head. The tattered pieces soaked up the seawater and disappeared under the waves as she dug her fingers into the wet sand and threw clumps out into the darkened ocean with defeated and broken cries.

Exhausted, she flopped down onto the sand, numb to the water seeping into her clothes. She stared out into the empty sky. Even the stars had abandoned her. If that god

Zeek believed in really did live up there, would he hear her prayer?

Would he kill her if she asked nicely?

The cold finally reached a part of her that still lived, and she sat up, shivering. Hugging her arms, she dragged herself to a nearby outcropping of rocks and sat on the dry sand, the air nipping at her wet hair and skin. Footsteps caught her attention, but she didn't have to wait long to find out who they belonged to.

"You will catch a cold if you stay like that for too long." Perryn stood in front of her wearing his trench coat, the black cloak draped over his arm.

She lowered her head to her knees as she continued to shiver. "No offense, but I don't really wanna see you right now." She sniffled, her throat weak and swollen.

Sudden warmth covered her whole body as Perryn's trench coat cascaded over her shoulders. She wasn't sure how much time had passed, but when she looked up, he was already walking back toward the base.

Something tugged at her as his figure grew smaller in the distance.

She jumped up and ran down the beach after him, clutching the open ends of his trench coat against her chest. When she was close enough, she reached out and grabbed his gloved hand.

"Please don't leave me behind!"

She yelled much louder than she was expecting.

They both froze.

For a moment, the ocean breeze danced through the silence, playing with the ends of their hair. Then the muscles in Perryn's hand twitched, and Al let go with a startled gasp.

"I—" Her words faltered as if her mouth had lost the will to speak. He kept his back to her, but she still needed to look at the ground. "If you always knew...why were you so cold to me?"

Perryn grimaced before he spoke. "It was an assignment. I felt it wise to keep my distance."

"But in the cave...?"

"An accident. You were never meant to know I was working with Maddox, so I needed you to believe I was your enemy to hide why I was keeping you alive. It was a coincidence that there were not enough biosuits for my bodyguards to accompany us. If I had not followed his orders, Maddox—" Perryn clenched his fists. "I did not mean for it to go as far as it did."

"Were you the one who changed my clothes at the trauma center?"

"Yes."

Al gripped the coat tighter. "And those times you picked on me and made me do all those pointless things...was that really to keep me safe?"

"Capital Scanners always perform routine sweeps. If I knew where you were, I could make sure they did not." Perryn's voice was losing its even temperament. "But—" Then, for the first time since she had known him, he choked back his words. "There was a time I did those things because...I hated you."

She moved to face him. "Because I'm just an unobservant, ugly, stupid little girl that should be dead, right?"

"No, Al! That—" He stopped, his hands hovering on either side of her.

Al opened her mouth to speak, but something warm trickled from her eyes. She touched her cheek and then stared at her wet fingers.

Tears?

She smiled as strange laughter fell from her lips.

Tears.

She had almost forgotten what they felt like.

"Al?" Like a fissure, his voice pierced the dam that held back a lifetime of feelings.

Her broken laughter turned into choked sobs. After all this time, this was when her body decided it wanted to cry? In front of Perryn? This wasn't fair. None of this was fair. She covered her eyes as her tears gushed out, her sobs turning into desperate cries. *No! Go back inside! Not now!* The words stuck to her tongue as she gasped for air.

Her wailing grew louder, and her body trembled. Would she be cursed to cry forever now? She pulled her hands away as her throat threatened to close and dizziness blurred her vision. Perryn caught her just as her legs gave out and they both dropped to their knees in the sand.

"Goddammit." He drew her to his chest, and all the sound in the world other than his heartbeat vanished. He smelled faintly of salt, but the comforting scent of pine overcame it. Her heart crashed against her lungs, but she didn't pull away. They stayed this way until her sobs quieted into breaths that resembled hiccups.

He released her and she wiped her eyes and nose with the long sleeves of his coat. Then they both stared at the ground for what felt like an eternity, with only the rolling waves to fill the silence between them.

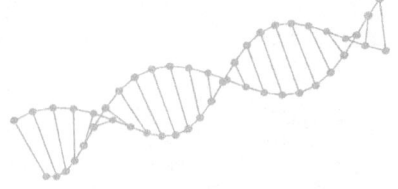

PART 2

WHAT IS
A GIRL?

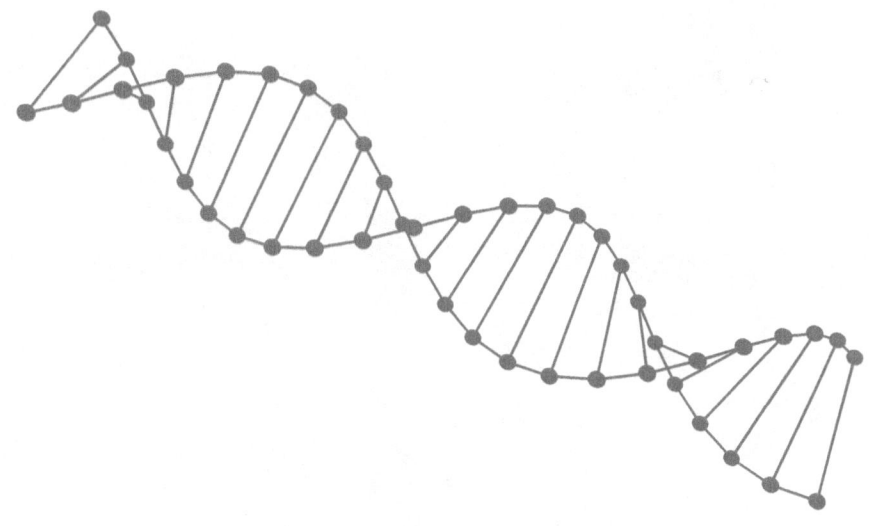

CHAPTER 14

Perryn stared at his gloved hand as he waited with Al in front of the stone door of the base. He had embraced her without thinking, letting her tears and wet sandy clothes stain his shirt. She was vulnerable, soft, something he never thought she would allow him to see.

He clenched his fist.

A fire once flourished in her eyes, but he had helped snuff it out. How was he any different from his father?

The scabbed cut on his cheek itched. Marcus, *his father*, was dead, his body charred beyond recognition and yet, his presence still lingered within Perryn's veins, within his very DNA. Instead of freedom, his soul ached with heavier chains—a grave miscalculation.

He tugged his hood farther down over his eyes as the door rolled open and the pair stepped inside. A few cloaked figures on pushing duty let out clenched grunts and disapproving murmurs as they passed.

The halls were almost empty, the late hour halting the sounds of construction or talk of revolution. He led Al down another circular corridor in the opposite direction as before and descended a flight of red, clay stairs.

MICHELLE A. MARIE

The space widened out into an open mess hall with walls made of a creamy orange stucco. A blue circular table that could seat at least thirty people stood in the center of the room, and a white kitchenette stuck out from the back wall.

They walked past the table and under an archway framed with silver wood, traveling down yet another corridor that stretched so far, the numbered, oval doors lining each side grew too small to read.

He stopped at her designated door and scowled.

Room four nine—the two most unlucky numbers in one place. Either Maddox had a dark sense of humor or he hated this girl as much as his outburst had suggested.

"Do you want your coat back?" She kept her head down as she loosened her grip on his jacket.

The thought of foreign germs teaming within the folds of the fabric made him shudder. "Not after you have cried in it."

"Oh..." Tears brimmed at the edges of her eyes again.

Perryn stiffened. Her timidness was abnormal. "I can always acquire another, so please do not trouble yourself." He pulled a keycard from his pocket and held it out to her. When she lifted her head to accept it, he averted his gaze.

She inserted the card into a thin slot on the wall and after a blue light above the arched metal lit up, the door slid open. As soon as she stepped inside, her shoulders started to shake.

He reached toward her, but the door shut with a smooth click before he could say anything. His hand dropped to his side as Al's muffled sobs stabbed him in the chest.

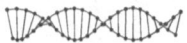

The faint light of a new sun hit Al's face, but her eyes were already open. After enduring endless nightmares in her sleep, she had kept herself awake. A bunched-up heap of blankets rested on the floor next to the metal bed she was lying in. If they could talk, maybe they'd express their distaste for her midnight triathlon that left them in such a state. She rolled to her side, and the damp pillow pushed against her cheek. The soft fabric smelled like salt and sea.

Across the room, Perryn's trench coat hung over the back of a metal folding chair.

Forcing energy into her limbs, she pushed herself up from the bed, her hair crispy with sand and tangled bits of dried seaweed. The mirror that hung on the opposite wall also revealed remnants of crusty blood on her forehead.

She frowned. "I look like a sea witch."

The nerves in her bare feet throbbed as she forced herself to the metal table in the corner, crossing over a shaft of light from a small window that made a warm spot on the otherwise cold concrete floor.

Curled up in a ball on top of the table, Cogs hummed in a steady rhythm, his gears clicking. He had spooked her last night, flying straight into her face as she sat on the bed. Unable to do anything but cry, she cuddled him as she tried to sleep, grateful she wasn't alone.

"At least I still got you on my side." She stroked his cool beak with her index finger, and he stirred with tiny twisting and twirling tones.

"Morning. Morning. Al. Today. Halloween?" He unfurled his wings like accordion blinds, his green eyes sparkling.

Al gripped a strand of her crisp hair and released it with a sigh. "No, but I like getting a *head* start. Were you brought here against your will too?"

"Cogs. Nap. Maddox. Darkness. Residence. Potentially compromised."

Al frowned. Did that mean she couldn't go home? Kera's picture was still there.

Cogs' antenna shot straight up as he circled her like a fly. "Cogs. No. Nose. But. Al. Needs. Clean." He landed back on the desk and jolted his head back and forth as he squawked.

"Yes Cogs. I know."

Pulling off her stiff clothes and tossing them to the floor, Al entered the bathroom and turned the squeaky nob. Freezing water shot down from a crooked and bent spout that looked like it could come loose from the tiled wall at any moment. Al gripped her elbows as chills danced across her body. Steam soon began to fog up the cylindrical blue glass divider, and she zoomed inside, the warmth hugging her skin.

Several spots stung as she scrubbed herself with a bar of red soap. While the smell of salt faded, the new smell that replaced it made her queasy. The shampoo offered a much more bearable scent, but still reminded her of something unnatural, something chemical.

She rested her forearms against the tiles, letting the water run down her back. Her list of allies had dwindled to a metal bird, a moody man, and herself. Zeek was an outlier. Would he even accept her now? Some secrets were just too big.

She turned off the water and closed her eyes, listening to the remnants drip down the drain. The finality of the vanishing droplets made her chest hurt.

Stepping out from behind the shower, she wiped away the fog from a section of the mirror. Swollen, hollow eyes, a drained and ugly face. She knew the girl staring back at her all too well. Fresh purple bruises dappled her torso like wine stains.

She threw the towel around her body with a broken sigh. "I'm never wearing that stupid binding ever again!"

"Al. Al. Clean. Cogs. Clean. Too." Her bird friend flew several laps around the room before landing on her bare shoulder. His tiny metal talons tickled her skin.

"Oh, did you organize your data? You're a very smart bird, Cogs."

"Yes. Yes. Cogs. Smart birb." He shuffled across her shoulder as if dancing.

She scooped him up and tucked him into a soft part of her bed before she rubbed the towel through her wet hair. Flattening his wings and antenna against his body, Cogs hopped to the top of her pillow and then rolled down like it was a slide. Once he had lost his momentum, he let out a water splashing sound effect from his beak and then hopped back to the top of the pillow to repeat his one-crow acrobat show. Al smiled and hung the towel over her bedpost.

Opening a tall gray locker that stuck out from the wall at a weird angle, she stared at the clothes waiting inside, a simple short-sleeved brown shirt, black pants, and the pair of black boots from Perryn. She noted the soft microfiber undergarments folded on the shelf. *Molly*. She was the only one who knew what Al liked.

Scrunching her nose, Al dressed like a boy yet again.

After she brushed her hair, she checked her appearance in the mirror. "Less witch now, but still far from a mermaid."

Her chest, without its white tethers, felt strange and naked even with a fitted bandeau giving it support. Her stomach rumbled. It felt like days since she had eaten. She picked up the keycard from the desk and placed it in her back pocket, the memory of pancakes and moose steaks traveling over her taste buds.

"See you in a bit, Cogs." She saluted him with a smile.

"Cogs. Will. Birb. The. Fort." He saluted her back with his antenna, then drew his wings tight against his body and began pacing the perimeter of the bed.

Al walked out into the hall, her footsteps faint against the concrete, as if the covert base also wished to erase her presence. She wondered if the other doors she passed housed more people or just more secrets. As she approached the archway that led to the kitchen, the hushed voices of two men arguing seeped into the hallway. The language they spoke seemed familiar, but she couldn't understand the words.

She pressed her back against the bumpy wall and crept closer to the opening.

"Perryn!" It was Maddox. He said something else in a biting tone.

Perryn scoffed. "Kudaranai."

"No," Maddox spoke in English again. "What's bullshit is you bringing Al here and trying to stop the bombing. You signed up for this. You don't get to jump ship now."

"What difference does it make? Marcus is dead and Al is safe. I never agreed to be a terrorist."

"Oh please. Don't act like you're an innocent bystander here, kid. Take your guilt and shove it up your ass."

Perryn let out a strained noise, as if trying to prevent himself from yelling. "And your conscience is so clear? After what you said to her last night? After what you put her through? *You* are the one who forced her into all of this, not me. You are not even related to her."

"I don't have to explain myself to you."

"No." Perryn's voice was harsh. "But what about Al?"

Al scrunched her nose. Neither of them understood her. She poked her head out from behind the wall, but when Perryn stood up from the table and turned toward her, she ducked back.

"You no longer have any leverage over me, Maddox."

"If you leave like this, I'll have no choice but to consider you an enemy."

"Kamawanai. We were only momentary allies anyway."

A gun's safety lock clicked off. "You think it will be that easy?"

Another click. "Try it."

This was ridiculous.

Al jumped out from behind the wall. "Will the both of you just shut up!"

Perryn and Maddox stood in front of the table, their guns pointed at each other's heads, still wearing yesterday's clothes. They turned and stared at her with dazed expressions.

She marched toward them. "Oh, I'm so powerfully strong and mighty. Oh, my words are so smart. Oh look, a gun! Just stop!"

Maddox and Perryn exchanged a tense glance before stowing their guns.

"I take it you heard everything then?" Maddox rubbed the back of his neck.

"How could I not? What with you arguing in broad..." She paused and looked up. "...underground bunker light. Just make a deal on whatever it is you need to already."

Perryn closed his eyes and pinched the bridge of his nose with a gloved hand. "In honor of our past arrangement, I suppose for the time being a truce could be enacted."

"Also, don't get the wrong idea. I still haven't forgiven *either* of you." Al continued her one-woman parade to the fridge and began rummaging through the shelves. "The only reason I'm intervening is because I wanna eat my breakfast in peace without a bunch of gun-slinging weirdos putting on a variety show I didn't ask for." She kicked the door closed with her foot, her arms full of eggs, moose meat, and oil.

Maddox sighed. Pulling a case from his back pocket, he tapped out a cigarette. "I'm too old for all this excitement." He turned and disappeared up the stairs.

Good. Leave.

Al dumped the ingredients on the counter and searched the cupboards for breakfast utensils as Perryn filled the kettle with water from the sink at the opposite end of the counter. She found a frying pan and set it on the stove, but when she turned, Perryn was standing next to her, placing the kettle on an adjacent burner.

She flinched. He was too close.

Did their encounter last night suddenly make him think he could invade her personal space whenever he wanted to? That had been a moment of weakness. It wouldn't happen again.

She swallowed and retreated to the ingredient pile, opening the metallic package of raw moose meat. Keeping her eyes focused on her hands, she arranged the thin strips in the pan and turned on the gas. The meat crackled and popped as a delicious, hearty aroma filled the room.

"Now where is the—"

"This?" Perryn held a muted-green spatula out to her.

The darkness had protected her from his eyes last night, but she hadn't forgotten how dangerous they were. She yanked the utensil from his hand. "Thank you." Holding the pan, she worked the flat rubber stick under a strip of meat and tried not to look at him.

"That is the third time you have said that to me."

"What?" The meat slipped from the spatula and splashed back into the pan, spraying droplets of grease and oil that seared her skin. "Ow!" She clutched her left hand to her chest, wincing, and the spatula clattered to the floor.

"Al!" Perryn rushed to the sink and flicked on the faucet. Pulling off his gloves, he stuck his hand into the water and after a few seconds, ushered her injury into the rushing stream. She breathed through her teeth as the lukewarm water hit the parts of her skin that still burned, but when she looked at her hand, she froze.

Perryn was touching her without the protection of his gloves.

His unblemished skin was softer than hers, and the warm pressure of his fingers seemed hotter than the oil. She turned her head, squishing her mouth against her shoulder. *Please don't squeak again, Al!*

"Burns are best treated in room-temperature water to prevent scarring." Perryn's gentle voice was unbearable. Why couldn't he be a jerk right now?

"It doesn't matter if it scars." She frowned, mumbling, "My ugly hand will just end up blending in better with the rest of me."

His fingers twitched against her skin. "*I* think it matters."

"Well, you—" Al whipped her head around, but her snarky comeback evaporated as his serious, diamond-black eyes bored through her.

Why? How could he look at her like that, like he cared? Trapped, swimming inside his dark pools, she drifted closer to the deep end—where she knew she would drown.

The kettle let out a high-pitched whistle and Perryn released her to lift it from the stove.

She turned off the water and cradled her burnt hand, her face still flushed. Her skin had cooled and turned pink like a faint sunburn, but every nerve he had touched was still on fire. The smell of something burning wafted into her nose.

"My moose thins!" She leaped to switch off the gas and fanned the smoke away. All that remained were black and brittle chunks of a breakfast that once held so much potential tastiness. With a heavy sigh, she tossed the pan into the sink and slumped into a chair, face-planting onto the table. Her stomach was empty, but her exhaustion meter was full.

"Tea?" Perryn stood beside her holding two mugs with spoons sticking out from them, his hands tucked back into his black gloves.

What is he, a butler now? Al nodded, and he set one cup in front of her and sat in the chair next to her. "When I said your kindness was weird, I meant it." She stuck her spoon into her mouth, its heat threatening to burn her tongue. It hurt, but it was a good distraction.

Perryn rested his chin on his hand. "Would you prefer I return to being a *jerk-ass buttface*?"

Al coughed. "Oh! So you, uh, know about that, huh?"

"I know about the field journal you compiled on me as well."

Of course he did. He was Perryn Keevie, after all.

"It's not that I want you to be mean. I just don't know how to react when you're not." She frowned and pointed her spoon at him. "Considering what's happened, I'm still debating on whether or not to forgive you for having your goons stuff me in that trash can."

"I know it is no excuse, but there was an unexpected health check during gym that day and I panicked. A trash can was the safest place to hide you at the time."

Al's face softened. A frantic Perryn was hard to imagine. "You said this was the third time I'd said something. What do you mean?"

"'The day I thank you is the day you die and disappear from this Earth, you pompous ass,' is what I believe you said, correct?" Perryn pointed his spoon at her. "You have thanked me multiple times and yet I am still very much alive."

Al squirmed in her chair. "Well that—that's just—those were freebies!"

"What?" Perryn stifled a laugh.

"I mean, what about you? You're the blanket fairy, aren't you?"

"Haa?"

"Yeah!" She stood, the chair scooting behind her. "Always covering me up when I fall asleep. It happened in the cave, at the library, on your ship..." She jerked the chair back so hard it squeaked on the floor, then plopped down in it with a pout. "I'm still mad at you, but...I'm sorry for saying such horrible things behind your back, for...what I did to you in the motel, and for insinuating you should die." She wrapped her arms around herself. "No one should be told that."

Perryn leaped up, his chair almost toppling over. He bowed with his hands at his sides. "I apologize for the sandwich, for the trash can, for making you sanitize my books, for changing your clothes at the trauma center, for pointing a gun at you, for lying, for—" He clenched his fists as he stood upright. "I understand how this sounds coming from me, but please do not believe anyone who says there is no place for you in this world."

There it was again, that feeling she couldn't name, bubbling out of her heart and onto her cheeks. She fiddled with her fingers in her lap. "Why are you telling me all this?"

Perryn covered his mouth with the back of his hand as he sighed. "I really would have rather not said anything, but I heard my mother's voice in my head, telling me to apologize."

"Your mother?"

Perryn stiffened, his face draining of all emotion. "Warui—I mean, sorry, but can we talk about something else?"

A complicated child-mother relationship, huh? They had that in common.

"So, um, how did you even get tangled up with Maddox anyway?"

Perryn took a sip of tea and folded his hands on the table. "When I was seventeen, I secretly went to the Underground, looking to hire someone to kill Marcus. When Maddox approached me, I got the impression he already knew who I was and why I was there. The way he spoke about Marcus also made it seem as if he held some sort of grudge against him. That worked in my favor. When he told me he was the leader of the Altered, however, I knew he had trapped me. Both of us were committing different types of treason, but it was treason nevertheless."

"Am I allowed to ask why you wanted to kill your father yet?"

"No."

Al scrunched her nose. "It seems out of character for Maddox to trust a kid." Or maybe he just didn't trust her.

"Our arrangement was never about trust. At the time, the probability of finding a better ally was essentially zero. We met again to discuss specifics, and that was when your name entered the conversation. He told me I had to keep you hidden from Vilroy at all costs."

"Vilroy?" Al slammed her hands on the table as she stood. "Did he tell you why?"

Perryn shook his head. "His request seemed odd, but I did not need that information to complete my task, so I never asked for further clarification."

Al leaned back in her chair, letting all her limbs hang limp like some sort of strange human plant. "More dead ends and secrets. My favorite."

The only thing she knew for certain now was that Maddox's actual intentions for forcing her to live as a boy were not as altruistic as he had raised her to believe. Like a captured flag or a coveted jewel, Maddox's only goal was to keep her from Vilroy. But why?

Vilroy used to be a scientist, just like Kera. *Is it possible that I really am the Eternal Child?*

She couldn't rule anything out yet. Did the child have any limitations? Did "eternal" mean they stopped aging at some point, or were they truly unable to die? Maddox thought she shouldn't exist, so maybe she was some horrible monster. *All this time, did he even love me at all?*

The smell of tobacco drifted into her nose.

"Your ship's cleared to leave." Maddox descended the steps and Al refused to look at him.

"Osokatta na." Perryn stood up from the table and set his empty mug in the sink.

"You're lucky I'm letting you leave at all. There are still a few things that need ironing out, so if you please, follow me."

"So it would seem."

Their footsteps faded up the stairs, and she sat at the table in silence until her tea grew cold and her stomach remembered it was hungry.

Al rested against a boulder as Perryn prepared his ship for departure. In her delirium, she hadn't noticed that only one other person, the pilot, had accompanied them. Though not the safest procedure for flying, it was probably the most prudent way to visit a secret base on a secret island.

Gray-blue clouds colored the sky, and the waves had receded beyond the first three rock formations, attracting seabirds that shrieked and fought over the newly unveiled buffet.

Perryn called out orders to the pilot in the front, double-checking the clipboard he held in his hands as he circled the ship. His eyes met Al's, and he nodded, his face softening into a small smile.

She tensed and turned away. "Okay what, Al? It's just a smile. It's not like he's—" She flung her hands over her mouth as she crouched on the sandy ground, shaking her head. *No! Brain, shut up!*

Perryn called her name, and she rocketed to her feet, turning to face him.

"You alright?" His voice was breathy from running. It was distracting.

"Me? Oh yeah. I'm great. So great." She laughed in broken bursts.

"You left this on the ship." He handed her the rucksack she had left behind and their fingers touched. He pulled away like a spring in a trapdoor. "I was not sure if you wanted the boot..."

"Keep it." Al clutched her bag for dear life. "Turn it into a flowerpot or something."

"Innovative..."

The screeching seabirds didn't lessen the awkward tension flying around them as they tried not to meet each other's eyes.

"See you around then, I guess?" She extended her hand and hoped her smile would hide the tremble in her voice.

"Al..." Perryn stared at her hand, his own remaining at his side. "This is the last time we should see each other."

Her bag dropped to the sand. "What?"

"I am the prime minister now. To remain involved to the degree I have been in the past would present a level of danger too great, not only for myself, but for everyone here at this base. Despite Maddox's expectations, I never intended to stay tethered forever."

His words stacked on top of each other like thick books, threatening to squish the air from her lungs. He was leaving. Why was that a bad thing?

"I see." She folded her hands behind her back. "So you got what you wanted, cleared your conscience and now you get to ride off into the sunset. Pretty sweet deal."

"Al—"

"No, it makes perfect sense. Really."

"I only—" He looked away.

"Well, I wish you a favorable wind then." She saluted him, trying to ignore the tightness forming in her chest.

He stood there for a moment longer before squaring his shoulders and saluting her with perfect precision. "To you as well." He turned and walked back toward the ship. The way he ascended the ramp made her think of what someone going off to war might look like. Was this how those left behind felt?

The door sealed shut, cracking a hole in the dam behind her eyes. A stream spilled down her cheek.

Wait.

The engine revved up, exploding into the silence and shooting more holes in the dam.

Wait!

She took a step forward as the ship lifted into the air, its downwash sending flustered birds shooting past her and clouds of scratchy particles into her face. With an exasperated cry, she crouched and shielded her eyes with her arms. When she looked up again, the ship had vanished. Only imprints of the landing gear remained on the beach.

Al slumped into the sand and wrapped her hands around her knees. This was infuriating. Instead of doing cartwheels down the beach, here she was, crumpled up and pathetic. She stared at her hand, the one he had held with such gentleness, and smiled as tears dripped off her chin. "I don't think lukewarm water will fix any of this."

CHAPTER 15

Even before Maddox forbade her from leaving the island, Al already knew her fate. The stadium bombing sent Astova into a panicked lockdown, ceasing all travel in and out of the country. Local Scanners joined forces with the military to search their neighborhoods for traitors, and they made hundreds of arrests—all Altered.

An old radio in the kitchen announced updates, but the dates of the news reports always lagged two or three days behind. Did a cloaking device cause the delay? Maybe the island was just that far from the mainland. Either way, the reports served as a reminder. There was no going back to her old life. Her home was now a gloomy metal cave with an uncomfortable bed, a foreboding shower, and a living room full of colorful strangers. Ironically, she missed her stifled life in Astova. At least there she had privacy.

Avoiding the resident rainbow people proved difficult, so she spent most of her time outside, jogging down the beach before sunrise and after sunset, sometimes eating her lunch on the rocks under the leafy canopy. The lemurdogs that lived above soon grew brave enough to sit near her to steal a stray berry or crust of bread.

As she explored the island, she planned her escape. There was no way she was staying in another prison. She was surprised Maddox hadn't assigned someone else to babysit her. He had yet to apologize for anything, but even if he wasn't always off-island, she didn't want to talk to him. There was nothing to say, not to him or Molly.

She joined Al in the kitchen some mornings and though her moose meat sandwiches tasted the best, they didn't taste the same. Their brief conversations only consisted of superficial topics, and Molly did most of the talking. Being in her presence was too painful. Was all the love and warmth she had given Al a lie too? She wanted to believe her bond with Molly was real, but what proof did she have?

Her nightmares returned and after waking up yelling her lungs out on several occasions without anyone noticing, she was convinced her room was soundproof. Cogs provided the only comfort, playing vintage lullabies and nuzzling her with his cool beak.

Perryn's trench coat had been relocated from the back of her chair to a box under her bed. Al did everything she could to distract herself from thoughts of him, but her mind had a mind of its own. Looking at the table in the kitchen reminded her of what he had said while sitting there. Touching the faucet made her remember the way his fingers had caressed hers. Within the swell of the waves, she thought she heard the faint hum of an engine. Before Perryn, being alone used to be easier.

She needed to leave this island, but where could she go? Al frowned as she entered the kitchen, trapped even inside her own mind.

A large group of people crowded around the radio as one man with orange hair and green eyes kept adjusting the antennae. Only white noise spewed from the silver box. About half the size of the refrigerator, it took up most of a table they had pushed against the wall.

Al swiped a roll from the lunch buffet laid out on the center table and watched the rainbow people argue about how to make the box work. She was about to turn back to her room when a robust melody, crackling with a static hiss, burst from the mesh speakers.

"Astova's anthem?" Al swallowed a bite of soft bread.

"Oh, it's an anthem alright." A green-haired woman with pink eyes stood next to her, stabbing at the noodles on her tray. "That's the sound of oppression."

Al scooted away and stuck the rest of the roll in her mouth.

Several men and women marched around the tables, mocking the way the Astovan soldiers patrolled the city, removing invisible hats and bowing.

An older man with close-cropped black hair and bright red eyes pushed through the crowd. "'Eers what I think 'bout that song!" He unzipped his pants and mooned the radio and all the people sitting near the table. Al shielded her eyes with more rolls and the crowd scrambled to pull him out of the way, some laughing and others muttering under their breath.

"Oh, sit down, Orion!" The orange-haired man shooed the half-dressed man away, pressing his ear against the radio and adjusting more knobs. After more static and a warbling sound came out of the speakers, a low rumbling voice cut through.

"My dear Astovans, I speak to you today during the direst of times."

The blood rushed from Al's face as she dropped the rolls. *Vilroy.*

His voice echoed like he was speaking inside a large hall, or some sort of mechanical effect was going ham with the reverb. "Our beloved Prime Minister Marcus Keevie was brutally murdered in a cowardly attack by the Altered mere weeks ago."

The radio spectators let out curses and angry shouts, some even tossing food toward the talking box. Al's class had reacted much in the same way, but for exactly the opposite side.

"Hush!" A woman in the crowd rapped a fork against her glass and the room grew quiet, with a few curses straggling behind.

"But fear not, my brave Astovans. Now, as the firstborn son and rightful heir, a new prime minister comes to us today, ready and willing to serve this great nation against the Altered threat. Place your trust in him. A perfect natural born. A mighty protector to serve as my right hand. Perryn Keevie."

Al's chest tightened, and she gripped the hem of her shirt. *Perryn.*

"Losing the prime minister came as a shock to my family, but his horrific death will not go unpunished. I assure you, I will find the ones responsible and bring them to justice."

A few people laughed. "Good luck finding us, rich boy."

"Yeah, big talk for a child. What does a twenty-one-year-old know 'bout being a leader? Typical Naturalists with their hereditary succession BS." Orion slammed his fist on the table.

They had never noticed Perryn among them? Then again, it seemed like until that meeting she witnessed, not even the members knew each other. These people had also worked for Maddox without knowing his true identity. He was no different from Vilroy in that respect.

"This has been a recording from our most beloved leader, Vilroy Vax." A new voice, rich with tenor undertones, poured out. The man cleared his throat and the sound of shuffling paper followed. "And now, in memoriam, we continue the list of names of identified bodies from the attack at the Keev-ship races."

Al looked down. She didn't want to remember that day. As she turned to walk back to her room, the names of the dead followed her.

"Ervin Niklas." She passed the table.

"Toven and Merrek Raschke." She reached the hallway.

"Alec Finn."

She jerked to a stop and gripped the archway. The other names blurred into the background as only one thought screamed in her head. *Zeek!*

She bolted down the hall to her room, jammed the key-card into the slot, and before the door could open all the way, she rushed through, scraping her shoulder against the metal. Wincing as she rubbed it, she yanked her bag from the locker and threw it on the bed.

Cogs, who had gathered a homemade nest of paper scraps, bobbed his head up and down from inside the pile. "Al. Busy. Busy. Bee."

"I can't stay here, Cogs." Al rummaged through her bag and found a thin black elastic tie. She gathered her shoulder-length hair into a messy ponytail. "Zeek probably heard that broadcast. If he thinks the Altered killed me, he's gonna lose it."

Cogs bobbed his head from side to side and squawked. "Gone. Forever. Bye."

"Cogs, please." Al pulled a water jug from her bag and began filling it in the sink. "I bet Maddox is behind this. To make it easier to explain why I just disappeared. But I won't let his plan play out the way he wants."

When the bottle overflowed, she capped it and threw it into her pack. Opening the locker, she pulled out a clean set of clothes and stuffed it down inside the already plump bag. As she turned, she saw her reflection in the mirror and grimaced. "I know I promised you I wouldn't, but it looks like you gotta be a boy one more time."

With an angry grunt, she reached down into the bottom of the bag, some of the already packed contents spilling out onto the bed. Yanking the fabric free, she pulled off her shirt and let the white boa constrictor slither its way around her chest again. She tied the ends together, the familiar, uncomfortable tightness returning. She'd worry about a sock later.

As she repacked her bag, Cogs landed in the middle of the mound and let out a timid squeak.

She sighed and scooped him up. "Cogs, I don't think you can go with me. It's not safe for you out there."

Cogs fluttered his wings as he hopped. "Not. Safe. Al. Cogs. Protect. Friend."

Something twinged in her chest as she set him on her pillow. He would be impossible to conceal in the outside world, but if he went with her, she wouldn't be alone.

"Okay." She smiled. "You'll finally get to be my mascot then."

"Hashtag cute birb."

As Al rescued her shirt from the floor and shuffled the thin material over her head, Cogs gripped a piece of crumpled paper in his beak and stuffed it into an open pocket in Al's bag. He hopped around his pile, tilting his head, before he selected another piece to pack.

Al took her holster and Scanner gun from the locker and situated them at her side—lucky she had packed her weapon before leaving home. Buckling the double straps of her bag, she swung it over one shoulder. Cogs perched himself on the other. She headed for the door, but just as she reached it, she stopped.

"Al. Broken?" Cogs tugged on a strand of her hair as she turned back toward the bed.

Ducking underneath, she dragged out a dusty brown box and set it on top of the unkempt sheets. She opened the lid and pulled out Perryn's folded trench coat. Hugging it to her chest, she closed her eyes. Al could've sworn it still smelled of pine. She wrapped the coat over her shoulders, remembering the warmth of the arms that had once surrounded her.

"Al. Sleepy time?" Cogs squirmed on her shoulder, the new layer of fabric over his head rippling with every bounce.

"No Cogs. It's time to focus." She fastened the top clasp so the trench coat hung like a cape. "I need you to keep quiet until we get outside. Can you do that for me?"

"Sneaky. Sneaky. Birb. Is. Mouse."

Al took a deep breath and stepped up to the door. When it slid open, her mind launched into another Keev-ship race. But unlike any other race, freedom was the prize.

Stepping out into the hall, she tried to be as casual as possible, or at least as nonchalant as a girl pretending to be a boy hiding a metal crow under a trench coat could be. Thankfully, the halls were empty, and only a few men and women remained in the kitchen area chatting in their seats or standing at the sink washing dishes.

She resisted the urge to sprint, her heart thundering in her ears like an engine. Now only the giant rock door stood in the way of her freedom. She swallowed and flexed her fingers as beads of sweat formed on her back. "Here we go."

She was about to step out of the hallway, but Molly crossed in front of her from an adjacent one, conversing with two people, one Altered man and one woman who looked like a Naturalist.

Al stiffened, then tapped against the wall as she spoke in a harsh whisper. "Come on. Come on. Hurry up!"

Molly waved at the man as he headed back down the corridor they had entered from and continued toward the opposite hall with the other woman.

"Dox—I mean, Mr. Finn has instructed us to move to Site C tomorrow, so be sure to prepare the teams. He also has requested—"

Molly disappeared around the corner and Al closed her eyes, the tightness returning to her chest. *Goodbye, Molly.* Maddox was Maddox, so he wouldn't receive a farewell, not even from the confines of her mind.

She ran to the door.

Six men wearing tank tops and shorts sat on the rocky floor, patting their sweating foreheads with micro towels wrapped around their necks. Not moving made the heat within the trench coat worse.

"Where you going, boy?" A man with purple stubble and golden eyes looked up at her.

She smiled as she rocked back on her heels. "For a hike in the hills, sir."

The men laughed. "In that getup? Okay, kid."

They were right. A trench coat in summer was strange, but she needed to conceal Cogs. Never mind that the item belonged to Perryn.

Just as Al was starting to worry that her hydrogen had been blown, the men groaned to their feet, stretching their arms and legs. They moved to their respective positions at the door, and with loud, strenuous grunts, they pushed the slab open. Al thanked them with a salute and stepped outside. The door slammed shut behind her almost instantly.

"Hang on tight, Cogs." Al felt a tiny pinch on her shoulder as she sprinted forward through the rock path.

The lemurdogs howled down at her and followed her as far as the vines allowed. Her boots reached sand, and while her pace slowed, she continued to run. The evil sun wasted no time in trying to cook her alive inside the black oven she wore. Even though the cold waves seemed inviting, she couldn't risk being caught.

Run now. Rest later. She pulled the top of the trench coat over her head and trudged onward.

With the base almost a tiny speck behind her, she reached the bottom of a few hills lined with leafy, green, and cone-like vegetation. She opened the trench coat and fell to her knees, the rubbery material sticking to her skin like glue.

"You...you okay Cogs?" she panted.

"Dizzy." His little coiled feet unhooked themselves from her shirt, leaving pin-sized holes in the fabric and her skin. She rubbed her shoulder. It wasn't his fault she had run so fast.

Cogs zipped out from underneath the coat and circled above her before nestling himself on top of her head. "World. Is big. Outside."

Al peeled off the coat, a breeze instantly sweeping over her skin. "Well, it's about to get even bigger."

Throwing the trench coat over her shoulder, she re-situated her pack and hiked up the steep hill, with Cogs squawking a song about a bear hunt. They reached the top of the hill and Al dropped to the ground on her stomach, the lemon-colored grass barely concealing her. "Look Cogs," she whispered.

"Birbs!" His antenna shot straight up.

"Shh. No." She laughed. "Our way outta here."

Towering before them, a gigantic hangar housed hundreds of pointy black Scraper Sharks, all with a red *A* painted on the wings. Several men dressed in grungy green flight suits ran about, loading cargo into the open backs of ships or hanging upside down by their knees with drills, hammers, and sparks.

"I found this place during one of my runs."

"A-plus. Reconnaissance. Captain." Cogs bobbed his head, his antenna swaying in the opposite direction.

"That mark's gonna get us in trouble though. No way we even get halfway across the ocean with that thing. If there isn't a support ship in the back of the assembly line, we'll just have to hope we're not spotted before we can paint over it."

Cogs clicked his tongue. "Redecorate. Girl."

Al laughed and patted him on the head. "We'll hang out on this hill until nightfall and then make our move." She could do this. She had to do this. With thoughts of a nap on her mind, she rested her head on her arms and closed her eyes.

A whining alarm pierced the air and the men below yelled as they ran, swinging their arms above their heads.

"Did they discover me?" Al sprang to her feet and turned to rush down the hill.

Ear-shattering thunder and a violent gust of wind sent her tumbling the rest of the way down. Groaning, she grabbed her head. "Cogs! Cogs!" Her words were dampened and distant as a high-pitched ringing filled her ears.

The dust floating around her made it hard to see, and the smell of hot metal and smoke clung to the inside of her nose. A familiar weight landed on her shoulder and she felt a tug on her hair. Cogs had returned unharmed. Al let out a sigh she couldn't hear and hugged him against her face. *What the hell happened?* She lumbered back up the hill, the burnt smell growing stronger. When she reached the top, she felt herself scream.

Where the hangar had stood, a deep crater with twisted metal pieces crumpling inward had taken its place. Fire ravaged the remains and splintered Scraper Sharks sparked in sporadic bursts. Dead bodies, many charred with a black crust, were strewn about, while some fleshy-looking ones hung in pieces that melted against the remaining rubble. Al felt bile rise in her throat and she fell to her knees.

Air from the crow's wings wafted against her head as he circled her, his beak opening and closing with words she still couldn't hear.

A dark shadow blocked out the sun as a capital warship, gray, red, and massive, glided above her, the doors on its belly folding open. She followed its trajectory with her head and wobbled to her feet. In the distance, more warships headed toward the base. Her stomach twisted. Molly was still there.

"Al. Danger. Danger."

She could finally hear again, but she couldn't see her bird friend anywhere. "Cogs! I don't know what to do!" Every second ticked by, stabbing her in the gut.

"Well, this is embarrassing. A survivor?" A young man's chiding voice came from behind and she spun around. Two Capital Scanners stood wearing smug smiles and red-and-white uniforms. They looked around the same age as Zeek.

"Yeah, I think you missed." The young man with a buzz cut hit his partner on the shoulder.

"Eh, ninety-nine percent is still pretty good if you ask me." This one had curly brown hair that rested around his ears. He took a step toward Al and she pulled the gun from her holster, switched off the safety, and aimed.

With a sharp warbling sound, a shot pierced through the middle of her gun, knocking it out of her hand. She clutched her wrist and glared at them as the pain from the shockwave reverberated through her fingers. Cogs was still missing.

"Wooo, fast reflexes. Glad you're on *my* team." The curly-haired man rested his hands on his hips and laughed.

"You're gonna come with us, nice and easy." Buzzcut kept his gun pointed at her.

She continued to glare as she took a step forward, raising her hands.

Please stay hidden, Cogs! He was smart. Molly and Maddox would escape the base in time and Cogs would find a way back to them. He would be safe.

Al took a few more steps and Buzzcut twisted her arm behind her back, shoving her face into the grass. Her muffled cries mixed with the dirt in her mouth as the sound of metallic clicking zoomed past her.

"What the—!" The young men let out frantic yells, swiping their arms above their heads as Cogs dive-bombed them, biting, pecking, and squawking.

"Cogs! No! Fly away!" Al broke free from her captor and waved her hands. "Please!"

"Al. Friend. Harm. Friend. You. Bad." Cogs continued to side-swipe his enemies, cutting the curly-haired man's face with his wing.

"Damn robot!" He clutched his cheek, blood trickling down his fingers. The bleeding man pulled out his gun and aimed it at Cogs, and Al sprinted toward him.

No! She slammed into his body just as the shot left his gun.

With a high-pitched squeaking, Cogs plummeted to the ground, tiny parts jettisoning off in all directions on impact.

Al crawled to the bird, her mouth agape, and her lungs filled with too much pressure to speak. She reached his resting place and cupped his broken body in her hands. The one wing still attached twitched, and gears and screws spilled out from his insides.

"C—" she choked on her words.

"A—A—Allllll. Al Al. Al. Aaa." The crow's green eyes sparkled one last time before they dimmed to black.

Al's whole body tensed, preparing to scream, but as she opened her mouth, she felt a sharp strike against the back of her neck. She toppled over, hitting the ground as her tears cascaded over her nose. Reaching out a wobbling hand, she touched Cogs' beak and her consciousness faded into nothing.

CHAPTER 16

A l's cheek pressed against a pitted metal surface. Other than her face, she couldn't feel her body. With her vision warped, shapes appeared with undefined lines and blurring colors swirled with pinwheels where the light in the space was the brightest. The smell of rubber and metal clung to the air.

Two tall blobs stood in front of her.

"So, what are we gonna do with her?" The blob's voice sounded as if he was talking from behind several sheets of glass.

A long sigh came from the blob next to him, his voice just as suppressed. *"Dumping her at the capital is the proper procedure, but since we're in the area, we could always take her to the Menagerie."*

"Oh yeah, and make some extra money, I feel ya. But she doesn't look Altered. Won't—"

Al's mind blanked out, causing a momentary lapse in her hearing.

"Don't worry. We'll make something up," the first blob sneered. *"And by the time the warden finds out, we'll be long gone."*

The blurry shapes moved toward her in jagged spirals as they laughed, and Al's consciousness faded back to an empty void.

The air was thick with steam and pungent chemicals.

Al's back and feet rested against cold tile, but her arms, that were under attack by a scratchy material, felt warm and irritated in comparison.

Faint murmurs and sighs, splashing, dripping, wooden, hollow sounds—she could just make out other bodies milling around her. With her eyesight still impaired, she couldn't tell what the two women standing on either side of her looked like. Their firm hands, rough with calluses, fussed over her body, moving a soft, lubricating substance over her skin before the harsh scrubbing returned. They dumped a bucket of lukewarm water over her head, and she gasped for air, coughing.

"Hold still! We're almost finished." The woman's voice was sharp and warbly, like a generator warming up in the winter.

Two sets of hands grabbed at her again, one pair scrubbing her feet and the other ripping at the roots of her hair with boney fingers and a stinging gel. After a few more buckets of cold water cascaded over her head, the two women hooked their arms under hers and dragged her through the steamy room, through a pair of double doors, and out into a bright lounge that hurt her eyes.

Dark blue lockers and shiny brass benches with red cushions lined the walls, occupied by other women and young girls in various stages of undress. The women dropped Al onto a bench and flitted about the room, gathering items from cupboards painted in the same dark blue. They returned with coarse towels, twisting sections of her hair between their fingers. Once they had deemed her dry enough, they fitted her with white underwear that felt too short to be functional. Despite its softness, the sides of the garment dug into her hips.

Forcing her arms above her head, the women wrapped a strange garment around her chest. She had seen something similar once when she was younger, having walked in on Molly changing. *Molly!* Was she alright? There wasn't conclusive evidence to point to her survival, but there was always a chance she got out in time.

With a click, a tiny clasp at the front of the garment locked closed and a pair of lacey white circles now cupped her chest. This garment provided the same amount of comfort as its matching counterpart—absolutely none. With Al securely fastened into her new undergarments, the women pulled a short-sleeved white dress over her head. They kept trying to yank it down farther past her knees, but with irritated sighs, they gave up and hooked their elbows under Al's arms once more.

The party of three moved down the length of the room, passing fake plants and disturbing, abstract art pieces mounted on the beige walls. They pushed through another set of doors, and a dark, windowless hallway greeted them. As the women dragged her down the hall, Al tried to memorize her surroundings, the urge to escape already sinking in, like the elastic in her new clothes.

Thick doors with black windows, and more strange art between them, lined the walls. Some had foreboding wording above them. *Surgery. Playroom. Furnace.* Wherever she was, she had a feeling people didn't last very long here.

They passed several other hallways that branched out into more until they began climbing a set of stairs.

The woman on the right let out a strained breath, almost letting Al's body slump to the floor. "How much did they put in her system? It's like carrying a log."

Al was too numb to frown or snap back, but she would've.

"Just bear with it for now." The other woman gripped Al's wrist, pulling her left side over her shoulder. "She's the last one for the day and then we can go home."

Home.

Still unable to move her head, Al shifted her eyes as far against their corners as she could. The women were Naturalists, perhaps as old as Molly, and both wore white apron-like smocks over the top of their ankle-length dresses. Panting and huffing, they reached the top of the stairs.

The landing widened into a short, undecorated hallway with doors on either side. Turning left, the women approached a door marked with an engraving of a small sun. Half of Al drooped to the side like a deflated balloon as the woman on the right let her go to punch a code into the keypad mounted on the door. It slid open and after the woman returned to Al's side, they dragged her into the room that was pitch-black except for the sliver of light entering at the bottom of the door.

"Finally!" The women dropped Al like a bag of dirty laundry. Her cheek throbbed from the impact.

After brushing their hands on their aprons, the women headed out the door. Al tried to lift herself, but her arms buckled, once again receiving a cold slap to the face from the floor.

"I'm thinking moose steaks tonight. My husband just loves them."

"Oh, how fancy!"

The door slammed shut, their voices fading beyond its thickness. Nothing but darkness and silence surrounded her now. Al wished that whatever they did to freeze her body would've frozen her mind as well. What was she supposed to do now? Would anyone come to save her? Did anyone even know where she was? Did anyone even care?

Cogs. Her brave little crow friend was gone. Gone forever.

Zeek. By now, he had to think she was dead and was probably beating himself up or doing something rash.

She was alone with nothing. She was nothing.

Perryn...

Her thoughts continued to stab the back of her eyes until they grew too heavy to keep open and she cried herself to sleep.

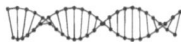

"She doesn't look Altered to me!" A child's bright voice exploded into her ear.

"Shhh! Punch! You'll wake her. The poor girl needs her sleep." This girl's voice was the exact opposite—mature and gentle.

Al tried to move her fingers and hope shot through her when they brushed against a soft blanket.

"*She's* a poor girl? We're all poor girls here." Another spoke, her voice vibrant and bell-like.

Al willed her feet to move, and they wiggled unhindered, hanging off the edge of the bed.

"Yeah! We think so, too!" This girl's voice was youthful and melodic.

The vibrant girl tsked. "Ribbon, you always say that. Let your sister speak for herself. You're not the same person."

Al opened her eyes to a blue ceiling painted with fluffy white clouds. One giant domed light protruded from the middle of the scene with squiggling orange rays radiating out on all sides. The room's temperature was on the colder side and bubble bumps had already formed along her bare arms. *I can feel things again!* But did she have full control?

She sprang up with all her strength, causing the bed to squeak.

A small girl with navy-blue eyes and red-orange hair ran away from her with a yelp. Her white dress was similar to Al's, but ruffles ran along her sleeves, showing her darker beige skin. What looked like red and purple puncture wounds dotted her arms.

"Swan! I'm scared!" The small girl retreated to hide behind a much older girl whose chest-length, dark-brown hair ended in gentle curls of light pink.

Swan laughed as she stroked the trembling girl's head. "There, there, Punch. She's not that scary. We only need to introduce ourselves and the scary will go away, remember?" She corralled the fidgety child back toward Al, smiling with her beautiful amber eyes.

Punch knotted up the material of Swan's white dress in her fingers and sent shy glances between the ground, Al, and then up at the taller girl. "My name is Punch. I am six years old. I like colors."

Al nodded with a pinched smile. "Hey there, Punch. Sorry. Didn't mean to scare you. Colors are awesome." Was that how you talked to a little girl?

Punch ducked back behind Swan, but her face relaxed into a pout.

Windowless walls painted with the same faint sky blue as the ceiling boxed them in. Several seemingly random sections of the floor had tiles with a different shade of white from the rest. The off-white splotches concentrated the most around the bed next to hers, which had orange sheets. A bathroom stood in the corner, but instead of a mirror above the sink, only a waxy rectangle remained on the tiled wall. Al rubbed her sore cheek. At least she wouldn't have to see how hideous she looked.

"Nice to meet you! I'm Swan." The older girl poked her head into Al's line of sight, her brown skin warm like her smile. "My bed is that one if you ever need to chat." She pointed to a bed with pink sheets near the bathroom.

Al looked down. Swan's enthusiasm would've been more contagious if Al didn't feel so uneasy.

"I guess I'm like the mom of the group."

A loud snicker resounded behind Swan. "I thought you hated being called that." The vibrant voice finally had a face.

Across the room, a teenage girl with soft umber skin sat on the edge of a bed with purple sheets. Her coily black hair sat in two space buns on either side of her head, and she too wore a white dress. She put a small book back on the shelf leaning against the wall next to her bed.

Swan raised her eyebrows as she hooked her arm under Al's. "Only when it's said sarcastically. Come and meet the others!" Al let the shorter girl pull her from the bed and guide her, almost tripping over her own feet. "This is Pulchra! She's the smart one!"

Pulchra crossed her arms with a toothy grin, revealing her pointy and pushed-up eye teeth. "Did you know Pulchra means beautiful in Latin? It's also the name of an extinct tarantula!" Her violet eyes looked like the midnight sky had crystalized into jewels within them.

"No, I didn't..." Al stared at her arm where Swan still gripped her. Was it normal for girls to be so familiar with someone they just met?

"And finally, these two are Lace and Ribbon! The hot and cold sisters." Swan gestured to two preteen girls near a bunk bed.

One girl sat in a silver chair with clear wheels, while the other stood behind her, gripping the chair's handles. The girls looked almost identical. Both wore matching white dresses, but their braided black ponytails sat on opposite sides of their heads. Their eyes, one green, one brown, were mirror images of each other.

"My name is Heejin, not Ribbon." The girl sitting in her mechanical throne crossed her arms.

"I'm Lace. I mean Jang-mi. I mean Lace!" She sank behind the back of her sister's chair, covering her eyes.

"Girls." Swan crossed her arms. "You have to forget those names while you're here."

"You make it seem like we'll actually get out someday." Pulchra fell backward onto her bed.

"No! These are the precious names Omma and Ahppa gave us!" Ribbon hit the side rests of her chair and Lace nodded from her crouched position on the floor.

"I understand that, but as I explained before—"

"I'm sorry." Al interrupted as she fumbled with a loose strand of her hair. "I don't mean to be insensitive, but where are we exactly?"

"Hell."

"Pul!" Swan rested her hands on her hips, turning to frown at the girl.

"What? It's not a lie."

Al stared at her scarred hand. "If that's the case, then I've been here before."

Pulchra stared at the ceiling as she continued. "It's a lab. Not sure what the purpose of their tests are, but they only bring Altered girls with superpowers here. I've heard the guards talking. We're on an island in the middle of nowhere."

Was it possible that this place was Marn? The high-security prison would be a perfect place to separate Altered individuals with special abilities from society. Al slumped to the floor. "Right, Hell."

Swan puffed up her cheeks. "I know you just got here, dear, but please don't encourage Pul's use of language. Punch is still a child and we need—"

"Stop acting like you can protect her, Swan." Pulchra stood from the bed, her eyes narrowing. "You'll drive yourself insane trying to protect any of us. You know better than anyone what kind of messed-up place this is."

"Stop picking on Big Sis Swan!" Punch slammed her fists into the floor and the force of her impact created two fractured holes in the tile, jagged pieces and multiple cracks spiraling out.

Al stared with wide eyes. "I think I understand why her name is Punch now..."

"Oh, sweetheart, not again! I hope they're in a good mood today." Swan rushed over to the distraught child, who wrapped her arms around her.

Al shook her head, collecting herself. "But if Punch's so strong, why haven't you used her ability to escape yet?"

Pulchra raised an eyebrow. "You think we haven't considered that already? Even if we got out of here, past all the guards and security checkpoints, we've got trackers in our legs. They'd find us before we even stepped outside our room." She lifted her white dress and gestured to a dark spot on her thigh that looked like a beauty mark.

Al tensed and looked down at her own leg. A new bruise was darkening on the outside of her knee. She sighed through her nose. *Figures it wouldn't be that easy.* "What if we found a way to disable them?"

"New girl, what part of 'on an island in the middle of nowhere' don't you get?" Pulchra picked up a book from the shelf and plopped back-first onto her bed. "Some advice, you'll last a lot longer if you lose your false hope first instead of your mind."

Watching Pulchra turn the pages in her book was too familiar. What would Perryn's stance be in this situation? What did it matter? He left her behind. Everyone did. Maybe this was where fate meant for her life to end. She wouldn't have to fight anymore.

"You don't have to worry about me." Al's shoulders slumped as she stared at her scarred hand. "I'm pretty sure I lost both of those things already."

Swan sucked in her cheeks and sighed. "We've all suffered more than we should, but at least we have each other."

"Yeah! I have so many family now!" Punch waved her hand as if a teacher had asked a question, her tears still fresh on her cheeks.

"That's right!" Swan snatched Punch up into a tight hug. "But oh no! What's this? I'm actually a tickle monster in disguise?" Punch squealed with laughter as she tried to break free.

Ribbon smirked and puffed up her chest. "Fear not! I, the flower queen, shall rescue you using my magic! Come, Dandelion! We fly!"

Lace popped up with a squeak, spreading out her hands above her head like petals. "Um, yes, my queen!"

Ribbon rolled herself forward, pausing to wiggle her arms at Swan, while Lace mimicked her actions with less confidence and from a much farther distance. Swan released Punch, falling over in mock defeat as the girls cheered.

A weak smile crossed Al's face. Swan was right. These girls were strangers, but at least Al wasn't alone. When she died here, there would still be someone who could hold her hand as her soul left the world.

Swan rolled to her feet and knelt beside Al, touching her shoulder. "It's alright if you still have hope. Whatever you have to stay alive, use it." Her smile faded as she looked toward Al's bed. "I don't want to lose anyone else."

"Anyone else?" Al's stomach heaved. "Swan? What happened to the other girl before me?"

With a cold metallic beep, the door to their room clicked open, and the girls abandoned their make-believe, lining up in front of their respective beds. Al sat alone in the middle of the floor. She glanced at Swan, who motioned with her head for Al to stand in front of her own bed, but Al stayed in her spot.

A man with black hair pulled into a short ponytail entered. Wearing a medical mask and a long white lab coat, he held a clipboard in his gloved hands. He glanced at the new craters on the floor and sighed. "Subject Three-Six-Three, still showing signs of aggression despite medication." Lifting the clipboard, he jotted down a few sentences.

Was he the one responsible for the marks on Punch's arm? Al clenched her fists.

The doctor finished his notes, and the clipboard retracted back to his side with a violent zipping sound. He then looked at Al. "Subject Four-Zero-One, you're due for processing. Follow me."

"And if I don't?" Al glared up at him.

The other girls gasped and Ribbon and Lace gripped each other's hands.

"Subject Four-Zero-One, if you choose not to cooperate, I am permitted to use a sedative." The doctor rapped his knuckles against the door and four other men dressed in black coats and pants ducked into the room. One of them opened a thin silver case, revealing a syringe filled with a yellowish liquid.

Is that the stuff that knocked me out yesterday? Al shuddered and then scrunched her nose as she stood. "I've decided to make it easier for you. You're welcome."

She walked to the door and followed the doctor into the hallway, the other men surrounding her on all sides like the directions on a compass. The cold floor bit into her bare feet. She looked over her shoulder and the wide-eyed faces of the girls pressed up against the window stared back behind the now-closed door.

The men led Al down the stairwell, which had a lot more stairs than she remembered. When they turned down the hallway that Al had been dragged down the day before, it looked the same, but the images were much sharper now that she wasn't drugged. The reflective linoleum floor was just as cold as the steps and granules of dirt and other particles stuck to the bottom of her feet. When she stopped to wipe her foot on the inside of her other leg, the tall men pushed her along, almost causing her to careen into the floor.

Passing the odd art pieces once more, they stopped in front of a white double-door entrance. The sign above them read *Playroom*.

Al grabbed her hand. *This is where I die.* In the end, her soul would leave the world without anyone beside her. Only she could comfort herself now.

The doctor pushed a button on a keypad mounted on the wall. "Subject Four-Zero-One, sir."

With a deep clicking sound, the double doors opened and a whoosh of sterile-smelling air hit Al in the face, making her cough. The doctor entered the room, and the four men pushed Al through.

"Okay, okay! Sheesh! I can walk, you know." She squinted as she stepped inside.

This room was also windowless, but unlike the hallway, bright and blinding rows of square lights hung from the ceiling like old-fashioned ice-cube trays. In one corner above a long metal bed with straps, several strange silver arms dipped down like a metal beast immobilized in ice. Clear film-like skin wrapped around the bulk of each arm, and each one ended in a sharp or twisted utensil.

Al stiffened. *So that's the type of play that happens here.*

In the middle of the room, a metal chair waited with open restraints on either side. Suspended above it, a giant magnifying glass, surrounded by a ring of bright light, stuck out from an adjustable arm. Next to the chair was a rolling cart with an old-fashioned monitor. The screen showed a time—eleven hundred hours.

Finally, a reference point.

Against the wall, several cylindrical tanks bubbled with liquid, and small orbs swirled around inside. Al walked closer and peered through the glass. The floating objects were eyeballs, the red fleshy strings still dangling from some of them. She jumped back with a startled cry, almost tripping on the many thick cords that ran along the length of the floor.

"Do you like my collection?" A deep and resonant voice emerged from the corner of the room.

The man leaning against the wall looked about Maddox's age with slicked-back brown hair. He swayed toward her, his hands tucked into two of the many pockets of his lab coat. His brown right eye hid behind a half pair of glasses, his left eye closed with a scar slicing down from his eyebrow to his beige cheek.

Al took a step back as she looked up, tucking her arms to her chest.

The man leaned down, his hand on his chin, and his good eye pointed toward her. "Don't worry, love. I only take the pretty ones."

Al snapped her head down as her shoulders shook. *The eye-dye!* She had left it in her bag. The last time she had used it was at the base. How much time had passed since then? How much time did she have left before the color faded? Would he think her eyes were pretty enough to gouge out then?

"Come now. Let's get acquainted, shall we?" The man turned toward the blue chair. "That will be all, Dr. Mubarak."

The doctor who had led her to this horrible place bowed his head before entering a code on the inside keypad and leaving the room. The four men dressed in black remained near the door, their backs straight and hands clasped in front of them.

Al remained motionless, her lungs tightening as she tried to steady her sporadic breathing.

"Please, love. I do not wish to use force on such a fragile creature."

Al gritted her teeth. She would have to comply for now. Her mind wasn't giving her any other options.

She made her way to the chair, the grooved floor leaving round indents on the soles of her feet. When she sat, the hardness of the seat forced her spine upright.

"Now, let's take a look at you." The man pulled the giant magnifying glass toward her and peered in with his one good eye, distorting him like some sort of gelatinous being, round and fat in some parts, skinny and long in others.

Half of her wanted to laugh, and the other half wanted to scream.

"Ah, clever. You're using eye pigmentation, aren't you?"

All humor evaporated from her system.

"We'll just have to wait for the big reveal, then. I'm rather excited!" He clapped his hands together, his one eye taking up most of the magnifying glass.

She looked down, squeezing the armrests. Tears poked into the corners of her eyes, but when the man turned his back to her, she rubbed them away. *Stay strong.*

"So, what do they call you, dear?" He turned toward the monitor and typed something on the keyboard. "I'm the warden, Mr. Benje."

Al glared at him, keeping her mouth shut.

He gave her a weak frown. "No matter. I will find out." He reached toward her and something inside her snapped.

She slapped his hand away and shot out of the chair, running toward the door. The four men surrounded her, but she kicked one of them in the face and he fell to his knees, holding his bleeding nose. Dashing past him, she reached the door, digging and scratching at the edges. The other three men descended upon her, grabbing her limbs. They pinned her back into the chair, fastening re-straints around her wrists and ankles, and she winced as the metal clasps dug into her skin.

The warden laughed. "Well! You're certainly a lot stron-ger than I expected." He waved away the men, and they returned to their post at the door. "I was suspicious when they told me you could fly, but after seeing your reaction, I see that it really was a lie. No matter. You are most in-triguing."

That's the superpower the Scanners made up? That I could just flap my arms and fly? A thin line of blood trickled from Al's wrist, but she continued to twist her body, trying to pull herself free.

Icy fingers caressed her cheek and when she turned her head away, his oily voice filled her ear. "I told you to cooperate, love. Now you've gone and made me damage your soft skin." He moved his hands over hers and she flinched. When he touched the scar on her right hand, he snickered. "Seems like I'm not your first."

Al continued to avert her gaze, her heartbeat pounding against her eardrums.

Mr. Benje rolled the cart closer to the chair and took a square device with a green grid and a long, coiled wire attached to the monitor. *A fingerprint reader.* Al clenched her fists as tight as she could, but the warden forced her index finger upon its flat surface. The machine beeped, and he released her with a strained grunt, the reader falling to the floor.

"Alright, love. Let's see who you really are."

A clear bar appeared on the monitor and as it filled with orange, the numeric percentage on the screen increased.

Her chest tightened again. Despite the danger, she wondered if this machine might reveal a clue about her past, even though it could very well be the last clue she ever received.

The monitor made a loud droning sound.

"Oh, most interesting indeed!" Mr. Benje turned the monitor toward Al with feverish delight. "How ever did you manage *this*?"

The monitor displayed a white outline of a human body and a sentence written in green.

Unidentified. Unable to locate.

Al closed her eyes and relaxed. Maddox had somehow erased her from the database. She thanked him inside her mind and opened her eyes to see the warden's face close to hers.

"I'm disappointed I didn't find out much."

"Good!" Al snapped, her courage growing.

Sighing, Mr. Benje plopped down onto his rolling chair and spun himself, his feet kicking off the ground every so often. "Hm...what to do?" He continued to swivel, and just when Al felt queasy from watching him, he sprang from the chair. It toppled to the floor, an amusement ride no longer worth riding.

"I know!" His face twisted into a strange ecstasy that made Al want to bash her head against the back of the chair just so she could avoid his gaze. "I'll send your file to Vilroy! He's the one who set up this entire operation, you know. Trying to heal these poor Altered. Bless him."

Al stayed silent, even though her insides wanted to explode from her mouth.

Mr. Benje mumbled to himself as he picked up his chair and sat back down on its squishy blue seat. He scooted toward her. "Then again, if I send him this information, he'll probably steal you away from me...I'll have to weigh my options further."

Al clenched the armrests again. Disgusting logic had warped this man's mind. If this was how he treated her, what horrible things had he done to the other girls trapped here?

Touching his chin as he stood, Mr. Benje called to the men at the door, and they released Al from the chair. She stretched out her sore limbs and rubbed the dried blood from her wrist.

No broken bones, just more bruises. She could still use her hands. She could still fight.

"Off with you now, my mystery girl." Mr. Benje rubbed his chin again. "Hah, that's a perfect name for you." He took a pen and notepad from his pocket and wrote down his discovery as the men pushed Al toward the double doors.

After the same deep clicking sound, the exit swung open, and the men corralled her out into the hall where Dr. Mubarak was waiting. As the doors shut behind her, Al heard the faint words of the warden, "See you again soon, Mystery."

Al made sure to send her harsh glare to the men around her before they started their trek back down the hall. Their faces remained emotionless, but the man with a dry bloody nose kicked her calf and she took a stumbling step forward. Her left heel stung as a thin layer of raw skin started to peel. Letting out an exasperated yell, she turned and pointed a finger at her aggressor. "You're on my list, buddy!"

She faced forward and continued to march in silence. Pulchra was right. This place was hell. Death was supposed to be peaceful, a release, not a torturous playground where powerful men could abuse and torment who they pleased. She had to get out. There had to be a way.

From the other end of the hall, two men wearing attire similar to Dr. Mubarak pushed a gurney toward them. The white sheet draped over the top covered something long and lumpy. As they passed, the cart jerked to a stop.

"Careful or you'll spill everywhere!" The leader turned to scold the man who steered behind him.

Flustered, the man offered a quick apology and bent down to adjust the wheel. Once situated, they both nodded at Dr. Mubarak and pushed the cart toward their destination, the door marked with the word *Furnace*.

Al felt numb.

A light-brown arm sticking out from under the cloth leaked dark red from a sliced wrist. The drops of blood followed the cart as it disappeared beyond the doors of the furnace room, dotting the cold ground with a trail of a life that used to exist.

CHAPTER 17

The men shoved Al back into the room, and she stumbled to her knees. She turned to yell something unsavory, but the door had already shut.

"Are you alright?" Swan's voice quivered as she wrapped her arms around Al. "What did he do to you? Do you still have all your fingers? Do you remember who I am?"

Had Swan worried this whole time? Al smiled. She had forgotten how nice a hug could be. "Yes Swan, I'm still in one piece." Her smile faded. *For now.*

Swan embraced her tighter. "Oh, thank goodness!"

"It's probably because you look so boring." Pulchra took a loud bite out of a crisp blue pear. She and the other girls sat on a checkered blanket spread out in the middle of the room, covering the impacts of meteor shower Punch. Arranged in the center, silver platters held colorful fruit and sweet rolls with dollops of red jam.

"Pul! That's rude." Swan released Al, her hands going straight to her hips. Pulchra took another bite of fruit without breaking eye contact or changing her vacant expression.

"No, she's right." Al sat next to her on the blanket. "But I'm glad *eye* was boring." She pointed to her right pupil. "Get it? Cuz he only had one..."

The room fell silent as everyone stared at her.

"Wow, fine. Pun rescinded." Al shoved a melon slice into her mouth and Pulchra snickered.

"I'm a berry bee!" Punch jumped to her feet, raising her jam-covered fingers as cherry globs fell to the floor. Crumbs stuck to her cheeks like freckles.

"Oh, Punch..." Swan tried to capture her, but the sticky child galloped away, circling the room as she squealed with laughter and licked her fingers. Swan finally corralled her into the bathroom and shut the door behind them.

The melon was sour and soggy, but Al forced herself to swallow. Regardless of whether she could actually escape or not, she needed strength to survive long enough to find out. She frowned at the fruit. "Are you sure they're not poisoning us?"

"I had the same thought when I first got here." Pulchra finished eating her blue pear and leaned back on her hands. "*Logically,* it doesn't make sense for them to kill us. We wouldn't be much use to them *scientifically* then. Still though, I tested my *hypothesis.*" Pulchra swung her head and smiled as she emphasized certain words. "I waited a few days watching the other girls, knowing that any poison would've taken effect by then if it was there."

Ribbon crossed her arms, causing a triangular orange to topple off her lap. "You mean you used us like tree mice?"

Pulchra gave the girl a harsh glare. "That's what we're all being used like anyway."

"I like tree mice." Lace cradled her roll above her head, rotating it from side to side as she smiled.

The door to the bathroom burst open and Punch bounded out, the front of her dress now stained with pink splotches. "Clean!" She ran to her bed and bounced face-first into her orange covers.

Swan shook her head and sat sideways on the blanket next to Al. "Our little earth shaker is definitely a handful." She faced Al and smiled. "But I'm grateful for her. I'm grateful for all of you."

Al blushed and stuffed an entire roll into her mouth, shifting her gaze around the room as she chewed. Being around other girls was strange. "So…how long have you all been here?"

"I suppose since I'm the oldest, I should go first." Swan folded her hands in her lap. "My father built our house as a gift to my mother when they got married. We didn't have much, but we were happy. Anytime we needed something the sea couldn't provide, my father would disappear for days. When he returned, he'd always have so many glittering and fancy things. I remember the bracelet he brought me for my tenth birthday. I never took it off…" She touched her bare wrist, staring at the wall with wistful eyes.

"One day, when my father returned from his usual absence, two soldiers from the capital were following him. They were smiling, laughing. We welcomed them into our home. I didn't know I was Altered or even what that meant until I saw my reflection in the ship's window as it was taking off. My parents and little brother were waving happily from down below, bags of coins surrounding their feet. It's been five years now, I think. It's hard to keep track."

"So, they just—sold you?" Al almost touched Swan's shoulder but stopped herself. Girl rules were still unclear.

"I'd like to believe they thought they were giving me a better life, but I'm honestly not sure." Swan's face morphed back into a warm smile. "Anyway, Pul? You up for storytime?"

Pulchra sighed and leaned back onto the floor, folding her hands under her head. "It's not much of a story. I've always been good at remembering things, so I helped my mom and dad keep track of inventory and manage the money when we sold our bread in the city. That's how we survived outside the wall. Soldiers followed us home and I've been here ever since. Okay, someone else go." Pulchra turned her back to them.

Lace shot her hand into the air. "Ooo! I want to tell a story next, please." Her determination melted from her face as she gripped her sister's arm. "Actually, let's tell it together."

Ribbon frowned. "Omma and Aphha loved us so much they kept us hidden from the bad guys for a long time. Going outside was not allowed, so it was very boring."

Ah, a comrade in arms.

"We made lots of things with Omma while we were inside though. Lots of yummy noodles in yummy sauces and meat buns and bibimbap and tteok-bokki and bulgogi, but it's not really bulgogi since the moo moos don't exist anymore. Oh, and sometimes hwajeon!"

"You silly, they didn't ask for a cookbook."

Lace lowered her head, her mouth sliding upward. "Sorry, I got hungry."

"Even though you're already eating?"

All the girls laughed, a much-needed dose of endorphins for their broken souls.

Ribbon straightened her dress. "We were out in the garden when the soldiers walked by. They saw us and they took us, crushing all the flowers with their mean boots."

"Omma and Ahppa were crying and asking them not to, but they didn't listen."

"I'm so sorry..." Al pulled her knees to her chest. "I can't believe Naturalists would be that cruel, that there's a man who—" She clenched her teeth. How many other girls had stories like these? Why didn't anyone care? "I feel so stupid for not realizing how bad things were, that it's been happening for so long..."

Was this what Maddox and Molly were trying to protect her from? Al let out a bitter chuckle. "Can't say the Altered are any better though. They killed so many innocent people with their bombs. I guess it doesn't really matter what side you're on. The ones without power are the ones who suffer and die."

No one spoke or touched their food for a while.

"So, what's *your* story? Are you actually Altered?" Pulchra sat up, resting her arm on her knee.

Al nodded as she twisted a strand of hair between her fingers. "My eyes and hair...aren't really brown."

"Wow! Really?" Lace rocked back and forth. "How?"

"With a special dye."

"What superpower do you have?" Ribbon chimed in next.

"Flying apparently. The Scanners who dumped me here told Mr. Creepo I was some kind of human-bird thing, but unless you count sarcasm as a special ability, I'm just a blank canvas."

Swan chuckled. "Funny enough, I know all about being a human-bird thing. I have a few webbed toes. See?" She lifted her left foot and wiggled her digits like worms. Lace and Ribbon giggled and wiggled their fingers at each other. "I also have a beautiful singing voice."

Pulchra choked on her laughter. "Oh yes, a voice so lovely it puts people straight to sleep."

Swan crossed her arms and smirked. "How rude."

Al smiled and then her eyes widened as a realization crossed her mind. "Actually, wait! I do have a superpower. I can get us out of here!"

Pulchra groaned. "You're still going on about that?"

"There's gotta be Keev-ships around here, right? People don't just walk out into the middle of nowhere, right?"

"Yeah, but none of us know how to fly them." Lace shrugged.

"That's just it. In a strange twist of irony, I do."

"But you're a girl!" Punch lifted her head from her bed, her nose wrinkled in confusion.

"That's right." Al stood and put her hands on her hips. "And they messed up big time bringing me here."

"For real?" Ribbon raised her eyebrows. "You really know how to fly?"

"More than that! I know everything about Keev-ships! You're looking at a trophy-winning mechanic here!" The faces staring back at her didn't look convinced. Hope was a foreign language that none of them seemed to speak anymore.

"I think I have an idea." Pulchra dashed to her bookshelf and pulled out a book. She flipped it open on the floor in front of them. The colorful but faded pages showed smudged pictures of extinct animals. "In exchange for cooperating peacefully with the experiments, they give us things like this as rewards." Pulchra smirked. "If I'm sneaky enough, I can search for a book about how to disable the tracking devices in the library during free time. It might take me a while, but if I can find it, one look, and I'll be able to memorize it."

Al stared at the book. "But would they really just leave that kind of information lying around?"

Pulchra laughed. "Yeah, because they're not that observant. They think I don't know how to read. That's why they always send me picture books."

Al's eyes moved from side to side as she constructed a plan in her head. "I think this might work!"

Swan stood, gripping her elbows. "Well, I don't think so." Her voice was stern again and all the girls tensed. Al frowned and was about to start an impassioned speech to convince her, but Swan scooped her into another hug. "I don't know your name yet, so how are we supposed to work together? I can't keep calling you, *you!*"

Swan let go and Al's cheeks warmed like the rolls she had eaten. "Well, I guess, uh...I guess just call me Brownie for now?"

"Brownie!" All the girls called out her new name.

"You promise we'll get out?" Punch stood behind them, a piece of paper in her hands, and her mouth squished into a pout.

Al crouched to Punch's eye level. "I promise."

"Okay, because I have only been here a little bit, but I hate it." The seismic child looked down, rocking on her heels. "I used all my color sticks to draw this. This is us, outside. That one is you." Punch held up her page and pointed to a brown scribble in the corner.

Al laughed. "Oh yeah! It looks just like me."

Swan put her arm up, flexing her triceps muscles. "Okay! It's settled then. We're getting the hell out of here as fast as we can! So, where do we start?"

Pulchra raised her eyebrows, her mouth falling open with a shocked laugh and Ribbon and Lace exchanged glances, covering their mouths that exploded with toothy snickers.

Al took a deep breath, the determination she thought had been scrubbed away in the shower flowing back through her veins. "Hey Punch, can we borrow your colors for a super important project?"

"Yeah! Yeah!" Punch nodded several times and rushed back to her bed. She returned with a container and turned it upside down, dumping a heaping pile of color sticks onto the floor. "This will be the bestest picture ever!"

Many days passed, though it was difficult for Al to keep track without access to calendars, clocks, or light from the outside. At first, she thought to keep a tally on the paper Punch shared with them, but for fear it might give away their plan, she opted to draw the lines on the underside of the wooden plank that held up her bed. Though more comfortable than the one she had at Petram, the atmosphere was anything but pleasant.

Often, she would wake up to the sound of Swan's muffled sobbing coming from the bathroom or Punch's wild screams as she thrashed in her sleep. There was even a time when Al heard Lace mumbling incoherently under her blanket in a feverish chant and laughing to herself. No one mentioned these events after they happened, so Al didn't either.

The daily routine was simple enough for her to grasp, spending most of the time stuck in their room, with only two meals to break up the monotony, one arriving soon after the lights turned on and the other, Al estimated, arriving a few hours before the lights turned off. Every other day was "activity day," when the guards in black escorted them out of their room to a different part of the complex for a few hours.

The first event of the week was storytime, held in a dusty library where about forty Altered girls packed together like sardines. The Naturalist women who read to them always seemed to have an air of self-importance to their words, like their effort to blurt out letters in the proper order somehow entitled them to a community service award. When the readings finished, only the youngest ones clapped, too innocent to understand that stories couldn't save them.

Two more days passed, and the six girls visited the Playroom.

Several men dressed in black stood by the door as more strapped Punch to the metal chair. Al and the other girls huddled together on the floor.

Mr. Benje situated a strange wire-infested hat on Punch's head and turned back to his computer. "Delivering wave one, in three, two..."

The helmet emitted an electric high-pitched buzz, sending Punch into mild convulsions. She whimpered as tears squeezed from the corners of her clenched eyes.

"Stop!" Al ripped away from Swan, lunging toward him, but the men yanked at her limbs and once they had a firm grasp on her, one slapped her across the face. Lace screamed and buried her head in her arms behind Ribbon's chair.

The warden stood up from his blue rolling seat. "Punch here is the strongest girl at the facility and I am merely testing her pain tolerance as a control for the rest of you. But I can see you're much too excited to try it out for yourself." He turned back to his computer, and after flicking a switch, the buzzing stopped. Punch relaxed into the chair, her eyes still closed. The men lifted her limp body and dragged her to a spot on the floor next to the other girls, dropping her like garbage. Swan caught her and cradled her against her chest. The men then forced Al into the chair, once again subduing her wrists under the straps.

Mr. Benje situated the helmet atop Al's head. "I'm very curious to find out how much pain you can tolerate, my beautiful Mystery." He stroked her slapped cheek, now warm and stinging. Al twisted her head away, spitting in his face. The warden smirked, wiping away the saliva with his fingertips. "Let's take you down to level two."

Without time to process what was happening, the buzzing sound emitted from the device, and a wave of hot, searing pain shot through Al's body. She thrashed in the chair, letting out strained screams, her fists opening and closing and her legs twitching against the bottom of the chair. Her mind was a wash of flashing images fading into white.

Perryn! Perryn!

Just as quickly as the pain surged through her, it stopped and she sank into the chair, gasping for air.

The warden clapped his hands. "Ohhh! Very good, Mystery. You didn't pass out. I'll add that information to your file."

The men didn't face resistance as they unstrapped her from the chair and dragged her back to the girls, throwing her on top of Swan. She resituated Punch on her lap so that Al could rest her head there as well and her cold tears dripped onto Al's face. Al reached out a shaky hand to interlock her fingers with Punch's. One by one, the remaining girls had their turn in the chair, their screams and crying resounding in the metal room like a gruesome shrieking thunderstorm.

The strange experiments continued for several days, though they weren't as painful as that first one had felt. Maybe Al's nerves were too damaged to tell the difference. She didn't know. Time blurred together and sometimes she caught herself drifting in and out of consciousness. The thought of freedom faded from her mind. She stopped eating. Swan was the only one who seemed to remain hopeful, rubbing their backs and humming through her tears when they couldn't sleep.

Then everything horrible stopped abruptly, and they remained in their room undisturbed. Al started to eat again and feeling returned to her body.

The next activity day sent them to a gym with an arched roof that looked like the inside of a soup can and a floor littered with broken boards. Scowling women holding baskets collected their dresses and instructed them to change into tight blue shorts and loose-fitting white shirts.

There were other girls, new ones Al hadn't seen before. Most of them shivered together in circled groups, their breath fogging in the air.

What month was it? Had Zeek's birthday passed already?

Void of equipment, there wasn't anything to do except run laps, which Al had no desire or energy to do, but when she spotted a window on the opposite side of the gym, she suddenly found both. Trying not to make it seem obvious, she stole glances as she ran past.

Across a grassy field covered in orange and red leaves, a hangar stood tall in the distance. Al tried to keep her triumphant smile hidden as she passed the men watching over them. The escape vehicle was located. Now to find the way out.

After several visits, they had discovered a map of the building's floor plan hanging in the gym office, but Pulchra never had enough time to stare through the window without raising suspicion.

A few weeks later, they enacted phase one.

When the guards ushered the girls from the gym, Swan and Al lingered by the door to distract the remaining two, while Pulchra ducked behind a set of bleachers. Al prayed she'd be convincing in her role.

"Stop stalling. Back to your rooms." One of the guards gestured toward the door.

"I bet being a guard is so boring." Swan's voice was sweet and thick, the way Angel's had sounded when Al first met her. "I bet I could help with that."

"Swan…" The other guard rolled back his shoulders as he faced them. "You miss me that much? And what about this one?"

Maybe it was nerves, or residual brain fog from the experiments, but as the man turned toward her, all the lines Al had rehearsed vanished. "I—I'm…" She glanced behind him, watching Pulchra sneak across the floor toward the office.

The man laughed and placed his arm on the wall above her head. "Don't worry. I like shy girls." He lifted her chin and Al could feel her face giving her away. How long did she have to stall?

Swan moved to the first guard at the door and whispered something in his ear, letting out a seductive giggle when she pulled away. He wrapped his arms around her waist, his smile growing bigger.

Pulchra gave a thumbs-up behind them.

"Well, anyway. Wouldn't wanna get in trouble now, would we? Maybe see you another time?" Al ducked under the second guard's arm.

He grabbed her wrist. "You can't just walk away."

Al's stomach lurched. *Oh, please! Why not?*

"Actually!" Swan sidestepped and touched the man's arm, laughing again. "You don't want her. She just got here. Plus, her technique isn't nearly as good as mine."

"You gonna take us both on, then?" The man smirked, releasing Al.

Swan touched her bottom lip with her index finger and cocked her head. "I've done it before."

Al clenched her fists, ready to fight, but Swan smiled and mouthed the words *I'll be fine.*

"I'll take this one back to her room, then." The first man pushed Al toward the door, just as Pulchra zoomed to her side. "And where did you come from?"

Pulchra chuckled. "Oh uh, sorry about that. I took a really long nap. Just woke up."

The man sighed as he forced the door open with his hand. "Come on, let's go. Don't start without me, Joe!"

They entered the hall and Al looked over her shoulder, watching Swan's form shrink in the crevice between the swinging doors.

Al's stomach twisted with a hollow gnawing. Swan had bravely stood her ground, but Al had abandoned her. What horrible things were those men doing to her? Al had vague ideas, but it was limited to what she heard in locker rooms or during lunchtime. She pulled her knees to her chest. Swan had to sacrifice herself because Al was defective, a girl in name only. When Swan returned to the room much later, her face still held her usual warm demeanor, but Al couldn't look her in the eye.

"I got it!" Pulchra held up a piece of paper with lines and boxes drawn in a circular pattern. "I drew the layout of the building just like I saw it!"

"Any luck on figuring out how to deactivate these bugs in our legs?" Al stared at the drawing, trying to purge the image of Swan's last smile from her mind.

Pulchra scratched her head with the blunt end of the color stick. "Yeah, about that. I looked several times, but I couldn't find anything. There weren't even instructions on how to assemble a portable water bottle."

"How are we going to leave, then?" Lace poked her head out of the bathroom.

"Instead of deactivating them, could we remove them?" Swan ran a brush through her thick hair as she sat on her bed.

"Hmm…" Pulchra bit the end of the colored stick. "Not without the proper tool. I don't know what it looks like either. Otherwise, we'd have to dig it out. And without these people even allowing us spoons, I'm not sure how we would even do that."

Al stared at the ground. The girls were working hard, doing everything they could, and she was just dead weight. Was there anything in her Scanner training that might be useful? The face of the Altered woman she encountered with Zeek flashed in her mind and she jumped from the bed. There was.

She hurried over to Punch, who was lying on the floor scribbling another masterpiece. "Punch, can I borrow a color stick and a piece of paper?"

"Yeah. You can have this one." Punch handed her the pink stick she had just used and then returned to her drawing, adding a layer of green circles on top of the already colorful twister-like spirals.

"I know what it looks like!" Al rushed to the center of the room and dropped to the floor, sketching a long stick-thin object. "During my training as a Scanner, they told us about these trackers. You have to jam this retrieval device directly into the skin and pull it out. It's like using tweezers." She moved around the room, showing the drawing to each girl. "Have any of you seen something like this? Obviously, it would be silver or black, not pink."

"I've seen it!" Lace raised her hand. "The big scary guy has it in his coat."

"Who?"

Lace looked down. "The one who hurts us…Mr. Ben."

Al smiled grimly. "Of course he does."

"We'll come up with something." Swan gave her a determined smile. "For now, we should try to get some sleep."

"Sleep sounds nice." Pulchra climbed into her bed, wrapping a blue silk scarf around her bow-shaped hair.

"Lace! Hurry up in the bathroom." Ribbon rolled her chair toward the open door. "The light will turn off soon and I don't want to get into bed in the dark."

"Sorry!" Lace's tiny voice squeaked and repetitive splashing followed.

As she dashed out of the bathroom and helped her sister into bed, Swan tucked Punch underneath her covers. "What do you want to dream about tonight, dear?"

"A magical warrior princess who comes and saves us!"

Swan stroked the little fighter's hair. "That sounds wonderful. I hope I have the same dream."

Al pulled the blue blankets up to her neck and stared at the cloudy ceiling. Closing her eyes, she sent a silent prayer out from her mind. She felt silly, but what could it hurt? Maybe a magical savior really would come and rescue them. She opened her eyes again, and it was pitch black, the sun-shaped light dimmed by an automatic switchboard hidden somewhere inside the building.

She dreamed she was floating with the other girls, their bodies made of sparkling beams of light and magic. Holding hands, they flew over the tall walls of Marn to freedom.

When Al awoke, Punch was standing over her with wide eyes. Al yawned into a laugh. "Good morning, Punch. You okay?"

Punch nodded vigorously. "Brownie! The top of your head looks like snow fell on it!"

"What do you—" She stopped as the other girls crowded around her, staring with the same expression.

With a sinking coldness spreading through her lungs, Al gripped a chunk of her hair and yanked it forward. No longer chestnut brown, a milky-white hue diluted the strands. She ripped the covers from her body and steadied herself on the side of her bed. "What color are my eyes?"

"Blue. Icy-blue." Swan looked like she was going to cry as she covered her mouth.

Al gripped the bed, her stomach twisting. *No. Not now. Not like this. Not here. Not with him.* "S—Swan!" Al's words stuck in her throat.

"Everything will be okay!" Swan rushed to her side.

A metallic clicking sound came from the door. It slid open and Dr. Mubarak stepped inside with his clipboard. "Subject Four-Zero-One, the warden will see you now."

CHAPTER 18

Al kept her eyes on the ground. Why did she have to change now? They were so close. If she faced the warden as she was, would she even come back alive? She knew her sudden costume change would excite him in dangerous ways.

"Subject Four-Zero-One?" Dr. Mubarak rapped his pen against his clipboard.

Al forced herself to stand, steeling her nerves as she headed toward the door.

"You can't take Brownie away!" Punch jumped in front of Al with her arms spread out. "I'll beat you up if you do!"

"Punch!" Swan gasped and took a hesitant step toward them.

Al knelt and embraced the small girl. "Thank you, Punch. You're very brave, but this is my fight now. You stay and protect the others." Pulling away, she tried to give the girl a confident smile.

Punch pouted as she nodded. "Okay…" She returned to stand in front of her bed.

"Subject Four-Zero-One—" Dr. Mubarak's voice cracked as Al glared at him.

Walking out into the hall, every step sent tremors through her legs. She had to be brave, or she'd break.

They reached the Playroom.

"Oh, Mystery! What a surprise!" Mr. Benje stood in the doorway, his face twisted into a dark smile. "You've completely ruined my plans for today showing up looking like this, but no worries. I'm flexible!" Hearing his squeaky laugh felt like spiders had crawled into her ears. "Bring her to the table."

Al's confidence left her, and she pushed off from the floor like a rocket escaping Earth. Her ship was immediately grounded as the four men each grabbed her and pulled her toward the metal bed in the back of the room, her body hanging like a sheet. She struggled with exasperated cries as they restrained her wrists, ankles, and head to the chilly table.

"Go. Go now!" The warden waved away the guards as he sauntered toward the table. He took off his jacket and threw it over his blue chair. "I wish to be alone with my work." The men scurried out of the room and the doors slid closed behind them, leaving Al and the warden alone in the silver horror house.

He started to hum.

Al's eyes darted around the room, her mind a flurry of screaming thoughts. With the strap squished across her head, it was difficult to see anything but the ceiling.

His face loomed above her, his mouth spread in a toothy grin. "Comfortable, love?"

"Let me go!" She lurched forward, the straps pinching her skin.

He sighed as he pulled away and began digging through a drawer of metal tools. "If you weren't so difficult, I wouldn't have to restrain you like this. You're really making me look like the bad guy here, but science is neutral, you know."

"What you're doing here is wrong! This isn't science! You're a monster!"

He snickered. "Me? A monster?" His eye turned wild as he pointed a surgeon's knife at her nose. "You're the one who's Altered. I'm more human than you'll ever be."

Al stiffened as he pressed the blade flat against her left cheek and then caressed the other with his rough fingertips. He smelled like sweat and chemicals. "Your eyes are mesmerizing, Mystery, like tiny snowstorms trapped behind glass. I would love to add them to my collection."

Al squeezed her eyes shut, letting out a tiny whimper.

"Ha! Who knew you could make a face like that?" He trailed the blade down her cheek, down her neck, and over her chest, stopping above her belly button.

Al bit down over her lips. Her reactions only seemed to add fuel to his poisonous fire.

He whispered into her ear. "I wonder what other faces you can make."

Al gasped as his hands traveled up the inside of her legs and underneath her dress. "Ss—sto—!" Her words were just as trapped as the rest of her, and she writhed with each malicious caress.

"Wonderful! Wonderful faces!" The warden let out an enraptured laugh, his hands continuing to move upwards. "Just one eye? Please?"

A sickening feeling consumed every breath, every nerve, every muscle, like a virus, burrowing into her soul. Is this what Swan felt with those men? How could she act like everything was fine when she returned to the room? This was wrong.

His fingers felt like hungry worms squirming their way through the dirt looking to devour a decomposing body. This was different from when Perryn had touched her.

Tears spilled down her cheeks and onto the cold table as she kept her eyes and mouth clamped shut.

The door to the room slid open, and Mr. Benje let out a disappointed sigh. "Dr. Mubarak, I told you never to interrupt me during my therapy sessions!" He pulled away, the sickness loosening its hold on her.

Dr. Mubarak stuttered. "Yes! Yes, sir, I understand but—"

"Is there a reason you are refusing to meet at our appointed time, Mr. Benje?"

Al's eyes burst open. *It couldn't be.*

"No, Prime Minister Keevie! I apologize. I was just so involved with my work that it slipped my mind."

Perryn!

"Your work?" Footsteps moved into the room. "Given your past, I feel I must remind you that genetic engineering is illegal in Astova, even for the criminals of Marn."

I'm right here!

"Oh, yes, but of course, Prime Minister!" Mr. Benje's words tumbled from his mouth like a rockslide. "This young woman was having seizures, and I was helping to relieve them."

How can I convince you it's me?

"I see." His footsteps turned toward the door.

Please, don't go!

Al opened her mouth and yelled with every ounce of strength she had left. "You're gonna leave? Just like that? You jerk-ass buttface!"

Mr. Benje floundered. "I sincerely apologize, Prime Minister! I will punish this Altered criminal right away!"

"No." Perryn stepped back into the room. "I will do it myself."

"But—but Prime Minister Keevie, with all due respect, as the warden I—"

"Leave."

With the scrambling of boots and an irritated grunt, Mr. Benje and the other men hurried from the room. Then the door closed and only one pair of boots squeaked across the floor.

"Al?" Perryn's voice was hushed and feverish at the same time. "Is that you?"

The moment his face appeared above her, more tears clouded her vision, spilling down her cheeks and flooding into her ears. "Of course it's me." She choked on her broken laughter. "Do you think anyone else would be brave enough to insult you like that?"

"Al!" Perryn freed her from the restraints and helped her to sit upright. His usual trench coat covered his frame and the comforting scent of pine had returned. She wiped her eyes, the familiar touch of his gloves lingering on her skin. He hadn't changed at all, unlike her. "Why do you look like that?"

She avoided his gaze. "I'm sorry...I guess you didn't remember I was Altered..."

Perryn clenched his fists as he looked at the door. "That is not what I meant." He moved closer to her. "How are you here? The base was bombed. I thought..."

"I was actually trying to run away, but then I was caught by Capital Scanners, and they brought me here. I don't even know how long it's been since then."

"Three months."

"What?" Al's head shot up, but she forced herself to look back down. "What about Molly? And...Maddox?"

"Unfortunately, I have no knowledge of their whereabouts. I stopped communicating with them the day I left the island."

"Oh..." Al continued to stare at the ground. "Did you...were you the one who gave the order?"

"No..." Perryn gritted his teeth. "Despite being the prime minister, military affairs are not within my jurisdiction. I was not even aware of the attack until after it happened. If I had known…Al, why do you keep—" Perryn touched her shoulder, and she flinched. He took a step back, dropping his hand to his side. "Sorry…"

She shook her head. "You're not the reason I—"

"Al, we can leave right now. I can take you away from here."

She smiled as her stomach twisted with the warmth of his words, but she had to douse the fire. "As perfectly wonderful as that sounds, I can't…"

"What! What are you saying?"

"I made a promise to the other girls in my cell. I won't leave them behind!" She clutched the metal table. "I'm tired of running away and being scared. I'm tired of being saved, of being powerless…"

"Al, stop being irrational. I will take all of you then. You know who I am, right?"

"Yeah. The prime minister. You think Vilroy won't notice his right hand waltzing a bunch of superpowered Altered 'criminals' outta Marn? How would you explain yourself? You'd be implicated for sure. Plus, Creepo might have already told him I'm here."

"…what if you die?"

Al smiled. "Life's a terminal illness, remember?" She finally lifted her head and Perryn's diamond-black eyes stared back at her. Her throat tightened, her resolve slipping. It would've been better if she had been strong enough not to look at him, but he was Perryn Keevie, after all. She touched his cheek where a faint scar clung to his skin, her gaze unwavering. "At least I got to see you again."

Perryn stiffened, his eyes widening. He reached up, but before he could touch her, she hopped down from the table. She walked over to Benje's forgotten lab coat and rummaged through the pockets until she found the tracker retrieval device.

"Gotcha!" She lifted her dress to lodge the thin metal stick between her hip and her underwear, flinching when her hand brushed against her bare skin. The warden's corruption was still fresh. "If all goes well, I'll meet you at Oceanside in three days."

Perryn remained silent.

"I guess I'll need your help to make my exit realistic though." She reached the door and lifted her arm, feeling his gaze searing into her back.

Moving to stand beside her, he took her arm and knocked, nodding at the guards through the window. The door slid open, and Al stumbled forward with an exaggerated fall.

"Take the prisoner back to her room."

"Right away, Prime Minister!" The guards surrounded Al, two on either side. "Come on! Hurry up!" They pushed her and she heard Perryn grit his teeth.

Her mind screamed at her, but she fought the urge to turn around. Just as she was about to round the corner to ascend the stairs, she gave in and glanced back, but Perryn had disappeared. Her breath heaved in her chest as she swallowed the tears that threatened to fall.

The door to the room slid open and Al was once again shoved through. Swan shot up from her bed and smothered her in a hug as the other girls surrounded them like a mother bird being reunited with a lost egg. Al returned the hug, Swan's body quivering with sobs as she hid her face in Al's shoulder.

Punch gripped Al's dress, a few tears bubbling in her dark whirlpools. "I thought you would go forever, like the last friend!"

Al patted her on the head. "Don't worry, Punch. I promised we were gonna get out of here, right? And we will. Tonight!"

"Really?"

Pulchra leaned against the wall with a small smile. "And how do you think we'll do that?"

Al reached under her dress and pulled the retrieval device from her hip. "With this!" She pushed the top and the short metal rod extended out into a pin-sized needle.

"The device thingy!" Lace jumped up and down, using her sister's shoulders like a springboard. Ribbon shooed her away, but she couldn't hide her smile for long.

Swan wiped her eyes. "How did you get this?"

Al tried to smile. "That doesn't matter."

Swan frowned like she might start crying again, but she clapped her hands together. "Alright everyone, once the light goes out, we're leaving this horrid place behind!" The other girls looked almost as teary-eyed as Swan.

"But first we have to remove these pesky trackers from our legs." Al lifted the rod as if directing an orchestra. "Lace and Punch, can you tear some strips from the sheets and get them wet with soap and water?"

"On it!"

"You got it, Brownie!"

Ribbon rolled forward. "You can try that thing on me first, since I won't feel any pain if you mess up." The girl placed her hands on her hips and grinned. "Finally, all of you are relying on me for a change."

Al nodded. "I promise I won't mess up." She helped Ribbon prop her left leg on her bed and Ribbon gathered the ends of her dress, stuffing them into the sides of her chair.

Lace and Punch returned with their damp scraps, though Punch's were more soap than water. A white trail of suds followed them from the bathroom. Al chuckled as she wiped her hands and then a large section of Ribbon's calf. She then positioned the device over the dark spot on the girl's skin. As the other girls watched with wide eyes and fidgeting fingers, Al stuck the needle end of the rod into Ribbon's leg.

Ribbon tilted her head without flinching. "That looks so weird…like a metal mosquito."

The rod began beeping as Al pushed the needle farther through more layers of skin, the beeps soon blurring together into a continuous repetitive tone.

"I think I found it!" Al pushed a button on the top and another beep followed. "Got it!" With a steady hand, she pulled until the syringe-like end re-entered the air. She grabbed one of the wet rags and wrapped it around Ribbon's leg. "You'll have to hold that there for a bit, but you did great, Ribbon!"

"Of course I did!"

Pulchra rolled her eyes with a soft smile and then turned toward Lace with a mischievous grin. "Lace should go next, since she is related. It will reduce the transfer of blood-borne pathogens."

"I don't know what a bath-egin is, but I don't wanna go next!" Lace sank to the floor, covering her legs with her dress.

"Oh, come on, Sis. It didn't hurt at all." Ribbon laughed and chased Lace around the room in her chair.

"A patient needs to rest after surgery!" Swan waved her arms, running after them like her animal namesake.

Al lifted the end of the rod to her eye level. Though almost too tiny to see, the square green chip it held had lots of round ridges and lines that formed looped patterns over the back.

"So that's what nanotech looks like up close." Pulchra squinted as she sat next to Al on the bed. "It would be so much cooler if it wasn't helping to trap us here. Kind of hate it now."

Al chuckled. "You wanna know something, Pulchra? I think you're one of the smartest people I know."

Pulchra turned away, her face curling into a smile she was failing to suppress. "Well, yeah, that's what I do. Being smart is my thing."

With much struggling, the girls managed to capture Lace and hold her down as Al removed the device from her leg. After, Lace sat on her bed, sniffling under her half-ripped blanket. Punch was next, sitting perfectly still, but she left a decent dent on the floor when her foot touched back down. Swan followed, enduring the process with gritted teeth and quick in-and-out breaths. Then Pulchra, who kept her eyes clamped shut the entire time. Al was last, pushing the needle into her own leg with Pulchra's help, as it pinched and burned through layers of skin. Finally, all the girls were free from the robotic ticks.

They laid the miniature squares out on top of a blanket in the middle of the room. Punch almost smashed them, but Pulchra and Al were quick to stop her. Destroying the devices might send out a signal, a signal that might bring guards and the end of any hope they had for escape.

They stashed them and the retrieval device under Al's bed before the attendants brought their last meal for the day. The girls ate with nervous laughter and twitching fingers, except for Punch, who kept pouting as she stared at the plates of food.

"Punch dear, you should eat." Swan offered her a meatless sandwich.

"We don't know when we'll have another meal, so you should stuff yourself silly." Al puffed out her cheeks, bringing her hands to her stomach.

"Swan? Brownie? I want to bring my color sticks with me, but I don't have pockets and I can only fit five in my hands. But don't I need my hands to help us run away?"

Swan and Al looked at each other and smiled. "How about you choose a color for everyone, and they'll hold it for you," Al offered. "That way you can bring six, no problem!"

Punch shot up from the ground. "Okay!" She rushed over to her bin and began sorting the colors into piles, mumbling her reasonings.

Al smiled as she looked down. "Just in case we don't make it out of this, I want you all to know that I'm so glad I met you."

"Hey!" Pulchra took an aggressive bite out of her sandwich. "None of that!" Her face softened. "Save that for the finish line when we're on the other side. You'll jinx us."

"I picked the best ones!" Punch ran back to the group, holding a few color sticks in her hands. As she announced the girls and their chosen colors, she walked around, handing them out. "Pulchra gets purple! Lace gets red! Ribbon gets blue. Swan gets green. Brownie gets brown and Punch gets pink!" She flopped down on the blanket, abandoning her pink stick for fistfuls of bread.

Al traced the scar on her right hand. *Only one more hurdle left to clear.* She only hoped they all could make the jump.

They huddled around the door, waiting in silence, the floor behind them sprinkled with dinner crumbs and a few extra holes Punch had inflicted on the tile. Any moment now, the sun in the middle of the room would go out. Al's heart pounded in her ears and her stomach complained about being too full. Once they stepped through the door, they'd be sailing through uncharted waters with unknown sea monsters lurking in the depths.

Al took a deep breath and let it out. "Remember everyone, until we get to the Keev-ship, no talking and move fast."

They all nodded.

The light went out.

Al tensed. "Ribbon, Punch, you're up."

Ribbon rolled her chair close to the door and placed her hands against its metal surface. Closing her eyes, she furrowed her eyebrows and clenched her mouth. Soon, the air around them grew colder and the metal in the door creaked as it shrank in on itself, leaving a gap between it and the wall. Swan lifted the ice child from her chair into her arms.

Punch stepped forward, and after letting out a breath through her nose, she stuck her fingers through the tiny opening and pulled. The door started to budge. Grunting through gritted teeth, Punch continued until the gap spread wide enough for them all to fit through.

"Let's go." Al stepped out into the hall.

After looking around, she motioned with her head for the others to follow. They dashed from the room, their bare feet slapping against the floor. Al spun around and placed her finger against her lips and the frightened girls froze, then lightened their steps.

They hid under the stairs once they reached the bottom, looking over the map Pulchra had drawn them. With silent nods, they snuck out from beneath them and turned down a hallway they had never traveled. The lights above them shone with a strange green harshness.

As they moved through the hall, their white dresses floated around their bodies like ghosts. Suspiciously, there were no guards like she had expected, but Al had no time to doubt their plan. They could only move forward and hope for the best.

Rooms with names that Al ignored sped by them as they ran, turning and winding through the metal maze and down another flight of stairs. At the bottom, two men in plainclothes stood in the hallway, their backs to them. Al raised her hand for the rest of the girls to stop and they crouched, pressing themselves as close to the wall as they could.

One man sighed. "Man, this compliance training is such bullshit. I hate my coworkers and no amount of team building is gonna fix that."

The other laughed. "I hear ya, but if the prime minister is leading it personally, you'll have to have a pretty good excuse to get out of it."

"Yeah, but it's so impromptu! I thought he was just here to check shit and leave. So much for getting off early."

Al scrunched her lips as she squinted. Was Perryn helping her escape?

The second man hit his buddy on the shoulder and turned to leave. "Come on, *coworker*, we're already late as it is."

Al waited until she could no longer hear their footsteps thundering down the hall before she turned back to survey the faces of her group. They looked terrified. Even Swan's face lacked its normal hopefulness. Al nodded at them before she turned back to face their path. She had to lead them out of here. She had to protect them.

Stepping out into the middle of the hall, she looked from side to side before motioning to the group to follow. The only thoughts that occupied her mind were the ones that propelled her feet to move and her lungs to breathe.

They continued down another flight of stairs until they reached a tunnel-like hallway with a low ceiling. An unguarded door waited at the very end. The oval window at the top revealed the hangar outside, red lights blinking amid the darkness.

"Okay, Ribbon and Punch, you're up again."

"You said we weren't supposed to talk, Brownie!" Punch's booming voice echoed in the small space as she pointed at her rule-breaking guide.

Al tensed, but then sighed. "I guess this is close enough." She turned toward Swan, helping her steady Ribbon at the door. As the girl's hands shriveled the metal inward, detaching it from the wall, a loud and high-pitched siren started to wail.

"What's that?" Lace crouched to the floor.

Pulchra backed up against the wall. "Something bad."

"Punch!" Al yelled. "Open the door!"

Punch stiffened like a board and shook her head. Her eyes were wide, like a bugle bird caught in a Keev-ship spotlight.

"Punch, please!" Al barreled toward her, but Swan stood in her way.

She handed off Ribbon to Al, and then wrapped Punch in a hug. "Punch. You have been so brave. So brave." She pulled away and held up her green color stick. "Would you mind using your special gift one more time? I know you can do it. You're our super warrior princess."

Al could feel her tears brimming and she glanced at the other girls. They were crying too.

Punch rubbed her eyes and nodded. "I'm going to kick that door's butt!" She put her pink color stick in her mouth and marched past the girls, sticking her hands around the edge of the door. In one loud burst of mighty fury, she wrenched it open and fell to her knees.

A gust of fresh, cold air flooded into the tunnel. Without hesitating, the girls dashed through the door, Swan grabbing Punch's hand.

The air bit with chilly teeth and the hard gravel dug into Al's feet as she and the girls ran across the tarmac toward the blinking red lights.

Suddenly, floodlights lit their path.

"Stop now!"

"Return to your cells!"

Behind them, men in dark uniforms flooded from the crumpled door, their guns drawn. Energy shots blasted through the girls' fleeing formation, just missing their heads and bouncing off the rocky ground. The girls ducked and stumbled, all screaming except for Al who glared at the men as she shielded Ribbon. If only she had a gun too.

The sound of heavy boots thundered closer.

"Punch! Go with Brownie!" Swan pushed the girl forward, dropping her hand.

"No!" Punch reached for her, but the older girl pulled away.

"I'll catch up. I promise."

Punch ran toward Al, screaming and crying. "Brownie! Brownie! Swan! Swan!"

Swan turned her back to them, spreading her arms out wide. As the guards continued to shoot, she took a breath, and then an ear-piercing screeching exploded from her mouth. The men running after them dropped to their knees, clawing at their ears and writhing in pain as blood spilled from their eyes and noses.

Ribbon covered her ears, and Al cringed. "Wow Pulchra! You weren't kidding about her voice!"

"Told ya!"

Swan continued her song until all the men remained motionless on the ground and then dropped to her knees, panting.

"Swan! Swan!" Punch fell on top of the girl, squeezing her dress as she sobbed.

"I'm okay, Punch." She stood once more and took the girl's hand. "Now let's go, shall we?"

After the two reunited with the rest of the group, the girl squad ran into the tall, domed hangar. Open on both ends, wires and lights dripped down from the high ceiling like industrial rain. The ships inside slept in three symmetrical rows, some looming above their heads like giant birds. They sped past fuel tanks, spare wings, and layers of boxes stacked high against the wall.

As they approached the other end, Perryn's ship came into view and the wiring for her heartbeat short-circuited and sent a painful shock through her chest. *You'll see him again soon.*

They hid behind the bullet-ship as Al set Ribbon on the ground. Her arms felt like jelly and her legs ached, but she had to keep going. Sticking her head out, she counted five men in blue-and-white uniforms loading wooden crates and barrels into a black ship—a cargo ferry. She kept her voice low. "That's the ship we want, but we're gonna have to work together to take out the crew."

"Can't we just ask them politely to leave?" Lace let a hopeful look cross her face.

Pulchra raised her eyebrows. "You're joking, right?"

"We'll have to run as fast as we can." Al turned back to face her team. "I'll take the lead. Swan? Can you protect Ribbon this time around?"

"You can count on me."

Ribbon waved her hand. "Yes peasant, carry your queen." Swan gave her a questioning glance as she picked her up. "What? If I go down, it will be with grace."

Pulchra stiffened. "I told you! Don't jinx us!"

"Head straight for that ramp and don't stop." Al pointed out their path. "Once we're inside, strap yourselves in and I'll fly us out of here. Ready?"

The girls nodded, the muscles in their faces tensing.

Al closed her eyes. "Please grant us a favorable wind..."

The moment she opened her eyes she charged across the hangar floor toward the men, with the girls trailing behind her. Al reached the ramp first, kicking the unsuspecting man carrying a crate in the back of his knee, causing him to tumble to the ground. He let out a weakened grunt as the box fell on his stomach.

"Hey!" Another man dropped his clipboard and grabbed Al's wrist. She twisted his arm around and yanked herself free just as Punch appeared behind him.

"Leave Brownie alone!" She punched him in the gut, and he went flying into a pile of crates, knocking him out on impact.

Al laughed in nervous bursts. "Well, okay then...thanks, Punch!"

Punch beamed.

The man Al had brought down earlier grabbed her ankle, pulling her to the ground. She groaned in pain and tried to kick herself free from his grasp, but before she could, Punch grabbed the man's collar and catapulted him into the rafters. He let out a high-pitched scream as he flew, clinging to the edges of a round light once he started to fall. Punch stuck her tongue out and brushed her hands together.

Swan's sudden cries for help sent Al and Punch toward her as a man pinned her to the ground. Ribbon lay crumpled up on her stomach next to them, another man looming over her. Lace reached him first, clamping onto his arm with both hands. "Don't touch my sister!"

The man screamed in terrified agony as his skin sizzled. He hit her and tried to break free, but she held on tight, tears streaming down her face. When her hold slipped, the man tore away, gripping his arm that now had two handprint-sized burns on his skin.

Punch pulled the other man off Swan and kicked him and he landed face-first inside of a garbage can, his limbs going limp with a defeated groan. As Al helped Swan up from the ground, Lace embraced her sister, tears raining over everything.

Nervous breathing caught Al's attention. The cargo attendant stepped out from behind a crate, shaking the wrong end of a gun at them. "M—m—monsters! All of you! Monsters!"

"You should probably run away then." Pulchra stood behind him with a smirk.

The man let out a strained cry as he backed away. "And wha—what do *you* do?"

Pulchra shrugged as she moved closer. "Oh, you know. I melt people's brains with my mind."

The man let out a string of frightened yells and ran down the middle of the hangar toward the compound as the girls cheered and laughed.

"I hate to break up the party, but we have to get out of here. More guards could show up any minute." Al scooped Ribbon into her arms and though she needed to focus, she couldn't help but smile. "Everyone in! It's time to get our freedom back!"

Freedom. A word that had felt so distant and elusive for so long.

Swan, Punch, Pulchra, and Lace hurried up the ramp, their white dresses dusty and torn, their feet blistered and cut, but their steps and faces light with hope. Al followed behind them, Ribbon clapping in her arms, letting her smile grow even brighter as she reached the top of the ramp. They were going to get out of this. All of them. They were going to live.

Behind her, a gun's safety lock clicked off.

"I'm afraid I can't let you leave just yet, my Mystery."

Al turned. Mr. Benje stood below them at the base of the ramp, a gun in his outstretched hand. She bent down and propped Ribbon against the inner wall of the ship, the gun's muzzle following her every move, and then faced him with a hateful glare. The girls behind her huddled together, gripping each other's hands and giving the same angry stare.

Mr. Benje chuckled as he moved up the ramp. "You're the most interesting patient I have ever seen. You act all innocent, but I know now that you're far from being tamed. So, let's be reasonable. Come back to the lab so I can teach you how to be good, and I'll let the others go."

Al's mind was clear despite the angry storm clouds brewing inside. She looked at the man before her, seeing his greasy hair, his lazy fighting stance, his horrible smug face, the hands that violated her, and his one good eye. Angel's advice flickered through her clouds like a descending lightning bolt.

"Pulchra." Al's voice was monotone and cold. "The flying manual is in the top left-hand drawer of the dash. Page twenty-seven. Start the ship."

Pulchra didn't move at first, but then she spun around. "Got it!"

"You won't get far, love." Mr. Benje aimed his gun.

Letting an intense yell burst from her lips, Al lunged forward and pummeled the crooked man in the groin with all the strength she had. He toppled to the metal ramp, clutching himself and groaning, the gun clacking out of his hand.

"Hmm. After seeing your reaction, I see that was a lie. Watch me fly now, asshole!" Al shoved him with her foot, and he slid down the ramp and off onto the ground like a beanbag.

Jumping back into the ship, she slammed her fist against a red button near the opening and the ramp rose with a heavy lurching sound. She picked up Ribbon and headed toward the front of the ship, the stunned girls following behind her. After she set the little ice queen down on a seat, she hopped into the rotating pilot chair next to Pulchra. "Strap yourselves in, girls. We're getting the hell outta Marn!"

CHAPTER 19

They flew for two days across the sea. Pulchra watched the autopilot while Al slept, but she didn't sleep much. Her dreams were short and always about Perryn. Would he really meet her at Oceanside? If she didn't make it in time, she might never know.

Inside the crates that had made it onto the ship before they stole it, the girls discovered dried fruit and meat. Free from any restricting schedule, they feasted whenever they liked. The scenery surrounded them in continuous blue frothy waves, though Punch kept announcing she spotted a whale shark or a king flipper bursting from the water.

Sprawled out on the floor, Swan turned to one side, gripping her knees to her stomach, her face pale and sweaty. "I think I hate flying." Her stomach let out a strange gurgle, and she groaned.

"Sorry you're not feeling nice, Swan." Punch rubbed the sick girl's back. "Don't worry. I'll take care of you."

"Hang in there, Swan," Al called over her shoulder. "We're almost back to the mainland."

Lace pulled her legs up onto the seat. "Do you think our parents are waiting for us out there?"

Ribbon leaned against her sister, their heads touching. "Maybe..."

Al rested her chin and hands on top of the pegged brass steering wheel, staring out at the grayish-blue horizon that seemed to stretch on forever. A thin layer of ice crystals had formed on the outside of the windshield and every so often, a small cluster broke free to join the wind.

"My real name is Alisa, but Al's okay too." She swiveled her seat to face the other girls. "I figured since we don't belong to anyone anymore, we should get our real names back. Don't cha think?"

"Yay! Well, you already know us! I'm Jang-mi." Lace raised her hand, causing her sister to bounce against her side.

Ribbon's eyebrows lifted in irritation as her head slid down to hit the seat. "And I'm Heejin."

"Nice to re-meet you both. Sorry we had to leave your chair behind, Heejin."

The ice queen straightened up as a smugness crept into her smile. "It *is* inconvenient, but it belonged to the bad guys. I don't want their fake throne. I'll extend a royal pardon to you since you're my friend."

Al chuckled. "Thanks."

"The name's Nia." Pulchra stuck her hand out toward Al from the copilot chair. "It means 'brilliance' in Swahili."

"Well, it means friend in my book." Al took her hand and Nia finally let the smile she had been hiding burst to life upon her face.

Swan groaned again as she turned to her other side. "I would love to give you a proper greeting, but seeing as my stomach has other plans, I will introduce myself from down here. I'm Amira."

"Amira, thank you...I mean it." Al stared out the portside window. "I wish I was as strong as you..."

Amira let out a gentle laugh. "Everyone is strong in their own way. You just do what you can to help others, even if it's a tiny bit. One day, that tiny bit from someone else might be what you need to keep going."

Al smiled. Amira had given her more than she probably realized.

"Ooo! Me next! My name is Itzel!" Punch raised both of her hands, interrupting the brief reflective silence.

"You have a pretty name, Itzel. I like it." Al gripped her elbows. "I'm sorry I yelled at you to open the door. I was scared, but I shouldn't have been so harsh to you."

Itzel swung her hands in an uneven rhythm as she rocked side to side. "I was scared too, but we all got out together. Now we're safe!" She thrust her pink color stick above her head.

Al picked up her brown color stick from the dashboard and held it out at eye level. One by one, the other girls held up their respective colors, with Amira's stick being the lowest.

"I think you accidentally jinxed me by giving me green, Itzel." Amira let out a strained laugh.

"Oh no! Is jinxed bad?" Itzel hid her mouth behind her clenched hands.

Nia pushed up from her seat and ruffled the child's hair as she passed. "Everything's fine now. Don't worry, kiddo."

The nickname ripped open an old wound in Al's heart and she turned back to face the bow of the ship, gripping the steering wheel. Was Maddox still alive? Was Molly? What about Zeek? Was he okay? How had the world changed since she last belonged to it?

"Look!" Itzel's voice pummeled the tiny space with sound as she hopped up and down next to the starboard window. "It's a king flipper!"

Nia, who had been stretching against the wall, stopped and sighed. "Pun—Itzel, you've been saying that all day."

"But this time I really do see one! Look!"

Nia squinted as she scanned the water below. "Woah. It really is a king flipper!"

Jang-mi hopped off her chair and pressed her face against the glass. "Hello, animal friend!"

"No fair! I wanna see too!" Heejin swayed back and forth, trying to peek out the window now almost entirely blocked by the three girls.

Al sprang from her chair, leaning against the dashboard as she looked out the window.

A giant white koi fish with reddish-orange splotches covering its body leaped from the water, its translucent fins fluttering in the wind as it crashed in and out of its self-made waves. Reflections from its glittering scales bathed Al's face in golden light.

She plopped back into her seat and stuck her color stick behind her ear. Pulling up on the steering wheel, she unlocked it from its gliding position and flicked a few switches on the roof of the cockpit. "We're gonna join the race too!"

Nia, Jang-mi, and Itzel crowded around her with laughter and feverish squeals, as Amira trudged behind them with Heejin in her arms. After buckling the little queen into the copilot seat, she lowered herself onto her knees, gripping the edge of the dashboard. She gave Al a nod and the other girls turned toward the window with wide-eyed anticipation.

"Come on, Al! Show us how you really fly!" Nia called out.

"Yeah!" The younger girls jumped up and down chiming in with cheers of their own.

Al beamed. "Hang on! We're gonna ride the wind!"

She surged the ship downward, flying parallel to the fish's path, and its giant black eye almost took up the entire window as it splashed in and out of the water. The mist from the runoff sprayed across the windshield each time, and the girls giggled and "awed". Al leaned back and let out an excited yell, shaking her head from side to side, and the other girls copied her gesture and call.

The king flipper dove deeper and after a much longer absence, it jettisoned out of the water. As the fish jumped over their ship, its glittering stomach passed overhead, followed by the webby fibers of its tailfin, creating a trailing waterfall like a sudden monsoon. The fish crashed back under the waves it caused and continued its solitary voyage across the sea.

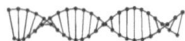

They landed a few hours later, a few miles outside the west wall of the frying pan, using the dense forest that grew there like an invisibility shield for the ship. Unlike Death Desert in the north, the foliage here still looked alive. Being so close to the ocean had kept the area clean, making it the ideal spot to stop.

The sun hung high in the center of the sky, but the temperature inside the ship began to drop as soon as the engine powered down.

Al hopped up from her seat and addressed the girls with her hands on her hips. "Alright, let's tear this ship apart and see what supplies we have." She looked down at her bare feet. "Maybe we'll be lucky and find some shoes?"

"Shoes would be lovely!" Amira rose from the floor like a zombie coming back to life.

The girls pulled open compartments, drawers, and storage bins, dumping their findings in the middle of the floor as Heejin directed them with her arms and snappy commands. They managed to find one rucksack, three cloaks, and exactly one pair of boots.

"Well, that's not much." Al wrapped her arms around herself.

"It's a start." Nia rubbed her chin. "If it's still there, I think there's an Altered camp not too far from here. We can take the extra food and barter for warmer clothing." She pulled on a cloak and pointed to herself with her thumb. "I know how to talk to them. This is my original circuit board after all."

"I'm the one who will be carrying Heejin, so these are for me." Amira snatched the boots and pulled them on. Even as she laced them, the sizable gap on either side of her ankles didn't lessen. With a sigh and clopping steps, she wrapped a cloak around Itzel and threw the last one around herself.

Al touched the back of her neck. "Are you sure you'll be warm enough?"

"It's okay! I'm my own personal heater, so if it gets too chilly, you can all just hug me!" Jang-mi hugged herself and smiled with her teeth.

"And I'm used to the cold. Original snow queen here!"

"I'd leave you the ship to sleep in, but I'm sure it would attract too much attention...ya know, seeing as it's stolen and has a clearly visible serial number on the outside..." Al forced a laugh and fiddled with her hair. "I plan to sink it in the ocean when—"

"Wait. You make it sound like you're not coming with us." Nia eyed her with tightened lips.

"You're not?" Itzel gripped her dress.

"I can't..."

"Brownie nooo!" Itzel's eyes burst with waterfalls as she ran to Al, almost tripping on the cloak dragging at her feet.

Al stroked the sobbing girl's hair. "I have somewhere I have to go. Things I need to figure out...someone I need to see..." She took the brown color stick from behind her ear and offered it to Itzel.

The teary child shook her head. "You have to keep it, Brownie! So we can see each other again."

Al smiled, her words sticking in her throat. "I'm sure we will." As she stood, Nia lightly punched her in the back. Small droplets dotted her cheeks. "Don't go and die out there, okay? That would make our escape look so uncool."

Al gave her a toothy smile as her tears continued to gather at the sides of her eyes. "Hey now. Don't jinx it, Pul." She moved toward the twins. "Take care, you two."

"We will!" they replied in unison.

Al turned toward Amira, and her throat tightened. The songbird smiled like she always did and they embraced, holding each other's shaking shoulders.

"Be safe, Amira."

"You too, Alisa."

Al's heart ached. Hearing her real name spoken for the first time by another person felt beautiful and sad at the same time.

After stuffing the bag with food, Nia threw it over her shoulders. Al followed her and the others to the back of the ship and pushed the red button to lower the ramp, which shuddered downward with squeaky hinges. A bitter gust of wind rushed into the belly of the ship, bathing Al's body in a wave of shivers.

With their cloaks secured around their necks and Heejin hoisted on Amira's back, the group of five descended the ramp one after the other, taking extra care to not lose their footing on the uneven metal. The dark ground crunched with frost beneath their feet, and the sun reflected through the white dusted trees like sparkling glass.

"I wish you a favorable wind..." Al clenched her fists and forced herself to smile as she watched the girls head toward the center of the trees.

Itzel whipped around, waving both of her hands in the air. "Thank you, Brownie! Oops!" Her hands stopped as she giggled. "Thank you, Al!!"

The little earthshaker turned to catch up with the rest of the group and Al sank to the floor. She stayed there, tears flowing from her eyes until her friends' footsteps and outlines disappeared into the forest like the rays of light dipping behind the trees.

The sunset reflected across the water in messy waves of pink, green, and purple as Al steered the ship back out over the ocean. With blurry vision and the bridge of her nose raw from rubbing, she kept the shrinking outline of the city on her right as her guidepost. When the pillars of the electric wall were no longer visible, Al headed toward the shore. She landed on the water below a tall cliff, leaving the engine running.

"I'm sorry I have to sink you, girl." She touched the smooth dashboard. "Thank you for saving us."

She unbuckled her restraint and took the color stick from her ear, gripping it tight. Heading to the back of the ship, she steadied herself against the hull before hitting the red button with her fist. As the ramp began its final descent, the water poured in through the opening. It would have been nice to use the life vest under her seat, but the built-in distress beacon would activate upon contact with a heartbeat. She had to make this "accident" look convincing.

The water level reached her ankles.

She tried to regulate her breathing as she waited, but the ocean's icy teeth forced her lungs into shallow gasps as it bit into her stomach. When the ramp fully extended, the ship lurched downward.

She took a deep breath and plunged into the dark water.

Cold crushed her body from all sides, ripping at her skin with burning needles, and her dress clung to her like a thick layer of excess skin, hindering her desperate movements. The darkness of the twilight blended with the deep water, suspending her in a black hole of disorientation. Sudden bursts of light almost blinded her as the ship's flickering headlights reflected off something made of glass.

Below her, clusters of shattered towers, broken highways with bridges snapped in half, free-floating wires, and strange giant vehicles covered in barnacles and algae slept forever in a watery grave. The devastated cityscape spanned the length of the ocean floor like the insides of a murky snow globe.

Her foot brushed against the tailfin. She bent her knees and pushed off.

Gasping for air, she broke through the surface of the water, the light of the full halfmoon bathing her in soft shadows. Coughing, she pushed her wet bangs out of her face and swiveled around, searching for the shore. It was behind her.

With labored strokes, she swam toward the beach, taking advantage of the sporadic rock outcroppings to rest. Several seabirds who didn't appreciate their unexpected dinner guest honked and pecked at her head. She swung her brown color stick at them like a sword, shooing them away.

When her feet finally hit the sandy bottom, she stood upright and stumbled and splashed toward the beach, her heavy, soaked clothes sticking to her skin, and her teeth chattering.

A nearby receptacle overflowed with reflective packaging and leftovers being pecked at by more squawking seabirds, a trendy location for their late-night rave. Several boot-print paths that stepped on and into each other covered the sand leading toward a set of salt-encrusted wood stairs. Beyond them, a metallic road led up a hill lined with stacked houses.

She emerged from the water and flopped back-first onto the sand, shivering. As she caught her breath, she stared at the dark sky, the tiny stars flickering as if congratulating her for not dying. Though her shaking muscles yearned for rest, her gut urged her to move. Whoever made those tracks could come back.

Staggering to her knees, she scanned the beach and noticed a closet-sized blue shack in the distance. She stood and trudged toward it, rough granules clumping and drying on her feet and ankles. The spaces between her toes scratched with every step.

When she reached the shack, she pulled the crusty door open, and the inside overflowed with sandy dust and discarded junk. Broken fishing poles and a ragged net rested against one wall and dark layers of filth blacked out a window on the adjacent one. The pungent air smelled of fish and seawater and Al gagged, a scowl crawling up her face.

As she entered the small stinking space, she attempted to step over a wooden board, but tripped, landing on top of the built-in bench that showed signs of severe rot. She let out an exasperated groan and laid motionless for a moment, face down on the wood. "If this is punishment for asking for 'too much help,' then I take it back, Mr. Deity In The Sky."

Between the splits in the wood, she noticed a bulky lump under the bench. She heaved herself up and crouched on her knees as she examined the form closer. A blanket. Her frozen fingers snatched at the brown fabric and she wrapped it around her shoulders. It too smelled of dead ocean, but warming her numb limbs mattered more.

With the last of her strength, she kicked the door shut and huddled inside the blanket as her eyes flickered closed and she tried to sleep.

When Al stirred, her whole body felt stiff. Her dress, though dry, was crispy, and her skin felt equally overbaked and seasoned with salt. A few threads of light snuck in through tiny holes in the walls. She shrugged off the blanket and stepped outside.

Squinting and sneezing, she made her way to the ocean waves and washed away the sand from her arms and legs. After shaking her hands dry, Al wiped the grime from her face. She grimaced and covered the back of her neck. Despite her unfortunate situation, the sun wasn't giving her any breaks.

Her stomach rumbled and her eyes landed on a nearby trash can. "No! We won't resort to that, Al. You're a Scanner. You've trained for this! Go back to your shelter." Marching, she ducked back inside her fishy cave, closed the door, and plopped down on the bench, bunching up the blanket around her wet limbs.

She stayed in the shack for the rest of the day, only stepping outside in brief intervals to search the skyline. "It's alright, Al. Perryn will come...he has to."

When the frosty night gripped the beach once more, Al stared at the paint-chipped ceiling. She pushed a portion of her white hair away from her face, the light and dark specks of sand squeaking between the strands. "Even now, I'm still a sea witch." Her stomach gurgled, and she sighed. "And I'm still hungry..."

She sneezed.

Curling up into a ball, she wiped her nose on the stinky blanket and closed her eyes, willing herself to sleep and praying that the new dawn would bring Perryn, or at least breakfast.

She stood outside in front of a beautiful giant Keev-ship, dressed in a glittering dress, waiting to board. Perched on her shoulder, Cogs wore a miniature top hat, complete with a tiny red flower stuck to his metal chest. Zeek, Molly, and Maddox stood smiling on one side and Itzel, Nia, Amira, Jang-mi, and Heejin surrounded her on the other, all wearing fancy, shimmering outfits.

A tap on her shoulder made her spin, causing the beautiful garment that reached her toes to flutter out like an upside-down flower. Perryn stood behind her dressed in a black suit, his arm extended. She took his hand, and his bare fingers tingled against her palm. Together, they headed toward the open door of the ship, the revving engine booming. Soon the noise grew so loud that her ears twinged with pain.

She stirred, rubbing her eyes, expecting the sound to fade, but when it didn't, she leaped up. There really was an engine outside.

Throwing the blanket to one side, she tripped over the board in the middle of the shack in her haste. After regaining her footing, she burst out onto the beach, running toward the sound, her heart pounding in her parched throat. She'd recognize that engine anywhere.

Faint pink light from the rising sun peeked out from behind the horizon, outlining a black bullet-like ship landing on the opposite end of the beach.

Perryn.

The wind tugged at her hair as she ran and though her stiff muscles and sore feet screamed against the sand, she pushed onward toward the figure stepping out from the ship.

Perryn. Perryn! Her mind repeated his name with every labored step, with every strained breath.

Their eyes locked, and he sprinted toward her.

Just before they might have crashed into each other, Al's knees buckled and she fell to the sand, panting. "You—you're late...you jerk..."

When he didn't respond, she looked up, and her face warmed. His diamond-black eyes held a softness that didn't belong to him, asking something she couldn't translate.

Before she could speak, he fell to his knees and embraced her, squeezing her against his chest. She remained motionless at first, but when the familiar scent of pine reached her nose, she closed her eyes and gripped the smooth fabric of his jacket, resting her head against his shoulder.

The sun rose above the horizon, showering the beach with heat, but Perryn's back shielded her from its reach.

Finally, she was free. Finally, she was home.

CHAPTER 20

"My original offer still stands. You need only tell me where you wish to go."

Al tensed. All at once, Perryn was warm, soft, and much too close.

"I mean, going to your place is better than nothing, right?" She tried to pull away, her words tumbling from her trembling lips. "But thinking about it now, being with you actually sounds kind of unbearable!"

"I can just as easily leave you here." He released her, and she tipped backward onto the sand. Sighing as he stood, he dusted off his pants. "It is quite extraordinary how you managed to escape despite your inherent clumsiness."

"Excuse me?" Al shot to her feet. "I got everyone out, didn't I? I'm alive, aren't I?"

He turned and entered his ship, ascending the winding steps. "Like I said...a true miracle..."

"What was that?" Al thundered after him. "And why were you so late picking me up?" She entered the main cabin and was greeted with a blanket to the face.

"Preparing for your arrival, obviously."

With muffled protests, she pulled away the fabric just as Perryn stepped into the cockpit and closed the door. She let out a disgruntled sigh and slumped down into a seat.

Still pouting, she wrapped the thick fuzzy blanket around herself so only her head was visible, like a blizzard bear peeking out of the snow. "See? I knew you were the blanket fairy..." She stopped, noticing the veggie sticks, protein bars, and a box of water resting on the floating tray table in front of her. Her stomach rumbled.

Tearing open the packages, she scarfed down the food and quenched her thirst. Her eyes soon grew heavy as the cozy warmth of the blanket enveloped her tired, cold limbs, escorting her first class to dreamland.

When she awoke, the cabin was swaying, and a vibrating hum gripped the air. She rubbed her eyes and a few wrappers fell to the floor. "How long have we been flying?"

Light breathing caught her attention.

Across the aisle, the dark prince was asleep, his lips parted and his messy hair falling over his eyes as he rested his forehead against his hand. Though sand and dirt dusted his wrinkled clothing, he still looked regal somehow.

Al bunched the blanket up around her mouth as she frowned. This was ridiculous. He was only sleeping, just existing, and yet it somehow seemed special. Perryn shifted, furrowing his eyebrows, and she gasped, pulling the blanket over her head.

A muffled crackling poured out over the intercom, followed by a man's voice. "Mamonaku. Hayashi shima ni tochakushimasu. We will soon be arriving at Hayashi Island."

Al popped out of her fabric fort with the intensity of a baby bird reaching for a worm. Scooting closer to the window, she pressed her face against the glass. "Wow...I finally get to see it up close..."

Peeking through the white wisps of clouds that dissipated as the ship surged forward, an immense green island floated untethered in the sky. Rising from the most distant edge, a five-tiered mountain range decreased in size like steps, and a thick, dark, evergreen forest grew from each earthy platform. The topmost hill housed a shrine with a roof that curled toward the sky like a red-painted smile and red-orange Torii-gates marked the winding path leading up it.

Two slopes down, an ornate castle-like building with dark-blue shingles hid among the trees, its white, tiered towers stacked like upside-down flowers. Nestled on the last hill was a much simpler and much smaller building with a green-shingled roof. More curved roofs in red, blue, and gold dotted the wide and grassy valley below it, where miniature people milled about on paved roads. As their ship flew closer, the gold-colored roof of a hangar gleamed in the sun.

Al looked back at Perryn. He was still asleep. She untangled herself from the blanket and stood over him, tapping his shoulder. "Perryn? We're almost—"

He startled awake, grabbing her wrist, and she froze as their eyes met.

"Warui." He cleared his throat and released her. "Sorry. Reflex." He brushed the hair out of his face and walked past her down the aisle.

Al held the wrist he had touched against her chest, her heart pounding. "I think I'm gonna die..."

Perryn let the swinging cockpit door rest against his back as he spoke with the pilots, his hair partially shrouding his intense eyes in dark fringe.

She hid her face in her hands. "Yep. Definitely gonna die!"

They docked in the hangar, where only a few transport ships slept, and two flight attendants hurried down the aisle. They were new. Al surveyed the ship. Still no sign of Perryn's bodyguards.

The men continued down the spiral steps and opened the hatch door, letting fresh air flood the ship. Jumping out, they shouted over the rumbling of the dying engine to the ground attendants that greeted them in the language Perryn often spoke.

Al descended the stairs and poked her head outside the ship. The atmosphere felt colder than the beach air, but it smelled clean and earthy and the gentle wind swirling through the hangar felt familiar. She smiled. "Freedom."

Metal tools crashed against the pavement as a ground attendant shook his pointed finger at her, his face drained of color. "Yuki Onna!"

Al scurried back inside, feeling like the man had insulted her, but not knowing how. Warmth and the smell of pine enveloped her as Perryn draped his trench coat over her head and stepped outside. She stood dazed at the door, watching as he called something out to the attendants who approached with hesitant steps and bowed. He said something else and their eyes widened and one raised his head to speak, but the glare Perryn gave him sent the young man's words back inside his mouth.

The men continued to bow as Perryn made his way across the tarmac toward a red taxi-ship hovering near the opposite side of the runway. He paused for a moment and then walked back toward her, his face plastered with a deep frown. As he extended his hand to her, Al couldn't help but remember her dream.

With his coat hanging over both sides of her head, she timidly reached out, her mouth threatening to spill all the strange noises colliding inside. Their fingers met, and she stepped over the lip of the door. The moment seemed to last forever, but when she blinked again, he had let go, and already walked halfway back to the taxi-ship. She rushed after him, ignoring the men's suspicious stares and the cold creeping into her bare feet.

A young man in a blue uniform and mittens bowed as he opened the passenger door. Al and Perryn situated themselves inside and the young man took his seat at the left-hand side of the pilot who wore similar attire.

The ship floated forward, hovering magnetically above a metal track that ran through the length of the town and up the hill, like veins leading to a heart. They passed under a tall archway and the charming buildings stretched out before them in organized blocks.

A hand-carved, flower-and-leaf trim ran along the side of a flower shop, and gold accents brushed across the lettering of the bakery that housed happy customers munching on hand-sized loaves. Outside the restaurants, realistic models of soba noodles, okonomiyaki, curry, and colorful drinks with star-shaped fruit spilling from their tops filled display cases. In front of many of these businesses, a tri-color cat figure with closed, smiling eyes, beckoned all to enter with its right paw bending up and down.

The taxi-ship continued, passing streets marked with round, red lanterns bearing symbols Al couldn't read, families with many children, all dressed in colorful and stylish fashions, and individuals with baskets overflowing with fresh produce, rolls of fabric, and gardening supplies. Like the rest of Astova, the only girls Al saw were babies and mother-aged women. She frowned.

As the ship ascended the hill, the green-roofed house she had seen from the air came into view on her right and when they rose above it, the force of gravity pushed her against the back of her seat. Beyond the building's white rocky walls, a courtyard separated the main entrance from a glass-paneled living room. Though the exterior architecture looked like something out of a feudal fantasy, the inside of the home was minimalist and modern.

"Who lives there?" Al craned her neck and the trench coat fell to her shoulders.

"Ah, ojou-chan, that is the new governor Mitobe's home." The pilot was an older gentleman with a long gray beard and a spirited, raspy voice. "He is a sakeya-san, best one on the island and not just because he's the only one."

"A what?"

"He makes his own alcohol and sells it to the local restaurants." Perryn closed his eyes as he rubbed his temples and then muttered something under his breath.

The pilot chuckled. "Hai yo."

Al scrunched her nose. *They better not be making fun of me for not understanding.*

The ship reached the top of the second hill, where the ground leveled out. Off to the right was the huge castle. Hanging in the middle of the arched, double-doored gate that greeted them was a metal symbol: 林. Al couldn't read it, but she thought it resembled two trees standing next to each other.

"Hai. Mairimashita." The pilot nodded and his youthful attendant jumped out of the ship, once again bowing low as he held the passenger door open.

Al gave a clumsy bow as she left the ship, her eyebrows scrunched in uncertainty and Perryn tilted his head as he followed her. The attendant returned to his seat and the red taxi-ship headed back down the mountain over an adjacent metal track.

With a loud creak, the wooden gate doors swung open, revealing several men and women dressed in black-and-white uniforms. "Okairi-nasai Hayashi-sama." Their voices resounded in unison as they bowed at a ninety-degree angle.

Al took a step back, pulling the trench coat over her head. So many people. Would they also be afraid of her? She ducked behind Perryn, though her head stuck out from behind the top of his.

He addressed the group in the same language, instructing them to do quite a few things. Al thought she heard him say her name, as a woman with kind brown eyes and black hair resting just under her ears approached them. Wearing a muted orange-and-brown outfit with a thick pink scarf wrapped around her neck, she looked vibrant and spunky, only her hard-working hands giving away her age.

Perryn didn't turn around. "Al, this is Matsumura-san and she will look after you while you are here."

Mrs. Matsumura bowed with a soft smile. "Hajime-mashite, Al-san. Nice to meet you."

Al stumbled forward and gave another awkward bow, clutching the trench coat so it wouldn't slip off her head. As she stood upright, Perryn had already stepped through the gate.

She prepared to chase after him. "Perryn!"

"Al-san, it is best if you leave him for now." Mrs. Matsumura bowed again as Perryn turned, his icy stare softening before he disappeared out of Al's line of sight. "He looks like he has much to think about, and I am sure you are tired after your journey. Perhaps you would enjoy a hot bath?"

Al spun around, her bare feet leaping for joy. "Yes, please! A hot bath sounds amazing!"

She followed the spry woman through the gates, past the men and women who still maintained their bows, and into a cobblestone courtyard lined with wooden boxes where budless flowers slept. Several faded green trees with puffy needles sprouted in patches on either side. The white towers looming above had solar panels seamlessly integrated into the blue tiling on the roof.

"This house was modeled after Hiroshima Castle and has been in the Hayashi family for many generations." Mrs. Matsumura shuffled along with graceful steps. "My family has served them for just as long."

"Hiroshima?" Al tilted her head. "Where's that?"

"An ancient city that no longer exists, much like the rest of our home country, but in a way, it still exists here, I suppose."

They reached a wooden entryway where many pairs of shoes lined the outside in straight rows. Mrs. Matsumura slipped off her shoes and stepped up into a pair of closed-toe slippers. After asking Al to wait, she pushed open a marbled glass door and floated with grace into the hallway beyond. She returned with another pair and set them down and Al stepped up into toasty clouds, wiggling her toes against the cushioned insides.

Across the entryway, another set of sliding doors stood before her, hiding their secrets behind more marbled glass, and to the left and right of the room, long hallways stretched out with lemon-brown flooring. Everything was warm and clean, in stark contrast to how Al looked and felt. Still, she refused to remove the trench coat just yet, taking advantage of any protection it might offer her in this new land without confirmed allies.

The white jewel-shaped lights complemented the wall divided between an upper white section and a lower wooden-paneled one made of the same wood as the floor. Mrs. Matsumura turned down the long hallway on the left, and Al followed.

"You said the Hayashi family, right? Who are they? And why do they let Perryn stay here?" Al rattled off her questions like a sputtering engine as her grateful feet thawed in her slippers.

"As per tradition, this house is passed on to the eldest child of the Hayashi family. The young master you know as Perryn is in fact the eldest son."

Al skidded to a stop. "Hold up. You're telling me that Perryn isn't just the prime minister, but he owns a whole freaking island too? Great! Something else for him to be smug about. How irritating!" She slapped her hands over her mouth, the trench coat falling to her shoulders, and her accusatory voice echoing in the hallway. "I um, I mean…"

Mrs. Matsumura chuckled. "Do not mind me. I helped raise the young master, so I am well aware of his temperament. Though he has always treated me fairly, I have seen firsthand what happens to those who disagree with him. Has he done something to offend you?"

"One minute he's doing something nice, but then he's all aloof and mysterious and gloom city." Al crossed her arms. "I wish he'd make up his mind on whether he wants to be kind or ignore me because it's super confusing! Like, pick one!"

Mrs. Matsumura pursed her lips in an inquisitive smile. "Ohh. How very frustrating indeed."

"I mean, he seems to be getting better, um—you said you helped raise him? What about his mother? Is she here? He only spoke of her briefly, but I would love to meet her!" Maybe she'd spare a few tips on how to rein in her ill-tempered son.

Mrs. Matsumura stopped, a frown deepening the lines on her face. "I am very sorry, Al-san, but it appears you do not know."

"Know what?"

"She passed away several years ago. Today is actually her death anniversary."

Al's stomach lurched. "I'm...I'm so sorry..."

"He does not speak of her often, so I find it encouraging that he spoke to you." Mrs. Matsumura continued down the hall, another sliding glass door coming into view at the end. Al followed, her feet scuffling across the floor like jammed landing gear.

"Yui-sama was very kind and loved butterflies. Some of them will show up here in the spring if we are lucky. I like to think she became one and comes to visit us sometimes. Here we are." Mrs. Matsumura stopped in front of the marbled glass door and turned to Al. "You will find everything you need inside and though this bath is for all residents of the house, I have made sure you will not be disturbed, so take your time. Go-yukkuri dozo. I will lead you to your room when both you and it are ready." She bowed and walked back down the hall.

As the woman disappeared around the corner, Al pushed open the door, her soul heavy like the glass. *Well, that was a depressing conversation.*

The bathroom was pristine, almost sterile, a fact that comforted her. Leaf and bamboo arrangements sprouted from pots amid the wooden benches and various shelves were filled with soft towels, almost as if the bathroom doubled as an exotic greenhouse.

A bath that could easily fit ten people sat against the back wall and the clear glass roof above it revealed the afternoon sun peeking through misty cloud puffs, shifting across the sky like white sand inside of a kaleidoscope. Foxes carved from the dark marble that matched the floor studded the edge of the bath at even intervals. They all had different expressions, but each had an open mouth and a tiny red scarf wrapped around its neck.

Al swapped her fuzzy slippers for a rubber pair she found near the entrance and approached the bath. After she failed several times to configure the thermostat on the wall, the bath finally filled with steaming water that flowed from the foxes' mouths. Her relief evaporated when the water seemed like it would overflow beyond its marble rim, but a beep echoed from the machine and it stopped.

Al rested her hand against the wall, her voice strained with pent-up panic. "Fish on a stick! How embarrassing would it be if I had to explain—oh yes, hi, my name is Al and I don't know how to fill a bathtub."

She pulled off the trench coat, her stiff, salty dress, and scratchy undergarments, stacking them in a pile beside her. As she stepped out of her slippers and into the hot water, all her cuts and bruises stung. She winced, but forced herself lower. "Have to get clean, even if it hurts, or else an infection will spread...if it hasn't already."

Taking a deep breath, she dunked her head in the water, staying under until she felt her lungs would explode. She burst from the water, gasping, and once her breathing had settled back into its usual rhythm, she stared up at the clear ceiling that had fogged up with steam, obscuring the sky.

"So his mom is gone too, huh...?" Perryn's brooding seemed natural, so the thought that something could've made him that way had never crossed her mind. "Is that why you ran away? Because you didn't want me to see that you were sad?" She dunked her head back under the water, blowing bubbles that popped in rapid succession as they reached the surface.

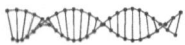

Al sat on the edge of a very large and very fluffy bed, swinging her legs and humming. Wrapped in a white robe, her body was now free from any granules and grime and her feet were toasty inside her slippers.

The room had the same wall and light design as the halls outside, but above her white canopy bed was an un-lit crystal chandelier. On either side, two dark-brown side tables with ornate, curling legs held a radio and an analog clock resting on top of a lace doily. The sliding glass door to her room was marbled as if snowflakes had frozen inside the panes. To her right was a closed and insulated window and along the wall, a closet stood next to a golden vanity with an ornate mirror. The molding along the top looked old and hand-crafted. In the middle of the room was a low table with a thick blanket draping from underneath the glass top. Mrs. Matsumura had called it a kotatsu.

A knock on the door brought Al to her feet. "Yes?" She pushed the button to open the door and Mrs. Matsumura entered, carrying a tray of delicious-smelling food. Sitting on her ankles, she set the tray on the kotatsu. Al zoomed to the table, the heated blanket warming her legs as she stuck them into the open space underneath.

"Tonight's dinner is fresh cloud fish and rice with a side of miso soup and pickled daikon. I brought both types of utensils for you since hashi can be difficult to use if you have not practiced." Mrs. Matsumura's eyes sparkled as she gestured to each dish.

"Well, I can give it a try at least." Al picked up the sticks with both hands and Mrs. Matsumura touched Al's wrist.

"Try using one hand, resting them between your fore-finger and thumb, like this." Mrs. Matsumura demon-strated a few times.

Sticking her tongue out in concentration, Al tried to pick up a piece of daikon with her chopsticks. It slipped and kept slipping each time. Sighing in defeat, Al relinquished her tiny food swords to the napkin and picked up the fork. "It feels wrong to use this on such a pretty meal..." She stabbed the pickled vegetable and placed it in her mouth and with a satisfying crunch, the sour but sweet taste washed over her cheeks.

"Just keep practicing and it will get easier."

"I'm sure one day I'll get a *hand-le* on it." Al lifted her fork, but Mrs. Matsumura's neutral disposition didn't change. Al scrunched her nose as she bit into the fish.

"I wanted to let you know, you are free to explore the house and outside as you please, but the young master insisted I tell you to take care not to break anything."

Al frowned as she scooped rice into her mouth. *Of course he did.*

"If you wish to leave the Hayashi residence, please inform me and I will prepare an escort. Going down the mountain without the taxi is almost impossible because of the steepness and the people living in the town are not used to seeing someone who looks like you. Your safety may be a concern."

Al paused with the fork still inside her mouth as she remembered what the man at the hangar had called her. "I see...I'll keep that in mind. Thank you for your hospitality."

Mrs. Matsumura nodded. "Mochiron. Oh! One moment, please." She stood and glided to the door, the panel sliding open and closed as she stepped into the hall. A few moments later, she returned with a fabric box tied with a purple bow and placed it on the bed.

"While I do not know the full details of your journey, the young master informed me you have no possessions and thus no pajamas to wear! Kawaisou ne." She touched her heart. "I personally chose these for you and hope they are to your liking."

"Oh! Thank you so much!" Al almost knocked the tray from the table as she stood.

Mrs. Matsumura bowed with a smile and left the room, her quiet footsteps disappearing down the hall as Al hopped onto the bed on her knees and tore off the lid.

Nestled between layers of tissue paper was a sleeveless pastel-purple nightdress and matching undergarments. Along the top and threaded over the straps was a lacey finish with a purple ribbon woven through the middle. She held up the items one by one, her smile growing as she changed into them.

Standing in front of the mirror, she twirled several times, the lacey edge of the garment swishing just above her knees. It didn't matter that the garment was short. The material was soft and warm and even the underwear felt comfortable, unlike her previous pair.

She giggled and twirled across the room, addressing the different Als reflected within the various objects around her. "Maybe today I'm more of a mermaid."

Another knock against the glass.

"Did Mrs. Matsumura forget something?" Al pranced to the door and pushed the button to open it.

Perryn stood on the other side, his hair and clothes still disheveled. The scent of pine permeated him, coating the air in the thick, relaxing scent.

Al grabbed her elbows as she avoided his eyes. "Can I help you?"

"I just wanted to check on you and—why do you smell like that?" Perryn covered his nose.

You're one to talk. "Hey!" Al pointed at him as she stepped out into the hall. "I took a bath, okay? I'm actually super clean right now."

He backed away. "You don't smell bad, you just smell strange..."

"Oh, well you see..." She gave him a toothy grin as her shoulders scrunched up. "There were so many types of shampoo and soap that I couldn't decide. So, I just sort of used all of them...at once."

"As I said, you do not smell bad just—" Perryn tensed. "Al, where is your robe?"

"Huh? Why?"

"You have to wear a robe with that kind of nightgown." His voice was strained, and he refused to look at her.

"Oh. Really?" Al looked down, her shoulders slumping as she gripped her elbows again. "I'm sorry. I don't wear girl clothes, so I don't know how they work..."

Perryn turned away. "Well, you appear to be stable, so I will let you rest now." He strode down the hallway.

"Perryn!" Al called after him. "I really am sorry!"

"What? No need to apologize for—"

"No, I mean. I'm really sorry about...your mother."

Perryn halted abruptly. "Matsumura-san told you what happened to her?"

"She didn't give me the details, just that she had passed. I didn't know...I'm so sorry. Mothers are really special people."

Perryn tightened his fists.

"I know how it feels to not have a mom. It's like a piece of you is missing. I'm not exactly like you since I had Molly, but still. I guess I just..." She bit her lip. "You asked me back in the cave why I freaked out after seeing that girl in the hologram. It's because that was my mom. Kera Lacey's Altered like me..."

Perryn laughed through his nose. "Yes, all of that is quite obvious now, but I appreciate you telling me the truth outright."

Al puffed up her cheeks. "I—"

"And thank you."

"Huh?"

"Thank you for caring about my mother."

She fumbled with her hair, which was an even lighter shade than before. "I—yeah, I mean, that's what a normal person does, right? And just because I'm Altered, doesn't mean I can't be normal, ya know. The not-normal one is you, cuz—"

He spun around and marched toward her, his eyebrows scrunched and his face tinged with a faint pink. "If you keep going on about it like that, I will have no choice but to rescind my compliment!"

Al stared at him and then burst into laughter, holding her sides. "Your face! I can't—you look—"

She continued her hysterics as Perryn closed his eyes and pinched the bridge of his nose. "Well, now that we have both confirmed the other is fine, I have no reason to stay."

"Wait!" Al jumped in front of him, moving closer until she had cornered him. "How do you say goodnight?"

"Why...do you want to know that?" Perryn continued to avert his gaze as his back hit against the wall.

"Oh, come on, just tell me!" She hit his shoulder with a smile.

His eyes retraced the invisible path her hand took with furrowed eyebrows. "Oyasumi." He cleared his throat. "It is oyasumi."

Al turned away, her hands clasped behind her back as she took a few steps. She recited the word several times until her mouth registered the new diction. "Oh, I see now! Got it!" She turned back around, and with a giant smile, she leaned toward him. "Oyasumi!"

Perryn's body stiffened as his eyes went wide. Then, his usual scowl returned to his face and he sighed. Moving past her to march back down the hallway, he mumbled words Al couldn't understand until he disappeared down the stairs.

She put her hands on her hips and shook her head. "I don't get him at all."

CHAPTER 21

Al stared up at the canopy as she lay on her bed. She had gone to the beach out of reflex, her desire to see Perryn again something she didn't understand. It was probably just a side effect from experiencing such horrible things at Marn. His familiar face, no matter how annoying, was still comforting. Now that the magic of Maddox's inventions had worn off and with Asotva's military arresting anyone who looked even remotely Altered, it wasn't safe anywhere else. For the time being, she had to put her search for Kera on hold.

Al welcomed the break more than she thought she would as she spent her days exploring the vast Hayashi Manor. Perryn was gone for most of them, having flown back to the capital to attend to his duties as prime minister. Sitting in the living room with Mrs. Matsumura, she listened to his speeches over the radio while sipping green tea or eating roasted satsumaimo, noting with irritation how striking his voice sounded.

The topics ranged from new water allocation laws and electricity rations to his proposed plans to rebuild infrastructure destroyed by the Altered. He accused Mr. Benje of illegal genetic engineering and removed him from Marn, but during his transfer to the capital, he "mysteriously" died in his cell. He was the most horrible person she had ever met, but was it okay to feel happy about his death?

Al found her closet stocked with new clothes, but, while winter appropriate, they weren't like the feminine outfits Angel had worn, or like her nightgown, the only thing she wore during her indoor adventures. When her pajamas needed to visit the wash, or she ventured outside for late-night runs around the building, she grudgingly wore pants. On one such run, she discovered a garden near the back of the house with towering red-and-gold trees.

Bald, child-like statues smiling with their palms pressed together dotted the trimmed, mossy grounds. In the middle of the foliage, an arched footbridge painted in a dusty red overlooked a fishless pond that ran the length of the garden. One end of the bridge ended in a stone pagoda, where tiny paper lanterns dangled from the edges. She often sipped hot barley tea under its arches, learning Japanese from Mrs. Matsumura as her pink scarf danced in the wind. Al would also join her when she went to town to purchase food and supplies for the household.

Trying not to draw attention to her unique attributes, she wore dark sunglasses and wrapped a scarf over her hair, which had turned completely white. Though this hid her true colors, it did nothing to lessen the stares she received as she and Mrs. Matsumura moved from store to store or loaded the red taxi-ship with their bags. Dyeing her hair again would've been smarter, but something deep within her rebelled against the very thought.

Though she enjoyed the fresh air, the many floors and secret corners of Hayashi Manor enticed her to stay inside.

She ventured to an upper level and found a grand library taking up the entire floor. With wall-to-wall shelves and tall bookcases spread out like wooden hedges, it was a literary labyrinth. Plastic casings preserved all the books, pages and covers alike, many of which were old or written in different languages. Lacking central heating, the library was cold, but organized, much like the aloof prince who had compiled the impressive collection.

Each of the five rooms on this level had a set of armchairs, a table, a reading couch, and a different color scheme that seemed to reflect the genre of the books they housed. Al spent days in the middle room, lying on a pastel-red carpet, surrounded by cushions as she visited the lands of fantasy and romance.

At night, the diamond-shaped wall fixtures provided light, and during the day, the sun poured in from a window that overlooked the entire town. She often awoke to the sound of the groundskeepers raking orange and red leaves across the smooth cobblestone, piling them high into mounds as their breath hung in the air.

On a particularly chilly day, Al discovered a glass case tucked away in the back corner with a single book inside. The weathered tome rested on a velvet cushion and a few of its crumbling pages lay off to the side, covered in a plastic film.

She recognized the cover. The expression Perryn made when she had presented it to him in the cave was priceless. She giggled. "So it really was a special book then." Raising her hands to minimize the glare, she peered into the glass. "*The Tale of Genji* by Murasaki Shikibu. Huh. Maybe he'll let me read it sometime."

"I could."

Al yelped, rocking the glass case as she jumped.

Behind her, Perryn leaned against a bookcase, a plate of cookies in one hand and a blue blanket draped over his arm. He looked well-rested in his black cable-knit sweater and black pants, and his hair had returned to its proper smoothness.

Is black seriously the only color he owns?

Al scrunched her nose and marched toward him. "I told you to stop sneaking up on me!" She grabbed a cookie from the plate and snapped it with her teeth.

Perryn scoffed through his nose. "After all this time, you still struggle with your spatial awareness. Good to know some things have not changed. And do you always talk out loud like that?"

Al paused mid-bite, the cookie still held to her lips. "Wow. And here I thought you knew everything. It's because I'm not in combat mode, or at least I wasn't until *you* showed up. Why are you here anyway?"

"Well, this *is* my house."

"I mean up here." Al stuffed the rest of the cookie into her mouth. "You can't bribe me with baked goods, ya know."

"Matsumura-san forced me to bring them. She informed me you have been visiting the library often and that you refuse to wear anything but your nightgown."

Al threw her arms around her silky dress and pouted. "It's pretty, that's why."

Perryn set the plate on the table, and with a graceful swoop, draped the blanket around Al's head. Holding her shoulders, he stared straight into her eyes. "Wearing such a thin nightgown without a robe could have consequences. Are you aware of that?"

Al tensed. He did it again, freezing her with only his gaze. Despite his stern warning, something soft lingered beneath his words. Why did he seem so worried?

"Consequences? You mean...like hypothermia?"

Perryn broke his eye contact with a frustrated sigh. "Never mind."

What? What did I do?

He walked over to a shelf and grabbed a book as Al yanked the material off her head. Tossing the blanket over an armchair, she stormed to his side. "What's your problem?"

Perryn returned the book to its home. "And here I thought reading would be a peaceful experience." He turned to leave.

Oh no you don't! With a frustrated grunt, she ran up behind him and scrunched his hair into a tangled mess.

Perryn crumpled to the floor, clutching his head. "What the hell are you doing?"

Al put her hands on her hips. "If you aren't gonna be nice, then right back at 'cha! It's kochira-koso, buddy!"

Perryn stared up at her, his eyes wild and huge. His face relaxed into a frown as he stood and slumped into the blanket-less armchair, not bothering to fix his hair. "So, you remembered that?"

"I told you I'd use it against you later. Well, welcome to the future!" With an exasperated huff, Al flung herself into the other chair, wrapping the blanket around her bare shoulders. "Why are you so annoying?"

"Kochira-koso." Perryn looked away as he covered his mouth with the back of his hand.

Is he pouting? "You are seriously the most irritating person in the world! If you really hate me that much, then why do you keep spending time with me?"

"I do not hate you. You are just very...frustrating..."

"Then why? Why even put up with me then?"

Perryn remained silent for a long time, but she endured the wait with crossed arms and a tapping foot. "I feel...like I have to watch out for you."

Al jumped from her chair. "Oh! Because I'm a little baby who can't take care of herself, right?" Waiting to hear his response and then being presented with such an obnoxious answer was unacceptable.

"No! Dammit, Al!" Perryn shot up. "How unobservant can you be? Do you know how worried I was? I thought you were dead! How do you expect me to act?"

Al took a step back. *Why does he care so much about that?*

Perryn retreated to his chair, his eyebrows wrinkling below his palm as he touched his forehead. "When I heard they bombed the compound, I went back. The place was decimated. There were no survivors. And when I contacted the other bases, I only heard static or the retreat sequence. After two months of hearing nothing from anyone and the lack of Altered attacks, I assumed you were all dead."

Al dropped into her chair, covering her mouth. Molly and Maddox really were gone then.

"Then I find you alive and some pervert is torturing you and instead of letting me rescue you, you want to escape on your own. You are so very frustrating."

Al wrapped the blanket around her shoulders again. "I wanted you to rescue me too, ya know..."

Perryn dropped his hand and stared at her.

"But—" Al averted her gaze. "I had to know if I could save myself." She chuckled. "I realize how stupid and risky all of that was, but now that I know I can, I feel stronger, less afraid." She pointed at him. "That's why you have to trust that I can take care of myself. Also, stop being so mean, ya buttface!"

Perryn smiled as he rested his cheek on his hand. "Should I come up with a nickname for you too?"

Al glared at him. "What?"

He lifted his hands in defense. "I will stop hovering. I was not aware you felt so suffocated."

"Oh." Al's face softened. "I will also try my best not to bite your head off so much." She stood up and extended her hand. "Deal?"

Perryn furrowed his eyebrows before he stood and took her hand. "Fine. I submit."

Even though he wore his gloves, his touch sent sparks down her arm. "So!" Al hopped toward a nearby bookcase, the blanket trailing behind her like a cape. "You wanna read something together?" She scanned the shelf, unable to hide her smile.

"I believe that was originally my idea, so yes."

"Oh please. I'm the one who suggested it first."

They continued to banter, shooting witty comebacks at each other as they added books to their potential reading stack. While Perryn browsed the historical fiction section, Al gathered a few oversized cushions for them to sit on. In the end, they narrowed their book selections down to two.

"*The Magic Engine!*" Al held out the thick tome. Moving pictures of engine parts combining and separating flickered on repeat across the cover.

"Ha." Perryn pushed up his glasses as he turned back to face the shelf. "*Sitting by Myself at The Edge of The World* is clearly the superior choice."

Al set her book down. "Looks like there's only one way to settle this…" With a cheeky grin, she picked up a cushion.

"Coercion?"

"Nope!" She whacked him over the head. "A con-*cushion!*"

Perryn turned, removing his dislodged glasses with a pinched smile. "Prepare for your demise."

"You'll have to catch me first!" She ditched her blanket with a crazed giggle and dashed toward a line of bookcases, clutching her fluffy ammo. As she rounded the end, he appeared out of nowhere.

"Surrender!" He swung his cotton cartridge with a wide smile and his attack collided with her shoulder.

Al squealed. "Never!" She returned fire, but he blocked it with his arm.

Laughing and taunting, they continued their pillow fight, chasing after each other between the bookcases until their voices grew fatigued. Al crouched with her back against the thick end of a bookcase and peered over her shoulder. Perryn stood near their book pile, his hands on his knees and his cushion abandoned at his feet.

Al smirked. Victory was at hand. "You left yourself wide open!" She zoomed out from her hiding place, cushion above her head. But as she ran toward him, she slipped on her discarded blanket and lost her footing.

"Al!" Perryn rushed toward her.

They fell to the floor, knocking over a few books that flailed and crashed around them like dying plastic birds.

His fluttering heartbeat ebbed against her cheeks, her face momentarily buried in the heavy pine scent of his sweater. Perryn winced, reaching for the back of his head to remove a book.

"Oh! I'm sorry!" She lifted her head from his chest. Her knees straddled his, the soft fabric of his pants touching her bare legs. "Are you okay?"

This situation was familiar.

"Your hair is getting longer..." The deep midnight in his eyes captured her once again as he tucked a strand of her white hair behind her ear. She plunged heart-first into his darkness.

"I've been wondering for a long time..." She gripped his sweater as he leaned toward her. "Why did you let me go...that day at the bunker?"

His lips were so close.

"I was tired of lying to you..." His fingers grazed her cheek and she closed her eyes.

"Hayashi-sama?" Mrs. Matsumura's spunky voice broke into the room and the two scrambled away from each other.

Perryn sprang to his feet, clearing his throat. "I should see what she wants."

"R—right!" Al's voice squeaked as she sat on her knees, staring at the floor.

He headed for the door but paused at a bookcase, his voice tentative. "Molly and Maddox may be gone, but you are not as alone as you think."

She thought she heard him curse under his breath as he left the room, but her overwhelming thoughts distracted her too much to be sure.

"Did he just—?" Al held her head. "And was I just gonna go with it?" She hugged a cushion to her chest and flopped backward onto the floor, staring at the ceiling. Her cheeks burned. "No! There's no way he wanted to kiss you. You're just imagining it, Al!" She flung the cushion against her face with a strained squeak and lay motionless until the sun had set beneath the island.

The next afternoon, Perryn left the manor again. From her bedroom window, she could just make out his ship—a tiny, black smudge taking off from the hangar. Resting her chin on the windowsill, she watched until the dot disappeared behind the clouds. Her face scrunched into a disgruntled pout as the tingling sensation of his fingers against her ear returned.

"Yeah, that's right. Run away..."

Leaning up from the window, she dipped her feet into her slippers and headed into the hall wearing a red sweater and black pants. As she mapped a new house trip in her head, she spotted Mrs. Matsumura about to descend a flight of stairs, carrying a basket of fruit and boxed goods. She took her first step and the contents tumbled to the floor. "Arama!"

Al rushed to her side. "Matsumura-san! Let me help!"

"Arigatou Al-san. That is kind of you. These steps are hard to use when they are hard to see." She chuckled as she retrieved a few pieces of runaway fruit.

After collecting the fallen boxes and taking the basket from Mrs. Matsumura, Al followed her down the stairs.

"This is where we helpers live. It is nice and cool during the summer, but during the winter it can be too much."

The staircase emptied into another hallway lined with closed sliding doors and an even larger one waited at the end. Mrs. Matsumura pointed down the hallway. "Right through there." Once they reached the door, she pushed the button on the wall to open it and Al passed through. The dark room felt like a refrigerator, and the potent scent of pine filled her nose.

"You can set the basket down near the table." Mrs. Matsumura entered and motion-sensitive lights flickered on.

Moving portraits of men and women ran along the top like wallpaper, their clothes becoming more modern as they wound closer to the middle. Several thin red cushions and a wide altar filled with fruit, sweets, flowers, and unopened boxes of foodstuffs sat at the front of the room. Above this, an ornate box with shutters held an incense stick and two moving portraits.

The first was of a petite young woman with a soft smile and black hair pulled high into a twisted bun. She wore a multi-layered purple kimono, and a long gold pin with butterfly charms and jewels dangling from its end, stuck out from her hair. The other portrait showed a young man with shaggy black hair in a black suit. His stern expression only changed when he blinked.

Al set the basket down and studied their faces. "Is that woman Perryn's...?"

Mrs. Matsumura nodded. "Hai. That is Yui-sama. In this place, we honor our loved ones who have passed and give them gifts in case they wish to visit us." Mrs. Matsumura took items from the basket and set them on the table, replacing the brown and more squishy-looking fruit with fresh pieces.

"She seems lovely."

"She was. Shall I introduce you?" Mrs. Matsumura sat on her knees on the cushion and lit the incense in the box. Small wisps of a familiar fragrance wafted from the stick.

Al sat beside her. "Is that...pine?"

"Yes, it was Yui-sama's favorite. She loved the forest where the butterflies were."

Mrs. Matsumura picked up a metal bowl and tapped it with a round dowel, producing a clear warbling sound. The tone pierced Al's heart and tears crowded the corners of her eyes.

Pine.

The smell that comforted her was the same smell that connected Perryn to his mother. He always smelled like pine, which meant he came here often. He missed her.

Al let her tears fall as Mrs. Matsumura pressed her hands together and closed her eyes. Al did the same, praying that wherever Yui Hayashi was, she was at peace.

"Are you alright, Al-san?"

Al nodded. "I'm okay...it's just...I think I'm starting to understand him more."

"I am sure his mother would be happy to know her son has found a friend."

Al smiled, her eyes still foggy with leftover tears. "I'm honored that you would share such a personal part of your life with me, even though I'm a stranger."

"Oh, you are no stranger. Hayashi-sama would never bring a stranger to his house. He even refused to let his own father, his father's wife, and their children visit..." Her voice trailed off.

"What?" Al scanned the room. Marcus Keevie's face was missing from the lineup. They must really have been on bad terms for him not to join the family, even in the afterlife. Perryn had a stepmother and siblings? "Who's that in the other photo, next to Yui-sama?"

"Ah. That is her younger brother, Calvin-sama. He sadly passed before the young master was born, so now Hayashi-sama is the last of his line."

"Calvin?" Al felt the room closing in around her. "As in Calvin Hayashi, the scientist?" Why hadn't she realized it earlier?

"Ara! I suppose Hayashi-sama has told you about him then? Yes, he was a scientist. His work kept him very busy, and he rarely visited after he moved to the capital. Yui-sama would sometimes travel there, but I had to manage the home. Too many things to attend to, you see."

It was a long shot, but Al had to ask. "Did he ever tell you what he was working on?"

"Oh no. Calvin-sama always kept to himself. Very quiet, with loud results. His mother would always say that." She covered her mouth as she chuckled. "So it was not surprising to learn he had suddenly married a coworker without telling anyone."

A coworker? Al tried to steady her breathing. "Do you know what his wife's name was?"

Mrs. Matsumura bowed her head. "I apologize. I never met her in person and it has been quite some time since they passed."

Al gripped the pillow, her knuckles turning white. "What happened to them?"

"It seems sad events often plague the Hayashi family. A terrible fire burned down their home, taking them both. They told us it was an accident, started by a stray cigarette. No pictures remained for us to place his wife in our family shrine."

Al released her death grip on the cushion. "I'm sorry. That must have been terrible."

Mrs. Matsumura looked wistfully at the moving photographs. "Yui-sama cried so much, I thought she would never smile again. But when Hayashi-sama was born, it was like her happiness was reborn too. Oh! I think there is something I can check."

Mrs. Matsumura stood, and with graceful steps, shuffled over to a wooden chest that sat near the door behind them. "Now if I can just find..." She sorted through papers, photos, and other keepsakes, spreading them out into stacked piles on the wood floor.

"Mitsukemashita!" She returned to Al and handed her a golden card tied shut by a swirling red cord. "This is their marriage announcement."

Al unwound the braided tassel from the sparkling paper and opened the tri-fold card. Stringed music flowed out of the panel as delicate flowers fluttered across the screen in a storm of pink petals. As they dissipated, Calvin Hayashi's name appeared in fancy letters. His wife's name emerged below his and Al froze.

"Al-san?"

Nothing was making sense again.

"I—I think I need some air..." She choked out her words and ran.

Abandoning her slippers at the front door, she stumbled across the cobblestone and into the garden with bare feet. Crossing the bridge, she ducked down inside the pagoda and clutched her knees to her chest as she trembled.

Kera Lacey—that's who Calvin Hayashi married.

CHAPTER 22

For the next several days, Al hardly left her room as she processed her thoughts. She finally knew how her mother died, the same way Maddox and Molly did. Burning. Choking. Unable to escape. They didn't deserve an end like that. Did Perryn know they might be related? Was that why he brought her to his house? What other reason could there be? The realization made her heart hurt.

I thought I'd be happier to know who my birth father might be. Al had waited so long to understand her past, she no longer understood herself.

The next morning, she woke up with an intense headache and heat radiating under her skin. Mrs. Matsumura arrived at her usual time with breakfast and almost dropped her tray in a panic as she left. She returned with a few attendants and all of them wore white masks over their mouths and noses. Even though Al didn't understand the commands Mrs. Matsumura gave them, she recognized several of the words—window, fresh, germs, sleep.

"Am I actually dying and just no one has the heart to tell me?" Al's throat hurt as much as her hoarse voice made it sound. *This is what I get for not wearing my robe.*

Mrs. Matsumura shook her head as she flipped the dangling end of her pink scarf over her shoulder. "You will be better in no time." She took a bottle from her apron pocket, uncorked the lid, and poured a clear liquid onto a spoon.

Al struggled to sit up as Mrs. Matsumura fed her the spoon's contents. Though her churning stomach threatened to trigger a tsunami, the sweet, earthy syrup quelled the waves. Al recognized the taste—Cave Moons.

So much had changed since she last had them—from hiding in the dirt to sleeping in the clouds. Other Altered girls could only dream of such a grand life, girls like Amira, Nia, Itzel, Heejin, and Jang-Mi. *Why am I the lucky one?*

Al fell back and shifted under the comforter, with only enough strength for a half-scrunched nose. "Matsumura-san...why are you so nice to me?"

The woman chuckled as she wrung the water out of a cloth, the droplets hitting the metal bowl below it like a dull wind chime. "Is there a reason I should be mean?"

"I'm Altered..."

"Yes. My eyesight is still good enough to see that, Al-san."

Al gave a weak smile. "You're a Naturalist, so shouldn't you at least distrust me?"

Mrs. Matsumura placed the washcloth on Al's forehead. "I suppose it must be because Calvin-sama was Altered, though no one would have been able to tell by looking at him."

"He was?" Cold relief spread out from the damp cloth. "How so?"

"His memory was like a computer." The older woman's eyes seemed to sparkle as she touched her pink scarf. "It made him very good at finding lost things."

"Do you think he was a good person?"

Mrs. Matsumura folded her hands in her lap with an amused smile. "Human souls are never one shade, but his was certainly bright. His smoking habit may have turned his insides a different color though."

"My dad also had that habit." Al froze and a sad smile traced her lips. The words had fallen out so easily. How ironic. She had finally acknowledged Maddox, but he was dead.

Mrs. Matsumura clasped Al's hand. "If you have a picture of him, we could make a special place for him to visit."

"I don't have any pictures, not of anyone..." A few tears slipped down her cheek. Her only memento of Kera was lost forever, just like the rest of her family—unless, she was a Hayashi.

"Was Yui-sama Altered?"

Mrs. Matsumura's face fell as she stared out at nothing, but her regularly scheduled happiness returned with lightning speed. "As the eldest, Yui-sama carried the family name, so she remained natural. Now, enough questions. It is time for you to rest." She tucked the covers around Al and turned toward the door.

"Matsumura-san?" Al struggled to lift her head, the muscles in her neck pinching. "Arigatou."

Mrs. Matsumura bowed with a gentle smile. "Doitashimashite." She filed out of the room with the attendants, leaving Al in silence.

"So...Perryn is one hundred percent natural, huh? Well, that's annoying..." She tried to roll her eyes, but they felt heavier than usual and she gave up.

"If Calvin Hayashi really is my father..." She frowned. "Then Perryn and I could never be..." She pulled the covers over her mouth, not sure if the new wave of heat rushing through her body was from the fever or something else.

She was running barefoot through a long dark hallway, the space around her pitch black except for the lemon-brown floor that reflected her mirror image in its smooth panels. With each step, another digitized voice mingled with the others in the thick humid air as if multiple radios were broadcasting their programs at the same time. The frantic voices delivered news reports of Altered attacks, Vilroy's conquests, and the deaths of the people she loved, all layering on top of each other.

"Shut up! Shut up!" Tears clouded her sight, but she didn't stop running.

Four figures appeared at the end of the hallway, and as she approached, she recognized their faces. Calvin and Kera stood smiling, their hands outstretched, and next to them, Maddox and Molly did the same. Al's lungs burned for air as she reached for them.

Just as she was about to touch their fingertips, tall hot flames burst from the invisible dark walls, engulfing them all. With soundless screams and curled fingers clawing toward the sky, they disintegrated into a pile of gray ash before her.

Her eyes shot open. Both of her hands were extended, grasping at the air. Fresh tears soaked her cheeks and sweat drenched her entire body. She sat up and held her head as her breathing settled.

What day was it? Since getting sick, her consciousness had blurred into a mess of undefined nonsense. Her nightmares didn't help to define reality, either. The moonlight pouring through the window told her she was alive, at least. Unpacking herself from the heavy layers of blankets, she stepped into her slippers, steadying herself on the bed.

She reached for the glass on the bedside table, but when she brought it to her dry lips, it was empty. With a defeated sigh, she headed to the sliding glass door and pushed the button. When it opened and she stepped out into the hall, she almost dropped the glass.

Perryn was asleep in an armchair, leaning in an awkward position as his head rested on his fist.

He was back.

The top buttons of his white shirt were undone, and the bottom was untucked from his black pants. As he sat there, his chest rising and falling, Al drifted to a dimension vacant of time. A shiver snapped her back.

With a scrunched nose, she set the glass out of the way and disappeared back inside her room. She returned with a blanket that dragged on the floor and draped it over Perryn's lap, tucking the ends behind the chair. After she finished sealing him in fluff, she picked up her glass and smiled. "Now we're even."

Perryn shifted in his sleep, and Al clenched the cup as she held her breath. When he settled into a different position, a faint smile formed on his lips. She released her chokehold on the glass, but when he moved again, she fled to the kitchen.

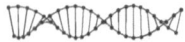

Al's gloved fists collided with a black sandbag that hung from the ceiling as she circled it with nimble steps. Her white hair, pulled high into a messy ponytail, swished behind her, and her tight black microfiber crop top and ankle-length pants let her skin breathe.

Though the worst of her sickness had passed, Al had felt off ever since she saw her mother's marriage announcement. Despite Mrs. Matsumura's protests, Al needed to reset herself by returning to something she understood. Working out made much more sense than a brooding boy and family secrets.

The manor's gym was much smaller than the school's, and many ancient exercise machines Al had never seen before filled the space. A wall of mirrors covered the right, and on the left, large windows let the winter sun warm the room.

She sent two more punches and a high kick deep into the sandbag, her breaths resting in the air as blurry clouds before they dissipated. With more concentrated exhales, she sent another barrage of punches and kicks into the sturdy material as the door behind her opened. She didn't break her concentration, but his presence was far too familiar to not recognize him.

"So, how long will you be here this time?" She watched Perryn watching her in the mirror. The black shorts and lightweight jacket he wore looked good on him.

"My duties at the capital have been fulfilled until next year."

Stay focused. He's just a distraction. Whatever you feel for him isn't real. You can't.

Al sent a final kick into the sandbag. "Consider that the extent of my excitement."

"So much for our truce." Perryn let an amused side-smile slip as she walked past him to where her water bottle and towel rested against the wall. She sat, dabbing her bare neck and taking a long drink.

He walked toward her, holding his own water bottle. "I see your attitude lives on. Matsumura-san was worried about nothing."

Says the guy who stayed outside my room. Al slapped the towel over her shoulder. "So, *you* weren't the one who was worried? Good to know."

He rested his forearm on the wall above her head and looked down with a cocky smirk. "Did you want me to be?"

Her mouth fumbled for words as she scrambled out from underneath his shadow. "No! I'm a lone dragon! I can take care of myself, remember?" She let out several small roars as the air puffed from her mouth like smoke.

"Oh, of course." Perryn continued to smirk. "But perhaps the lone dragon would like a real sparring partner?"

"Fish on a stick, I just finished my workout! Let a girl rest first, you cheater." She sat farther away and took another sip.

"Fine." He unzipped his jacket and tossed it to the side, revealing his bare chest.

Al choked on her water.

"You alright?"

She flung her hands in front of her face. "I said I just need a minute!"

Perryn sighed and walked to the opposite side of the room to stretch.

Al held her head as she mumbled under her breath. "Come on, Al! You've seen chests before. It's not a big deal!" She looked up, her eyes narrowing. "I must conquer the chest." She jumped to her feet and called across the room. "You wanna fight? Then let's fight, Perryn!"

The half-dressed man, now sitting on an exercise machine, let the bar he held rise back into its resting position. As he walked toward her, drinking from his water bottle, her resolve weakened, but she prayed it didn't show on her face.

He stood in front of her, his face alight with mischief. "A bold challenge from someone who has yet to defeat me in anything." A few water droplets trickled down his chin and onto his bare chest.

Al stiffened. *He's doing this on purpose.* "Ha! You're gonna eat...whatever this floor is made of! Yeah! That's what you're gonna eat!" She pointed at him with forced bravado.

Perryn held back his laughter as he set his water bottle against the wall. He called something out in Japanese as he returned to face her, and a computer voice responded. A timer with large numbers appeared on wall. As the clock began its pre-start countdown, the two fighters separated to stand on opposite sides of a large mat.

Perryn bent his knees, raising his fists. "Last one standing when the timer ends wins. Shall we wager something for a more interesting fight? Loser owes the winner one favor."

Al dug her heels into the squishy ground and brought her fists in front of her face. "Get ready to give me what I want then!"

Perryn smirked.

A beep echoed into the room, starting the real countdown, and the two moved in perfect tandem like a choreographed dance. Every punch Al threw, Perryn blocked with his forearm and every kick he delivered she dodged. As she tried to land another punch, he caught her fist in his hand and moved to hold her wrists. Their eyes locked as their rapid exhales created a cloudy haze around their faces. Even with his gloves, his pulse pounded against her skin.

She spun under his arms, twisting her hands free and jumped back in one fluid motion.

The numbers turned red as the last minute remained.

They locked eyes again.

Al knew she had to bring him down fast. There was no time. She zig-zagged forward. He stood his ground as she lunged with a two-armed push, attempting to knock him off balance. He caught her ankle with his foot and she fell to the mat with a cry mixed with pain and frustration.

"What happened, Al? Did you lose?" Perryn leaned over her.

She glanced at the clock. *Fifteen seconds left!*

"You should learn not to be so cocky!" She launched her foot up, catching the back of his knee, which buckled under him. Losing his balance, he fell to his side just as the clock reached zero and a buzzer cut through the air.

He rolled onto his back next to Al, their panting creating a misty canopy above their heads.

Al let out a breathy laugh. "Looks like we're both even again, huh?"

"So it seems." Perryn's voice was just as fatigued. He sat up, looking away from her. "What was it you wanted?"

"I dunno. I agreed to the bet so quickly, I actually didn't have anything in mind." As she sat up, her white hair draped over her shoulders like the fringe of a royal cape, most of it having fallen from her ponytail. "I'll save mine for later. What did you want, Perryn?"

He remained silent for so long, Al thought he might have fallen asleep. She was about to poke him when he responded. "I want you to go somewhere with me..."

She swallowed as the sweat gleamed across the ridges of his chest. "Why?"

He turned toward her, his eyebrows furrowing. "Explaining the rationale behind my request was not part of the terms of our duel, which you already accepted, need I remind you!"

His bare skin was too powerful.

Al threw out her hands. "Okay, okay, fine! I'll go with you!"

His eyes widened before he stood with his back to her.

Al lowered her arms and fidgeted with her hair. "So...where are we going?"

"If I told you anything more, it would ruin the surprise." He looked back at her, his face warming with such a gentle smile, she froze, stunned into silence. So much genuine happiness floated in his eyes, he looked like a different person. He left the room, swinging his jacket over his shoulder like some handsome protagonist in a romance novel. Al fell backward onto the mat, throwing her cold hands against her hot face.

In the coming days, the attendants ran about cleaning and changing the color scheme of the house from brown and orange to red and gold. Fruit-topped cakes, spiced cookies, and peppermint-dipped pastries filled the kitchen, the sweet aromas of which would drift into Al's room in the mornings. She began getting up earlier so she could watch the kitchen staff make them or to snag a free sample.

Mrs. Matsumura taught Al how to fold paper cranes and after creating a large flock, they strung them together and hung the different strands around the living room like garland. With frowns and protests, Perryn let Al tear him from the pages of his book to help her secure the bird chains to the walls.

He hadn't spoken about their potential adventure for weeks, and Al wondered if he had forgotten. But when she returned to her room after making a secret batch of cookies one night, she found a red envelope resting on her pillow. She tore open the letter and read the words.

Tomorrow at 18:00. Dress warmly.

~Perryn

Unable to sleep, she used her extra energy to divide her homemade treats into different metallic bags and tie them with matching ribbons.

When the brilliant white of the rising sun greeted the room, Al awoke to find herself under the kotatsu table. Uncoiled ribbon and other supplies lay strewn about on its glass top. She shot up. Their outing was tonight.

She visited the library, folded more cranes, and took up another round of exercise in the gym, but her nerves continued to eat at her. Even soaking in a warm bath couldn't calm her racing mind. As she dried herself with a fluffy towel, she froze when her gaze fell upon her sides. She had been so busy with everything else, she hadn't noticed. The familiar purple bruises and cuts that had tormented her for almost three years had nearly faded.

Her eyes welled up with emotions her smile couldn't contain and she fell to her knees.

Her body was finally free.

She hugged herself as she laughed through her tears.

The curse was lifting.

She stood, wiping her eyes. "Maybe I can be a mermaid after all."

After returning to her room, Al examined her new skin and tried on different combinations of sweaters and pants, an activity that now seemed fun. She settled on a red, knitted one with poofy sleeves and a pair of tight black pants. Just as she pulled on her socks, someone knocked on her door.

Al glanced at the clock. He was right on time.

Stumbling as she jumped from her bed to the door, her hand hovered over the button as she took a deep breath. She pushed the door open. "I'm almost—"

Perryn's hair was shiny and combed, but framed his face with generous bounce. Underneath his trademark black trench coat, he wore a dark-blue turtleneck and black pants. A gray scarf with a dark-blue pattern wrapped around his neck, and his trusty black gloves covered his hands.

Al swallowed as her mind circled through the compliments she refused to say out loud.

"Ready?" His handsome diamond-black eyes didn't hide behind a pair of glasses tonight and greeted her with undisguised warmth.

She tried not to look at him. "Yeah, just need to grab my wig and I'll be good..."

"Go without it."

"But people might—"

"Never mind what they think." He smiled. "For one night, especially tonight, you should be who you really are."

Her legs turned to jelly. "Y—yeah um, sure...that's... I think..." She wanted to bolt down the hallway, or slam the door and duck under the covers, never to come out again. How could his kindness disarm her so much? "You can come in and wait if you want! I—I'll just do something with my hair." She bounded back inside her room, her words spilling from her mouth.

He stood near the door with his hands in his pockets, as if the very air in the room would stick to him if he moved. As he watched her gather her long hair into a low side ponytail near the vanity, his shoulders relaxed. Al pretended not to see him staring at her in the mirror as she pulled a few of the shorter hairs from the red velvet scrunchie so they framed her face.

This looks girly, right?

"Okay! I'm ready!" She spun around, trying not to let her nerves take over.

"Finally." Perryn grinned, pulling his hands from his pockets.

Al scrunched her nose and grabbed her white thermal coat from the closet. "The outing hasn't even started and already you're acting uppity. I don't have faith in the success rate of this mission—" She put her hands on her hips. "Hayashi-sama."

Perryn laughed through his nose. "Welcome back."

"What do you mean by that?"

"Oh, nothing at all." He moved to stand in the doorway, the smug smile still on his face. "Shall we go?"

Al pulled her arms through her coat and marched out into the hallway. He was acting weird again, like he had in the gym. Before, his teasing use to feel mean and distant, but now, it almost seemed friendly.

As Al stepped into her boots at the front door, she lost her balance and fell into Perryn's waiting arms. The feelings that bubbled across her cheeks as they touched forced her to admit that she was being just as weird as he was.

They descended the snow-packed mountain in the same taxi-ship with the same spirited gentlemen as before. Colorful lights below sparkled brighter than the few lone stars sprinkled in the dark above them, and as the buildings grew closer, so too did the giant light sculptures.

"You're taking me to the snow festival!" Her enthusiasm illuminated her face as she pressed it against the window.

"My plan is ruined. Oh no." His mock concern made her giggle.

"Yes! I found you out, sir."

Al allowed the tiniest whisper of hope to enter her mind as the vehicle reached the bottom of the mountain. Maybe just for tonight, it was okay that they were both being weird. Maybe just for tonight, she didn't have to hide.

CHAPTER 23

The taxi-ship continued down the main road, passing buildings and trees outlined in colorful bulbs. People bundled in thick clothing swarmed the sidewalks, pointing with bright smiles, or cuddling on benches as they sipped steaming beverages. Al continued to press her face against the window, her excitement building like the snow mounds on either side of the main road.

When the taxi-ship reached a wooden barrier that kept the rest of the road open for foot traffic, it stopped. Al yanked the door handle down, unable to contain her enthusiasm. "Arigatou gozaimasu!" She barreled out into the street.

"Al!" Perryn's voice died behind her as she shot past the barrier, her boots crunching against the white ground.

As she ran, intricate structures made of wires and lights towered amid the trees, their shapes resembling Keev-ships, snowflakes, and cute winter animals. Below them, couples had their pictures drawn, and families enjoyed picnic dinners atop thermal blankets.

Al spun in circles as she stared at the illuminated canopy. "So, this is how fancy people use their electricity."

She giggled and veered off the main path toward a muffin-shaped building.

Though the bakery was closed, the pink and purple lights dangling from the windows blinked as though greeting her. She rounded the corner and youthful voices pierced the air with laughter, taunts, and playful screams as two groups of boys chucked snowballs at each other. One side hid behind snow figures that resembled pastries, while the others braced themselves against an uneven snow wall. Hats and scarfs littered the battleground between them.

Al approached with a friendly smile and using what she could remember from Mrs. Matsumura's teachings, she shouted an encouraging phrase. "Ganbare!"

Their giant smiles morphed into trembling lips as they looked at her. A boy with rosy cheeks yelled something, and both sides huddled in a circle. Al waited, fidgeting with her fingers, and regretting she had opened her mouth.

After a moment, the same boy swaggered toward her, hands in his pockets. "Kaere! Yuki Onna!" He kicked the snow and the sloshy mixture splattered across her face and clothes. Too stunned to move, Al let the residue slide down her cheek.

A barrage of snowballs followed as the other boys chucked them at her, chanting the same phrase, and Al shielded her face, sinking to the ground, her heart sinking with her. The snowstorm ceased, and the boys ran away with boastful laughter.

"See...I told him this would happen." She shivered and wrapped her arms around herself. "I can't be myself..."

"Al!" Perryn's footsteps rushed toward her. He crouched, placing his hands on her shoulders. "What happened?"

She kept her head down. "Perryn...what does Yuki Onna mean?"

His grip tightened. "We should go somewhere warm."

Perryn sat across from her on a white couch as she looked out into the room with a blank stare. Hosts had taken their coats at the door and ushered them to his chosen table inside a box-like seating area. Lined with red satin and framed with red curtains, the box provided fashionable, though unnecessary, privacy. The restaurant was empty other than the staff, consisting only of men dressed in velvet suits.

"Did you buy the whole building or something?" Al rested her chin on her palm, scrunching her mouth.

"Only for tonight." He smiled, hopeful his playful quip would jumpstart her spunk, like it had in her room. But she only offered a tiny, acknowledging sigh.

Perryn frowned. The atmosphere and decor should have been able to improve her mood. With delicate snowflake designs painted on the windows and fiber optic snowmen as centerpieces, the interior seemed like her aesthetic. Along the wall, gold frames held black-and-white sketches of extinct plants, and above their heads, red and gold orbs dangled from the curved legs of a chandelier. Festive and interesting, but clearly not enough to make her smile.

A waiter approached with a tray, and the smell of shortbread and cinnamon wafted into the dining room from the open kitchen door. He placed a porcelain teapot wrapped in a blue knitted tea cozy and two cups without handles onto the table, bowed, and untied the curtains. They fell with a quiet swoosh, surrounding the pair in soft red.

Perryn gripped the teapot with gloved hands and poured its thick dark contents into the teacups. When he had finished, he set one in front of Al. "Douzo."

She brought the cup to her lips and her eyes lit up. "What is this?"

He smiled with pride. Finally, he had done something right. "Hot chocolate."

"You serious? Isn't that extra expensive?" Al stared at her cup in wonder. "I've only ever heard of it and now I actually get to try it? Lucky!" She took another enthusiastic sip but pulled the cup away with a harsh slurping sound. "Ohw ohw ohw!" Her voice warped as she stuck out her tongue and fanned it with her hands.

Perryn held back his laughter with his fist. "Glad you enjoy it."

"So...are you gonna tell me what that name means?"

His face fell as he folded his hands on the table. *I wish she had forgotten that.* "There are many versions of the legend, but to summarize, a Yuki Onna is a beautiful spirit that appears during winter and usually kills the person she encounters. Some renditions mention that she only enchants her victims, usually men."

Al remained silent as her eyes darted from side to side and he frowned at his hot chocolate. Her dejected face would return, and all his planning would have gone to waste.

"So...what you're saying is, she's a winter siren."

"A what?" Perryn took a solemn sip from his cup. Her sadness was imminent.

"Yeah! A winter siren! She's a snow mermaid!" Al shot up and slammed her hands on the table, her face stretched with excitement. "That means *I'm* a snow mermaid!"

Perryn coughed several times as unbridled laughter interrupted his drink's scheduled path.

Al sat with crossed arms, and her nose scrunched. "What? That's what she is, right?"

Perryn cleared his throat and smiled. Her spark had returned. "I have no choice but to agree. Your evidence is overwhelming."

"Of course it is!" She nodded with a definitive huff.

Soon dinner arrived and their gurgling stomachs found relief in thick mashed potatoes and vegetable-stuffed moose-meatloaf, all drenched in a miso gravy. With their stomachs full and spirits recharged, they put on their coats and stepped back out into the frosty night.

"Thank you..." Al looked down. "For...all of that."

Perryn tried not to look too happy with himself as he sauntered ahead of her. "Douitashimashite."

"Oh! That means 'you're welcome,' right?"

"I see you actually managed to remember something."

"Hey now! I *have* been studying." With a grin, she ran ahead of him, toward a collection of red tents bustling with people, before she stopped and turned. Cupping her hands over her mouth, she called out to him. "You better be nice to me or else I'll enchant you with my snow powers!"

A warm smile tugged at his lips. "I think you already have."

The pale-blue lights from the trees illuminated the snow as Al and Perryn entered the tents. A few people noticed her and scurried away with unstifled gasps, but she marched forward unphased. She was a certified child of winter now.

Partitioned into different stalls, the vendors sold glittering metal trinkets, cloth ornaments, homemade candles, and hard candies. The scents of cinnamon, nutmeg, and cloves mixed with fresh citrus and other tangy spices.

Al picked up several candles and, after smelling them, pushed her favorites into Perryn's face. He cringed away, reciting a list of potential germs that lived on shared surfaces. The candle vendor laughed and called out something to her in Japanese.

"I'm sorry, I'm still learning." Al hunched her shoulders as she put the candle back on the table.

"I said I like your costume, miss! Yuki Onna, right? I've seen a few of them today, but yours is the most convincing."

"Costume?" Al turned toward Perryn, but he had already left the tent. Thanking the perplexed vendor with a bow, she hurried after her moody companion. She found him leaning against a tree near a crowd swarming a stage made of pure ice. Just as she was about to ask about his mysterious behavior, loud reverberations shook the air.

A group of men wearing traditional Japanese fishing garments entered the stage, their wrapped feet marching in time with the rhythm of the drums. They extended their legs and sank as their arms mimed pulling and throwing heavy nets. With uniform precision, they called out sharp chants as their heaving and gathering continued. The audience watched with hushed excitement until the drums reached a crescendo and the dancing men struck a final pose. Al joined in the enthusiastic clapping as the group left the stage, but when she looked at Perryn, he stared out with his old eyes, vacant and cold.

They stayed for a few more dance performances and a short kabuki play, and though Al couldn't understand the words, she understood the plot when an all-white being floated onto the stage. She clapped passionately when the male actor who played the snow woman bowed at the end. Several men and women dressed in snow-themed outfits and painted streaks of white staining their black hair crowded around him, holding pens.

Al glanced at Perryn and smiled. He knew all along.

They grabbed a hot snack and meandered down another path illuminated with colorful lights. It led them to a giant wire tunnel covered in paper flowers that changed color in a sweeping wave every few minutes.

Al zoomed inside, her arms spread out like wings. "How come you just left the tent?" She spun with her eyes fixed on the blue canopy above her.

"That man was suspicious."

She faced him with a cheeky grin. "Aww. Someone sounds Perryn-noid." She burst into laughter, and he shot her an unamused glare.

"And how long have you been planning to say that one?"

"Since the beginning actually." Still in the throes of giggles, she moved to his side. "I've got a ton more if you wanna hear them."

"Kekko desu. That means no."

Al smiled as the flowers above bathed them in pink light. "Ya know what? I'm really glad I went with you tonight. I had fun!"

Perryn's eyes widened before he looked away. "The snow festival is a cornerstone of Hayashi Island culture and should be experienced if one has the chance."

Al snickered. "Okay, brochure-san, but what did you get out of this then? I mean, you've been before, right?"

Perryn stopped as the lights above them turned red.

"Perryn?"

"When I was younger, my mother brought me to this festival. We would watch the performances, look at the lights. Then we would enter this tunnel, holding my hand until the end so I would not get lost." He clenched his fists, his voice shaking. "This is my first time being back since she died. I guess...I did not wish to go alone."

Al's heart squeezed inside her chest. This ache was familiar. She realized, more than anything, she wanted to see his smile.

"Then..." She stretched out her hand. "*I'll* be with you until the very end."

Perryn stared at her, shock spilling over his face like the wash of color from the lights. He hesitated, but then took her hand, their warm, gloved fingers intertwining.

They walked the rest of the way in silence with soft smiles, sneaking glances at each other. As they exited the tunnel, Perryn covered his eyes with his free hand.

"You okay?" She didn't let go.

He turned his face from her but maintained his firm grip. "The lights are too bright."

When they returned to Hayashi Manor, darkness had enveloped most of the house and only the sound of faint creaking broke the silence as Al and Perryn tiptoed through the halls with slippered feet.

They climbed the stairs to the second floor, and Perryn touched her arm as she turned toward her room. "Al, I need to give you something. Will you come to my room?"

"Ooo! Present time? Hold on! I'll get yours too!" She covered her loud mouth and smiled. Pulling off her jacket, she headed to her room and once inside, the overhead lights flickered on. She tossed her jacket onto the bed and searched through the names tied to the many bags stacked on top of the kotatsu table. After finding Perryn's, she galloped back out into the hall.

"Okay!" Her whisper still held all her enthusiasm. "Onward to happy land!"

Keeping his gift behind her back, she followed Perryn up two more flights of stairs until they came to another frosted glass door. He slid the door back, revealing a windowless one made of thick metal, and entered a code into a panel where a handle would be. The sound of gears twirled and clicked within before the thick slab slid open and tucked itself inside the opposite wall. They stepped inside and the door slid closed.

Perryn's room looked just like him. On one side, sleek black curtains framed a sliding glass door that led to the balcony outside, and a white couch with a few black pillows and a low black table sat in front. Both rested atop a gray rug with wood grain spilling out underneath over the rest of the floor. The walls alternated between thick vertical beige panels and thinner black ones with a gold circular pattern engraved into the wood. Black bookshelves built into the wall overflowed with volumes arranged in alpha-betical order.

"Wait here." He disappeared behind a pair of paneled paper walls that formed a half-hallway.

When his shadow vanished, Al set off to explore. No pictures or art hung on the walls, but she found sever-al pages of Keev-ship schematics preserved in plastic on a bookshelf. As she reached for them, something caught her eye.

"Is that...?" She crouched to examine the object and a warm smile crossed her face. Resting on the bottom shelf was the boot she gave him. Only now, it housed dirt and a flower beginning to unfurl its delicate white petals. From its center, yellow tendrils shot out like an explosion frozen in time. "What do ya know. He actually used it."

"It *was* an innovative suggestion."

Al stood and turned toward his voice. "Well yeah, but I didn't think—" Her words halted, and the bag of cook-ies fell to the floor with a soft crunch as her hands rose to cover her mouth. She took a shaky step forward. *How is this possible?*

Nestled within Perryn's cupped hands, a metallic crow with green eyes turned his head from side to side.

"C...Cogs?" Al's words squeaked from her like wisps of air.

"Yes. I am Cogs. Who. Be. You." His playful voice was just as she remembered.

"Al..." Her tears gushed out as her shoulders shook. "It's Al."

Cogs paused as his indicator light flashed, but it wasn't long before it turned green and his leaf antenna stood straight up.

"Al. Al. Al." Cogs launched himself from Perryn's fingers and flew straight for her. She extended her hands, and he fell into them, repeating her name. His coiled feet felt so nostalgic against her skin.

"Cogs!" Al crumpled to the floor, cradling her crow friend to her chest, her sobs mixing with broken laughter.

"Cogs. Was. In. Dark." He bit at the white strands of her hair that draped over his head. "Why? Al. Different. Now."

She held him up with a smile. "It's really complicated, Cogs."

"No worries. Cogs is. Smart birb."

"I really missed you..."

The crow hopped from her hand to the top of her head and buried himself between the strands of her hair.

"Cogs. Miss. Also. But. Reunited...now..." His words trailed off as her small friend powered down.

Al untangled him from her hair, her tears slowing. "Where did—? How did you even know about him?"

"Maddox mentioned him once or twice. Informed me you were so attached to this crow, you would compromise your safety to protect him." Perryn crouched to his knees beside her. "So when I returned to Petram and found him in pieces near the bombed hangar I felt I could not leave him there."

Her face warmed. *He really cared that much?*

He held her hand and looked straight into her eyes. "I apologize for not telling you earlier. The damage to his memory bank was extensive and the likelihood of him recovering was so low, I did not want to hurt you if I failed to reassemble him. As you can see, I only managed to restore half of his original power and I still—"

Al buried her teary face in his shoulder as she cradled Cogs. "I really mean it this time...thank you."

Perryn embraced her, resting his cheek against her head. They stayed this way, as she felt their breathing and heartbeats sync to the same calm rhythm. How did he know her heart so well? All the things she tried to hide, he always saw through her. He always saw everything.

They separated and Al walked to the fallen bag of cookies, pouting as she picked them up. "Well, my present is super underwhelming now. You reunited me with a long-lost loved one and me?" She held out the bag. "Amateur hour."

Perryn stood and retrieved his gift. "And what are these meant to be?"

Al puffed up her cheeks. "Don't make fun of me! I tried to make them into book shapes for *you* because *you* like books, but they look like weird continent blob things instead."

He untied the ribbon as he walked over to the couch and sat. After removing one of his gloves, he reached into the bag and pulled out a cookie piece. Al watched with anticipation as he chewed.

"These taste rather enjoyable." Just as Al's face flickered with pride, he flashed her a cocky smile. "And their broken state adds to their authenticity."

"Why?"

"Continental drift."

Al took a long breath in and let out a heavy sigh as she glared at him.

He laughed through his nose. "This is a perfect present. Thank you."

As much as she tried to keep her frown, she yielded to the feelings only he could awaken within her. She looked down at her crow friend sleeping in her hand. Cogs was alive. Against all odds, he had returned to her. Perryn had saved him. He had saved them both.

The next morning, an extravagant breakfast waited for her in the living room. Along with Perryn, and Mrs. Matsumura, the rest of the staff joined them, wearing comfortable holiday attire rather than their usual black-and-white uniforms.

Amid bites of spiced pancakes and sips of hot honey-fruit juice, Al handed out the rest of her strange cookies, receiving gracious laughter in return. The festivities continued late into the afternoon with games, stories, and even more delicious food. When Perryn had finished giving his staff their year-end bonuses in fancy paper envelopes, they all crowded near the entryway, pulling on their shoes and coats.

Soon the home grew quiet as the party moved outside. While the staff members picked teams for an adult snowball fight, Al ventured back into the living room where Perryn sat in an armchair reading yet another book. His glasses had returned to their usual place on his nose.

"Perryn?" Al rocked on her heels in front of him.

"Yes?"

"If it's alright, I would like to give your mom a present too…"

He stared at her, frozen for a moment, before taking off his glasses and folding them away into his shirt pocket. "Uh—um...sure..."

As he stood and headed for the stairway, Al stood motionless with her eyebrows scrunched in shock. That was the first time he had ever stuttered like that. She grabbed the remaining bag of cookies from the table and followed him down the stairs.

"How is Cogs?" Perryn reached the door first.

"He's okay. His new battery takes a while to charge so I don't wanna move him too much. He's sleeping now."

They both stepped inside the memorial room and once again, the potent scent of pine filled her nose. She approached the table decorated with other festive treats and placed her cookie bag in an open space. "I tried to make butterfly-shaped ones, but I hope she likes lily pads." She gave an awkward laugh.

"I am sure she will." Perryn lit the incense, and they both sat on their knees and closed their eyes.

Al silently thanked Yui for being a good mother to Perryn and apologized for her clumsy baking. She opened her eyes again, but Perryn still had his closed. Trying not to disturb him, she folded her hands and waited.

"When I was born, I was very sick." Perryn's voice cut through the silence.

Al turned to look at him. He was staring at the ceiling.

"Despite what the physicians told her, my mother refused to believe I would die. She refused to give up on me. So, I lived. I spent most of my childhood inside sterile environments without interactions with others. Books were my only connection to the outside world. She would read them to me." He gave a sad laugh as he leaned back on his hands. "They were not books about talking animals or heroes saving the world. She read me anthologies, books about history and science. Kaa-chan was strange like that."

Al smiled as she resituated herself to face him.

"By the time I surprisingly reached the age of ten, my health had improved enough that I could venture outside for short amounts of time. That was why the snow festival was special." His words turned caustic. "But my body was still weak. Marcus blamed my mother for producing such a pathetic heir and accused her of possessing tainted genes, of being Altered. He told me countless times that it was a mistake that I was born."

Al covered her mouth as her heart pinched again. Perryn understood her, because they were the same.

"Under the guise of tough love, he would push me through strenuous physical trials and when my mother stood in his way, his anger turned violent." Perryn clenched his fists and lowered his head, his hair obscuring his eyes.

"Then one day when I woke up, she was gone. Her body was found a week later, and not two days after that..." His voice twisted and cracked. "...that son of a bitch Keevie married another woman. As the prime minister, he prevented any investigation, and her death was ruled a suicide. That is why he had to die! I was the only one who could bring him to justice!" He clutched his heart. "But nothing changed! He is still here and Kaa-chan is still dead!"

Al threw her arms around him, and he clung to her as breathy, almost voiceless sobs wracked his body. His pain was his own, but she still felt it ripping into her soul.

She pulled away and cupped his face, the scar on his cheek now a faint line. His eyes were red, clouded with tears, and the way he stared at her broke her heart. "It's not your fault, Perryn." Al forced strength into her voice. "It's not your fault your mom died."

His eyes widened, and he crumpled into his hands. "Gomen...I am so sorry, Al..." His voice was weak, but returning. "I never wanted you to see me like this."

"Everyone's broken, Perryn." She smiled through her forming tears. "You just have to find people with the right glue to hold you together."

He looked up, his face softening as he brushed away her tears with his thumb. "That sounds expensive."

She cupped his hand against her cheek and smiled. "Don't worry. You can afford it. I'll send you a bill."

Their eyes met and Perryn moved toward her, pulling her face closer to his. Her eyelids started to lower, but then her gaze fell upon the altar where Yui and Calvin's moving photos watched with judgmental stares. Al froze, panic shooting through her.

"No!" She shoved Perryn away, closing her eyes. *What are you doing, Al?*

The night and all its wonderful moments had distracted her, comforted her with warm feelings she couldn't explain. She realized she didn't want it to be true. She didn't want Calvin to be her father. Al opened her eyes and the look on Perryn's face made her sick with guilt. She was hurting him.

"I'm sorry..." Her voice shook as she looked down. "We can't...your mom and uncle are watching..."

Perryn rose to his feet, his fists tucked at his sides. As he walked past her, Al reached toward him. "Perr—"

"My mistake." He avoided her touch and left the room, the door sliding closed behind him.

CHAPTER 24

Al sat on her bed with her knees pulled to her chest and a blanket wrapped over her head. Perryn's face and the rigid way he left kept replaying in her mind like a conveyor belt.

They hadn't spoken in days, no longer ate together in the dining room, and if they saw each other, they would turn down different corridors. She caught him slipping away from a back door one day and it wasn't until she heard footsteps in the hall late at night that she realized he had stayed out all day.

She wanted to talk to him, wanted to explain, but that would mean admitting something she wasn't brave enough to say. This time, it was clear Perryn intended to kiss her, but that meant he had no idea they might be related. How in Astova could she explain herself and her strange feelings knowing that?

Why would Perryn wanna kiss me anyway? With a heavy sigh, she rested her head on her knees, the blanket slipping to her shoulders.

Cogs circled around the room, darting in and out of the bathroom as he squawked a stream of numbers. "...98.

99. 100." He landed on Al's head with a triumphant fan-fare escaping from his beak. "Al. Bad. Hider. Cogs. Wins. Again."

When Al didn't respond, Cogs hopped off her head and plopped his cool beak against her bare foot. "If. Al. Sad. Cogs can. Lose. Game?" He let out a gentle clicking noise as the gears inside his stomach twirled.

Al lifted her heavy head. "I'm not sad, Cogs. My mind is just so full I can't think."

"Cogs suggests a defrag."

"Yeah. Wouldn't that be nice?" She stroked under his chin and the bird closed his eyes. "Cogs, do you know what love is?"

"Baby. Don't. Shoot. Me." He squawked a song.

"What?" She shook her head. "I mean, how do you define it? I love *you,* Cogs, but that's because you're my friend."

"Cogs. Loves. Al. Too." He pushed his beak against her hand, which earned him more scratches.

"I love my mother, but I don't remember meeting her. I love flying, but that's not a person. Is it all the same or are there different kinds of love out there?"

"Cogs is. Smart birb. But. Not. Psychologist." He hopped onto the bed and paced, tilting his head from side to side. "Cogs will. Play recording." Her crow friend squawked to a stop. "Error. Unable to retrieve."

Al sighed. "It's okay, Cogs. My head hurts, too."

A hearty knock snapped her attention to the door, and her body stiffened. Perryn might be lurking beyond the glass.

"Al-san? Are you dressed? We will be late for the shogat-su parade if we do not leave soon." Mrs. Matsumura's presence soothed her panic, but it returned when she realized she was nowhere near being ready.

She leaped from the bed, catapulting Cogs into the air. "Danger. Danger." His cute voice spun in circles with his body as he let out a whirling siren.

As Al yanked on her clothes, Cogs landed on top of her closet and peered down with a tilted head and a disapproving squawk.

"Sorry, Cogs..." She offered him a smile as she pushed her head through the top of a blue sweater.

"Al. Is. Lucky. Cogs is great. Circus. Birb." He coasted down from his perch and landed on her shoulder. As she pulled on a black wig, he bit at the ends.

"I'll be back." Al touched her cheek to his wing. "So birb the fort for me until then, okay?"

Cogs flew to the bed and began pacing its squishy perimeter, his wings at attention against his sides. "Talons. On the. Ground."

Al saluted the patrolling passerine and stepped out into the hall.

Mrs. Matsumura stood near the stairs, bundled in many layers of orange and brown, her sparkling scarf wrapped over her head like delicate pink icing. She greeted Al with a nod and resituated the thick red blanket tucked under her arm. "Saa-te. Shall we go?"

"Will Perryn be going too?" Al slammed her mouth shut, the question refusing to stay in her mind.

Mrs. Matsumura shook her head with a sigh. "He has not left his room for three days, but he is not the sort to go to these things."

Al looked down, as pain like a hot gear spun inside her chest. "I see..." Her feet dragged as she followed Mrs. Matsumura down the steps.

The decor had changed again to match the upcoming holiday, now featuring art pieces of alternating lengths of green bamboo shoots wrapped together with a grass-like twine and golden fans with red and white paper flowers arranged in a semicircle. Small mounds of mochi, stacked like edible snowmen, sat on the windowsills with fresh Emperor Oranges and clay figures of smiling goats with golden horns arranged at their sides.

The smell of seafood and datemaki drifted from the kitchen as Al pulled on her shoes at the door, but the delicious scents soured as the gear of shame continued to rip its way through her body.

As she stepped into the taxi-ship, she glanced back toward the manor and thought she saw Perryn staring down from his balcony, but when she looked again, the black curtains seemed like they hadn't been disturbed in years.

Al huddled under the thick red blanket next to Mrs. Matsumura. Even with her sweater and jacket, the cold still seeped past her skin and into her bones. She sneezed into her arm and readjusted the pair of dark sunglasses that had slid down her nose.

They sat on top of a wooden platform in an open area near the hangar, the snow scraped out from underneath them. Other groups sat on similar platforms, some enjoying hot tea and food from many-tiered, lacquered bento boxes. Several boys gathered against the guardrail, looking over the edge of the island into the cloudy mist below and when one of them began to climb it, a worried shout from a mother brought him back to the ground.

The outdoor decorations from the winter festival still surrounded them, though unlit, and flags with the same smiling goat fluttered from the light poles. A wide tapestry with the image of a goat piloting a Keev-ship hung across the archway that Al and Perryn had passed under the day they arrived on the island.

Al sighed and scanned the crowd behind her with a blank stare. Was he okay?

She flinched. His bodyguards sat together a few yards behind her, wrapped under the same red blanket. They both held a pair of magni-scopes to their eyes, aimed straight at her.

"I guess his goons are okay now." Al ducked farther underneath the blanket. "But why are they with us and not Perryn?"

"Endo-san and Yamazaki-san have always followed us. Hayashi-sama is quite protected at the manor." Mrs. Matsumura sipped tea from a porcelain cup, stifling a small laugh. "Since we will be stationary for quite some time, they are visible for today."

"Every time, huh...?" If Al sank any lower, she'd be as flat as the boards they sat on.

Mrs. Matsumura nodded at them before turning back to face front. "The only time they stayed behind was the night of the winter festival. Hayashi-sama was very insistent on attending alone."

Al's cheeks warmed, but her shoulders soon slumped as melancholy once again held her feelings hostage.

The sound of a high-pitched musical instrument echoed out over the loudspeakers and a man's voice followed. Though he spoke too fast for Al to catch many of the words, a loud cheer from the crowd told her the parade was about to start.

The rumble of revving engines emanated from the hangar and then two Keev-ships shot out from the metal structure like a blast from a stun gun. They dove straight down over the edge of the island, the rippling sound of their engines disappearing into the clouds that swirled into spirals where the ships had ripped through them.

More boys rushed to the railing and stood shoulder to face as they stuck their necks out as far as they could. With a gust of wind, the ships returned, soaring straight into the sky, twisting into a helix pattern. The boys let out excited yells and chased after the shadows of the ships as they passed over the crowd. Al fell back against the wood platform as she stared blankly at the sky. She had performed the same maneuver with Zeek once.

Zeek! She had completely forgotten about him since arriving on the island. Was he okay? The last time she saw him they were plummeting to the ground. More sharp gears stabbed her gut, and a bitter taste reached her smile. *Are Keev-ships seriously making me feel miserable right now? I deserve it though.*

She stood, letting the blanket fall to the wooden platform. "I need to stretch my legs."

"Alright, Al-san." Mrs. Matsumura's eyes flashed with worry, but Al jogged away before she could say anything.

She headed toward the hangar, checking over her shoulder to confirm Perryn's bodyguards hadn't left their spots behind Mrs. Matsumura. When she was far enough away, she slowed, dragging her feet through the snow. How could she enjoy anything when she had hurt someone she cared about and ditched her best friend like a used bandage?

"Your disregard for the safety of others will not be tolerated!" A familiar voice exploded from inside the hangar.

Mr. Lann? Al skidded to a stop before she crouched flush against the cold metal, poking her head into the enclosure.

Her former instructor wore a flying outfit of many dark layers and straps, and a pair of goggles dangled from his neck. In front of him, a young pilot wearing the same outfit leaned against a ship, holding a glass bottle filled with a brown liquid. Several men, tinkering with their engines or tying their boots, tried not to make their stares obvious.

"I was lenient this past season because of your loss, but this was your final warning. You're done. Leave."

"Yeeeaaah? Well fuuuuuck youuu!" The young man's voice slurred with agitation.

"I said take a walk, Mr. Landers."

Al's heart almost soared out of her chest. *Zeek!*

He snickered. "Oooo fun. Walkin' round a flooooating island. Hope I don't get lost!" He took another sip from the bottle as he sauntered in Al's direction, his gait wide and overly pronounced. She scooted out of the way and watched him pass, her lungs suffocating with too many conflicting emotions to sort through.

Mr. Lann sighed. "Alright men, the next phase will commence with Chavez and Marteen—"

His voice faded behind her as she ran after Zeek like a mother goose trailing her gosling. She hid behind buildings and mounds of snow, watching every wobbly step he took. He almost tripped and fell backward as he lifted the bottle for another sip, but he regained his balance and continued his teeter-tottering trot through town. Al almost jumped out to catch him, but stopped herself with locked knees. If she approached him, things wouldn't end well. She was a girl now and an Altered one too.

After turning down a narrow dead-end alley, Zeek stopped and stumbled to sit on the snowy ground. Fatigue darkened his eyes and the unkempt stubble on his chin made him look several years older. With his back against a brick wall, he brought the bottle to his lips, but when no liquid reached him, he let out an angry grunt and threw the empty bottle against the opposite wall. The glass shattered and Al ducked behind an adjacent brick corner

"Al...I'm sorry I couldn't save you either..."

The burning gear dug deeper into her heart. She wanted nothing more than to run out to him and tell him she was fine, that she was alive, that he didn't have to torture himself anymore. She shut her eyes and covered her quivering lips for fear that they would give away her position. Wasn't there something she could do for him? Keeping her hands over her mouth, she glanced beyond the wall again.

Zeek passed a piece of broken glass between his fingers and over his knuckles. As it traveled over his thumb, it nicked the side and blood trickled down his wrist and into the snow. He stared at the shard with a dark smile.

"Don't you dare, Zeek Landers!" Al hid behind the wall as her voice echoed down the corridor.

"Al?" The shard clinked as it hit the snow and an icy silence gripped the air. "And I'm hearing your voice again...you came back to haunt me some more..."

Al remained frozen against the wall.

"I guess that's what I get for having a guilty conscience." Zeek let out a pained laugh. "If I finally confess, will you leave me alone?"

She hesitated as the air chilled her lungs. "...yes..."

When Zeek remained silent, Al feared she had doomed herself, but his soft and slurred speech continued with the crunch of snow as he resituated himself.

"It's my fault you died..."

Al relaxed her shoulders and shook her head.

"Instead of protecting you, I let you die just like Evie..." His voice grew manic as he rambled. "I wanted the Alts to pay for what they did to her. Vilroy said he could help me, but I had to find someone. His daughter. The Alts stole her from him. He said she might be disguised, even as a boy. I didn't think it was you. You were weird, but you were a guy, my best friend..." His words caught in his throat and his tone turned dark.

"But when you stayed in the tent, I found out you lied. You lied...I wanted to protect you, but I was stupid, so stupid. I should've never given you that tracker. While I was unconscious, he followed it and bombed their base...before I could explain...before I could get to you..."

Al froze, not comprehending or believing anything he had said. Her binding had been loose when she woke up on race day. *That was him?* Zeek knew she was a girl and didn't say anything? Why? Maybe there was a chance she could change his mind about the Altered too.

But hold up! The Altered kidnapped Vilroy's daughter? But that means he might be my father! Though terrifying in its own right, Al preferred that lineage over being a Hayashi. She had to talk to Perryn.

And what tracker? Al closed her eyes and steadied herself on the wall as she tried to remember. Her eyes shot open. *The charm!* Zeek had given it to her right before they took off and she had taken it to Petram. Al covered her mouth and swallowed to prevent herself from throwing up. Zeek had been working for Vilroy the whole time. That's how the Capital Scanners found their way to that place, to her, because of Zeek's horrible gift.

Memories flooded her mind—Cogs and his parts scattered out amid the grass, the cold floor, the fake sun she used to live under, the smiling faces of Amira and the other girls, the leering eyes of Mr. Benje. Hot tears streamed from her eyes as she fell to her knees.

"I'm so sorry Al..." Zeek's voice strained with sobs. "I'll never know if you were his daughter or just a regular girl trying to hide, but I..." His voice shook. "I loved you..."

She bit back the cries that tore at her lips for release. Her best friend and she never noticed. The talk they had

on the hill, the way he had changed after they visited Angel, it all made sense, but it didn't matter anymore. Zeek
was right. The Al he knew was dead. Unable to hear anything more, she stood and bolted from the brick wall, racing back toward the parade.

Night had reached the island by the time she returned
to the house with Mrs. Matsumura. After kicking off her
shoes at the front door and tossing her wig and sunglasses
as she ran, she barreled through the hallways and up the
stairs, all the while calling out Perryn's name. She reached
his door, but before she could knock, it slid open.

He stood on the other side, his gaze intense and focused. "Why are you yelling? What happened?"

"I need to talk to you!" She dashed into his room and
the door closed behind her.

"Maybe you should catch your breath first."

"I don't have time to breathe!" She put her hands on
her knees as she panted. "Vilroy might be my father."

Perryn spun around to face her. "What? How?"

"Well uh, I ran into Zeek and—"

"Did he see you?" Perryn rushed over to grip her shoulders. "Zeek works for Vilroy directly, so if he were to—"

"I know. Wait." She shrugged away from him. "You
knew, and you didn't tell me?"

He pinched the bridge of his nose. "Al, I just—Zeek is
dangerous."

"How long have you known?"

"Since I became prime minister. I am sorry for not telling you, but I thought you would be safer that way."

Al frowned and clenched her fists. "I thought I told
you I can take care of myself."

"Al…" His expression softened. "Please, just tell me what happened."

Her stubbornness was no match for his adamant eyes. She relaxed her hands with a heavy sigh. "He didn't see me. Zeek was drunk and rambling, but I managed to piece together that he gave me some sort of tracker that led the Capital Scanners to Petram. He told me Vilroy asked him to find his daughter that the Altered kidnapped and—" Al shifted her gaze. No need to tell him everything Zeek said. "I really think he was talking about me."

Perryn looked away. "What evidence do you have?"

My heart, you annoying jerk-face! "It all makes perfect sense!" She paced around the room as she spoke. "Maddox told you to keep me away from Vilroy, right? Well surprise, Maddox was the Altered leader! He hates Vilroy, so what better way to get back at him than to kidnap his daughter?"

"Al—"

"Besides, why else would Vilroy care about me so much unless I'm related to him? I mean, come on! He and my mom were close because they used to work together. So maybe they had a—"

"Al!" Perryn's forceful voice halted her feet. "Kera Lacey never gave birth to a child." He kept his gaze to the ground as he frowned. "It was medically impossible for her…"

Al held her hands against her heart as her shoulders slumped. "How do you know that?"

Perryn furrowed his eyebrows before turning and disappearing behind the paper screens. He returned moments later with the P.M.D. and clicked the side. The grainy, blue-tinted scene that had played for them in the cave burst to life on the ceiling.

"I can't believe you still have it!" Al smiled. It had been so long since she had seen her mother's face.

"I never knew what my aunt looked like until I found this, so I thought I could add it to our family shrine." Perryn switched off the device, set it on the table and began pacing around the room. "It was strange that you knew her too, but after Petram, it made sense. I confronted Maddox, but he refused to tell me anything."

Al gripped her shirt. "Yup. Sounds like Maddox."

"I searched through the old capital databases, but Kera's name had been erased from the system. Even records of my uncle's marriage were missing. So, I decided to access the restricted archives and found remnants of an experiment called The Eternal Child project. Along with my uncle, Kera and Vilroy manufactured an immortal child using Kera's DNA as the base. It is plausible that Vilroy provided the other necessary genetic material."

He walked over to the sofa and slumped down with his hand against his forehead. "Al, I think you might be that child…"

"So, it *is* me…" She looked down with a faint smile. It only stung a little. Being born from an experiment meant she wasn't natural, but she already knew that. When she raised her head, Perryn was staring at her, his face contorting into a mixture of shock and irritation.

"Oh, right!" She hunched her shoulders. "An explanation. I've kind of been conducting my own investigation. I have been since the day Maddox drunk-screamed at me that he and Molly weren't my real parents. So what if Kera didn't give birth to me? She still created me. She's still my mom! And I know she loved me."

If she didn't, why else would Kera have looked so happy holding her in the photo? Why else would Kera have given her a name?

"She named me Alisa. That's my real name…but you can still call me Al if you want. I'm not used to Alisa yet."

Al smiled and nodded. "Now all I have to do is meet Vilroy and the quest will be complete!"

"What?" Perryn shot to his feet. "That is the exact opposite of what you should do!"

She scrunched her nose and stormed over to face him. "My whole life I've been lied to and I'm sick of it! He's the only one left alive who might have answers about who—what I am! Besides, since he's my father, maybe I could convince him to stop persecuting the Altered if I returned!" Her breath caught in her throat. "Maybe that's the whole reason he started this war against them..." *How many people have died because of me?*

"I understand, I do, but just think about the danger you would be putting yourself in!"

Al let out a frustrated growl. "I'm not fragile!"

"I know." Perryn smiled, his diamond-black eyes softening. "But I am."

She stiffened as bubbles rose in her chest, suffocating her. "Well, um, that just means I'll have to protect you when we go together. Seeing as I'm the Eternal Child, I've got some immunity to death, right? And speaking of that, I—uh, wanna use my favor now—for this." She fiddled with a strand of her hair as she avoided his gaze.

"Al—"

"I'll go without you if I have to. Just straight-up announce myself at the front door."

Perryn pinched the bridge of his nose again. "I know." He sighed. "Fine, I will accompany you."

"Thank you." Her stubbornness had made her speak harshly without thinking, but he hadn't abandoned her. "That means a lot..."

Perryn reached out to embrace her, but then pulled back with a stunted grunt.

"You okay?"

"Well, if you recall the—the incident—um..."

"Oh!" Al tilted her head with a shrug. "That was because I thought you were my cousin."

Perryn's lips scrunched into a pinched smile as he took a deep breath through his nose. "What?"

"Yeah! Calvin and Kera got married so I—"

"And here I thought it was due to what you experienced at the prison and I was overstepping." Perryn let out a heavy sigh. "Why are you like this?"

"Me? What about you? Why'd you go look up all that sneaky stuff about Kera, huh? You thought we were related too, didn't you! Even Matsumura-san said you only bring family here."

"Honki ka yo..." Perryn hid his mouth with the back of his hand. "Matsumura-san needs to keep some things to herself."

"Oh!" Al hit her hand with her fist. "I guess that means my mom technically cheated on your uncle with..." She shuddered. "Vilroy..."

Perryn moved to her side with a smirk. "So, Al. Is there a reason you were so concerned about me being your cousin?"

"Concerned?" She stiffened as her eyes darted around the room. She wasn't ready to tell him the truth. "I just think it would be horrible to be related to you is all. No thank you, please!"

Perryn's arms cascaded around her, and the comforting scent of pine once again embraced her heart. Al relaxed against him. Were these feelings allowed now? She gripped his shirt. *Please let them be okay.* She missed this. She missed him.

He pulled her closer. "I cannot believe how ridiculously irritating you are..."

Al closed her eyes as she hugged him back. "Kochira-koso, buddy."

CHAPTER 25

During the coming weeks, they stayed up late brainstorming ways to infiltrate the capital, schematics, miniature diagrams, and scribbled plans strewn across Perryn's bedroom floor amid pillows and green tea. Many times, Al would wake up on the couch with a blanket draped over her shoulders and the distant sound of Perryn breathing drifting from beyond the paper dividers. He could easily request an audience with Vilroy, but how would he take her, a random girl, along with him?

While celebrating his golden birthday near the end of January, a letter arrived from the capital with their answer. Perryn tore open the envelope and pulled out a thin card. He scanned the words and scoffed, tossing the invitation onto the table, where it almost landed in a slice of cake. "It appears Vilroy will be attending the annual Founder's Day Ball this year."

"Well, that sure makes it easier to see him." The tassel on Al's party hat bobbed as she shifted on his couch and a pillow landed in her lap. "But it seems suspicious."

"I agree. Choosing to advertise his first public appearance is a risky move, unless he is expecting someone to show up." He sat next to her. "I still do not think you should meet him."

Al hugged the pillow to her chest. "Why would he wanna hurt me if I'm his daughter? If he loved Kera enough to make me and if he had Zeek looking for me this whole time, it's clear he cares about me. I'm more worried about you. If Vilroy finds out you've been working with the Altered and have been keeping me here, he might execute you..."

Perryn took her hands into his. "Let him."

Al's face warmed before her nose scrunched. "If he tries anything, I'll kick his ass!"

Perryn chuckled. "Now that I would love to see."

In the month that followed, Al prepared for her mission. Going undercover as a Personal Girl would be her best bet at sneaking into the capital. As a new P.G., no one would expect her to know the inner workings of the high court and their allies. The fewer questions, the better.

Many dance lessons and a pair of sore feet later, the day before the Founder's Day Ball arrived.

Al had never known the true number of attendants Hayashi Manor housed until she awoke with a yelp, finding them surrounding her bed. After an awkward breakfast of eggs and stares, they ushered her to the bath, where, despite her protests, they scrubbed her with floral scented soaps, trimmed her nails, and re-cut her bangs so she could see again.

She spent the rest of the afternoon trying on stylish dresses of different lengths and textures. Forgetting her earlier discomfort as the attendants strapped or buttoned her into the garments, Al twirled, the fluttering material gliding around her hips like a tent. Distracted by her transformations, time froze like the icicles hanging outside her window and it wasn't until Mrs. Matsumura clapped her hands together that she even realized the sun had set.

"Kore ga ii! I think this one."

The attendants parted, and Al stared at her feet as she walked forward until the bottom of the mirror came into view. A tight knot formed in her chest. Who would she see staring back? A sea witch or a mermaid? She squeezed her eyes shut and lifted her head. After counting to three, she opened her eyes.

Her breath stopped in her throat.

She wore a knee-length, bell-shaped dress the color of fresh snow that draped with scalloped edges. Delicate, swirling blue-tinted icicles lined the bottom and her bodice crisscrossed, leading to short sparkling sleeves that resembled fairy wings.

An elegant snow mermaid stared at her with her mouth frozen open. Without breaking eye contact with the magical being, Al lifted her shaking hand and touched the mirror. Her reflection touched back.

Blue eyes, white hair, a girl's body—she was forced to hide everything, taught that she could never be accepted. The dress was gorgeous, maybe even prettier than Angel's, but it wasn't the clothes that made Al's chest hurt. After all this time, Al had finally found herself.

Her lips quivered as tears trickled down her cheeks.

Mrs. Matsumura bowed with a smile and ushered the attendants from the room. As soon as the door clicked closed, Al's knees gave way, and she crumpled to the ground, crying. Lifting her head, she stared at her reflection, a tiny smile finding its way out.

"There you are, me. I thought I lost you."

The door behind her slid open again.

"Al, how is—Al?" Perryn fell to his knees beside her, and she laughed, wiping the tears from her eyes.

"I'm just being silly." She looked at him with a beaming smile. "For the first time in my life, I finally feel beautiful."

Perryn straightened and faced her with his gloved fists against his knees. "Of course you are beautiful. You have been for a long time."

Al stared at him, the computer in her head taking forever to process the data he had just inputted into her ears. When his words reached her inbox, her face turned bright red. "Wha—y—you can't just say that! Take it back!"

"Kotowaru! I will never take it back!"

Al's mouth fell open with incoherent squeaks before she turned her head with a pout. "You—you're really sneaky!"

"I am?"

"Yes! All it takes is one of your perfect smiles, or one of your warm hugs, or that annoyingly cute way you get excited about books and my mind goes completely blank!"

Perryn touched his chin with mock contemplativeness. "Sounds terrible."

"It is! Also, the lack of care you have for my mental health when you take off your shirt is so unbelievably rude!"

Perryn smirked. "I do apologize."

Al lowered her head. "But...the sneakiest thing you do is make me feel things I don't understand..." Her lips trembled. "And it's not just unfair, it's annoying! How am I supposed to think straight when all I think about is you? How am I supposed to be strong when seeing you hurt makes me feel so helpless?" She lifted her head, tears streaming down her cheeks. "Why! Why do you make me feel like it's okay that I exist?"

"Because I want you to!" Perryn threw his arms around her, squeezing almost too tight. "For the longest time, my only purpose in life was revenge. I hated everyone, and they hated me. Then I met you. Your naivety irritated the hell out of me, but I was just jealous. Jealous you still had hope. Your hope is beautiful, Al. It taught me there was something else to live for." He released her and warmth radiated from his eyes. "I want you to exist because I love you."

She flung her hands over her mouth as she sniffled. "You do? You really, really do?"

"Yes." He chuckled as he wiped away her tears with his thumbs.

"Then..." Al gripped her dress as her gaze wavered. "...aren't you supposed to...kiss me?"

His smile faded. Then, unflinching as he stared, he removed his gloves and tossed them to the side. He cupped her chin, pulling her closer to his diamond-black eyes.

She was ready to drown.

"Bold of you to tell me what to do..."

His soft lips touched hers and a current shot through her body as her mind swirled with bright light. Pine. Her heart beat in her ears. Heat. His breath escaped his parted lips. As his bare fingers burned her cheek, his other hand moved to hold her at the small of her back. Surrender. Her shoulders relaxed, and she closed her eyes, pushing back against him and gripping the fabric of his shirt.

So this is what it feels like to love you.

Perryn continued to kiss her, and she fell back against the floor, the icicles on her dress clinking together. Lightheaded, she opened her eyes, and he pulled away, trailing kisses down the side of her face and neck. She flinched, disoriented from her rapid breaths.

More. He pulled down one of her sleeves, and kissed her exposed shoulder, his touch sending electric chills across her skin.

She gripped his hair. *More!* She wanted him to devour everything. Her loneliness. Her doubt. Her fear. When he was with her, she wasn't a boy or a girl. She just was. His lips returned to her ear, and he whispered her name, his hungry voice invading her sanity as his hands moved farther down. She let out a breathy squeak as her body spasmed.

"Warui!" Perryn jerked away and turned his back to her.

Al sat up, blinking. "Did—did I do something wrong?"

"No…" He touched his forehead, his shoulders slumping. "But I almost did."

Al hid her mouth behind her hands. "I don't—"

"We will take it slow." He turned around and pulled her to his chest. "I promise I will cherish you."

With flushed cheeks, she let him hug her as their heartbeats pounded against each other. What just happened? What was going to happen if he didn't stop? Why did she make such a strange sound? She didn't even know she could make a sound like that. Her body had acted on its own. She buried her face in his shoulder, shaking her head. He loved her. Nothing else mattered.

They parted ways until dinner, which they ate in silence with timid smiles snuck between bites. The staff whispered amongst themselves as they passed, and Al couldn't help but wonder if they had heard her upstairs. That's why Perryn had stopped after all, because she had made a strange noise. She sank lower in her chair, hiding her face with her turtleneck sweater.

After they finished eating, he escorted her back to her room.

"I…um…" With a goofy grin, she tried to stall for time.

Perryn kissed her forehead. "Get some rest. I will see you tomorrow."

As he ascended the stairs, the airy feeling that had hugged her for hours vanished. *Tomorrow.* She rushed into her room and as the door shut behind her, she slid to the ground, staring out into the darkness. Tomorrow might be the end of everything.

Her eyes, tired from nightmares, opened to the sun stabbing her from the window. She rolled over with a groan, pulling the covers over her head and disrupting Cogs in the process. He pushed his way out from underneath the blanket and unfurled his wings.

"Morning. Morning. Up. Up. Al." He jumped on her shoulder and nibbled at her ear under the sheets.

"That's the problem Cogs, I have been." She yanked down the blankets and sat up.

"Today. Adventure. Yes?" His antenna bobbed from side to side.

Al scooped him up and kissed the top of his head. "I'm sorry, Cogs. You have to stay here this time. I can't let anything happen to you, not again."

"Cogs is. Worried. Al. Disappear. Again."

His words tugged at her heart. "I'll come back this time. I promise."

Cogs hopped to her knee and lifted one of his legs. "Phalanges promise."

Al stuck out her pinky, and his coiled talon curled around her finger. "Phalanges promise."

With an approving squawk, Cogs released her and flew to the window, spreading out his reflective wings to catch the sun. Al gripped the sheets. She was going to find out who she was tonight. She would make Vilroy tell her everything.

Al sat inside Perryn's ship with her hands clenched in her lap as she stared out the window. Her reflection looked different from the girl she had seen yesterday in the mirror, her lips now painted with a light pink, and her pure blue eyes outlined with a charcoal and peach color. She looked more mature, like a future version of herself.

Dressed in her snowy gown, the black wig she wore curled into an intricate twist secured with a matching headpiece. Delicate snowflake jewelry, attached by clips, dangled from her ears, and an elegant woven choker hugged her neck. Her feet, crammed inside a pair of ornate blue crystal heels, felt like they would cave under her the moment she stood. She scrunched her nose and turned to face front.

Perryn sat next to her dressed in a dark suit, his hair pulled back and his bare eyes narrowed in concentration. Her heart fluttered.

"I wonder if that..." His mumbling voice trailed off like he had more to say, but he wrapped his gloved fingers around her bare ones and kissed the back of her hand. "I will not let anything happen to you. I promise."

Al stiffened as her cheeks flushed. She still wasn't used to him being so casual with his touch. "This is no time for you to be charming. We're about to go into enemy territory..." She pulled her hand free.

Perryn smirked and turned her chin toward him. "Right, another mission together. Perhaps I should start deducting points for your impertinent behavior?"

She let out a strained squeak. "Stop messing around! The goons are watching!" She glanced behind her and met the intense stares of Endo and Yamazaki from the back row.

"Let them."

"You—fine, then!" She grabbed Perryn's collar and pulled him into a rough kiss. As she released him, her cheeks exploded with red. "There! How do you like being messed with?" She crossed her arms and sank lower into her seat.

Perryn froze as he stared at her and then burst into laughter. "Okay, okay. Wakatta yo." His laughter settled. "Sorry. Now that I can be honest with you, it is difficult to hold back how much I love you."

With her cheeks still burning, she rested her head against his shoulder. "Just...try not to go overboard."

A voice over the loudspeaker announced their arrival at the capital and Perryn interlocked his fingers with hers again, his face turning solemn. "I will try."

They landed at the royal hangar and when they exited their ship, another one waited for them. Small and silver, the automated transporter wound through the neon-lit metal veins of Astova City until it shot out and the purple obelisks of Vilroy Towers loomed above them. The light of the crescent halfmoon cast dark smiles on the ground that blended with their shadows as they walked to the entrance. Trying not to stumble in her new footwear, Al gripped the white shawl that hung on her shoulders.

Without natural vegetation, the bare landscape felt lifeless, and other than a slight icy sheen that clung to the buildings, all signs of winter had vanished. When their party of four fell in line, Al looked up at the massive tower, the top of which disappeared above the clouds. Her stomach churned. *Vilroy.* She gripped Perryn's arm.

They stepped up to the door, where several armed guards dressed in red greeted them. Perryn presented his invitation, Endo and Yamazaki declared their weapons, and a young man who seemed to enjoy his job too much checked Al for contraband. She remained as stoic as she could as his wormy fingers grazed her skin, but it didn't last long. Perryn grabbed the man's wrist with a death glare.

"My apologies, Prime Minister!" the man gasped in pain.

Perryn released him and hooked his arm under Al's, escorting her inside and leaving the man to nurse his wounded hand.

A pristine golden lobby waited beyond the door with men and women checking their coats, lounging on soft couches, and milling about in front of the double elevators. After Al relinquished her shawl, the elevator attendants cleared the area so the prime minister and his party could enter alone. The thick smell of cinnamon and tobacco overwhelmed her once the doors closed.

Perryn stood beside her, his bodyguards in front of them blocking the doors. She gripped his hand and he squeezed back. *No matter what happens, I'll protect you, too.*

When the doors opened again, a gust of fresh air flooded in, as though the elevator had inhaled. They stepped out and the dull roar of voices bounced off the golden walls and vaulted ceiling as hundreds of gorgeous and strangely dressed characters laughed, ate, and disappeared around corners with each other.

A semicircle of firelight hung above their heads, and tall pillars, extending out like the support beams of a bridge, had red banners with Vilroy's crest draped between them. Carved out like the gills of a giant fish, the ballroom walls showed marbled depictions of ancient machinery and important scenes from Astova's history. On the other end of the room, a gold throne sat in the middle of an indoor balcony and behind it, several floor-to-ceiling windows overlooked the glittering cityscape.

Several armed soldiers approached and after saluting Perryn as they passed stood on either side of the elevator behind him. He nodded at Endo and Yamazaki, and they disappeared into the crowd on either side of the room.

"My lady." Perryn extended his hand, and she took it with a timid smile. As they walked farther into the hall, hundreds of eyes made no attempt to hide their glares, and she shrank closer to her partner. Even though she was pretending to be a P.G. the judgement still felt real. "Ignore them. Their opinions matter not."

Al squeezed his hand. That's right. She wasn't alone this time.

Boisterous laughter resounded from a group of men in front of them and it wasn't long before one man turned around. "Well, if it isn't Mr. Important himself."

Al's confidence froze beneath layers of pain and betrayal that came bubbling up from the hole in her heart.

"I see a promotion has made you rather arrogant, Mr. Landers." Perryn glared down his nose.

"Whoa!" Zeek stepped away from his group and sauntered toward them wearing a fancier version of a capital soldier's uniform. The three triangles on his left shoulder were new, a reward for Zeek's unwavering allegiance to Vilroy at the battle of Petram. "Only jokin', prime minister. It's a party. You should loosen up." His haughty tone didn't match his signature smile. Now clean-shaven, Zeek looked like his old self again, his eyes no longer the broken windows Al once saw.

He turned his attention to her with a smirk. "And who's this?"

She threw her gaze down. Would he recognize her?

"Blue eyes?" He took an exaggerated step backward. "Is she an Alt, Prime Minister? You should be careful. Some may question your loyalty, even if she is just a girl."

Perryn stepped in front of her. "Watch your tone, Landers."

"Pfft. You may be the prime minister now, but I ain't gonna kiss your feet like the rest of these plebs here. I'm part of Vilroy's elite team now. I'm on another level." He flung his hands out and he and his sneering entourage headed to the snack table.

Al held her elbows as her heart sank. "Guess we've always lived in different worlds. Just now I can see the walls."

Perryn frowned. "Shall we find some fresh air?"

She nodded, keeping her hands pulled against her body. As they made their way through the crowded ballroom, she glanced over at Zeek, who was taking a bite out of an oversized drumstick. Their eyes met and he sent her a disgusted glare.

Walking under the balcony, they traveled down a smaller corridor, passing more guests in eccentric outfits. Soon the air cooled as the hallway opened onto a rounded outdoor balcony. They were so far above the city, any noise from daily life below couldn't reach them. Despite the circumstances, the night was almost peaceful.

"Perryn Keevie! That's you, isn't it?"

Almost.

Al recognized the girl's melodic frequency even before she turned around.

Angel bid the drunk man she had been kissing adieu and skipped toward them. The thin lines of golden fabric that crisscrossed above her belly button and ample chest left nothing to the imagination. Without hesitation, Perryn grabbed Al's hand and turned back toward the hallway.

"Oh, come on. Don't you want to spend some time with me, too?" Angel wrapped herself around his free arm and pressed her chest against him. "You weren't here last year, or the year before that, or even the year before that. I mean, you're practically a unicorn in this sea of boring regulars. I miss you!"

Al's heart tried to force its way out through her throat. They knew each other.

Perryn yanked his arm away with a glare, and Angel turned to Al with a sly smile. "Oh! Is this the new one?"

New one?

"Hi there. I'm Angel." She waved a glittering hand. "Oh, by the way, you should prepare yourself if you haven't already. This one has major mommy issues and likes it real rough, too."

"Angel!" Perryn's harsh voice echoed across the balcony.

"Aww." Angel put her hand to her mouth and cocked her hip to the side. "Did I upset the little prince? Whoopsie."

Perryn stepped toward her, his voice low. "One word from me could end you."

"Wow! So scary!" Her voice glittered like her clothes, but something dark lurked beneath her words. "You know, in my experience, you really suck at keeping promises, Perr. Maybe...you should leave the sucking to me."

Perryn tensed. "That—"

Al felt sick. "Juice...I'm gonna get juice."

Perryn reached for her, but she turned and ran.

The sound of her heels clacking on the marble floor echoed down the hallway until the crowd of voices drowned it out. She walked past the refreshment table and headed for an unoccupied corner of the room. Pressing her back against the wall, she stared at the ground.

Why are you surprised, Al? Of course, he's experienced with girls. Don't you dare cry!

Was that why Perryn had stopped kissing her? Because he knew he'd be rough? Or was it because she wasn't as beautiful as Angel? *How many times did they—?* She squeezed her eyes tight.

"Pardon me, miss, you seem to be in some distress." A charismatic voice reached her ears.

She opened her eyes and a man in his late forties wearing a dark blue suit smiled at her. Streaks of white peppered his thick black hair, and his well-trimmed beard and sideburns hugged his brown face. He wore a pair of glasses over his brown eyes, the lenses rippling with a digital surge every so often. Though she had never met him before, his demeanor reminded her of a kind grandfather, like Mr. Shrub.

She wiped her eyes with the back of her hand. "Oh. I'm—" She stopped and shifted her voice to a more saccharine-sweet timbre. "I'm afraid I'm not quite used to these shoes yet." She swallowed the irritation clogging her throat and did her best to smile like a real girl, just like Mrs. Matsumura had taught her.

"Ah yes, the price of beauty. My wife would always fuss over those things, but she was beautiful, even without fancy accessories." He reached into his back pocket and presented her with a bandage. "Not sure why I have this. Force of habit, I suppose."

She hesitated as she took it. "Thank you, sir."

He bowed, and Al gave him a clumsy curtsy as he walked back into the crowd.

She stared at the bandage. "That was close..." Her voice dropped back into place. "He seemed like a nice guy, but I'm still not a fan of handing out fake smiles."

Trumpeting fanfare erupted into the hall, drowning out the crowd's conversations. Al stuffed the bandage into her pocket as the lights dimmed and a blue-tinted spotlight fell on the throne on the balcony. Soon, a figure wearing a regal white suit entered from one side, waving as he walked. Al couldn't see his face, but his forced purity was so bright it could probably be seen from the moon.

He lifted his hands. "My fellow Astovans. I know it has been quite some time since I appeared in front of you, but with the Altered threat neutralized, peace has returned." Al knew this voice. She had heard his distinct tone too many times. *Vilroy.* Her mouth went dry.

"And what could be a more wondrous occasion to celebrate this peace than on our beloved Astova's founding day?"

The audience clapped as they rushed closer to the balcony as if their brains had suddenly remembered their civic duty to praise. Al tried to steady her erratic breathing as she scanned their darkened faces. Perryn had not returned from "heaven" yet.

"Fine. I'll do this on my own." Al clenched her fists and marched forward, but something in the windows behind the balcony made her stop. The air outside seemed to ripple. She didn't have time to confirm her suspicions before a masked man burst onto the balcony and pointed a blaster at Vilroy.

"The future belongs to the Altered!" He fired a shot, the blast ripping a hole through Vilroy's chest just as the windows behind them shattered. Figures in black burst in, glass raining down around them as they rolled onto the balcony. Several black Scraper Sharks materialized out of thin air, their engines roaring and pushing gusts of wind through the hall. Terrified screams rang out and bodies careened into her as guests scrambled to reach elevators or stairwells.

Vilroy's lifeless body slumped over the chair, blood and internal organs splattered across his white clothes. "No!" Al covered her mouth. He could never answer her questions now.

Capital soldiers arrived in droves, flipping tables over for coverage as they fired at the intruders on the balcony. Glasses, plates of food, and silverware crashed to the floor.

Shots from the balcony reigned down near her and she dashed off to the side, knocking over a table and ducking behind it. She poked her head out and noted several other masked figures pouring in from the stairwell and hallways. They fired upon the soldiers in the middle and dashed off when they shot back, a few of their comrades dying before they could get away.

Without a weapon, Al wouldn't be of much use. She decided to wait for a break in the skirmish and make for the stairwell. Her plan derailed when Zeek dashed across the hall, shooting at the balcony. He braced himself against a deep lip in the wall. Occupied by his opponents, he couldn't see the masked figure sneaking up behind him from the adjacent hallway.

Al sighed as she kicked off her shoes. "If I actually die this time, I'll haunt you for real, you jerk." She let out an exasperated cry and dashed forward, jumping on the masked figure's back.

In the confusion, he dropped his gun as he tried to pull her off. Just as Al fell and hit the floor, Zeek shot the man, who dropped beside her with a pained groan. Al scrambled away from the body, glancing around the room. It was obvious which side was winning, and it wasn't the away team. Zeek must have killed or wounded his aerial attackers because the shots had stopped raining down.

Al stood and brushed her hands on her dress. "So much for being a lady." She frowned at the smudges staining her once pure white dress. *Forget this.* Scrunching her nose, she stormed toward Zeek, who had stowed his gun, his back now turned to her. "Zeek! You could've killed me!"

He spun around and the color drained from his face. "You—"

Al sighed and clenched her fists. It was time to tell him the truth. "Yes, Zeek, it's me. It's—"

"I was right! You really are a damn Alt!"

"What—?" Al stopped and grabbed the top of her head. The wig had fallen off.

Before she had time to think, Zeek lunged at her with a feral yell, squeezing her neck, his eyes wild and huge.

He slammed her to the ground and Al wheezed within the momentary spaces he took to resituate his grip. She clawed at his arms, her legs thrashing against the cold marble floor. Her choker dug into her neck as his weight crushed her lungs.

"I knew it!" Zeek's heartless tone tore into her. "I knew you terrorists were still out there. Vilroy's plan worked. You all showed up here just like he said you would! I bet you're a spy. And you thought I'd go easy on you because you're a girl. But all you filthy Alts are the same! Every last one of you!"

She tried to say his name, but only air escaped. Her vision blurred, her arms growing heavy as her strength waned.

"Let her go, Zeek!" Perryn rushed toward them and punched Zeek in the face. He tumbled off, his fingers releasing. Al gasped for air between coughs and quick breaths as Perryn knelt at her side, his expression uncharacteristically broken.

"Well, well. Isn't this interesting." Zeek wiped the blood dripping from his nose with the back of his hand as he stood. "Really didn't take you for an Alt-lover, Keevie, but she must taste pretty damn good for you to completely lose your mind and betray your country, you traitor!"

Perryn held Al in his arms, the tidal waves in his dark eyes raging. "You are so blinded by your hatred for the Altered that your moral compass has warped beyond repair. Do not lecture me on loyalty, you immature child."

Zeek gritted his teeth. "Oh sure! That high and mighty act of yours might make you feel invincible, but it's not gonna save you when Vilroy hears what you did!"

"Zeek..." Al winced. "I really did wanna go to the moon with you one day."

He tensed, his eyes growing wide and frantic. "What the hell are you talking about?"

She lifted herself from Perryn's chest and swooped a wobbly hand low like a landing ship. Bending her arm up straight, she showed him the scar on her right hand. "Coming in for a landing..."

"...Al?" Zeek's eyes softened and for a moment he looked like the carefree boy who had once only cared about flying and adventures. "It can't be...I thought you— but then, how can...I don't—" He fell to his knees, his voice shaking. "Why...why did you have to be Altered?"

Al fell forward, shutting her eyes. The colors and shapes in her vision made her too dizzy. "That day in the snow, I heard everything." She forced her eyes open. "I'm sorry I didn't understand you back then...I understand now, but I can't return your feelings..."

Zeek stared at Al and then Perryn before his face turned dark again. "Wow. You really played me. I thought you might be some poor kidnapped girl, but in reality, you're a fucking Alt. And what? Perryn's supposed to be the hero now? You gotta be shitting me." He scrambled to his feet. "Bastard! You knew about Al this whole time, didn't you? Liars! Both of you!"

Perryn pushed Al out of the way as Zeek lunged toward them, blocking the blow with his forearm, but Zeek slammed him in the side with his other hand. Perryn let out a pained grimace.

"Perryn!" Al tried to stand, but her limbs collapsed under her.

He jumped to his feet and sent a punch toward Zeek's face, who blocked it with an irritated yell, his feet skidding backward toward the wall. They continued, Perryn's sharp eyes and attacks never wavering from his target, and Zeek, swinging and kicking wildly with relentless strength and unbridled hate. Soon Perryn had cornered him against the wall, ready to lunge forward.

"Stop!" Al reached toward them. "Just stop! Both of you! I don't want anyone to get hurt anymore!"

Perryn hesitated, his fist hovering above Zeek's bloody face. His twisted smile dared him to continue.

"Perryn, please!"

Perryn let out a breath before punching Zeek in the stomach and turning away. Zeek fell to the ground coughing and after a moment, his gasping turned to laughter. "Ha! That's it? You're not gonna finish me off?" Zeek staggered to his feet. "Maybe you should get Al to do it then. I'd love to be her first."

Perryn grabbed Zeek's collar and slammed him against the wall. "For her sake, I am giving you mercy, but if you *ever* touch her again, I will kill you."

Zeek's eyes narrowed. "Oh really?"

The thundering of a gunshot ricocheted through the air.

Al screamed as Perryn fell backward, blood pouring from a wound in his torso.

"You bastard..." He gritted his teeth as he hit the floor.

Al stumbled toward Perryn, crying out his name. When she reached him, she tore a piece of fabric from her dress and pressed it against his wound. He grimaced every time she touched him.

"How could you?" Al glared up at Zeek, tears filling her eyes. "Why should it matter if I'm Altered or not? Did our friendship mean nothing to you?"

Zeek knelt in front of her with a cold stare, touching the barrel of his gun to her forehead. "You promised me once that I wouldn't lose you."

Al froze, but her intense expression didn't change.

His stare traveled the length of her torn dress until he reached her eyes. "Don't worry. You lost me instead."

Her tears burst free as all the strength faded from her face. Her best friend was gone, lost under the rubble of her secrets and lies, killed by the heartless imposter that took his place.

"Hey, Mr. Important." Zeek's stony expression didn't change as he lowered his gun and turned his harsh gaze to Perryn, making sure their eyes locked. "If I *ever* touch her again, it'll be to kill her."

Perryn lunged at him with a guttural yell, but he fell backward, clutching his stomach.

"No! Please stay still!" Al propped his head against her lap and stroked the hair out of his eyes. "You'll lose more blood and then you might—" Her words choked in her throat. He had to stay alive. She'd be alone again.

"Who have you caught this time, Captain Landers?" A charming voice resounded from behind as armed capital soldiers surrounded them. Even before the man in the blue suit approached and even before Zeek knelt on one knee in front of him, Al somehow already knew who he was. The corpse on the balcony had been a stand-in.

"Vilroy..." She glared up at him.

"Nice to finally meet you properly, my dear."

CHAPTER 26

I see *you're* alive." Al wrapped her arms around Perryn, drawing him closer.

Vilroy smiled and rubbed his chin. "Yes, well, what's a good dinner party without a little show?"

Perryn coughed, spitting flecks of blood across the front of his already-stained white shirt. "Perryn!" Al loosened her grip, letting him fall back into her lap. His face was turning pale, and his skin felt clammy against the back of her hand. She stared at him a moment longer before kissing his forehead and moving him to the ground.

"You've been lookin' for me, right?" She glared at Vilroy as she stood. "Well, let me tell you how this is gonna go. You're gonna save Perryn and then you're gonna answer all of my questions. Got it?"

Vilroy cocked his head with an amused grin. "And what exactly makes you think you're in a position to demand any of that?"

Al narrowed her eyes and then, without hesitation, ran up behind Zeek and twisted his arm. With a pained grunt, his fingers released his gun. She snatched it from the ground and pointed it straight at Vilroy.

The capital soldiers drew their blasters, aiming at her with uniform precision, but Al didn't flinch. Maintaining her glare, she set the gun against the side of her head and unlocked the safety. "I'm no good to you dead, right?"

"Al—no!" Perryn tried to lift himself from the ground.

Vilroy let out a long-winded laugh as he applauded. "Most impressive!"

Al's eyes twitched, but she didn't loosen her grip on the gun. She wasn't keen to test if immortality could protect her from a bullet to the head, but her life was the only thing she could wager to save Perryn's. "I'm waiting."

"Very well." His voice settled, but a strange smile remained on his face. "We'll patch up Prime Minister Keevie. Can't have him die *before* his trial." Vilroy motioned to his guards, and they returned their blasters to their holsters. Two others bowed and ran off down the hall.

"Trial?" She stopped herself from looking down at her wounded partner.

Vilroy shrugged. "But of course. It's clear now our beloved prime minister has been aiding the Altered, perhaps even with the assassination of his own father." He smiled that strange smile again. "Good work, Captain Landers, your suspicions were correct."

Al sent a cold glare to Zeek, who was struggling to stand. The smeared blood across his cheek had dried and turned crispy.

"One of the most promising youths of his time, if my opinion means anything." Vilroy touched his chest with feigned modesty as he walked toward his star pupil. "Did you know I recruited him when he was only twelve? The Altered took away his childhood, so I gave him a new purpose, and now he has become a man both his family and his country can be proud of."

Al scowled, her words biting with sarcasm. "Yeah, a real man of the year."

Zeek avoided her eyes. He could pretend he was hiding from her all he wanted, but he couldn't hide which side he chose. Altered or Naturalist, it was beyond that now. He had abandoned her the moment his master called.

The circle of soldiers parted as the two men returned, a hovering medical gurney following behind them. Together with several other soldiers, they hoisted a grimacing Perryn onto the rubber bedding and buckled his ankles into the restraints.

As they stood back, tiny mechanical arms with various medical tools attached to their ends rose from compartments on the side. They ripped the soaked, dark-red cloth of Al's dress from his wound and tossed it into a built-in incinerator chute. The tiny metal beasts cut away Perryn's suit until they had cleared a large section, revealing the entry wound.

Al turned back to Vilroy. "You knew exactly who I was when you talked to me earlier, didn't you?"

He gestured behind him. "Come now, my dear. Let us go somewhere more private so we can *catch up*."

Al hesitated as she lowered the gun, but kept her finger on the trigger as she moved to Perryn's side and Vilroy to the other. The soldiers surrounded them like a human force field as they left the ballroom, the gurney floating forward on its own.

Zeek lagged behind. Did he feel guilty? *Good*. He did it to himself.

As they turned down the hallway, Perryn let out several pained yells before he forced his mouth closed, biting down on his lips. The tiny instruments cut and dug their way deep into his side, searching for the bullet as he writhed under the restraints.

"Forgive me, but it seems we are out of local anesthesia." Vilroy's smile twisted at the corners as he kept looking ahead.

Hate surged through her, but she forced herself to keep steady as she squeezed Perryn's hand. Just because her heart was breaking didn't mean her face had to.

The robotic arms finished tying their last stitch, and after they applied a blue-green gel to the length of the closed incisions, they slipped back into their home like metal vines retreating into the ground.

Perryn's convulsing slowed and soon his breathing returned to a normal rhythm and his grip relaxed. His dry blood splotched her sore fingers and her dress, stained in dark red, had torn up to her thigh. Al tightened her grip on the handle of the gun. She wouldn't break now. Not after everything she'd gone through. Not when she was so close to finding the truth. She forced herself to stare at the windowless walls.

Harsh firelight flickered from above and a smoky smell filled the hall, but cinnamon overpowered the musk. Al's mind wandered to Endo and Yamazaki. So much for their esteemed protection. Where were they?

They rounded another corner, and a single metallic-blue elevator appeared before them at the end of the corridor.

"Major De León, please escort the prime minister to medical bay five and await further instructions." Vilroy gave his order without turning around. "Captain Landers, take your unit and assist."

With a sharp affirmative call, Zeek and the major bent their arms and held their fists out over their hearts.

Al turned to Perryn, her eyes memorizing every detail of his face with frantic speed. She had to say goodbye.

"I want a refund." Perryn gave her a weak smile. "Your bedside manner was horrible..."

"Don't you dare die…" Al dropped the gun beside him and squeezed his hand. "If you die, I'm gonna kill you."

His smile faded. "About what happened on the balcony…"

Al shook her head. "I don't care about that right now. Just rest." She touched her forehead to his and closed her eyes. "Wait for me," she whispered. *I'll come back and save you.*

They locked eyes again, sharing a delicate smile just as the gurney pulled away. She picked up the gun and kept her opposite arm extended until their fingertips could no longer touch.

A barrage of blasts coming from an adjacent hallway pelted the group, taking down a few capital soldiers. They convulsed on the ground as fellow soldiers pulled out their blasters and closed the gap in the human circle.

Al ducked as Major De León stepped in front of her. "Protect our beloved leader!"

With a unified shout, the battalion separated into groups, one surrounding Vilroy, and began shooting back.

"Landers! I leave the prime minister to you!" The major held out his gun to Zeek, who rushed over and accepted the weapon with a stiff nod.

Al watched in horror as shots zipped past Perryn's immobilized body while Zeek and his squad moved him down the opposite hall.

"Okay. Now I'm mad." Al lifted her gun. "Will everybody just stop shooting at everybody? Fish on a stick, I hate guns! I don't care if you're Altered or Naturalist! Stop trying to kill the guy I love!"

She ducked and braced herself behind different soldiers as she weaved forward until she made it to a support pillar, where she fired at a few of the metal wires that held the lights. Several broke free and cascaded down, causing a wave of flames to spread out across the floor.

"Oh, look! Fire! Can't *fire* so well when there's *fire* blocking your view, can you?" Al yelled over her shoulder.

"Hold!" A familiar voice cut through the commotion. "Al?"

She pushed her back against the marble to steady herself as her eyes widened. The man's name could barely escape from the place she had locked it away. "Maddox...?"

"Cease fire!" Vilroy's crisp voice resounded from behind his human forcefield, as they moved with him, stepping over their dead and dying comrades. A whirling beeping cut through the hall and a dripping curtain of water turned into mist, dousing the fire. Al peered out from her position into the hazy air, and a few undefined figures stood in the distance.

"Al! That's you, right?" Maddox's frantic voice sounded the same as she remembered.

"Of course it is! Who else would it be?" Her lips trembled.

As the mist dissipated, a man stepped forward, wearing all black, his face covered except for his eyes. The woman and two men standing on either side of him and the large group crowding behind them all wore the same uniform. The Altered had survived.

"Maddox!" Al took a step but stopped. Instinct told her not to believe in miracles. "No, you're dead!"

The man pulled down his mask. "That's my line, kiddo..." Maddox stared back, his glistening eyes rugged from war.

Al touched her chest as it tried to cave in on her. "And Molly?"

"I'm here, Al!" Molly's voice rang out, and a crack formed in Al's hardened heart. Relief seeped into her veins. They were alive.

Vilroy let out a loud, throaty laugh. "How many years has it been since we've been in the same room, old friend?" He waltzed toward Maddox, his armored entourage surrounding him. "I hardly recognize you."

"Shut up, you disgusting piece of shit!" Maddox lurched forward as he pointed his gun at him.

Vilroy tilted his head. "And calling her Al? You really must enjoy torturing yourself. Losing Kera wasn't enough, I guess."

Al stiffened. *Kera.*

"Don't you dare say her name!" Maddox fired a shot at Vilroy, but his bodyguard moved in front of the blast, which dissipated into the soldier's thick shield.

"Oh, Al!" Vilroy's voice bounced across the room as he continued his parade forward. "Would you like to know who he really is? He may have changed his name and given himself a brand-new face, but I know who he is!"

Maddox yelled as he shot more blasts toward Vilroy, but once again, they hit a soldier's shield.

Vilroy stood behind her, his hushed voice right in her ear. "He stole you from me because he missed Kera too much after he killed her. I think you know who he is."

Al's mind went blank as the name he uttered violated her ears. The gun fell from her hands. Pushing through the soldiers, she stumbled out into the middle of the hall.

Maddox rushed toward her. "Al! Whatever he told you, it's not—"

"Liar!" Her face turned dark and all the strength she had used to keep herself together fell down her cheeks. "Look me in the eye and tell me you're not Calvin Hayashi!"

Maddox froze as horror gripped his face. A thick silence fell over the room.

"Al—"

"Are you?"

Maddox's body lost its tension, like a puppet severed from its strings. "...yes..." His voice was the most broken sound Al had ever heard, but she didn't care. This whole time, Calvin had raised her. That's why he recruited Perryn. He dragged them both into his twisted revenge plot against Vilroy, the other man Kera loved. That fire she died in didn't seem like an accident anymore.

"So, you killed my mother in a jealous rage, faked your own death, became a different person, and then kidnapped me to hurt Vilroy?"

"No! That's not—Al, please!" He stumbled forward, his eyes brimming with panic. "You don't know—"

"No! I do know!" Al screamed. "I know that someone I trusted my whole life is a liar and someone I just met has only told me the truth!"

"Al! Please listen to us!" Molly clutched her chest as tears ran down her cheeks. "You really don't understand! Kera wasn't—"

"I think Al has made her decision clear." Vilroy's demeanor returned to that of an elegant gentleman as he turned on his heels. "Commence fire!"

Al's face remained cold and unmoving as the soldiers fired upon her once-treasured family. Maddox had killed her. He had killed her mother. He should have stayed dead.

"Fire!" Maddox raised his hand and Molly scrambled back into the black sea of armored people behind her.

Al turned and followed Vilroy as the blasts ricocheted through the air and bodies dropped around them. They reached the blue elevator and Al looked back down the hall, but Perryn had vanished. The garish door of the elevator slid open and Vilroy and two guards entered, standing single file. She didn't hesitate and stepped inside.

Something in her gut told her this was a mistake, that she should run. But she wouldn't. Her future was at the top of this elevator, and she had to know. She had sacrificed everything to find the truth. She couldn't back out now. When she turned around, the doors of the oval elevator had already closed.

The sounds of the ensuing battle were muffled as the overhead lights hummed and clicking mechanisms pulled the tube upwards. There were no windows, only an endless foamy-blue wall and buttons with symbols instead of numbers. No one spoke, which made it harder for Al to discern how long they had been rising.

The thought of her mother entangling herself with two men didn't exactly give Al warm fuzzy feelings, but if that was the type of person she was, at least it was something real that Al could hold onto. A light tap on her shoulder snapped her back to attention.

"We have arrived, my dear." Vilroy gave her a sincere smile, and she nodded, stepping out through the open doors onto a covered landing.

Clear glass windows boxed them in and when Al looked down, she couldn't see the ground anymore, only the tops of buildings and a sea of twinkling lights stared back. The landing ended with a round blue door that looked almost identical to the one that had led to Kera's lab. Once Vilroy entered his code in the box on the wall, the door split open down the middle.

"Welcome." Vilroy extended his hand and then turned toward his soldiers. "Wait outside." They bowed their heads, putting their fists out over their hearts, and Vilroy and Al stepped inside. The doors shut behind them.

The hexagon-shaped room had tall brown walls and under a skinny, gray carpet that ran the length of the room, golden, petal-shaped panels covered the floor, arranged in semicircles. Narrow windows lined the top of one wall above a *J*-shaped desk and a couch and lounge chair wrapped in the same foamy elevator-blue sat against another.

So this was where he lived while the world he ruled over crumbled, while his citizens killed each other and while Al grew up knowing nothing.

She turned toward him with a hard stare. "Are you really my father?"

Vilroy chuckled. "Straight to the point, I see." He walked across the room, ascending a shallow set of stairs, and when he reached a cupboard, he opened it and removed a wine glass. Placing it on the counter below, he filled it with a thick orange liquid from a tall twisty bottle. "Yes, if you wish to call me that. I'm your father."

Al kept her distance. "So I'm the Eternal Child...what does that mean? Will I live forever, or is it a regeneration thing? Do I have any special powers? Why did you make me? Are there more people like me, or am I the only one?"

Vilroy smiled as he swirled the liquid in his cup. "One question at a time, Al."

She stared at the ground. "I thought Molly and Mad—I thought...they cared about me. After what he did, how could they just pretend like it didn't matter?"

Vilroy took a sip of his drink as he approached her. "Denial, I imagine. His regret for murdering his wife caused him to seek the closest thing to her he could find. You, my beautiful daughter." He caressed her cheek with his index finger.

Al slapped his hand away. "And I'm supposed to believe your relationship with my mother had nothing to do with his actions?"

Vilroy raised his glass to her before taking another sip. "Deductive reasoning. Kera was good at that too."

"Stop avoiding my questions!"

"I'm sorry, my dear." He set the glass down on his desk. "But I'm troubled by your appearance. Why don't you clean up first and then we can continue our conversation."

Al looked at her crusty red hands. Though she could tell he was stalling for some reason, the thought of washing away some of her sins filled her with relief.

She glared at him. "After that, you'll answer my questions."

"I promise I will tell you everything. The bathroom is to the left, down the hall."

Continuing to glare as she passed him, she entered the silver bathroom and closed the door, locking it behind her.

She stared at the bloody mermaid in the mirror. Her makeup was smudged around her eyes making her resemble a panda, her hair was tangled like white seaweed, and red streaks and splotches covered the front of her dress. Her earrings were missing, and the choker had left red indentations on her neck.

She turned on the faucet and pulled open the drawers until she found a towel. Soaking the end with fresh water, she pulled off her choker and rubbed her bare skin, the blue towel turning purple. Adding soap, she scrubbed her face and hands. Her eyes burned.

A sudden knock on the door made her jump. "Al, are you alright in there?"

Vilroy might be her father, but she hated the way he said her name.

"Be out in a minute!" She waited until he had walked away before she continued.

There was no saving the dress. Al frowned and threw the towel into the shower behind her. Steadying herself against the sink, she took a breath.

Get your answers. Get Perryn. Then get out.

When she opened the bathroom door and walked back to the living room, Vilroy had moved to the armchair. With his legs crossed, he sipped his drink, and his holo-glasses rested on the side table. His green eyes stared at her.

She glared back as she swallowed the cough tickling her throat, like the dust from the lab had returned. "That's right. You're Altered too."

"Actually, I'm not." He uncrossed his legs and leaned forward. "You see, I am one of the few people in the world that nature gifted with green eyes. That's why I was so enamored with Kera. She was like me. A natural-born rarity."

"Wait. Are you saying Kera wasn't Altered?" Her eyes widened. "But that means—"

"Correct, you're not Altered either."

Then why did Maddox make me think I was?

Vilroy stood. "Kera's ethereal beauty was so rare the probability of the two of us ever meeting was astronomically low. I know the universe intended for us to be together, to return the world to a state where nature could once again create real humans. Not those fake made-to-order children. If the world became perfect, what would we strive for? Without adversity, the human race ceases to evolve."

"So that's the reason you pit us all against each other?"

Vilroy smirked as he swirled his drink. "Not entirely. The Naturalists need a common enemy, to keep the fabric of society intact as we start over."

Al clenched her fists. "That's not fair! You can't just manipulate people and then hide in the shadows while they suffer and die!"

Vilroy laughed long and hard, the way he had when he had spoken to Maddox. "Yes, now you sound like her.

You sound just like Kera." He set his drink on the table and moved toward her. Al's inner voice screamed at her to run, but her stiff legs could only reverse in slow motion. "Let me tell you a secret." Though his words were steady, a darkness brewed beneath them.

Al's back hit against the wall as he stood over her.

"It began much like this, actually. She had come to tell me she could no longer see me. That she couldn't lie to her precious Calvin any more. That setting off the bombs myself and framing the Altered for starting the war was morally unjust."

"That was you?" Her stomach twisted. Everything she knew about Astova's history was a lie, handcrafted to sell one man's depraved vision. "You're a coward! A horrible, disgusting coward!"

Vilroy tried to hold back his laughter. "It's uncanny how similar your accusations are. Are you going to ask me to turn myself in too?"

"Don't bother! *I'm* gonna tell everyone what you did!"

"Oh?" A nefarious smile crossed his face. "Kera thought she was clever too, recording our conversation via the implant in her eye to incriminate me." He moved closer, his eyes narrowing like his smile. "So I killed her. Right here in this very room."

Al stiffened against the wall, as every part of her gasped for air.

"But I made a mistake. I couldn't be in a relationship with a dead woman. What would people think of me?" He laughed and trailed his index finger down Al's cheek.

She couldn't move. "But—you said—I thought Kera died in a fire that Calvin started."

"Ah, yes. Discreetly arranging arson to look like they both died after he discovered the recording was such a pain, and as you know, wasn't even successful. Mistake number two." He grabbed the back of her head and yanked her closer to his wild darkness. "But at least I acted quickly before the lights left Kera's eyes."

A painful pinch radiated down Al's arm as Vilroy stabbed her shoulder with a syringe. He pushed down the stopper. "I saved her memories." He pulled away and she fell to the ground, her body growing numb and lifeless.

"You poor ignorant child." Vilroy stood over her, his smile wide and cruel. "Kera was never your mother. You *are* her."

Tears dripped from her frozen-open eyes. "No! You're lying!"

"I'm surprised you never figured it out considering you two look identical. Shame I couldn't see the look on Calvin's face when he realized who you were. Ha! I knew he wouldn't be able to kill you, but imagine. Raising a clone of your dead wife for eighteen years."

Al screamed, her air cutting short as she lost all feeling in her muscles. That's why Maddox kept his distance. That's why he was so harsh to her. That's why he lied. His wife had returned from the dead, but he couldn't love her.

Vilroy headed to the door and as it opened, the two soldiers ran in and hoisted her up by her arms. Dragging her limp body across the floor, they pulled her over the shallow set of stairs, down the hall, and into a sterile white room that looked like a medical facility.

This was Marn all over again.

They laid Al in an examination chair, pulling straps over her wrists and ankles, her head drooping forward until they secured it with a head restraint. Once they had finished, they bowed and left the room.

"Comfortable, dear?" Vilroy stood in front of her, pulling on a pair of blue rubber gloves.

Al couldn't feel her body anymore.

He disappeared from view and rummaged through drawers. When he returned, he popped in front of her, holding out a picture like a proud father. "This is the Eternal Child, *Al*." He mocked her name. "We called her Alisa."

Al tried to scream again, but only scratchy gasping noises escaped from her throat as the familiar scene of Kera holding the bundled baby flickered across the photo.

That's why Al could enter Kera's lab and why her fingerprints didn't show up in the system. Al wasn't the Eternal Child. She wasn't Altered or a Naturalist. She never even existed.

"Just one more step!" Vilroy rolled a mechanical contraption near her and pulled out a thin tube. It ended with another syringe.

No! Perryn! Perryn! Tears streamed down her face. *When he finds out, he won't love me anymore.* She'd be alone. She was always alone.

Vilroy pushed the needle into her left temple just above her ear, and her body spasmed against the restraints as her throat twisted in a dry, squeaky wheeze.

Pain. Sharp, bright pain.

He pushed a second syringe into her right temple, and she jerked again. Blood trickled down her cheeks.

"It's a memory diffuser! I created it myself." He pulled a thin vial from his pocket, and after kissing it, inserted it into an angled slot. His hand hovered above a switch as he turned toward her. "Well, my dear Al, it's been a pleasure, but goodbye now."

Al let out a single squeak before a searing, intense pain pooled around her right temple. Her eyes drooped closed, the memories leaving her body like a vacuum sucking away her soul. Scenes and people flashed across her eyes, but none of them seemed familiar, or maybe they did. She couldn't tell anymore.

A formless space surrounded her, pitch black except for the single light above her head. Where was she? How did she get here? Who even was she?

A name echoed out across the space.

"Al." Al spoke her name and knew it was hers.

A girl with blue eyes and white hair appeared in front of her.

"Who are you?" Al reached toward her.

"I am you." Their fingers touched and their hands clasped together.

"Where are we?"

The girl moved Al's hands to her heart. "Here."

"I don't think I'm supposed to exist. Can you tell me?"

"If you exist, you exist."

The bright light above their heads grew too bright, and Al shut her eyes.

Someone was shaking her, but she couldn't see them or hear their words. Her brain burned. She fell forward and a pair of strong arms embraced her. Warmth. They seemed familiar, but she wasn't sure.

All at once, her senses filtered their blockage and sound and sight rushed into her at full force. A piercing monotonous beep indicating an escape pod had been launched wailed like a siren and she cowered against the floor, holding her head. Who had escaped? And why? Wires and light fixtures dangled from the ceiling, and sparks flew off into the thick smoky air, swirling from the draft caused by a gaping hole in the wall. The faint glow of city lights flickered against the darkness outside.

The person in front of her shook her again. "Al! Did you hear me? I said we need to leave! Come on, Al! Tell me you're okay! Answer me, kiddo!"

"Al? Kiddo?" Her voice slurred as she gripped the thick black fabric of the man's shirt. "Who are you talking about? My name is Kera."

ACKNOWLEDGMENTS

Al Eyes began as an incomplete forty-one-page gar-
ble I wrote when I was sixteen. Then life happened, for
a long time, and I stopped working on it, but my characters and my dream of publishing a novel never left
me. After encouragement from a dear friend, I joined
NaNoWriMo in November 2019 and started a brand-new
draft. Though returning to the world I created was nostalgic and fun, formally organizing all my thoughts turned
out to be harder than I expected. I only managed to write
half of my novel. Covid started to surface soon after and
I threw myself into my story, determined to finish. Then
my grandma passed away and writing turned into a way
for me to cope with her loss.

Now, two years later, the characters have changed
and grown as I have, some even switching their allianc-
es. I poured my soul into these pages, especially into Al,
whose journey to find herself mirrors my own—wordplay
most definitely intended.

To help center my story as I rewrote it, I asked myself
a question: What does it mean to be human? In the end,
I found out what it means to be me instead. Being vul-

nerable and expressing myself to others has always been something I struggled with, but writing *Al Eyes* helped me be brave. Everyone has a story worth telling. Whether you decide to share it with others or not, I hope that you too can find and embrace the unique perspective you hold within yourself.

It feels surreal to have finally finished this book, and I couldn't have written it without the support of some very special people.

To my wonderful husband, my darling, who stayed up into the dark hours of countless mornings listening to me theorize character motivations and craft my world—thank you for being by my side and for letting me borrow your ears. I love you shou shou machi kudasai.

To my "book mentor" Morgan, for offering invaluable advice on where to start.

To my alpha readers, Jack and Cheyenne, for being so invested in and excited for the next chapter.

To my beta readers—Renae and Maddie, for taking the time to read such a long manuscript and for offering your helpful insights, and to Kate and Matt for doing all of that in addition to talking to me in-length about everything.

To my "soul twin" Breaugh, for inspiring me to start writing again.

To my mom and dad for loving me and always supporting my dreams.

To my amazing editor, Rebecca, for somehow knowing exactly what I meant even when I didn't.

And to Japan and my host families who helped me find an important piece of myself I was missing.

Thank you so much! 感謝しています 。

MICHELLE MARIE is a bilingual voice actress, singer, author, and full-time indoor cat. She did venture outside once, living in Japan for two years as an exchange student. Born and raised in Oregon, she now ~~hides~~ resides in Los Angeles with her childhood friend turned husband. A hopeless romantic at heart, Michelle adores puns, sheep, stoic softies, and has entirely too much tea in her house.

michelleamarie.com
Twitter: @MichelleAMarie

THE ALTERED ARCHIVES TRILOGY
CONTINUES IN BOOK 2...

KERA
CELL

COMING SOON!

www.ingramcontent.com/pod-product-compliance
Lightning Source LLC
Chambersburg PA
CBHW051311190726
48290CB00001B/103